Dear Reader,

In December 2010 we published our first set of holiday collections. I'm pleased that these collections have become an annual Carina Press holiday tradition.

For *Holiday Kisses,* I invited four amazing authors to participate in this contemporary holiday collection. Between them, Jaci Burton, HelenKay Dimon, Alison Kent and Shannon Stacey have decades of writing experience and have published dozens of books their fans have adored. I knew these four authors would bring together holiday stories that would capture our hearts and take us away from the holiday craziness for a few hours. And did they ever! They delivered a powerful, fantastic collection.

I'm thrilled and proud to share the heart-wrenching and wonderful holiday stories of the Holiday Kisses collection with you for the first time in print. I hope you love *A Rare Gift* by Jaci Burton, *It's Not Christmas Without You* by HelenKay Dimon, *This Time Next Year* by Alison Kent and *Mistletoe and Margaritas* by Shannon Stacey as much as I do. These are stories and characters that will live on for you, long after you've read the last page.

Happy reading!

~Angela James

Executive Editor, Carina Press

Holiday Kisses

JACI BURTON ✶ SHANNON STACEY
HELENKAY DIMON ✶ ALISON KENT

CARINA
PRESS™

CARINA PRESS™

Recycling programs
for this product may
not exist in your area.

ISBN-13: 978-0-373-00207-8

HOLIDAY KISSES

Copyright © 2011 by Carina Press

The publisher acknowledges the copyright holders of the individual works as follows:

THIS TIME NEXT YEAR
Copyright © 2011 by Alison Kent

A RARE GIFT
Copyright © 2011 by Jaci Burton

IT'S NOT CHRISTMAS WITHOUT YOU
Copyright © 2011 by HelenKay Dimon

MISTLETOE AND MARGARITAS
Copyright © 2011 by Shannon Stacey

www.CarinaPress.com

Printed in U.S.A.

CONTENTS

THIS TIME NEXT YEAR   7
Alison Kent

A RARE GIFT   107
Jaci Burton

IT'S NOT CHRISTMAS WITHOUT YOU   215
HelenKay Dimon

MISTLETOE AND MARGARITAS   325
Shannon Stacey

THIS TIME NEXT YEAR

Alison Kent

To my sister, Detective Leah Apple, Frisco, Texas P.D.,
for your service and your sacrifice.

ALISON KENT

A born reader, it wasn't until Alison Kent reached thirty that she knew she wanted to be a writer when she grew up. Not long after, she accepted an offer issued by the senior editor of Harlequin Temptation live on the "Isn't It Romantic?" episode of CBS's *48 Hours*. The resulting book, *Call Me,* was an *RT Book Reviews* finalist for Best First Series Book.

Alison's Harlequin Blaze title, *A Long, Hard Ride,* part of Harlequin's 60th Anniversary celebration, was nominated for an RT Reviewers' Choice Award, as was *Striptease* from her Harlequin Blaze gIRL-gEAR series. *No Limits,* book ten in her Smithson Group series, was excerpted in *Cosmopolitan* magazine as a Red-Hot Read, and *The Beach Alibi,* book four, was a National Quill Awards nominee.

In addition to more than forty works of fiction, Alison is also the author of *The Complete Idiot's Guide to Writing Erotic Romance* and a partner in DreamForge Media as a website designer. If there's a better career than romance writing to be had, she doesn't want to know about it, as penning lusty tales from her backyard is the best way she's found to convince her pack of rescue dogs they have her full attention.

CHAPTER ONE

Over the river. Check. Through the woods. Check. To grand-mother's *house*. Double check. And though corny enough to put a smile on Brenna Keating's face, the similarities between the song on the radio and her visit to Gran ended there.

Instead of relying on a horse to know the way through the oak-pine forests of the Blue Ridge Mountains, she had thirty-three years of memories. She also had a dash-mounted GPS unit, one she'd installed in the economy import her parents had surprised her with ten years ago to celebrate her degree. Kinda took the romance out of the wintry trip, but then she didn't know squat about sleighs.

Transportation was one thing she wouldn't have to worry about when she hit Malawi after the first of the year. Preparing to spend the next twelve months in the impoverished African nation, she'd invested instead in good shoes, cases of antibiotics and a copy of the *Oxford Handbook of Tropical Medicine*. And even then she knew the in-country experience would be just as valuable as the text and her master's in nursing.

Still, the car had served her well in getting around Raleigh—to the hospital where she worked, to Starbucks where the baristas knew her name and her drink, to the diner where once a week she had dinner with the girls.

And getting her to Gran's wasn't usually a problem. The car was more than capable of making the long scenic drive. Today, however, most of the scenery was hidden behind a whole lot of drifting white snow.

Four hours ago when she'd left home, the approaching storm had been predicted to hit Gran's mountain close to midnight. Because Brenna didn't have chains, she'd planned her drive accordingly.

She glanced at the clock on her dash. The digital numbers clearly read 2:45 p.m., and big fat flakes were coming down faster than her wipers set to High could clear. This was the last time she paid attention to the local weathermen.

At least her heater was having no trouble keeping the cold at bay. In fact, with her boots and thick socks, and her wool coat draped over her thighs like a blanket, and her gloves, the car's interior was a tad stuffy.

She slowed for the road's next switchback, careful as she braked, then again as she accelerated. Her headlights cut twin beams through the tall trees standing sentry on either side of the road—the road that hadn't seemed so narrow in the past.

She hated that this trip, more than any other she'd made up her grandmother's mountain, would be driven with white knuckles and near zero visibility. She wanted everything about this visit to be perfect—for herself and for Gran, too.

The next few days might be their last to spend together, and that realization had Brenna wishing for a cell signal so she could call the charity who'd been thrilled to have her on-board and tell them she'd changed her mind. She was staying here. Right here. In the only home she'd ever known. In the place that made her happy.

But doing that would disappoint Gran more than would transatlantic phone calls in lieu of spur-of-the-moment visits. Even more than the possible end of the Christmas holidays the two of them cherished. Gran was Brenna's biggest supporter, and her cheer at hearing the news of her only grandchild following in her footsteps had echoed off the mountain for days.

Leaving Gran was going to be so hard. Even harder was accepting the difficulty of getting back, what with the cost and logistics of international travel in and out of the third-world countries where she'd be putting her skills to good use.

But the hardest thing of all was realizing Gran wouldn't be around forever, and Brenna's new life of volunteer work, one her grandmother championed, meant after Christmas, they might never see each other again.

Sadness rising to choke her, Brenna glanced down to adjust the heater, looked back up—

Two eyes. Glowing. Unmoving. Frozen.

Oh, God! A deer!

She swerved, skidded, fishtailed and braked, then bounced off the road and plowed headfirst into a snowbank.

Cold. So cold. Her nose and left eye throbbing. Her foot jammed under the brake pedal. Teeth chattering, Brenna pushed away from the steering wheel to sit up. The airbag plopped onto her lap like a pancake.

Groaning, she remembered…the too-hot heat, the deer in her headlights, the amusement park ride into the ditch. Her car was nose down, no longer running. Her door, when she tried it, wouldn't budge. And her phone, when she found it, still had no bars.

She collapsed against her seat. Wasn't *she* the picture of a damsel in distress? Stupid deer. Stupid car. Stupid driver. At least Gran knew she was on her way and would eventually call out the cavalry, right?

Right?

For the love of Pete. If she'd pulled off her gloves and tossed her coat from her lap and left the car's heater alone, she'd be sitting in Gran's cozy kitchen by now. Drinking spiced cider. Filling up on glazed sugar cookies. Gran fussing over the biscuits in the oven and the soup on the stove.

Instead, visions of a tiny motherless Bambi had her stranded and now starting to shiver in the bone-cutting cold.

The tips of her fingers and toes were numb. Her breath frosted in the air as she blew it out in an attempt to remain calm. She grabbed her coat and struggled into it, then reached down to work her foot free.

Pain shot up her shin. She grimaced, pretty sure her ankle was sprained. Not that it mattered. She couldn't sit here and freeze to death. Unfortunately, getting out of her car wasn't going to be as simple as had been getting in.

She was pondering the nuts and bolts of climbing out one or the other of the—thank God—manually operated windows, when the wind began to howl and the already blowing snow whipped into what in minutes would be a full-on blizzard. Lovely.

With no street signs and a starburst crack in the center of the GPS screen, she couldn't be certain how far she was from Gran's. She'd driven this road often, but the accident and near whiteout conditions had her crazy disoriented. And mental confusion was one of the first signs of hypothermia.

She closed her eyes, swallowed and tried not to panic, but her teeth were chattering, gooseflesh pebbled her skin and the car's interior was rapidly turning into an icy tomb. Tears welled and she brushed them away, sniffing.

Cold. So cold. And tired. And very very scared.

Bang! Bang!
"Hello! Miss! Hello!"

Brenna's eyelids fluttered open. Had she been asleep? Dreaming?

"Miss! Hello!"

Thud! Thud!

She glanced toward her window, saw a fist, a coat…a man.

He leaned down, a big black Stetson pulled low on his face, and cupped his hands around his mouth. "Can you roll down your window?"

She cleared the glass with her sleeve and nodded, reaching for the handle. Frigid air sucked the remaining warmth from the car's interior, slapped her in the face, stole her breath, started her teeth chattering anew.

"Are you hurt? Can you move?"

"My ankle. It's sprained or bruised." It wasn't broken. Of that much she was sure. "I can move."

"Okay. If you can, turn your back to the window. I'm going to slide my arms under yours and lift you out."

Nodding again, she did as he instructed, ignoring what felt like nails hammering her head. Then he was there, big, strong, hefting her out of her seat. She pushed with her good foot, winced when she tried with her bad.

But she was sliding out, her shoulders, her butt, finally her legs. He eased her to her feet, and she hobbled to lean against the car.

"Thank you," she said, but the wind whipped her words away, the same wind pelting her with ice shards.

"C'mon," he yelled, reaching for her. "We've got to get you out of here and warmed up."

She needed her purse, her clothes, Gran's Christmas gifts. But he didn't give her a chance to tell him any of that. He scooped her up as if she weighed no more than a snowflake and turned, and that was when she saw his horse.

The big chestnut beast had snow-frosted lashes and a similarly dusted mane. His breath puffed out in clouds as he snorted. Her rescuer lifted her into the saddle, then swung up behind, scooting her onto his lap before wrapping his thick sheepskin coat around her.

He smelled like leather, like hay, like the deep green woods and the snow. His chest behind her was broad and warm, his thighs beneath hers solid. Like her, he wore gloves, but she could tell his hands were big, and obviously capable as he reined the horse around and away from her car.

She tilted her head back. "I almost hit a deer."

Having leaned down to catch her words, he nodded, then brought her tighter against him with an arm across her middle. She really should be much colder than she felt, and had to be nearly delirious because all she could think about was how treasured, how protected, how small and feminine and faint she felt.

And how romantic it was to be rescued by a knight in a black Stetson on horseback.

Brenna woke later to find herself in a bed, not hers, in a bedroom, not Gran's, and dressed in her socks, her panties and the long-sleeved pullover she'd been wearing with her jeans, which were missing. She had no idea what time it was, or how long she'd been asleep.

What she did know was that she was warm, her ankle sore but only slightly swollen beneath an elastic bandage. And she was safely out of the storm.

Beyond the walls, the wind screamed bloody murder. And on the other side of the door, a fire crackled and popped, its light flickering in long yellow tongues over the bedroom's hardwood floor.

Not sure why, she found herself hesitant to leave the cocoon of quilts and pillows. She assumed she'd find her knight in a black Stetson on the other side of the door, and before she faced him she'd like to have her jeans.

Still, she couldn't resist. She'd felt his strength as he'd lifted her from the car, as he'd guided his horse through the blizzard and kept her safe. She'd sat in his lap, and knew how he moved, his thighs, his abs, his hips, balancing the both of them.

Yet she had no idea what he looked like. He was a blur, a shadow. A sheepskin coat, and boots and jeans, and the sort of big black hat she'd always associated with bad guys. She wanted to see him. So hand on the knob, she turned and inched the door open.

Her first impression of being in a log cabin instead of a frame house like Gran's was spot-on—though this *cabin* was no rough-hewn shack. The stone fireplace containing the blaze took up a full wall of the structure. The flames provided the room's only light and more heat than did Gran's furnace.

Brenna supposed there was a lot more to see…furniture, fixtures, decorative design…but her gaze was snagged and held by the man sleeping on the sofa in front of the fire. He was stretched out on his back, his boots on the floor beside him, his socked feet crossed at the ankles, an arm thrown over his eyes.

All she could see of his face was his nose, his mouth, his very square and very strong jaw, and his end-of-day beard that appeared darker than his short hair crushed flat to his head by his hat. But his body…she could see almost all of it, and another of her first impressions was proved right.

He was a big man. Tall and fit and dressed like he belonged on horseback in a yoked Western shirt. His hat hung on a peg with two others beside the front door, and his heavy coat that had kept her so warm hung on a coat tree nearby.

The only item out of place was his brass belt buckle. She was too far away to make out the engraving, but thought it looked more military than rodeo cowboy. Interesting, and unexpected, here on Gran's mountain.

Who was this man? How soon could he get her to her grandmother's house, and why had he been out riding in the storm?

But the most important question was, what had he done with her pants?

CHAPTER TWO

Dillon Craig waited for the bedroom door to close then moved his forearm from his eyes and rolled up to the sofa's edge. He was pretty sure he had what his unexpected guest was looking for, but he hadn't wanted her to feel uncomfortable having to ask a strange man for her pants.

That would make it hard to avoid the subject of his having taken them off her, and he knew he'd never be able to have that conversation without looking at her legs. Panties at her hips, socks on her feet, all that bare skin between. He'd had a hard time thinking of anything else since undressing her.

Coming across her car like he had… He rubbed a gritty lack of sleep from his eyes and stared into the fire. Instead of the flames, he saw the white car's red taillight covers like reflectors in the snow. And instead of the warmth from the blaze, cold rushed like a river of ice over his skin. If he'd shown up any later…

He'd been on his way home, skirting the edge of the mountain's main road after his daily rounds. Even his routine check of his neighbors—some elderly and housebound, some chronically ill, some, like Donota Keating, just friends—had been cut short because of the storm. The buffeting winds had nearly lifted him out of Ranger's saddle, and the horse hadn't had a much easier time of battling the incoming blast.

Dillon had seen the car just in time. It was close to being buried. Snow had mounded on the roof, the back window, the lid of the trunk. Had piled to mid-rim on the wheels. Another couple of hours and her near hypothermia would've been a very real case, one requiring more treatment than dry clothes and a warm bed.

Being unable to climb through the window on her own had probably saved her life. She was still miles from the turnoff to Donota's place. A walk in the sub-freezing temps, even with a good internal compass, would've screwed her coordination, skewed her course and eventually killed her.

Before nodding off in his arms for the ride up the mountain, she'd told him that was where she'd been headed. And since he'd learned when seeing Donota earlier in the day that her granddaughter was expected, it hadn't been hard to put two and two together.

And now the woman he'd gotten to know through years of listening to her grandmother's stories was in his bedroom without her pants.

Clearing the image from his mind, Dillon got to his feet, made the trip to the laundry room to fetch her jeans from the dryer. They'd been soaked from the snow, though his own had fared better because of it. Her thighs had kept his warm and mostly dry.

Standing to the side of her door, he knocked. "I've got your jeans."

He waited no more than ten seconds. The door opened and she reached out her hand. The corner of his mouth pulled into a smile and he handed them to her. The door just as quickly closed, but did so on a muffled, "Thank you."

Still grinning, he headed to the kitchen and the pot of stew he'd put on to reheat after tucking her beneath enough quilts to warm a platoon. He'd figured it wouldn't take long for her body heat to rise, or that she'd need more than a power nap to shake off the brunt of her exhaustion.

He'd been right, and was stirring the stew fragrant with beef and draught beer when he heard the uneven slide of her socks on the floor behind him. He glanced back, but didn't linger. He didn't need to. Her sleep-tousled hair and eyes still not fully awake would stick with him a very long time.

As would the remnants of her fear. "How's your ankle?"

"It's okay. Sore, but I don't think it's sprained."

Her voice was low, a bit husky. With no door or bad weather between them, it was the first time he'd noticed the tone, and he let it settle, finding it unexpected, intriguing. Sexy. "Most likely it's bruised from being twisted. But you should still take it easy."

"I will. Thanks for drying my jeans. I guess they were pretty soaked."

Nodding, he set the business end of the ladle on the saucer beside the stove and turned to get his first real look at her. He knew she was tall from the way she'd fit against him on horseback. Knew, too, she was curvy.

But he hadn't had time to take her in and did so now. Admiring. Appreciating. Lusting inappropriately. He had a thing for long legs. "Sorry about…peeling them off without asking first, but it had to be done."

Shrugging, she tucked a lock of coffee-brown hair behind one ear. "No apologies necessary. I'm pretty sure I'd have frozen to death if you hadn't happened along. I'm not one to get bent out of shape over life-saving efforts."

He liked her attitude as much as her voice, and wondered how much came naturally, and how much was a result of her nurse's training. "Shucking a woman out of her pants is definitely more enjoyable than cracking open a chest behind a burned-out Humvee."

Her eyes widened. "You're a military doctor?"

"Army Reserves. For a while." He came closer, breathed in the soft scent of something outdoorsy, held out a hand to shake hers. "Dillon Craig."

"Brenna Keating."

"Donota's granddaughter."

"You know Gran?" She pulled her hand from his, wrapped her arms around her middle as if cold. Or uncertain.

Hmm. Strange. "Saw her this morning," he said, hoping to put her at ease. "She told me you'd be coming up tonight. When I saw the Duke Raleigh Hospital tag on your window, I was pretty sure it was you in that snowbank."

"Huh. You know Gran, and you know I work at Duke Raleigh." This time she was the one looking him over, her green-eyed gaze intense, unnerving. Inappropriate in its own way. "Why don't I know about you?"

That one was easy. The folks he took care of knew he wasn't up to the scrutiny, the speculation. The questions he wasn't sure he'd ever be able to answer.

The things he'd seen did that to a guy. "Can't think why I'd come up in conversation."

"Are you kidding?" Her hair again, falling forward, tucking it back. "Gran tells me everything that goes on up here."

He didn't want to get into this—not now, not with her, not yet—and turned back to the stove. "Are you hungry?"

"Actually, I'm starving. I'd planned to be at Gran's for an early dinner—" She cut herself off with a sharp inhalation. "Oh my God. She's got to be sick wondering where I am. My cell had no coverage so I couldn't let her know I was okay."

"She's good. She knows. I got through on the landline before the storm took out the service."

Brenna sank into a chair at the table, her knees together as she leaned forward. "Thank you. Oh God, thank you. I can't imagine how worried she must've been."

Dillon reached into the cabinet for two deep bowls, dished more stew into his than into hers, then thought better of it and gave hers another ladleful. "She said to tell you not to fret. Her words. That she'll put the cookie baking on hold till you get there."

"I guess it's too late to go tonight, huh."

It was only nine, but they weren't going anywhere anytime soon. He set the filled bowls on the table, the steam curling up from both. "Too late, and too dangerous. It doesn't look like it's going to get better for days."

"Days." She sat straighter, her gaze puzzled as it searched out his. "What do you mean, days?"

"I mean days." He took the chair opposite hers. They needed this conversation out of the way, the reality in the open, or else those days were going to be tough ones. "They're calling it the storm of the century. I'm afraid you're stuck here for the time being."

"But I can't be stuck here. I've got to get to Gran's. It's Christmas."

"You will. Eventually."

"Wait. Wait. Eventually?" She shook her head as if the motion would get rid of the truth. "No, that won't work."

"You don't have a choice."

"You brought me here on horseback. Just take me to Gran's the same way." It sounded so simple and obvious when she said it.

Knowing it was neither, he spooned up a bite of stew to let cool. "No can do. I'm not taking Ranger out in this mess. It's not safe for me, for you, or for him."

"I can't believe this. I cannot believe this." She collapsed in her chair, her eyes closing, her voice going painfully soft. "I'm going to miss Christmas with Gran."

The possibility was there, and he wasn't going to promise her anything, but if he could, he'd make sure it didn't happen. "Storm's predicted to blow itself out by the end of the week. It's still four days till Christmas."

"The storm wasn't predicted to arrive until midnight, and look what happened. And all my stuff's in my car. God, my car." She groaned, then opened her eyes. And finally she reached for her spoon and dug in. "Do you know anything about cars? Do you think it's still drivable? If it's not…"

He was better at putting bodies back together. "I know some."

"Will it be safe where it is? Will another driver hit it, do you think?"

"I can't imagine any driver being out on the road in this."

Her gaze narrowed. "It wasn't like *this* when I started out. It wasn't supposed to be like *this* for hours yet."

"Gotta love Mother Nature."

"Or not," she grumbled.

Time to move on. "You more the indoor type?"

"I'm more the not-wanting-to-die-in-a-snowbank type," she said, stirring her stew. "Other than that, I love being outdoors. It's why I love coming to Gran's so much. Besides seeing Gran, of course."

"She's a great lady."

"She is. I don't know what I'd do without her."

"Your folks are overseas somewhere, yes?"

"They've got an obstetrics clinic in rural Malaysia." Frowning, she shook her head, the line between her brows hooking right. "I can't believe you know that about them. And know what you do about me."

It wasn't a big deal. "Your grandmother talks about all of you. A lot. She's very proud of you and your dad."

"I guess that makes sense." She took another bite of stew. "And what about you? You have family nearby?"

He looked down at his bowl. "Nope. Just me."

"But not always, right?"

"No, not always." He stopped. Started again. Blamed the hot food for his loose tongue. "This used to be my father's place. Lost my mom when I was a kid, lost him during my second tour in Afghanistan. The mountain seemed like a good place to live after resigning my commission."

"How long did you serve?" She set down her spoon, gave him her full attention.

Attention that made him itch. "Eight years. Army Reserves. I'd done a couple in the E.R., then 9/11 happened. Seemed there were emergencies happening overseas I was suited to help with, so…"

"I'm sure your dad was proud."

He nodded, shook out more words. "It was tough to lose him that way. Being so far away and all."

"Was it sudden?"

"A heart attack."

"I'm sorry."

Losses. Not what he wanted to talk about over dinner. "You want more stew? Corn bread?"

"No, I'm fine. And this was wonderful," she said, though she hadn't eaten but half of what he'd served her. "Thank you."

"You're feeling okay? I mean, I know you're a nurse—"

"But you're still a doctor," she said, and laughed, the sound tickling and sweet. "No ill effects at all. I don't know what I would've done if you hadn't come along."

Thing was, his coming along hadn't been totally random. He'd known from Donota that her granddaughter was overdue, and storm or no, he'd ridden the long road home rather than shortcutting through the woods.

He hadn't expected to find Brenna stranded. He assumed she'd been delayed by the weather. That she might even have canceled her trip but been unable to reach her grandmother to let her know.

Taking the path he had had been instinct, not even a conscious choice. It was just how he operated these days. Looking out for others. Anticipating the next corner as well as eyeballing the here and now.

He could tell by her crooked frown that Brenna, too, was caught up in what might've happened instead of what had. "You want to warm up by the fire for a while?"

She looked at him then, shaking off the borrowed trouble. "I'm not really cold."

"I know. I've just found watching a good blaze is a great way to take your mind off things."

Her laugh was low and soft, and rolled over him like summer on the beach. "A glass of wine would help."

"I might have a bottle. I know I have beer." Beer. The beach. Brenna in a bikini.

"That works."

"Go get comfortable." He got to his feet, tried to remember the last time he'd equated sand and sun with sex. "I'll clean up here and bring you a drink."

She stood too. "I'm happy to do the dishes. You did cook, after all."

He found himself smiling. "I heated up a pot of stew. That's hardly cooking."

"And here I thought you'd whipped this up while I napped."

"Mrs. Calhoun whipped it up. Paid me with it when I looked in on her father yesterday."

"Paid you with it. You mean you barter your services?"

"Sometimes."

Her expression grew curious, as if she was looking for more than just an answer. As if she was looking for who he was in his response. "And other times?"

He wasn't sure how much he was comfortable telling her. "I give them away."

"That's very generous." Her voice was soft again, sultry and low because of it.

"I just consider it human. I'm not looking to be paid."

"I don't think I've ever heard a doctor say that."

Come to think of it... "I wouldn't have before Afghanistan. Now..."

The word hung between them, taking up space, pushing them apart. His past. His baggage. It would always be in the way.

Brenna moved her chair up under the table, wincing at the scrape of the feet on the floor. She gestured stiffly over her shoulder. "I'll go sit by the fire."

"I'll get the beer."

CHAPTER THREE

Legs crossed beneath her, Brenna sank into the corner of the sofa and thought she might never want to move. It was a big piece of furniture to fit a big man, and the rust-colored leather was ridiculously sumptuous for a log cabin in the woods.

It was also strangely out of place. As was the exquisite stone fireplace that took up an entire wall of the main room. As was the six-burner stove on which Dillon had heated the stew. Even the pot itself, a mustardy ceramic number, seemed better suited to a Food Network kitchen. Paula Deen. Rachael Ray.

In fact, nothing about the cabin fit.

And that included the owner.

Most of Gran's friends who lived on the mountain lived simply. Many were retirees on a fixed income. Others were the granola type, getting back to basics with vegetable gardens, chickens and goats, a couple of horses, dairy cows.

Some, like Gran, had lived here their whole lives. To outsiders, their places appeared haphazard, cluttered, when what they were was lived in.

She'd visited their homes with Gran and knew Dillon's décor was not the norm. Rustic, yes. Comfortable, definitely. But the simple look was deceptive.

And she couldn't help but wonder if he'd chosen the pieces

to create that impression in an effort to fit in. Or if this was who he was, the cabin reflecting the man who'd volunteered his services in places where his life was as much at risk as his patients.

His heavy steps drew closer. A bottle of dark beer appeared over her shoulder. She took it from his hand, their fingers brushing, hers tingling. "Thank you."

He folded his long body into the opposite end of the sofa, his legs outstretched, his ankles crossed. "I'm sure it's not your usual, but it gets the job done."

"Doctor's orders? A stout at bedtime and come see me in the morning?"

"Something like that." He was smiling when he lifted his bottle to his mouth, his eyes hooded beneath his dark lashes as he stared at the fire.

She studied his profile, the stubble covering his jaw, his hair, a dark dirty blond, clipped short though still long enough to show the fit of his hat. The vee of smooth skin in the open collar of his snap-front shirt. His belt buckle lying flat against his stomach. His...jeans.

She looked away, looked at the fire. She wanted to hear him talk about the war. It had been in the news for years, stories of soldiers lost, of ones saved, acts of bravery, of sacrifice. The man beside her was a hero. Whatever had happened to bring him home, that much she knew.

But she also knew not to ask. Gran hadn't mentioned him for a reason, and Brenna was certain it had to do with respecting his privacy. Whether by his direct request or Gran's sense of decency, only Gran could say.

Brenna chose a safer ground for conversation. "Do you have a practice here? On the mountain?"

"Of a sort," he said after another long pull on his beer. "I don't keep regular hours, but I've got a clinic. House out back was my dad's. Once this one was built, I converted it."

Interesting. "So people just drop in?"

"They usually call first, but yeah. I do rounds in the mornings, then the rest of the day I'm usually here."

"Doing what?"

Never turning his head, he cut his gaze toward her. "Kind of personal, isn't it?"

Her cheeks warmed as if she'd been sitting for an hour on the hearth. "Sorry. That didn't come out right. What I meant, was—"

"If I'm out of the service and have no family and no real clinic hours, what do I do with my time?"

She drank from her bottle, realizing first that he'd nailed her intent exactly, and second exactly how nosy her question was. "Yes. That."

He laughed, a gut-deep chuckle that made her want to curl against him and feel the vibration. Once the thought of doing so settled, she couldn't shake it. And the beer flowing through her, heavy and thick, only made things worse.

"I keep busy," he said, pulling her mind from its lusty travels. "I've got a good chunk of land here to keep up, and there's rarely a day someone doesn't stop by the clinic. I have to go into town to pick up lab results for the tests I can't do myself. Stuff like that."

"Do you have help? A nurse or physician's assistant?"

"It's just me working with the patients, though the wife of one of my regulars does my accounting and keeps up with the paperwork."

Very cool. "Sounds like you could give lessons in bartering."

"It works for me. It wouldn't for everyone."

It wouldn't for anyone needing cash. Which she took to

mean he didn't. "You mentioned doing rounds. Obviously not in a hospital."

"On the mountain." He cut her another side-eyed glance. "A big part of how I spend that time you were wondering about."

"You have that many patients?"

"Rounds aren't just about patients."

"How so?"

He took a minute, probably regretting he'd ever rescued her chatty self. "A lot of folks up here are housebound, maybe not sick but not able to get out. Some just don't want to, but still need a hand now and then. Most knew my dad, and would let him help, so they trust me where they wouldn't trust social services or a stranger."

Now *that* she understood. "Gran plants a bigger garden than one person could ever need for the same reason. She bakes dozens of loaves of bread, and always doubles her casserole recipes and freezes the extra for emergencies."

"I know," he said, and finished his beer. "She has me deliver them when she's not up to getting out."

His words sent a ripple of unease down Brenna's spine. "Is she okay? I mean, do I need to be worried about anything? She never complains, you know. And I don't think she'd tell me if something was really wrong."

"Nothing to worry about. She's healthy as a horse. Sharp as a tack." He got to his feet, waggled his empty bottle by the neck. "Be right back."

That took care of the physical and mental clichés and left Brenna to wonder about Gran's emotions. They talked two or three times a week. Sometimes more. Nothing unusual was going on in Gran's life. Except for one thing.

Dillon returned with two beers, set hers on the coffee table when she showed him she hadn't finished her first.

"She told you I'm going to Africa."

"She did," he said and sat.

"And you disapprove."

"I didn't say that. It's not my place."

"You didn't have to."

He turned to her then, shifting a bent knee onto the couch and looking at her. Looking into her, his eyes lit sharply by the glow of the fire. They weren't the brown she'd originally thought, but a golden gray, and they saw way too much of what she was thinking.

He glanced down at his bottle, returned his gaze to hers before speaking. "I'm not saying you're doing anything wrong. I just think it's going to be tougher than you realize to leave her behind."

Brenna fought the urge to jump to her feet, to leave the room and escape his words that felt like an accusation. That sort of defensive response would do nothing but prove him right. Already she was bracing herself for the guilt to come, the sorrow.

The longing to be in Gran's arms, to smell the butterscotch and roses. "I'm not leaving her behind. I'm doing exactly what she did, what she was doing, volunteering, when she met my grandfather. He was a doctor, you know."

"And she was a nurse. She's told me."

Again, with his knowing things about her and hers. "My folks are doing the same now. I'm just following in the family footsteps, and I'm doing it with her blessing."

He nodded, his eyes on the fire again. "My dad gave me the same blessing when I gave up my practice to enlist."

"Then you know firsthand what it's like to make that kind of career choice."

Several seconds passed before he gave her a response. "I

also know how tough it was to be seven thousand miles away when Dad's heart gave out."

Anger began to bubble in her blood but she stayed silent, unsure of the root of the emotion—his words, or her life's dream taking her away from Gran. The way their same dream had taken her parents from her.

She'd been fine with their going. She'd been eighteen, independent. And she'd be just as fine now... Wouldn't she? "I'm sorry that happened. To you and to him."

Dillon shrugged, took a long drink from his bottle, said nothing.

"At least I won't be in a war zone."

"The health conditions where you're going? Call it another kind of war. And you'll be fighting it *eight* thousand miles away."

So her extra thousand made a difference? "I live four hours from Gran now. If her heart gives out, I'm already too far away. And if you'd still been practicing medicine in the States instead of saving lives overseas..."

She stopped. His life wasn't her business. And making him feel worse would not make her feel better. Besides, it was wrongheaded and rude.

He sat forward then, his elbows on his knees, his hands between holding his beer, his head hung low. "I've told myself the same thing dozens of times. I don't know why it won't stick."

She thought of her struggles with leaving Gran. Then realized this wasn't all about her. That Dillon Craig, soldier, warrior, doctor, savior, shared her doubts.

Setting the rest of her beer on the table, she got to her feet. She was done for the night. Done doubting, done worrying, done letting guilt win. Done upsetting her very generous host because she still had issues.

At the door to the bedroom, she turned. "Maybe it's really not about the miles. Maybe it's not being sure we're doing the right thing."

Long after Brenna had turned in, Dillon was still sitting in front of the fire thinking about what she'd said. About making choices. About doing the right thing.

He knew without a doubt that serving his country had been a calling he had to answer. He didn't think he'd ever seen such pride in his father's eyes as when he'd stood with the rest of the military families seeing their loved ones off to war.

Brenna was right. It wasn't the miles as much as the choices. And he'd made some while in Afghanistan that had repercussions he'd live with the rest of his life.

No man left behind. And none had been. That didn't mean he hadn't had to choose who to save, and who to let go. Those were the faces he saw daily, faces he couldn't shake. Faces that would haunt him no matter how many others owed him their lives.

He wasn't looking for kudos or credit. What he wanted was to know he'd done his best, done all he could, the only things he could. To know that one extra step wouldn't have made a difference. That no family was suffering needlessly because he'd made a mistake.

From his bedroom came the sound of Brenna coughing. He frowned, listened closer, heard nothing else. He hadn't yet decided if she was the woman he'd expected after all of her grandmother's stories. Mostly because he hadn't known what to expect. Grandmothers had a way of sugarcoating even the tiniest of flaws.

So far, he hadn't found any. She was girl-next-door cute but bedroom-eyes sexy. She was smart, sharp. She challenged him, and he liked that most of all. But he meant every word he'd told her. Leaving loved ones behind for a career move didn't come easy.

At least she wouldn't have to deal with the life-and-death battlefield choices that still had him questioning if his move had done more harm than good.

CHAPTER FOUR

The first thing Brenna did when she woke the next morning was remind herself it was Friday, and Christmas was now three days away. The second thing she did was climb shivering from bed to pull back the curtains and check on the snow. The third thing she did was groan.

The drifts mounded against the house were indecipherable from those circling the trunks of the surrounding trees, creating one very wide and still deepening blanket. Or so she supposed was happening since she couldn't see much beyond her reflection in the glass.

She dropped the curtain into place, turned back to the room and clicked on the bedside lamp. The shade was an ordinary pleated linen in a color between eggshell and cream, but the base, a section of knotted tree branch housing the socket and wires, was obviously one of a kind, fitting in with what she'd seen of the rest of Dillon's décor.

She lifted it, turned it over, found a set of initials—W.T.— and a date—3/25/2007—burned into the bottom. But before she could think about what either meant, the smell of coffee wafted in from the kitchen, and her stomach growled.

After a quick shower in the bedroom's attached bath, she dressed in the same clothes she'd put on when leaving Raleigh yesterday. Minus a comb or brush, there was nothing but her fingers to run through her hair, though she did help herself to a new toothbrush, along with Dillon's toothpaste and soap.

She really needed her things. Especially if she was going to be stuck here for the next couple of days. It was bad enough that she'd driven him from his bed and would be sharing what food he'd laid in store. She didn't feel right using his toiletries, or asking if she could borrow a pair of pajamas so she could wash her things.

Still imagining the overlarge fit of his clothes—the hems of his bottoms rolled up to her ankles, the sleeves cuffed to her wrists, his scent of leather and pine enveloping her—she left the bedroom to find herself alone. A fire still blazed in the main room, and the pillow and blankets left rumpled on the sofa gave her another twinge of guilt.

Tonight, she slept there, Dillon in his bed. Hospitality didn't need to mean he sacrificed his comfort for hers, and she would fit the sofa better.

In the kitchen, the coffee was hot, and a cup sat on the counter next to the pot, but Dillon wasn't around. Now that dawn had given way to daylight, the window over the sink allowed for a better view of the storm. She sipped her coffee, noticing the wind had died to more breeze and less bluster. Snow flurried in soft swirls, tempting her outside to see how bad things were.

When she got to the rack where Dillon had hung her coat, she found her purse, her suitcase and her carryall of gifts sitting just inside the front door. She stared, confused, disbelieving, but curious most of all. Yes, she appreciated the gesture. But if he could make the trip to her car for her things, why couldn't he get her to Gran's?

Wanting an answer, she dug through her bag for her boots and a knit hat, grabbed her coat and her coffee and headed onto the porch. White powder had already begun to stake its claim on the recently swept boards. And the passage cleared from the steps around the cabin proved Dillon had been busy long before the sun had come up.

Pulling her hat low on her forehead, she cradled her mug to her chest and ducked into the wind. The path circled the cabin then branched in two directions. She couldn't see anything but trees and snow to the left, but the right leg dead-ended at a barn. A row of high windows shining brightly drew her that direction.

Packed snow crunched under her feet, but above the wind and the sound of her steps, she heard that of a motor grinding. The barn's main entrance was braced and bolted, but a sliver of light escaped from a door on the structure's side. She let herself in and eased the door closed behind her.

Breathing in the sharp pitch of pine, and those of burning wood, horseflesh and hay, she made her way around tables and tool chests and shelves of supplies—paint, stain, planes and chisels and knives—before she found Dillon. And then she stopped because the scene before her was so unexpected, she lost her bearings.

The largest part of the building was, indeed, a barn, and Dillon's horse happily feeding in his stall. A fan blew a stream of warmth along the floor, keeping the worst of the chill at bay. She set her coffee on the ledge of an empty stall, shrugged off her coat and draped it over the door. Then she headed for Dillon.

Boughs of pine needles and wood scraps and shredded bark lay on a table where he stood working with a section of tree branch. Without seeing more than that, she knew she was looking at the artist who'd created the lamp. Deducing that much didn't explain the initials or the date. In 2007, he'd still been overseas.

He hadn't acknowledged her presence, but she was pretty sure he knew she was there. Sure, too, that he wished she wasn't. He'd stiffened a bit, his shoulders, his back, the tilt of his head, and his hands had stilled, as had the air around them.

"Thanks for getting my things from my car." She said it to break the strangely uncomfortable silence, but also because she meant it. And because she wanted to broach the subject of his taking her to Gran's.

But that part she held off on. His stance told her it wasn't the right time. And when he finally turned from his work to face her, she knew hunting him down this way had been a mistake.

His face appeared ragged, as if he hadn't slept at all, and tortured, as if he'd been lost in a world she couldn't imagine. His eyes conveyed a sadness she swore hadn't been there previously. Swore, too, that the tight set of his mouth was all that kept the corners from turning down in a sorrow too deep to bear.

She didn't need to be here. She shouldn't have come here. She had to go, to leave him. Looking away, she reached for her coat. "I just wanted to say that. I didn't mean to intrude."

Three heavy steps brought him to her, and he grabbed her arm to keep her from walking out of the warm barn and back into the frigid morning. "Wait."

His hold was firm and gave her little choice. She stared at his hand, the hand of a stranger, a man much larger than her, a warrior who'd been damaged, and realized she wasn't frightened at all. Instead, compassion coiled in her center, and she did as he said.

Long, tense moments passed, the roar of the fan and the whiffling of Ranger feeding filled the air that seemed too thick to breathe. Brenna couldn't blink, she couldn't move. She could only wait for Dillon to shake his demon's grip.

"You're not intruding," he finally said and released her, returning to the table and giving her his back. "I should've left you a note, told you where I was. I didn't think."

He wasn't used to leaving notes, she thought, rubbing at her arm. She got that. He hadn't expected her to come looking for him. She got that, too. What she didn't get was what seeing him like this, hurting, had done to her, because without question it had changed everything about her reason for being here.

Why she was less concerned about getting to Gran's than she was with talking him off whatever ledge had him suffering alone?

"It's not a big deal." Striving to appear unaffected, she fetched her coffee, sipped at the brew that was lukewarm at best. "I was just excited to see my things and thought I'd ask you how my car is faring."

"Not too bad considering the driver's window was down all night."

"Crud. I hadn't even thought about the wet mess inside."

"It's wet, and it's a mess, but the airbag collected a lot of the snow. I rolled it up."

"I'd been planning to sell it before my move, but I wonder if it's going to be worth the cost to repair." Another swallow and her coffee was gone. She was also running out of conversation. "Really, though. I wasn't expecting that, so thank you."

"You're welcome." He pulled open a drawer in his table, stored away several saw blades. "I needed to clear the road to the clinic while there was a break in the storm, so made the trip down to your car with the tractor."

"Ah, I thought you went on horseback." And so much for her getting to Gran's the same way. "That must've taken a while. A tractor."

"I couldn't sleep." He picked up an awl, gave a gritty, humorless laugh. "Not that me not sleeping is anything new."

He'd said the words to himself, not to her, and she wondered if he knew he'd spoken them aloud, or if he was so wrapped up with his internal battles he'd forgotten for the moment she was there.

Eyes closed, she breathed a soft sigh. This wasn't her business. He was barely even a friend. Yet he was Gran's friend, and obviously a close one. Gran never let a hurt go uncared for, and had instilled in Brenna the same.

"Maybe you should see a doctor about that. The no sleeping thing."

"Yeah, well, if I knew one who had a clue what he was doing I might."

Her comment had been lighthearted, offhand, but his response... She was no good at this. She bandaged cuts and scrapes and gave injections and packed sprains in ice. She wasn't Gran who knew how to soothe, how to pull out deep-rooted poisons with words. And staring into her empty cup wasn't giving her an answer.

She returned the cup to the stall's railing, tucked her hands into her pockets and walked toward the table where Dillon stood. "I guess it's like the cobbler's kids who don't have any shoes."

He looked over at her then, his smile not quite reaching his eyes, though the bleakness had faded to what looked like acceptance. "Yeah. Something like that."

"I've heard doctors make terrible patients anyway."

"You've heard right."

And then, not knowing why, she pried. "Bad dreams keep you awake?"

"Not dreams. Memories. They're worse than the nightmares."

"The war?"

He shrugged. "Yeah, but not really. It's hard to explain."

Something told her he hadn't explained it to anyone, that he needed to, that doing so would go a long way to helping him sleep. "Mother Nature's made sure I'm not going anywhere. I've got time."

He turned, leaned against the table, crossed his arms. "Next you'll be telling me you're a good listener."

"I'm female. We specialize."

"So tell me more about nursing."

"Are you changing the subject?"

He gave her a wink. "I'm male. We specialize."

She grinned at that, and at the crow's-feet crinkling at the corner of his eye. He was trying, and that had her grinning too. "I'm a nurse because of Gran and her stories. About her and my grandfather meeting in a field hospital. About working with the Red Cross at Pearl Harbor. But I also blame my folks. Medicine runs in the Keating family veins."

"The clinic in Malaysia."

She nodded. "This is the longest they've ever stayed in one place. But the clinic's been a huge investment. I think this move was their last."

"Have you been there?"

She nodded again. "They wanted me to stay. And if not for Gran, I might have. I even talked to her about moving with me, but she's tied to the mountain."

"Most of the people here are."

"But not you."

"I wasn't. I am now."

Interesting distinction. "Because of what you saw in the war?"

"Because this is where I'm needed."

And yet, the only thing tying him here was his father. "Your skills, your experience, you could fill the need in a lot of places."

"I've done the E.R. thing. And this need is different. If I wasn't here, some of the folks would never see a doctor."

"They trust you."

"They knew my father."

"But they trust you."

"That's part of it, I guess."

It was a lot bigger than part of it. Trust was everything for the people Gran called friends. So why was Dillon reluctant to take the credit he so obviously deserved? And why had he chosen to live on his father's land when he could write his own ticket to anywhere?

"Did you get breakfast?" he asked before she could push the conversation further.

She'd table it for now, but she wasn't going to let it go. He intrigued her and puzzles were one of her favorite things. "No, and I'm actually starving."

"Mrs. Calhoun's stew didn't hold you?"

Oh, he had so much to learn. "And here I thought Gran had told you everything about me."

CHAPTER FIVE

Dillon got his wish. He got Brenna back to the cabin before she asked what he was doing in the barn. He could talk to her about the war, his life before the war, but he hadn't talked to anyone about his life after. The life he was living now, though a by-the-numbers existence, seemed a better way to look at his days.

Up at dawn, coffee and breakfast, seeing to Ranger then riding out for rounds. Most days he was back at the clinic for afternoon hours. Then he worked in the barn until exhaustion sent him to bed. Not that he slept when he got there, but he was a doctor and he knew, if nothing else, he needed the rest.

He'd found the woodworking tools behind boxes of books when going through his father's things. Up till then, he'd forgot about his father building the shelves he used in the clinic and the porch swing that creaked beneath any amount of weight. Forgot, too, about the toys his father had carved for the mountain kids—until he'd run across an unfinished pirate's sword while cleaning, organizing. Looking to connect.

Looking for forgiveness.

Enough.

He pulled open the refrigerator door. "Pancakes? Eggs?"

"If you've already eaten, I can fend for myself," Brenna said, shrugging out of her coat. "I don't want to get in the way of your schedule."

His schedule could use a dust-up. "I had the last wedge of corn bread with my coffee, and both wore off a while ago."

"Then let me cook." She came toward him, stopped, raised a brow in question. "Unless you've got a patient who's bartered meal prep for your services."

Interesting that she was still ignoring his woodworking. He wondered how long before it became the elephant in the room. "No. You're welcome to the kitchen. I try to cook as little as possible."

When he stepped away from the fridge, she moved to peer inside. "Because you can't, or because you don't want to?"

He snorted. "Because I make a worse cook than I do patient. And because most of the time I don't have to."

"How's that?" she asked, coming out with bacon and eggs. "The bartering thing?"

"Some of it, yes." He pulled his gaze from her ass. Tamped down his lust. "But folks drop dishes by a lot. I've got a freezer full. It's like I'm on a list, or something."

Setting the food on the counter, she pointed a finger his way. "I know exactly what list you're on."

"Yeah?"

"Sure. The mountain's most eligible bachelors."

"I don't think that's it."

Her look called him on his denial. "Do these folks who drop by have daughters? Single daughters of marrying age?"

His fault, this hell, for mentioning the list. "Some do."

She nodded sagely. "And others are single women themselves? Widowed young? Divorced even?"

He didn't respond.

"I knew it. You're the biggest catch around." She frowned, bent again to look for a skillet, the position of her body giving him a whole lot of grief. "Which makes me wonder again why Gran hasn't told me about you since she's always asking about my love life."

The grief had him rubbing at his forehead. "Do you have a love life?"

She turned, her eyes bright, curious. "Do you?"

He thought about what she'd said. "I've got a freezer full of casseroles, if that counts."

"Then you're doing better than me," she said, biting off a sharp laugh.

He found that hard to believe. She was smart, she was feisty. Her ass was as amazing as her legs were long. She'd made him laugh more in the last few hours than anyone had in a very long time. She'd also made him think, and forced him to re-visit the past that had brought him here—when he avoided doing both because neither one did him any good.

And, yeah, he liked the way she looked. Liked it a lot.

"The guys you date don't cook?"

Shaking her head, she pulled strips of bacon from the pack-age and lined them up in the pan. "And what guys would those be?"

"You don't date?"

Her back to him, she asked, "Do you?"

"No, but—"

"Exactly."

He crossed his arms, leaned a hip on the corner of the coun-ter. "Why don't you date?"

"You first," she said, lifting a finger.

"I don't have time."

"Neither do I."

"Nursing doesn't take all day."

"Oh, yeah? I've got regular hours and volunteer hours, then I teach and grade projects and tutor privately. The rest of my time I spend catching up with housework, seeing friends. Reading, sleeping. The usual."

"So you do go out."

"With girlfriends, yes. And I have a couple of guys I tap if I need a male escort. But I quit the blind-date thing after a guy who paid for the dinner and the movie expected me to pay him back in bed."

He didn't know what to say to that. He'd known men who thought similarly. That picking up the check entitled them to more than a woman's company. He enjoyed taking a woman to bed as much as the next guy, but he never expected or assumed, and he certainly never bartered for sex the way he bartered for other services.

But that was him. He still didn't get her. "What about dates that aren't blind?"

"You ask like it's the easiest thing in the world to meet someone."

He shrugged. "Sorry. Didn't mean to hit a sore spot."

She dropped the fork she was using, splattering bacon grease across the stove. "Oh, now my not dating is a sore spot?"

That made him smile. "Want me to finish the bacon?"

"I'm fine. I just thought we—" she picked up the fork, gestured with it "—and by *we* I mean society, not you and I...I just thought we'd gotten past thinking there was something wrong with a woman who wasn't attached to a man."

Ah, there was a sore spot. "There's nothing wrong with you, Brenna. If that's your takeaway from me wondering why you don't date, I apologize."

Her mouth tight, she flipped the bacon slices, checked each and transferred those already crisped to a waiting paper towel. "No need to apologize. I just get that a lot, or did before I threatened bodily harm to the friends who kept hounding me about being single."

"Being single's a good thing."

She spun on him, glared. "And now you're patronizing me?"

Prickly, wasn't she? Prickly and cute, though dangerous with a fork and bacon grease. "Sorry. That wasn't about you."

"Want to know the truth? This is why I don't date," she said with an expansive wave of her arms. "I'm a wreck at communication. The obvious come-ons I'm great at deflecting, but subtle is out of my league."

He could do obvious. "So if I wanted to kiss you I'd stand a better chance if I came out and asked?"

One heartbeat. Two. "Are you asking?"

He watched the beat of her pulse in her throat. "I dunno. Probably not a good idea when you're holding a fork."

Time ticked between them as if a clock were winding down, the second hand reaching for one more notch on the face before stopping. Dillon stayed where he was, waiting for Brenna to choose, her gaze searching his...tick...tick.

This wasn't the time or the place for attraction. They were snowbound with very few options for staying clear of each other. He shouldn't have pushed her into a decision that would change their dynamic. Because whatever happened next, this moment would always be in the way.

He was still waiting when Brenna looked away and turned off the fire beneath the skillet of bacon. She set the fork on the paper towel with the strips that were cooling. She wiped her palms on the seat of her jeans, tucked her hair behind her ears. Her chest rose and fell as she breathed, and Dillon's heart beat faster.

A step in reverse took her away from the stove, another brought her closer to his side of the kitchen. She moved slowly, though he didn't think her hesitance was uncertainty. Brenna

Keating didn't strike him as someone who had trouble making up her mind.

He moved his hands to the counter at his sides, curled his fingers over the edge to keep from reaching for her and dragging her against him. He admitted to being a caveman, but that could wait. This was Brenna's show. His job was to follow her lead, to ignore the lust coiling around the base of his spine.

Her gaze was still on the floor when she reached him. She brought it up slowly, starting with his feet and taking in his legs, lingering between his thighs and his belt buckle, rising again to take her time at his chest and the hollow of his throat.

He tried not to swallow, failed, watched her watch the movement of his muscles before she reached his mouth. She lingered there the longest, catching her bottom lip with her teeth, then finally, finally, lifted her gaze to his.

"Are you sure?" Her husky voice scraped his nerves.

He gave her a single nod in answer. He didn't trust himself to speak. He'd say the wrong thing and scare her away. He wanted her right where she was, doing exactly what she was doing, even if she had yet to do anything at all.

As she rose on her tiptoes, her lashes shuttered down. He hated that. He wanted to see her eyes. But then she was there and nothing else mattered.

It was a first contact that hummed, that danced and arced, that sizzled. Her lips were as soft as he'd expected, but they moved on his with purpose. She hadn't come to play or to tease or to test the waters. The kiss was real and she meant it.

Dillon wondered what was going through her mind, but he only wondered for a handful of seconds because he was a man, and she was pressing her body the length of his, and it had been a very long time since he'd felt what he was feeling now.

He couldn't put words to what that was, and he didn't stop to try. Instead, he kissed her back, slanting his lips over hers, wrapping her in a loose embrace. He kept himself from asking for too much too soon, even if he wanted her naked beneath him.

That thought had him kissing her harder. She responded in kind, parted her lips, invited him to do likewise and to use his tongue against hers. She didn't have to ask twice, and he didn't have to think about it at all. Nature took over. He just gave in.

He tightened his hold, his hands sliding down her back to the pockets of her jeans. He slipped his fingers deep inside to keep her as near as she'd let him. She wiggled, letting him, and she brought up her arms to loop around his neck, one hand cupping the base of his skull. Her fingers massaged him there, and her tongue learned the length of his.

Heat rose between them, a hazy column of lust and surprise. He'd never expected this, never expected her, but hell if he was going to question any of what was happening, or stop to define whatever this was making him feel so alive.

The coil at the base of his spine squeezed and desire grew. As close as she was, she had to feel him, lengthening, hardening, going thick. And when she pushed against him and sighed into his mouth, he had his answer. He dug his fingers into her backside, wanting to strip away the denim and get his hands on her skin.

The kiss changed then, becoming frantic, needy, the press of her lips to his harder, the thrust of his tongue against hers fevered. His thoughts raced, but he couldn't catch a single one. All he knew was this kiss, her body, his body. He wanted her. She wanted him. He tasted it. He smelled it.

He pulled his hands from her pockets and lifted the hem of her shirt. When he reached her bare back and the hooks of her bra, her shoulders went rigid, and she took a single step away.

It was enough.

She wasn't ready to take this trip. Not now. Not with him.

"Sorry," she mumbled, returning to the stove, the fork, when she lifted it, shaking in her hand. "I don't know why that ever seemed like a good idea."

He cleared his throat, willed down his erection, though the room's tension kept his nerves singing, his blood racing. He pressed his lips together, but she was still there.

The fork bobbled again, and she set it down. "I think I'm going to get my things out of the living room and change into some clean clothes. Maybe wash these if that's okay."

"Washer and dryer are in the utility room out that door." He inclined his head toward the kitchen's exit, even though she was looking at the skillet of unfinished bacon instead of at him.

"Thanks," she said, her head down as she left him standing there wondering how the hell they were supposed to get through the rest of the week after that.

CHAPTER SIX

Oh. Oh. What in the world was *that?*

What was wrong with her? What was she doing? Where was her brain?

Why did *that* have to be unlike any kiss ever? And with Dillon Craig, a man with baggage she didn't have the strength to lift?

A man her grandmother hadn't even wanted her to know.

Slumped against the door, Brenna pressed her fingers to her mouth, to her breasts, squeezed her thighs tight, but he remained. She felt him along her body, smelled him when she breathed in, tasted him when she dared touch her tongue to her lips.

For the love of Pete. She had no business kissing the man whose bed she was sleeping in!

Things between them were already tense. Now they would only get worse. She had to find a way to get to Gran's. And then she wondered what had gone through Gran's mind when she'd learned where Brenna had holed up to wait out the storm?

On a whim, she picked up the phone on the bedside table. Just as dead as Dillon had told her. That made her feel a little bit better. He hadn't been lying to keep her here. But he wouldn't need to lie, would he, when she was obviously open for business.

She fell into the center of the bed and stared up at the ceiling. And then she frowned. Like in Gran's house, Dillon had a fan over his bed. The blades hung without moving, the tip of each carved, a date cut into the abstract pattern. The design was repeated on each. But the dates were different, all earlier than the 2007 carved into the base of the lamp.

What she'd seen in Dillon's barn this morning left her with no doubt that he'd done the work. At the time she'd held off asking, the haunted look in his eyes tearing at her and the only thing that mattered. But now she wanted to know the meaning of the dates. Not that he'd tell her anything after that kiss.

Her brain had to be frostbit. Nothing else made sense. She did not kiss men she didn't know. She did not goad or dare or push men into letting her crawl all over them. And, no, she hadn't really crawled all over him, but God had she wanted to.

She pressed both fists to her forehead and groaned. She was snowbound with the man, dependent on his hospitality, and it hadn't taken her but twelve hours to go insane. She was sticking with the frostbit story. The hours she'd spent in the snowbank had to be at the root of her bizarre behavior.

Except she wasn't buying it. Dillon was at the root of her behavior. Her attraction to him. Her curiosity about who he was and why Gran had kept him a secret. Her empathy for what he'd suffered overseas, what his return to civilian life had cost him. Her interest in the drive behind his art. And now the kiss.

Oh, but the man could kiss. She touched the back of her hand to her lips, feeling him there, feeling, too, the scrape of his whiskers, the muscles in his neck and shoulders, the bristled ends of his short cropped hair, the heat of his hands.

Honestly, she hadn't meant to stop him. His skin on her

skin, his fingers at her bra had shocked her, and she'd stiffened—her spine, her shoulders, the tilt of her head. How could
Dillon not have been put off by her reaction to his touch?

What was done was done, and hiding in the bedroom for
the duration of her stay was out of the question. First of all,
she was not one to duck and run when things got heated. Sec-
ondly, she was starving.

She sat up, left the bed and grabbed her carryall to sort
through her things. She chose another pair of jeans and a
Christmas red sweater Gran had knitted last year. The yarn
was a softly glittered silk mohair, the shade perfect for her hair
and her skin and her eyes.

A shower and shampoo and fresh makeup, and she'd be
ready to finish cooking the breakfast she'd abandoned in lieu
of a bone-melting kiss. And hopefully she could convince Dillon Craig that she wasn't the jerk he was probably thinking.

Brenna cooked her breakfast alone, ate it alone and washed
up the dishes all by herself. And though she stretched out the
tasks for an hour, her host never showed, giving her no chance
to convince him of anything. *Fine. Be that way,* she mused,
walking through the cabin, looking for something to do.

She assumed he'd returned to the barn, or perhaps this time
to the clinic. Searching him out for the company seemed like
a very bad idea—especially since the storm had found new
footing. Squalls rattled the windows and wind gusts sent the
flames in the fireplace jumping. She figured the electricity
wasn't long for this world.

At least Dillon had a generator. He also had a television but
nothing but snow for reception. She didn't bother with her lap-
top; there was no using her smartphone for a hotspot in these
conditions. She did have her e-reader and hundreds of books,
so she settled into the corner of the sofa for a fictional escape.

One book then another lost her attention. Hardly surprising. Her attention had been caught by the kiss and pulling it free to focus elsewhere was proving to be a chore. If she were at Gran's she wouldn't be having this problem.

If she were at Gran's, she'd be baking cookies and decorating the tree. She'd bought new candy-cane-striped ribbons and cupcake ornaments with glass sprinkles to add to the tree's edible theme. She wondered if Dillon ever put up a tree.

He had a forest of pines around him just like her grandmother did. One friend or another always brought Gran a tree, and by the time Christmas morning arrived, Brenna and her grandmother had left no branch unadorned. They strung popcorn and cranberries, pierced cut-out cookies with ice picks before baking to make holes for threading with string.

She glanced toward the front door, wondering how far out she'd have to go to find a workable tree. It was Christmas, dang it all, and without a tree and baking and her week with Gran, things weren't going to be the same.

Though she couldn't blame herself for the accident—she hadn't been speeding, she'd listened to the forecast—she couldn't help but be filled with what-ifs. What if she'd left Raleigh ten minutes sooner, or ten minutes later? What if she'd been thinking about the conditions of the road instead of her upcoming move? What if she'd toughed out the heat in the car rather than reaching for the temperature controls at just that moment?

She closed her eyes, shook her head, looked back at the door and realized she had no way to chop a tree unless she made a visit to the barn for an ax or a saw. Plus, she'd have to rig a stand, and her luck, sharing close quarters with the pollen would set off an allergy attack.

But there was a seven-foot coat tree with, she counted, eight curved arms beside the front door...

She had ribbons and ornaments and hooks, and surely she could find a pinecone or two without getting lost in the forest. If Dillon objected, she could take it all down, though unless he was some kind of Grinch, she couldn't imagine why he would.

Bringing a semblance of Christmas into the house would help get her through the days to come, and he'd have to be a total scrooge to say no to a girl missing her Gran.

Brenna's kiss still on his mouth, Dillon stomped the snow from his boots on the mudroom floor, shrugged out of his coat and hung it on a peg to dry. Then he stopped, sniffed the air, and swore he smelled sugar cookies baking.

He was given more baked goods from friends and family of patients than one man could ever eat. He kept the cookies and brownies in the clinic to share. He ate a couple of slices of the cakes and pies, froze some, tossed the rest.

But since resigning his commission following his father's death, and his building and moving into this cabin, no one, in the two years he'd lived here, had ever baked anything in his kitchen. He was pretty sure he didn't even have cookie pans.

The thought of Brenna doing so…

He knew the back door squeaked, knew she'd hear him coming, but still he tried to sneak in so he could see her at work. Stupid, really, but he couldn't deny the purely caveman enjoyment of having a woman, especially this one, especially after that kiss, cooking in his kitchen.

"I hope you don't mind," she said before he even got a good look. "I read till my eyes crossed and I had to do something."

He pulled the door all the way open, letting in a rush of cold air from the mudroom before he got it closed. Her hair was caught back from her face with a band, and the dark strands fell in waves around her shoulders. Her cheeks were flushed from the heat of the stove, and the smile on her mouth was full of memories.

He knew that because of what he'd learned from Donota about her and Brenna's Christmas cookie tradition. "No. I don't mind. Smells great, in fact."

"I only made half a batch so I wouldn't use up all your flour."

"There's probably a bag in the freezer."

"Yeah, I saw it when I went looking for a casserole for dinner, but I didn't want to be anymore presumptuous than I've already been."

"The casseroles are there to be eaten, the staples used. And cookies are always welcome. Not presumptuous at all."

She had yet to look at him, her sweater sleeves pushed to her elbows as she used the side of a glass tumbler to roll out a small slab of dough. And she didn't look at him now, either. But she did pause, and the smile kicking him in the gut began to fade.

She scrunched up her nose. "It's not just cookies and a casserole."

He'd been working in the barn four hours or so. He hadn't noticed the time when he'd left the house, and he only noticed it now because he made for a lousy host, leaving her alone for so long. He hadn't thought that she'd have nothing to do.

So what besides cookies was he in for?

He followed the cant of her head, pushed off the back door and made his way from the kitchen to the main room. He didn't see it at first. The fire blazed brightly, lighting up the room where his blankets were folded rather than draped over the back of the sofa.

The television was off, the books stacked on the shelf in their usual disarray. She'd left his clutter—his reading glasses on the coffee table, his patient charts beneath them, his empty coffee cup on top, too—and he liked that she had.

It was when he glanced at the door that he saw the coat tree.

Red-and-white ribbon wrapped the trunk and the arms where, last he looked, coats had been hanging. Sparkly glass cupcakes weighted down the ribbon, hooked at alternating intervals with pinecones tied with sprigs of fragrant green needles.

On top of the rack perched his Stetson, the black beaver crown ringed with the same red and white. A star-shaped cluster of pinecones held the place of honor in the crease he'd spent a lot of time working to his liking.

"I didn't damage your hat, or the coat tree. And I can undo it all if you want—"

"No. Leave it."

"Are you sure? Because I don't mind taking it down."

She minded. He could tell by the tone of her voice. And that made all the difference.

"You might not even celebrate Christmas. I didn't think…"

He turned to her before she could talk herself into undoing all her work, because it was suddenly important to him that she not. "Brenna, trust me. It's fine."

Her gaze found his briefly before she glanced back at the only holiday decoration his cabin had ever seen. And as he watched, her mouth turned down, her chin trembled, her eyes grew red and damp.

"I miss Gran. Every year, for as long as I can remember, and especially since my parents moved to Malaysia, this has been our time. Mine and Gran's. And next year I might not be able to get back. If Gran's still here then."

Well, hell. "Don't say that."

"Why not? I think it often enough." She wrapped her arms over her middle. "I'm not trying to be morbid, just realistic.

That's why this Christmas meant everything, and now it's not going to happen." At the sound of the kitchen timer, she headed off to pull her cookies from the oven.

Dillon stared at the coat tree a few seconds longer, and swore on the lives of the men he'd lost, Brenna wouldn't lose Christmas.

CHAPTER SEVEN

Brenna pulled the last cake pan of cookies from the oven and slid the thawed casserole in to heat. To keep busy and from embarrassing herself further, she prepped a simple powdered-sugar-and-water icing for the cookies, taking Dillon up on his offer to use his supplies. He did have plenty, though not everything she would've liked.

At Gran's she'd have had access to food coloring and decorative sprinkles and colored sugars. Instead of finishing a half batch with a washed-out glaze, she and Gran would've baked dozens, then piped icing into ribbons and swirls and curlicues. And though just as scrumptious as cookies baked with Gran, these wouldn't be the same.

Nothing about this Christmas would be the same, and she'd planned so carefully to see that it was. Next year, things could change. This year, her last year in North Carolina, she wanted to surround herself with the comfort of the familiar.

There was nothing comfortable or familiar about the situation she found herself in. She didn't have a plan to deal with what Dillon was making her feel, and that left her flailing, left her…acting out. Because that was the only way she could describe that impetuous kiss.

"Can I help?"

His question was simple, the offer kind, but she couldn't find her voice to answer. She felt…unbalanced, and until she was stable, keeping her mouth closed seemed like a really good idea. Handing him the bowl and spoon, she held the vented pizza pan she'd used in lieu of a cooling rack over the sink.

"Like that?" he asked, the sugary ribbon dripping onto the first cookie and spreading to cover it. The excess ran into a bowl she'd placed beneath.

"Perfect," she finally said because not responding was more of an obstacle than acknowledging his effort to smooth the bumpy waters.

"This is the first time this kitchen has seen any cookie bak-ing, you know."

Having dug through his freezer, she wasn't surprised. At the rate food arrived as gifts or barter, the man could go years without ever having to feed himself.

"Too bad, because this is a great kitchen. Mine is half this size and I still manage to be a baking fiend. I can't imagine what I could do with all this space." *And please,* please *don't let him think I was asking for an invitation to use it on a permanent basis.*

"You've got a condo, right? I think that's what Donota said."

It was strange to hear Gran called anything but Gran, and it made her wonder again about the relationship Dillon had with her grandmother. "I do. Not too far from the hospital. It's a mess at the moment, boxes everywhere, and I'm not even halfway through packing."

"I got rid of most of my things when I enlisted. Stored what I wanted to keep in Dad's barn."

"What did you keep?" she asked, turning the pizza pan to bring more cookies close.

He laughed. "None of my baking sheets or wire racks for sure."

That gave her a chuckle, but it didn't answer her question.

It did, however, make her wonder why he'd had baking sheets in his previous life. *None of your business, Brenna. Don't ask.* "Easy enough to make do."

"You're pretty good at that. The cookies. The tree." He dipped up more glaze.

She shifted the pan again, nudging her hip against his and staying there. "Mostly I'm good at Christmas. I love it. The corny songs, stringing popcorn for the tree. Eating as much as ends up on the needle and thread."

"You do it by hand?"

"Gran and I do. Some folks buy finished strands, or fake plastic ones. But stuck fingers and Bing Crosby is our thing."

"What's Christmas without traditions, right?"

She thought again of the dates carved into his lamp and fan. "Do you have any?"

"Does spending it alone count?"

"You don't, do you?" The thought of him doing so broke her heart.

"I spent a half dozen in tents eating turkey and ham with thousands of other guys dressed just like me."

"Since then?"

"I get a lot of invitations," he said, and she heard the smile in his voice.

"Ah, the mountain's most eligible bachelor." One her grandmother had never mentioned. As soon as she and Gran were alone, Brenna was going to get to the bottom of the secret of Dillon Craig. "How do you decide which to accept?"

He shrugged, brought a knuckle to his mouth and licked away a blob of glaze. "I accept them all."

"Seriously?"

"I make rounds on Christmas day like any other. I just stick around longer for lunch or dinner or coffee and pie, depending on what time it is."

"Must make a long cold day for Ranger."

"He gets his share of oats and warm barns."

"Bet you bring home lots of presents."

"I've got enough scarves to wrap an army of mummies. Reb Curtis made my fireplace set. Dewey Moss made Ranger's saddle. And you've seen my freezer."

She had to ask… "Anyone hang mistletoe just for you?"

"I've been caught a time or two."

"I'll just bet you have," she said, and bumped his hip.

He bumped back. "And you haven't?"

She thought about last year's department party. About the bad karaoke. About Rob Merrill's thick lips. She shuddered, wishing for brain bleach to clean her memory.

"Thought so."

"Uh-uh. That was me remembering a night of bad karaoke caroling."

"If you say so."

"I do. Besides, we both know I don't need mistletoe." And there it was. The kiss and her big mouth. One big happy family. Or one big pile of poo. Either way, she'd stepped in it.

"Be a damn shame if you did."

Oh, but he tempted her. The tone of his voice, so soft, so seductive. Or was she imagining things she wanted to hear? She set the pan of glazed cookies on the counter, hesitated. "About that…"

"If you're thinking of apologizing, don't. I was there, and you have nothing to apologize for."

That didn't exactly set her at ease. "I don't want things between us to be uncomfortable."

"Are they?"

Avoiding the question, she found two pot holders and opened the oven for the casserole. "We've got a couple more days of being cooped up together. I think things will be less awkward if we forget that kiss happened."

He waited until she'd set the dish on the stovetop. Then he took her by the shoulders and turned her to face him. "I'm not ever going to forget that kiss happened. And I don't believe for a minute that's what you want."

And wasn't that her problem in a nutshell? Knowing what she wanted? "We can't get involved and kisses have a tendency to take things that direction."

"It's too late," he said before his mouth came down on hers and proved him right.

They *were* involved. There was no getting around it. The sweet touch of his lips, the gentle exploration of her face with his hands showed her that truth, as did her fast beating heart.

She reached for him, curled her fingers in the fabric of his shirt and felt the rise and fall of his very hard chest as he breathed in, breathed out, as his heart thudded to the rhythm of hers.

He was a beautiful man, he was a damaged man. He was a secret her grandmother had kept from her and she wanted to know why. His kiss only told her so many things, but she fell into him anyway, his bravery, his generosity, the heat of his skin, his strength.

Why now? The question worked to wedge between them but she pushed it away. All that mattered was the brush of his fingers along the curve of her ear, the press of his other hand to the small of her back. He was hungry, his mouth, his body. He wanted her.

And she wanted him. How could she not? She slid her tongue along his to play. To coax, to tease. To imagine what it would be like to have weeks, months, not just days.

She let out a moan at the thought, slid her hands to his shoulders. He smelled like the big outdoors, pine and cold earth and winter, and she tasted the cookie glaze he'd licked from his hand.

It was too much, all these conflicting emotions. Wanting what she couldn't have. Wishing he'd come into her life before she'd turned her world upside down. Wondering how hard it would be to make room for him, what it would cost her?

Breaking away from the kiss, she dropped her forehead to his chest and shuddered. "We've really got to stop doing this."

"And I'm really going to have to disagree."

She wanted to laugh, but found herself squeezing her eyes tightly shut. "Then we really need to stop doing it while I'm cooking because I'm going to starve if we don't."

"Does that mean we can pick up again when I don't have you slaving over a hot stove?"

She pulled back to look up at him, her enigma, his eyes so kind, so bleak, so full of arousal. "Did you just call me a slave?"

His laughter rattled off the kitchen walls and vibrated the length of her limbs. "Guess there's no way to convince you it was a compliment?"

"Not in this lifetime," she said, returning to the stove to dish up the casserole, and asking herself again, *why now?*

After dinner, Dillon sent Brenna to the main room while he cleaned the kitchen. He'd been kidding with the slave remark, but realized she'd been doing a whole lot of things he would never ask of a guest, and he was liking it. Liking both her taking charge, and taking care of him. Stupid when his job defined caring for others.

And, yeah. He got that all the casseroles weren't presented in trade or barter. That there were more than a few women on the mountain who'd made it clear they were ready and willing to take over the care and feeding of him.

He wasn't interested in any of them. And he didn't yet

know why Brenna was different, but he was definitely interested in her.

Maybe it was the close quarters. Conditions the last couple of days had made it impossible to do more than very limited rounds, and he admitted it. He didn't do well when he had nothing to do. Woodworking filled that void, but he didn't want Brenna asking about it. He was surprised she hadn't.

His woodworking was too connected to his years spent at war for him to explain where it came from. And as much as he wanted to take her to bed, he wouldn't barter for that pleasure by baring his soul. Nobody got that close. Ever.

Piling cookies onto a plate, he carried them along with two cups of coffee to the main room. Instead of curling up in her usual corner of the couch, Brenna sat cross-legged on the floor between the coffee table and the fireplace.

Lost in thought, she didn't respond to his setting down the drinks and eats, and only looked over when he joined her on the handspun rug he'd taken in payment from a patient.

"I'd say a penny for your thoughts, but that's too close to slave wages..."

She grinned. "You are a funny man. Anyone ever tell you that?"

"Your grandmother."

"Now that I believe. I don't know anyone with a better sense of humor than Gran." She took the coffee mug he handed her. "I tried to call her earlier. Your line's still down and there's no such thing as a cell signal up here."

"And somehow everyone manages just fine."

She looked over from the corner of her eye as she sipped. "You don't miss being plugged in?"

"I am plugged in." He pointed toward the ceiling and the roof above. "I'm a doctor. I've got satellite."

"A satellite phone? Or just internet and TV? Not that either seem to be working."

He'd watched her hopes rise. Hated dashing them. "No phone. Sorry."

Eyes closed, she dropped her head back against the table. "What does your satellite tell you about the storm?"

The wind howled outside the front door, scratched at the windows, rode flames up and down the chimney. Neither one of them needed satellite to know they weren't going anywhere anytime soon. "I'll get you to Donota's by Christmas, Brenna. I promise you that."

She turned her head, her gaze finding his, and he was lost. He wanted her. She wanted him. So what if the timing was all wrong and they'd have only this? It was more than the men he'd lost had been given.

Leaning forward, he set his mug on the hearth, took hers from her hands and did the same. Then he moved over her, urging her down, stretching his body the length of hers. The rug was soft, though little protection against the hard floor beneath.

And when he covered her, he did so gently, bearing the bulk of his weight with his arms, his elbows braced at her sides.

CHAPTER EIGHT

"Do you want this?" he asked, looking into her eyes. "Do you want me?"

"Both," she said, her voice barely a whisper, her body trembling, her eyes bright and sharp. "But—"

"Shh. I know you're leaving. I know we can't get involved." He also knew, but didn't tell her, that he wasn't fit to be any woman's partner. "But we're here, and we have now, and sometimes that's all we get."

She freed the arm wedged between them and brought her hand to his face. "I could fall for you in a heartbeat. That seems like a dangerous thing to put a match to."

Even so… He closed his eyes, opened them, stared into hers. "This is all I can promise." And then he watched her throat work as she swallowed.

"I don't want you to break my heart."

He couldn't give her that unless he moved away. Even then it could be too late. It was too late for him. Whatever happened this Christmas, he'd remember her for all the rest.

"Your call, sweetheart. Just know…"

And suddenly he couldn't say it. Couldn't tell her that he hadn't laughed in ages, that his cabin had never felt like a home as much as a place to hang his coat and hat.

That he'd dreamed of her the last two nights, not of blood and sand, not of reckless, needless loss, but of her.

He tried to tamp down memories that had no business in this moment, then realized his service was as much a part of the man Brenna wanted as was his childhood, his years in the E.R., his life on the mountain.

Before he could find words safe enough to say, she slid her hand from his cheek to his nape and pulled his head down, finding his mouth with hers.

This wasn't a kiss like the others. This one was simple, sweet. Pure. A kiss of caring, not desire, though he couldn't ignore the arousal winding through him with her touch, her scent, both as familiar as his name.

She kneaded the base of his skull, slid her tongue along the seam of his lips, opened her legs to cradle his weight. He wanted this, he needed this, the contact so intimately tender he thought he might break.

And then her kiss grew bolder, her tongue more insistent. She worked her arms beneath his to massage the muscles on either side of his spine. His erection thickened, and he pressed himself against her, losing the battle with taking things slow.

He slid his fingers into her hair, slanted his mouth harder, pushed his tongue deeper and began to rock his hips. She rocked with him, her hands roaming his back, her legs hooked over his to keep him close.

She was making this so easy, and he wasn't ready to finish so soon. They had all night. He wanted all night. He wanted her in his bed, naked, the storm raging. He wanted to bury the both of them with pillows and quilts until neither had the strength to stir.

The thought had him groaning, as did the touch of Brenna's hands against his back as she tugged his shirt from his belt to find skin. He rolled to the side, the fireplace crackling with a hard gust of wind, and reached for the hem of her sweater.

He bared her slowly, watching the play of light on her flesh. She was warm and soft, beautiful, perfect, and he held her gaze as he bent to kiss her belly, moving higher until his lips grazed her breast.

She caught her breath sharply, let it go with a sigh, and then she pulled away to sit up. With her eyes on his, she stripped her sweater over her head, then released the clasp of her bra. The straps slipped down her arms, then stopped. He used one finger to help them along until finally her breasts spilled free.

She was gorgeous, the color of peaches in the fire, her nipples blushed darker, her lips wet where her tongue had slicked over them. He reached for her and she came, crawling into his lap and looping her arms around his neck, leaning back in invitation.

He accepted, bending to take her into his mouth. She whimpered as he sucked her, moaned as he curled his tongue around the taut peak, gasped as he used his teeth.

And then she straightened, and her hands were at his shirt snaps, popping them open before shoving his sleeves from his shoulders. He brought her close, kept her there with one hand on her back and one in her hair, and kissed her until he was thinking with his cock.

"Do you think we could take this to the bedroom?" he asked against her mouth.

"I like the fire," she told him, nipping at his ear. "But, yeah. A bed would be good. Though really," she added in a gruff-voiced whisper, "all I need is you."

For a moment, her words froze him. How many others in need had he failed? Then he remembered where he was, who he was with, and he closed the door on the past.

"I'm all yours," he told her as he gained his feet, and with her legs around his waist, his arms around her, he carried her to bed.

The second they tumbled onto the mattress, Brenna rolled away to switch on the lamp. His legs dangling over the edge of the bed, Dillon raised up on to his elbows and frowned, but before he got out a word, she pushed him down.

"I want to see you," she said, tugging off her boots and jeans and giving him no time to argue. "I don't want to be in the dark. Not tonight."

Because he was right. They had tonight and might never be here again. She couldn't imagine spending this moment in darkness. Too much of her pleasure came from looking at him, from anticipating the touch of his hands, his mouth, from seeing his expression, his lust, the sweat on his skin.

Wearing only her panties, she straddled his thighs. Then looked down into his worried eyes, his haunted, hungry eyes, ready to put him at ease. "If we're going to do this, I want to make it unforgettable."

With that, she braced her hands on either side of his head and leaned down to kiss him. Her nipples brushed his bare chest, and she swayed, dragging them through the wedge of hair there that felt like strands of silk, tickling. He groaned, his hands settling at her hipbones and holding tight.

His fingers gouged her flesh and no doubt she'd have bruises, but those would fade and for a few days, anyway, she'd have the reminder of this night, of Dillon, an after Christmas gift to see her into the New Year when her life wouldn't be this life anymore.

The thought that she was creating one more thing to leave behind had her throat swelling, her eyes growing damp, and for a moment she wished she'd left off the light. But the moment passed, and she pulled her mouth from his to trail kisses along his jaw, down his neck, along his collar bone to his shoulder where she bit him. Not hard, but enough to leave a mark. She wanted him to have a reminder of her, too.

He gave a grunt, half pleasure, half pain, and she licked the wounded skin before moving to his chest. There she found a nipple, and swirled her tongue around it, and pinched the other until his grunt turned to a more visceral sound, one that rumbled through her, thunder with lightning sparking where they touched.

A final lick and she moved to the trail bisecting his abs. His erection thickened, lengthened, and she covered it with her hand when she stopped.

"I'd wondered what your belt buckle said." A gold caduceus in the center sat beneath the words *United States* and above the word *Army*. "Just didn't think I'd get close enough to see."

He crossed his arms beneath him like a pillow and rested his head on his wrists. "You could've asked."

"And admit I was checking you out?"

"You should have. Look at how much time we've wasted getting here."

She laughed, ran a fingertip over his lips then wet a path down his middle to the buckle holding her back. "Wasted? I didn't even wait two days before kissing you."

"That was two days too long." His gaze sizzled, singing her. A tic beat in the vein at his temple.

She released the buckle's hook from the hole in the worn leather and carefully freed each button of his fly. She did it all without looking but holding his gaze, watching his pupils dilate, watching his lids drop to half mast.

It was intoxicating, to know she affected him so, a heady feeling, to have this much power. She came to him with nothing more than desire, no years of experience to draw on. All she had was the last two days, and the things she'd learned about him, and desire.

When she spread open his jeans, he reached for her, his hands covering her breasts as she did the same to him through the white fabric of his briefs. He was gorgeously ridged, full and bold, urgent in his need. He swelled as she drew her fingers as far as she could, and still she looked nowhere but into his eyes.

What she saw there, his enjoyment, his hunger, stirred her, and she freed him, bending to take him into her mouth. He was smooth against her tongue, engorged to bursting, and he was warm and salty and weighty where she held him. She tongued the slit in his cock's head, tongued the underside seam, then wrapped her lips beneath the ridge and sucked.

He let her have her way for a minute at the most, then broke her hold and sat up, ridding himself of boots and jeans and his unbuttoned shirt and his socks. "Now. I'm all yours."

If only it were true. That he was hers for more than this moment. He was so beautiful, stretched out as he was, taking up most of the bed and hers to use.

His limbs were long, his arms muscled, his legs, too, his chest and abs sculpted as if he passed his time in the gym when she knew he didn't. She walked her fingers over the ridges defining his stomach, wondering how much of his body he'd built during the war, working out to keep from going stir crazy, to relieve the stress of the things he saw, of waiting for RPGs and gunfire.

The thought had her eyes closing, her chest aching. Fear trembled through her and he wasn't even there anymore. He was here and for tonight he was hers. She stretched out beside him, buried her face in the crook of his shoulder, hooked her leg over his and nestled her thigh against the warmth of his groin.

"You feel good."

"Yes. I do."

She grinned against his skin, plucked softly at the hair on his chest. "I like touching you. I like looking at you."

His cock stirred, nudging her leg. "Have at it. Just, you know, don't take too long."

"Take too long?" Oh, but the wait made the want that much better.

He grabbed her hand where she was toying with his nipple, moved it down his body and wrapped her fingers around his erection. "That's better."

"You're right. It is." She began to stroke him then, watching the motion of her hand on his shaft, the play of her thumb circling the tight skin on the head. Her own arousal blossomed, her nipples tightened, her sex grew full and damp. And then she rolled on top of him again. "But this is better still."

The look in his eyes said play time was over, and he proved it to be true. Opening the bedside drawer for a condom, he cupped the back of her head and pulled her against him before rolling it on. His mouth devoured hers, slanting and bringing her close, his tongue thrusting into her mouth to find hers.

When he pushed his hand between her legs, she gasped but made room. He parted her lips with the length of a finger, slid up and down to spread her moisture from her entrance to her clit. She ground against his hand, then against the bones of his pelvis, his hair scraping her tender flesh with unbearable friction.

She was ready, and he was ready, and she lifted her hips and guided him into place. Holding his gaze, she pushed herself onto him, taking him slowly, savoring the first breach as his body entered hers. He gripped her rib cage, his thumbs brushing the swell of her breasts.

The stubble on his face couldn't hide the tic in his jaw, and she loved that she made that happen. She lifted, lowered, rode him to a rhythm that he matched with the upward thrust of his hips. He filled her, stretched her. The base of his shaft rubbed against her clit as she writhed, seeking the sweet spot where her nerve endings sizzled, whimpering when she hit it.

"Good?" he asked, and she nodded.

"Unbelievable." It was true. Nothing had prepared her for the sensation setting her body on fire. It was more than what she'd known, bigger and consuming and potent. It devoured her and possessed her, and she was lost.

Lost in Dillon, lost in more than his touch. Lost in all the things he was, that he offered, safety and courage, compassion and generosity. She could so easily fall in love with him, love him, and she knew this moment held her future in its hands.

Dillon wrapped his arms around her waist and sat up, bodily forcing her to him. But with his gaze on hers, their connection became more than sex. Became her whole world. Became everything she knew and was, and *oh,* what a heady rush.

His forearms on either side of her spine, he hooked his hands over her shoulders and rocked her back and forth. Her breasts were crushed to his chest, her sex owned by his cock and his thighs and hard muscled abs. He was everywhere, and she couldn't get enough, couldn't think, could barely breathe.

She buried her face in the crook of his neck, gave up. Her core tightened, pressure built, scratching, urging. He whispered in her ear, words she couldn't make out but didn't need to. Sex words, sex sounds. Begging, desperate, demanding, hot.

She let go, cried out, drowning. She couldn't draw breath, and he followed her into the wake, groaning and shuddering for what seemed like forever. And just as they'd exploded together, then they calmed together, coming down to earth as different people, knowing nothing between them would ever be the same.

CHAPTER NINE

After the energy he'd expended the last few hours, Dillon was surprised to find himself still awake. Surprised, too, that Brenna hadn't slept at all. Dawn would be here soon, and if his senses were accurate, the storm that had brought her into his life was dying. That meant she'd be leaving, and if he slept he'd miss out on the rest of their time.

Then again, he didn't trust his senses for much of anything right now. They'd been scraped raw, peeled to the core, sanded down until they were numb. She'd done that to him, Brenna. Taken all he had. Demanded more. He couldn't remember the last time… No. There had been no last time. He'd never known a woman like Brenna Keating.

"It's okay if you sleep, you know," he told her, aiming his words down to where she lay curled at his side.

She shifted even closer, her head on his shoulder, her breasts flattened against his ribs. "I don't want to sleep. I'm afraid I'll miss something fun."

About that… "I'm pretty sure the show's over for tonight."

"That's probably a good thing," she said, yawning, toying with the hair on his chest. "I won't be walking straight for days as it is."

"Then my job here is done."

She tweaked his nipple, and he yelped. "Only because I say so."

"Bossy wench, aren't you?"

"I like to think of myself as a woman in charge."

He laced the fingers of his free hand through hers. "Something tells me you're damn good at getting your way."

"Not all the time, but it takes a lot for me to give up trying."

"I'll consider myself warned."

"Good, because I want to ask you something."

And this was where things went downhill. He turned away, gave her his back. "Good night."

"Uh-uh. Don't even think about it," she said, grabbing him by the shoulder and forcing him onto his back. To keep him there, she pinned him with a thigh thrown over his, and an arm across his chest.

Not that he couldn't move if he had a mind to, but she'd made her point. "You'd better ask quick. I'm fading."

She shook her head, her hair tickling where he'd caught it beneath his arm. "Don't pull that after-sex man disease excuse on me."

"How about the 3:00 a.m. excuse?"

"Are your eyes open?"

"I can talk with them closed."

"Open them," she ordered, lifting up onto her elbow to check that he had.

He gave her a side-eyed glance. "Satisfied?"

She was. She was also nervous, her palms damp when she squeezed her hands, so she dove right in. "What do the dates on your fan blades mean?"

The lines at his temples furrowed, his pupils went dark. His pulse beat like a tom-tom in the hollow of his throat. "I'd rather not answer that."

She ignored the razor crack in his voice and pushed on. "That's why I asked. That's why I want to know."

He cut his gaze from hers to the fan hanging overhead like the Sword of Damocles. But it took him a long time to respond, and she wasn't certain he would. Then beneath her leg, his stiffened. Beneath her arm, his heart pounded, and his chest rose and fell with his short rapid breaths as her question found its mark.

She'd hit a nerve. A big one. Bigger than she'd anticipated, though she'd been certain the dates weren't without purpose. And she was pretty sure she'd figured it out, but pressed one last time. "Do they have something to do with your military service?"

His muscles continued to twitch, his heart to race, though his breathing had slowed and grown measured as he stared up at the fan. "May thirty-first, two thousand six. Private Ford Weber's Humvee hit an IED. He needed more hours than I had and equipment I didn't. I made him comfortable for the flight to Landstuhl, then left him on the stretcher while I worked on the kid who'd been driving."

"Did he make it?" she asked softly, unsure how hard or far to push for the things she wanted to know, weighty things Dillon had carried with him a very long time. Things she had a feeling he'd never told anyone, that he'd committed to wood instead of voicing.

"The driver, yeah." He shifted the arm beneath her head to toy with the ends of her hair. "I felt Weber die while I was digging shrapnel out of the kid's chest."

"I'm so sorry." It sounded lame, but would anything sound any better? She had no idea what he'd seen, what he'd been through.

"February twenty seventh, two thousand five. Suicide bomber took out a market as a patrol was passing by. I lost

Specialist Len Waters that day. Spent hours working to stabilize him. I had six others to attend, six with better chances, and had to leave him to see to them."

It was the second time he'd used the word *leave,* or *left.* Brenna frowned. He'd also talked about leaving his father, about her leaving Gran. Sadness rose in her throat, hot and living and red like blood.

Was he blaming himself for the men who had died, or blaming the conditions he couldn't control? Was the woodworking his way to honor them, to remember, or his way to get through the damage those years had done?

She doubted he needed it to keep from forgetting. He would never forget. "Does it help? Having the dates as reminders?"

He barked out a gruff laugh. "I don't see the dates. I see the faces."

"I mean, does it help you to deal with things, pouring all of that...I don't know what to call it. Energy? Anger? Sorrow? Pouring it into your art?"

He fell silent, rolled away from her to sit on his side of the bed, and switched off the lamp. It was the middle of the night, but the moon was bright and the sky clear and the snow on the ground reflective. She took in his silhouette, his head hung low, chin tucked to his chest.

His shoulders flexed as he braced his palms on his thighs. He was hurting, and her efforts at pop psychology weren't helping relieve the pressure that had him burning into wood the dates men under his care had died. And yet she couldn't be sorry she'd asked. He was talking about his experience, and she was certain he hadn't done that often—if ever before.

"January second, two thousand three. Corporal Boyd Massey took a hit from an RPG. The medics did what they could in the field. I got him off the chopper, took one look and knew he was done. The grenade's explosive trigger hadn't detonated on impact. It was lodged in his chest." He swallowed, shuddered. "He was a live bomb."

"Oh, my God." The room fell away. There was only Dillon and his surgical tent and the sandblasting heat of the desert. She hadn't been there, but could feel it rolling off him as he made the trip back.

"He was awake when he came in, knew what was happening. No way was I going to walk out and leave him alone."

"What did you do?" she asked in a whisper.

He swallowed, cleared his throat. Shuddered. "One of the chopper crew was an explosives specialist. He and the medics stayed in the OR against protocol. After a hairy couple of hours, we got it out. Then lost Massey on the table."

Tears fell from her cheeks to her breasts. "You risked your own lives."

"It's part of the job."

"And breaking the rules?"

He leaned forward then, buried his face in his hands. "He was alive, but he was dead. And he knew it. He was so scared, but he was the bravest damn soldier I've ever seen."

Brenna rose up on her knees, pressed her front to his back. His skin had grown icy, and she rubbed her hands up and down his arms, wishing she could reach the part of him inside where she was certain he hadn't felt warm in years.

"I wish I could make it easier for you. Or make it go away."

He shook his head. "I don't want it to go away. Those men deserved to be remembered."

"As do you. For trying to save them."

He huffed. "I doubt their families feel the same way."

Was he kidding? "To know you did all you could? Why wouldn't they?"

"What if I didn't do all I could? What if I made wrong choices?"

"You know yourself. You made the only choices you could under the worst of circumstances. Tell me I'm not right."

"I don't know, Brenna. I don't know."

She leaned her cheek against his neck, breathed in the scent of his dried sweat and the chill on his skin. She was ill-equipped to offer counsel, but she could hold him. And it was easy to do when she cared for him so greatly, when what she felt had crossed the line from friends to lovers to a connection too deep and rich to define.

"Did you do anything you regret?"

It took him several seconds to answer. "No."

"If you could go back, is there anything you would do differently?"

This answer came more quickly with a shake of his head. "No."

"Did you ever look back, when you were in the E.R., and wonder if you'd done the right thing?"

"That was different—"

"No. It wasn't. Not really." And this was what he needed to see. "The setting was different, sure. The types of injuries. And you weren't working with combat gauze in a tent. But you dealt with trauma, life-and-death decisions. That part is the same."

"Patients in the E.R. weren't kids putting their lives on the line for their country."

"But were they putting their lives on the line for their family? Stepping into domestic violence situations and ending up beaten or knifed? Maybe you treated police officers who'd been gunned down, or firefighters who'd fallen through burning buildings."

When he didn't respond, she went on. "Aren't all these people heroes, too? They're serving their communities, their families, not the bigger picture. But it's still service. And it's still selfless. And you'll always be a hero because of what you've done. No matter where you were when you cracked open a chest."

He turned his head a bit, smiled back at her. "You know about combat gauze?"

"I watch the news. I read the papers."

"And you were a cheerleader in school?"

She rolled her eyes, but was happy to see the smile widen. "No."

"Debate team?"

This time she slapped at his shoulder. "I was an only child of parents who refused to spoil me so I learned to argue convincingly when I wanted something."

"You argue well."

"But do I convince?"

He rolled his head side to side. "It's more about convincing myself the argument is valid. It's one I've made to myself many times, but I'm still not there."

"I'd help if I could. Please know that," she said, and sat back on her knees.

"You've helped by being here. By asking. By listening."

Hmm. "I can't be the first one to offer."

He took a deep breath, shook his head. "No, but it's tough to know when to talk about it."

"Bad timing?"

"Wrong people asking."

Her heart swelled like a balloon, full and lifting, and the only thing she could say was, "Then I'm glad I asked."

"Me, too."

"Even if it didn't help."

"It helped. Trust me," he said, and reached for her hand.

His touch was strong, cold. Fierce. "Talking can be hard, but it usually does."

"I know. One of the folks I see on rounds always wants to know how I'm doing."

"Someone you trust?"

He nodded, looking at their joined fingers. "We talk sometimes. She tells me a lot of the same things."

A spark flared in Brenna's stomach. It felt like jealousy and she told herself that was dumb. She had no claim on this man. She'd known him but a matter of days. Of course he'd have other friends, a confidante, lovers...

God. Had she stepped into something? Not a relationship, because he was too honorable to cheat, but an arrangement? She moved back to her side of the bed. "Is this going to make things awkward for you?"

He turned, frowned. "What are you talking about?"

"You said you have someone. You said *she*."

It took a moment for her words to register, then he grinned. "I talk to my someone. That's it. If this causes any awkwardness, it'll be for you."

Uh-oh. "How so?"

"My someone is your grandmother," he said then rolled her beneath him and brought his mouth down firmly on hers.

CHAPTER TEN

When Brenna woke on Saturday, Dillon was gone, and judging by the chill on his side of the bed, had been for a while. She glanced at his alarm clock. Glanced again. For the love of Pete, it was nearly noon! When had she ever slept till noon? She hated that he'd left her alone, but noon? Seriously?

She stretched, yawned, groaned as rarely used muscles reminded her of last night. She could do with a repeat. Of the physical part, anyway. The emotional part had her hung out to dry. She couldn't imagine how Dillon was faring. The things he carried with him… She sat up, naked, and shivering from more than the cold as she left the bed. It was amazing he hadn't broken under the weight.

She showered and dressed quickly, sorting her things for the laundry she hadn't done yesterday. Sniffing the air for coffee or breakfast, she got nothing, then remembered the cookies on the coffee table as she opened the door. As long as Dillon hadn't gone all Suzy Homemaker on her and moved them…

Oh. *Oh.* She couldn't believe it!

Where her decorated coat tree had stood last she'd looked, Dillon had placed a perfectly shaped fir. Her ribbon had been threaded through the branches, and her cupcakes hung randomly to maximize the canvas. He'd even added his hat on top in the place of honor, and tucked the cookies she'd planned to eat here and there.

Her throat grew tight. Her eyes burned. She dropped her clothes bundle, bringing her steepled fingers to her mouth, pressing them to her trembling lips. And then she saw the gift sitting beneath. A square box, plain unwrapped brown cardboard, with a pinecone cluster on top like a bow.

She knelt in front of the tree, lifted the box. It was *so* hard not to peek, but she resisted, holding it in her lap. Laughter bubbled up, a heady, airy, happy burst of it. This was perfect. Just perfect, except... She had nothing to give Dillon.

She'd baked him cookies, yes, and she'd given him a night she hoped would be hard to forget. But he'd rescued her from the storm. He'd saved her life. He'd shown her heaven, and now he'd given her Christmas.

At the sound of the back door opening, she got to her feet, leaving the box on the floor. She turned just as Dillon entered the room. She was in his arms before he'd shed his coat. The sheepskin was cold against her face, but he was warm beneath, and she knew she couldn't have found a better man to love.

"I can't believe you did this," she said, pulling back to look at him. He was beautiful, and he was smiling, and his eyes weren't quite so sad anymore. "Did you sleep at all? And thank you. Thank you! This has to be the best Christmas gift ever."

He arched a stern brow. "Does that mean you peeked?"

"No! And I wasn't talking about the present. I meant the tree. And you decorated even."

"Ready for more?"

"Are you kidding me?" Did he mean...

He gave her a wink. "Dress warm. Ranger's saddled and ready for the trek to your Gran's."

While Dillon lived in a rather chichi log cabin, Gran's two-story farmhouse rambled in all directions, the inviting sprawl a perfect fit for the patch of land cleared years ago by the grandfather Brenna knew only through stories.

Riding in from the rear on horseback, rather than approaching the front by car, gave her a different perspective. And she was suddenly filled with tears of joy and belonging—yes *this* was where she belonged—tears that fell in icy pearls the moment Gran, bundled head to toe like a puffy patchwork quilt, stepped out on the back porch and waved.

Dillon leaned close to her scarf-wrapped ear. "I'll let you down then take Ranger to the barn."

She nodded, barely registering what he said as she vigorously returned her grandmother's wave. Then they were there, Dillon's hands beneath her arms to keep her from falling as she slid from Ranger's back to the ground.

She hurried the three steps it took her to reach the porch stairs, frozen snow crunching under her boots, the wooden boards creaking the way they always did. Gran's arms came around her and Brenna cried, breathing in the scents that made Gran, Gran. Butterscotch and roses and fresh mountain air. Finally, finally, it was Christmas.

"I didn't think I'd ever get here," she got out through her sobs. "I've been about to go out of my mind."

Gran chuckled, a deep thrumming sound, and rubbed Brenna's back through her heavy wool coat. "You've just spent several days snowbound with Dillon Craig. I can't imagine things were that bad."

"I guess that depends on your definition of bad," Brenna said, then pulled free to kiss her grandmother's cheek.

"I'd say tell me all about it—" Gran paused to adjust her glasses "—but he'll be up here shortly, and something tells me this is a story that will take hours to tell."

"I can tell you that the man is obstinate. He wouldn't let me bring anything but my toothbrush, a change of underwear, and one single gift. Said he wanted to keep Ranger's load as light as he could." She turned to guide Gran into the house and out of the cold that had them both shivering. "I'll have to get the rest to you later."

"You're here now, pumpkin." Gran laid an icy palm against Brenna's cheek, her eyes misty and red. "That's all I need."

Inside, the kitchen breathed toasty air, and the smells of garlic and tomatoes wafting from the oven had Brenna's stomach rumbling. "Lasagna and fresh baked Italian herb bread. Christmas Eve the way it's supposed to be."

"Or at least Christmas Eve the way you love it." Doffing her coat and hat, Gran slipped a mitt on her hand and pulled out the oven rack to test the top of the bread. "We're eating lunch instead of dinner, then leftovers tonight with dessert."

Mmm. Dessert. "Tiramisu?"

"I baked the ladyfingers yesterday. Dillon brought me the mascarpone and rum last week."

"Guess he's a handy man to have around." She left it at that, unsure how to play this Dillon thing, because letting Gran in on the truth didn't seem like a good idea.

"He is that."

Brenna pulled out a chair, sat sideways, tossed her coat on the table with Gran's. "Is that why you never mentioned him to me? Keeping him all to yourself? Because he certainly knew of my existence."

Gran smiled to herself and nodded, as if entertained by private thoughts she had no intention of sharing. Brenna held her tongue. If after all these years Gran was going to matchmake… Not that Brenna was about to let on that there was no need.

"Everyone knows of your existence, pumpkin," Gran said, bustling about gathering plates and flatware, and refusing Brenna's offer of help. "I talk about you at every opportunity. But I don't talk to you about everyone I know."

"You talk to me about the McGees and the Shepherds and the Martins. And the Alexanders and the Whites." When Gran glanced over, a guilty look in her eyes, Brenna grinned. *Gotcha.* "Should I go on?"

"That's enough I think," she said, but was stopped from saying more by Dillon opening the back door.

He stepped into the kitchen, searched out Brenna and held her gaze. His was smoky and golden, smoldering, the thoughts behind them publicly indecent. "Smells good in here."

"Let's get that wet coat hung to dry," Gran said, hurrying over to where he stood, hat in hand.

Brenna tried not to roll her eyes. She'd taken care of her own coat. Why couldn't he? "Five bucks says more than a couple of those dishes in your freezer hold lasagna."

He gave her a grin full of wicked that wasn't fit for Gran to see. "They do, but none of them are your Gran's."

Gran's voice came from the utility room. "That's because I don't make lasagna except when Brenna's here for Christmas. Used to do the same when her dad was a boy. Recipe came from my mother and her mother before. It's a lot of work, and I'm too old to be baking it for any occasion but Brenna's Christmas Eve."

"Then I'm glad the storm kept us from making the trip over until today. I wouldn't have wanted to miss out."

"You're welcome any Christmas you want to visit." Gran gave Dillon's arm a pat before returning to the stove. "You know that. And I've made up the downstairs guestroom for you."

"You didn't have to go to any trouble." Dillon tossed his hat to the table. "I'm fine with the couch or a pallet on the floor."

Gran shook her head. "Not under my roof. You spent enough years sleeping in bad conditions for me to give you anything but the best I have."

Just as long as it wasn't in the same room where her granddaughter was sleeping, Brenna mused, working hard to keep a straight face. Though she hated the idea of sleeping alone, it was probably a good thing they were reduced to a hands-off relationship.

It would give her a chance to see if the feelings growing out of the seeds planted earlier were based in some shallow attraction. Or if what she was feeling had the sort of roots that had tied her grandmother to this mountain her entire life.

"He likes you."

Brenna looked over to where Gran was dropping balls of powdered sugared dough for Chocolate Krinkles onto the silicone mat lining her cookie sheet. A saucy grin pulled at both corners of her mouth and the lines at her eyes deepened with mirth. But she kept her gaze on her task, leaving Brenna to make the next move.

Threading a ribbon through the hole at the top of the star-shaped sugar cookie now that the icing had set, she asked, "Let's get back to you never mentioning him to me."

Still grinning, Gran coated another ball of dough with powdered sugar. "I'm sure I've told you about seeing Dr. Craig."

Uh-uh. Gran could hedge like nobody's business, but Brenna wasn't having it. "Not that kind of mention."

"What kind of mention did you want, pumpkin?"

Pulling teeth. The woman should've been a dentist. Brenna shrugged. "I don't know. You've talked to him about me. He knew about my job and my move."

"Pshaw. Those are the things I tell anyone who'll listen to me ramble on about my only grandchild."

That didn't help. Brenna wanted to find out how much Gran knew, if Dillon had told her the same stories he'd shared last night in bed. But she wanted to find out without letting the bed part slip. "Have you seen his woodworking?"

"I have. He made that big bowl on my coffee table."

"Is it dated?" Brenna asked, resisting the urge to run to the living room and check.

Gran's hands slowed. Her smile faded. "It is."

"Do you know what the date means?"

Gran slid the cookie sheet into the oven, washed and dried her hands. "You've seen the dates?"

Brenna nodded, tying a bow in the ribbon for hanging.

"Did he tell you about them?"

She nodded again.

Gran took a minute to study Brenna's face, her gaze pensive, searching, then returned to her cookie dough, her grin back in place. "Then I'd say he more than likes you."

"Gran! You're not helping." Though she had to admit Gran's words had caused a blip in her pulse. He desired her, yes. He'd enjoyed her, and she imagined he cared for her to some degree.

But was her grandmother seeing, or sensing, more? This was what Brenna needed to know. She was about to make an eight-thousand-mile move that would change everything about her life. The idea that it might be a mistake, that she might have another reason to stay...

Was that what she was thinking? After one night in his bed? "You've never had a problem pointing out eligible bachelors in the past."

Gran brought her bowl of dough and next cookie sheet to the table where Brenna was working and took the chair to her left. "If Dillon has told you the same stories he's told me, you'll understand my hesitation."

"To do what? Tell me about him? Or..." surely Gran didn't mean "...consider him eligible?"

Her lips pinched, Gran focused on the sugar and the dough.

Her hands moved quickly, deftly, belying her swollen knuckles and age. After what felt to Brenna like an eternity spent wool gathering, Gran sat back and looked over.

"You're the most precious thing in my life, pumpkin. And Dillon Craig is probably the most honorable man I know. But he's also the most tormented, and I would never want to see you hurt."

"I don't think he would hurt me."

"Oh, I don't think so either. Not intentionally. But caring for someone with his type of baggage will take an emotional toll. That much I can guarantee."

Brenna dropped her gaze to her lap. "You're talking about Grandpa Keating."

"I'm talking about any man who has had to kill others. Or see his friends die in war."

"But a man like that..." She was so conflicted, so confused. "Maybe he needs to be loved more than most."

"Do you love him?"

"I only just met him three days ago."

"Do you love him, pumpkin?"

Even for Gran, Brenna wasn't ready to admit her feelings. "I think I could. But as soon as I get home, I finish packing, then come the new year, I'm off to Africa. So it really doesn't matter, does it?"

"Of course, it matters, Brenna." Reaching for Brenna's hand, Gran enclosed it in both of hers, and said softly, "Love is the only thing that does."

CHAPTER ELEVEN

Dillon stared at the tongue-in-groove ceiling of Donota Keating's guestroom, wondering if Brenna was sleeping in the room above. Or if her bed was farther down the hallway, as far away from his as her grandmother could manage.

The thought had him smiling, though his wry grin became more of a grimace as he sat up. He had no problem abiding by his hostess's rules, but he didn't like the idea that she'd kept him from Brenna for any reason but propriety.

And something told him grandmother and granddaughter had done a lot of talking at his expense while he'd tended to Ranger after dinner last night.

Really, though, what did he expect? Donota knew almost as much of his history as he'd spilled to Brenna, and he could hardly blame her for wanting her granddaughter to steer clear from damaged goods.

He tugged on his socks and his jeans, buckled his belt and found his boots. After yesterday's huge lunch and equally big dinner, not to mention the cookies he'd grazed on all day, his stomach shouldn't be rumbling, but it was. Rain or shine, breaking dawn meant coffee. And seeing to Ranger's feed.

He slipped on his shirt and, boots in hand, started toward the kitchen. Halfway down the hall, he passed the living room and glanced in, at the tree Brenna and her grandmother had decorated while laughing like schoolgirls, tossing popcorn and cranberries at each other and him, their squeals bringing down the house and breaking loose chunks of the armor he wore.

And that was when he saw her asleep on the floor, not in the room above his at all. She was wrapped in the quilt from the rack behind the sofa. Throw pillows from the pile he'd seen in the rocking chair were scattered around her, cushioning her head, tucked to her chest, trapped between her legs.

She looked warm and cozy and comfortable, and then he realized she wasn't asleep. Instead she was looking at him.

"Good morning," he said, leaving his boots at the room's entrance and crossing to the tree. "You're up early."

"Up late, you mean," she said, pushing to sit, her legs stretched out in front of her.

"You haven't been to sleep?"

She shook her head, scraped a fall of hair from her face. "Gran and I stayed up half the night talking."

"When I came in from tending Ranger, you said you were headed to bed."

She shrugged, smiled softly. "That had been the plan."

Hmm. "What changed it?"

"That," she said, inclining her head, her gaze searching out his gift boxed under the tree.

He hadn't planned to bring it, had stuffed it at the last minute into Ranger's saddlebag. Something told him giving it to her here, at her grandmother's house cloaked in the familiarity of Christmas, would make a bigger impact.

And making an impact was the whole point of the gift. "You want to open it?"

"Can I?"

"Your call," he said, crossing his ankles and folding down

to sit facing her. "You're the one who knows the house rules, not me."

"We don't really have house rules," she said with a laugh, reaching for the box and pulling it into her lap. "I don't have anything for you."

"It's not that big of a deal. Besides, you made me cookies."

"And then ate half of them myself."

"Some gifts are better when shared."

She dropped her gaze from his to her lap, her cheeks going pink. "I guess some are."

He thought about having her in his bed, wondered how he'd ever sleep again without her there. They'd be leaving Donota's after the big noon meal in order to get back to his cabin before dark. And with the storm over, he could get her to Raleigh tomorrow. Another week and she'd be looking down on the Atlantic from forty thousand feet.

He didn't want her to go. He had no expectation that she'd stay, no right to ask her, no claim to stake. This gift was all he had. "Are you going to open it?"

She pulled the pinecones from the top, stripped away the tape holding the flaps together. Then gripping two in her fists, she said, "You're making me nervous."

"Do you want me to leave?" He didn't want to, but he would.

"No," she said, shaking her head. "It's Christmas morning. This is where you belong."

He wasn't sure what she meant. Did he belong here because of the holiday, or was this about neither one of them being alone? "Do you want to wait for your grandmother?"

"No." And without another word, she lifted out the carving, holding it, studying it, turning it this way and that.

To anyone unfamiliar with the area, the chunk of wood would look like exactly what it was. A chunk of wood. But he could tell Brenna recognized the distinctive profile of the mountain he and Donota Keating called home.

"Figured you could use it as a paperweight or something."

She turned it over, traced the date he'd burned into the wood. The date they'd become lovers.

"It's beautiful," she said, her voice strangely flat. "But I can't accept it."

"Why not?" he asked as she returned it to the box.

"You were obviously carving this for someone else. I wouldn't feel right taking it."

He'd been carving it for no reason at all. He'd been carving it because that was what he did. "I wasn't carving it for anyone. And I want you to have it."

"Why?" She pushed to stand, crossed her arms over her chest and turned away. "You think I need a reminder of what I'm leaving behind? You think having this with me, seeing it every day will make things better?"

He stood, too, his jaw tight and aching. "I wasn't trying to make anything better, Brenna. I didn't know things weren't good."

Her hair flew as she spun on him then, her fists in balls of frustration. "Of course you did. We talked about it. I told you how guilty I feel for leaving Gran here with no one."

Uh-uh. Uh-uh. "She has friends. I'm here. She won't be left with no one."

"She won't be with family. She won't have me."

And neither will I, he thought as he picked up the box. He didn't need this shit. "It was a gift, Brenna. Not a guilt trip."

He was at the door, reaching for his boots when she spoke. "I'm sorry."

He turned. "For what?"

She shook her head, her eyes damp and red, her throat working as she fought back tears.

He hung his head, took a deep breath, looked back up. "If you're sorry for rejecting the gift, don't be. My feelings don't hurt easily. If you're sorry for leaving North Carolina, that's on you. If you're sorry for what we shared, well, I'm not."

He started to go, stopped. "If I'm sorry about anything, it's that we only had one night because given a chance, it could've been a hell of a ride."

Brenna stood on the back porch, wrapped in her grandmother's arms, her coat and gloves and her hat little protection against the cold seeping into her bones. This was it. She wouldn't see Gran for at least another year, and even that depended on things out of her control—staying healthy, her and Gran both, getting away from a position she knew would consume her, money to make the trip home.

Her stomach rebelled against the turkey and stuffing and mashed potatoes that she'd hardly tasted at lunch. The food sat like a rock, a heavy anchor keeping her in place. Keeping her where she wanted to be.

How could she leave North Carolina when this was where her heart belonged?

"Oh, my sweet pumpkin, I'm going to miss you so much."

"I'm a phone call away. A plane ride away." Brenna inhaled roses and butterscotch because she didn't ever want to forget. "You need me, I'm here."

"I don't want you worrying about me." Gran gripped the fabric of Brenna's coat and shook her. "I want you living your life, enjoying the adventure. Making new friends and having fun. Falling in love."

Behind them, Ranger snorted, ready to be on the way. Dillon waited beside him, giving her and Gran their time. He'd said little during the meal, focusing on the feast. After the callous way she'd refused his gift, she couldn't fault him for his silence.

She didn't want to talk to her either. She was an abominably rude bitch.

"Now, you go on with Dillon," Gran said, pulling away after a pat to her back. "He's waiting and it's cold. And you've got quite a ride in front of you."

A ride that would be nothing like the one yesterday morning. Then they'd been lovers. She didn't know what they were now. "What if I stay? I'm happy here. I don't need to make this move. I don't know why I ever thought I did."

"Isn't that why you're going? To find out what your life here is missing? And what's waiting for you overseas?"

What wasn't waiting for her was Dillon Craig. He'd be here. She'd be there. Those damn eight thousand miles between them. "I promise I'll be here for Christmas next year. I know I said I probably wouldn't be able to get back, but I'll make it happen. I promise."

"I hope you can, but it won't be the end of the world if you can't. I'll just have to do my baking early so you'll have cookies for your tree." Taking hold of Brenna's shoulders, Gran turned her around, then leaned close to say, "I love you, pumpkin. Now go."

Reluctantly, Brenna obeyed. Gran stayed on the porch, watching as Dillon gave her a leg up onto the horse and settled in behind her. He waved for the both of them as he spurred Ranger into motion. Within seconds the trees swallowed them, and Brenna closed her eyes.

If she could sleep for the whole of the ride, she wouldn't have to think about hurting him. She wouldn't have to feel his body around hers keeping her warm. She wouldn't have to think about choosing between career and family and losing whatever time she had left with Gran.

She wouldn't have to admit she was having second thoughts.

"I'm sorry about the gift," Dillon leaned close to say. "I never meant to make you feel bad."

"Why are you apologizing to me? I was horrible. I should be apologizing to you."

After a couple of seconds, he said, "I'm waiting."

She slapped at the hand he'd wrapped around her waist, then wrapped it even tighter. "I am sorry. I wasn't fair."

"Is this where I'm supposed to say life isn't fair?"

"It's not, you know." She sighed heavily. "Here you come, just as I'm about to start a new life, a new career. One that's been my dream forever. One Gran knows is my dream. It was her dream, too. What's fair about that?"

He nuzzled his cheek against the scarf Gran had tied like a hood over her head. "She's going to be okay, you know."

"No. I don't know. And neither do you."

"I'm a doctor. Trust me."

"I'm not talking about her health."

"Brenna, if she needs you, you can hop a plane and be here in a day. Two max. I can take care of her till then. You know I will."

"I'm going to miss her so much." Eyes closed, she let him bear her weight and the burden tiring her, and said what she couldn't hold back any longer. "I'm going to miss you, too."

She must've fallen asleep then. She didn't hear him respond. The next thing she knew, Ranger had stopped in front of the barn door and Dillon was nudging her awake. He dismounted, helped her down then inclined his head toward the cabin.

"If you want to pack up your things, I can drive you home."

She followed the direction of his gaze, saw the road had been cleared, the snow graded into banks on either side. "Santa stopped by?"

His laughter echoed as did the grating creaks of the barn door opening. He led Ranger inside. Brenna followed.

"Bud Travers. As soon as a storm blows itself out, mine is the first road he clears."

"On Christmas Day?"

"Upset stomachs, food poisoning. Happens every year."

She thought about that. "If folks are counting on you to be here, how can you drive me home?"

Tending to Ranger's needs, he finally shrugged as if making a decision he wasn't sure was the right one. "There's a doc in Asheville who handles emergencies and cases I can't. My patients know him. I'll put a sign at the end of the drive. I can spare the day."

"What about my car?"

"I'll have Bud tow it up here. Leave me your number. He can let you know how bad the damage is."

She could wait for her car. Stay here until she knew whether or not it was a total loss. And that would accomplish what? Give her another day or two in Dillon's bed? Time she'd set aside to pack up her life in Raleigh?

She'd made a commitment. She had obligations. She couldn't just up and change her mind. Who did that? She doubted Gran ever had, or her folks.

He was right. It was time to go home.

As homeless as she felt, it was time.

CHAPTER TWELVE

Dillon was starting to wonder if he'd ever catch up on his sleep. Since Brenna had plowed into the snowbank, he'd lost way too many hours thinking about her, worrying about her, wondering about a life with her. And yes, making love.

Being awake for the latter was the best loss of shut-eye he'd had in years. The best loss ever, if he was honest. Yeah, he'd dated during his days as an E.R. doc, and he'd hooked up a few times with female soldiers in need of the same intimate comfort.

But Brenna, for whatever reason, was the first woman ever to have him thinking beyond the next time he could get her into bed. And that surprised him. Since his service, he'd done no more than exist a day at a time. He doubted he had it in him to promise forever, and that's what she deserved.

She lay beside him now, in her bed in her Raleigh condo, on her side but facing away, her shoulders moving ever so slightly each time she inhaled. More than anything, he longed to fold himself around her, but resisted the urge so as not to wake her.

As long as she stayed sleeping, he wouldn't have to get up and get dressed and make the drive back to the mountain without her. He wouldn't have to think about never seeing her again, though that was the only thought he had and his throat burned with it, his chest a crushing weight he couldn't budge.

"I can hear you thinking," she said, her voice, already raspy, even more so with sleep.

He rolled toward her, bent his knees to fit behind hers, draped an arm over her waist and tucked his hand between her breasts. He was going to miss this. Miss her.

God, he was going to miss her, he admitted, fighting to swallow how much. "Didn't mean to wake you."

"I wasn't sleeping." She held his arm tight against her, wound her legs between his. "I just fake it better than you do."

"You're still talking about sleep, right?"

Laughing softly, she turned toward him, plucked at the hair on his chest. "None of last night was faked. Trust me. You… make things happen."

His ego wasn't the only thing swelling at that. "That's good to know."

"Please. Like you didn't know it already."

"A man can never hear the truth enough."

In the soft light of dawn filtering into her room, he saw her expression go from happy to sad. "All truths? Even the one about me not wanting you to leave? Wishing you could stay with me here until it's time for me to leave for Africa?"

That one he could do without. The thought of coming to terms with those eight thousand miles was already giving him hell. But his leaving Raleigh—and soon—wasn't an option. Ranger would be fine until he got back, but he'd skipped rounds yesterday, and sign or no sign, he had folks who'd be waiting, who he hadn't let know he'd be away.

Folks who counted on him. Folks he couldn't let down.

But if Brenna said the word… "I need to get back to the mountain."

She sent a searching look over his face, her eyes soft and

damp. "It's like I've known you forever. Like I'm leaving be-hind my best friend. I'm already having a hard time leaving Gran, but now there's you."

He reached over, brushed her hair from her forehead, said nothing but "Shh."

But that had her shaking her head, tears spilling from the corners of her eyes with the motion. She brought up her hand to cup his face, ran a thumb along his cheekbone, pressed her lips together, but still they quivered.

That quiver killed him. It goddamn killed him. "Brenna, sweetheart. Please don't cry."

"How am I going to leave you?" she asked, her voice crack-ing on the whisper. "How am I going to know you'll be okay?"

"I'll be fine." He reached for her wrist, turned her hand to kiss her palm, tasted the salt of tears he wasn't aware he'd let go. "I'll be fine."

"I'm going to make sure Gran looks after you," she said, moving her hand to his neck, his shoulder, caressing him until they both shivered and her nipples pebbled against his chest.

"She already does," he said, his lower body going hard. "We just pretend I'm the one checking on her."

"I'm glad." She rubbed her thigh against him where his erection prodded her, drawing a scratching, primal groan from his throat. "It'll be easier, knowing you two have each other."

"For you, maybe." Nothing would make this easier for him. She couldn't know what she'd given him in the short time they'd had, and to lose her so soon... He wasn't losing her. He couldn't think that way. Time healed all wounds, right? So far he hadn't found the old adage to be particularly true, but just maybe...

"It won't be that bad. You'll see." Her hand drifted down between their bodies, her thumb stroking his sensitive skin where it pulled tight. "Time will fly, and who knows. This time next year—"

"This time next year you'd better be in my bed." He growled out the words, believing nothing she was saying, not about time or how bad or easy things would or wouldn't be. Believing only in the connection he'd found with her and his body's need for hers.

He rolled over her, sheathed himself with a condom from her bedside table and didn't even let himself draw a full breath until he was buried deep. She hooked her heels against his lower back, shifted her hips to take him farther inside.

And then he began to move, slow measured strokes she met with synced rhythmic thrusts, keeping him close, keeping him safe. Keeping him balanced and certain. He didn't want to have all that taken away, and he told her with the movements he made, the steady rise of heat between them, the labored heartbeats they shared.

Her fingers walked up his spine, threaded into his hair, learned the curve of his ear and the ridges of his brow and the crooked slant of his nose. She kissed him as she touched him, her tongue slipping past his lips to find his, the noises she made—oofs and ohs and grunted sighs—like air puffed into his mouth.

Nothing in his life had prepared him for this…this respite, this escape. It bewildered him that she knew how to give him what he didn't have the words to request. And then words didn't matter. She rose up into him, heart to heart, hips to hips, crying out as she came apart. He came with her, the force of his feelings tearing into him, ripping him open.

Exhausted, he collapsed, his head next to hers on her pillow as he inhaled the scents of her hair and her skin. Long after they'd returned to reality, he remained inside her. It was the only reality he wanted to know.

★ ★ ★

Brenna swore the series of flights from Malawi to the States hadn't taken as long as the drive up Gran's mountain. Or maybe it was the delay in having to settle things in Raleigh making this last leg of her trip drag on. Since accepting her future had been set in motion when she'd plowed into that snowbank last Christmas, all she'd wanted to do was leave her old life behind for the new one she couldn't wait to start.

The to-do list between here and there had been way too long. The first thing she'd done after her December 22nd arrival in North Carolina was pick up the truck a nurse she'd worked with at Duke Raleigh had found her. That out of the way, she'd visited the storage unit where she'd kept the few things she hadn't been ready to part with, and loaded the pickup's bed with only those she couldn't live without.

She'd arranged for the rest to be donated. She'd closed out her bank accounts, changed her mail-forwarding orders from the London charity's address to Gran's. She'd had a long gossipy lunch with the girlfriends who'd had her back for years, promising to look them up when she was next in the city. And that was that. The end of the past. She'd hit the road for the four hour drive to her future.

The last year had been both the best of Brenna's life and the worst. She'd done so much good where good was needed, but oh, she'd missed Dillon and Gran. Gran she'd talked to every time she could get to a phone, and during their conversations had learned things about Dillon his letters didn't say. Things they couldn't say. Things Gran had noticed, tiny bits and pieces of his old self emerging as the damage he'd sustained as a warrior had healed.

Brenna had thought about calling him, too, but since writing him the first time on the long flight from DC to Ethiopia, their exchanges had all been by hand. She'd added paragraphs almost every night to the letters she'd penned on yellow legal pads, routing her tomes through the charity's headquarters rather than relying on the local post.

Dillon's letters had been similarly patched together, though never as rambling as hers. He'd reported on weeks' worth of life on the mountain at a time, but said very little about himself, and that was okay. He didn't have to open a vein and bleed. She was really good at reading between the lines.

The words he'd chosen, the change in the tone of his notes, they told her everything she needed to know. She could almost hear his laughter, imagined him smiling as the pen scratched over the page. And when put together with Gran's observations, Brenna knew her year away had been worth it.

Navigating the uphill length of his snowy drive, she wondered if he remembered what he'd said their last morning together. His words had stayed with her since. And when leaving her grandmother's this morning, after their reunion over lasagna last night, she'd told Gran to expect her back with a guest for dinner. Just not to expect them too soon.

His cabin came into view just then, and she saw him stop halfway up his front steps and turn at the sound of her truck. He held what looked like a patient file in his hand, one he'd been studying intently, head down and black Stetson pulled low. He wore the sheepskin coat she remembered, and the boots, jeans and snap-front shirt she'd pictured him in often, and her entire midsection fluttered as if tickled by butterfly wings.

Heart pounding, she pulled to a stop, parked, cut the engine. He watched her silently, somberly, and she wiped her palms on her thighs before climbing from the cab.

"Hi," she said, her hand close to her chest as she waved.

After an interminably long pause, he said, "You're quite a ways from home."

"Not really." She shoved her keys in her pocket, slammed the truck door.

He faced her, frowning. "Last I knew you were living eight thousand miles away."

"Yeah, well." A shrug. "You know how the mail service has been."

"Things have changed, you're saying."

"They have, yes. I'm actually looking for work."

"Work?"

She swallowed. Swallowed again. "You wouldn't know of anyone who could use a nurse, would you?"

He looked at her. Hard. Eyes glittering. "That mean you're done in Malawi?"

"All done," she said, trembling at the reaction of her body to his gaze. Oh, it was going to be hard to wait.

"What about Raleigh?"

She shook her head. "I gave up my place when I left. I'm going to stay with Gran until I can get settled on the mountain."

He looked over her and into the forest, let that sink in. "You're moving to the mountain?"

"I am," she said, and nodded.

"That's good to hear."

So was that. She walked toward him, shivering, shaking, teeth nearly chattering as she walked up the steps. "You know what today is, don't you?"

"I'm pretty sure it's Christmas." He pressed his lips together, narrowed his eyes.

Yeah, it was, but it was so much more. She held out her hand, her fingers unsteady, her future overflowing her palm until her heart ached with it. *Please*, please *let this go well.*

Nodding, her gaze holding his, she said the words she'd

practiced for the last twelve months. "It's also this time next year."

For several seconds, he remained still, an anchor dug in deep, and then he reached for her, pulled her to him, tucking their hands to his chest that rose and fell at the same pace as hers. He was warm and solid and her everything, and she blinked away her tears before they ruined the moment, hoping, wishing, waiting...

The hard line of his mouth cracked slowly, breaking into a wicked dimpled grin. Then he dragged her with him through the front door, kicking it shut behind them.

★ ★ ★ ★ ★

A RARE GIFT

Jaci Burton

For Charlie. I love you.

JACI BURTON

is a *New York Times* and *USA TODAY* bestselling, award-winning author of over fifty books. She lives in Oklahoma and when she isn't on deadline (which is often), she can usually be found wrestling with her uncooperative garden, wrangling her dogs, watching an unhealthy amount of television or completely losing track of time reading a great book. She's a total romantic and longs for the happily ever after in every story, which you'll find in all her books.

You can find Jaci on the web at www.jaciburton.com, on Twitter at twitter.com/jaciburton and on Facebook at www.facebook.com/jaci.burton.

CHAPTER ONE

Wyatt Kent stood outside Small Hands Day Care Center, debating whether or not he could actually go inside.

He was no coward, but it wasn't often he was faced with something like this.

He was about to give a bid on a construction job for his ex-wife's younger sister.

How he'd gotten stuck with this he didn't know. That was what he got for not paying attention in meetings. He'd been bulldozed by his two brothers along with Tori, Kent Construction's oh-so-efficient but manipulative office manager.

"No big deal, Wyatt."

"Calliope Andrews is nothing like your ex-wife, Cassandra."

"No one else can do the project, Wyatt. It's either you or the job doesn't get done."

Might as well suck it up and get this over with. The wood-frame house was painted shocking blue and blinding white. The sign out in the front yard was plastered with a bunch of multicolored handprints.

So it was cute. The house needed a new coat of paint. Probably would need a new roof within the next year or two, too. But that wasn't his problem. He stood at the end of the walkway and watched the endless parade of parents driving up to the side of the house. The side door opened, parents dashed in to retrieve kids, then the car drove through to the back alley and the next car pulled up.

Wyatt went up to the front door and rang the bell, then waited for someone to answer. And waited. And waited. He tried the door, figuring he'd let himself in, but it was locked.

Great.

He went around to the side and was halted by a tall, thick woman with short cropped black hair and likely more muscles than he had. She wore jeans and a T-shirt and looked more like a wrestler than a day care worker.

She frowned, gave him the head-to-toe once-over.

"Who are you?"

"Wyatt Kent. I have an appointment with Calliope Andrews."

She laid her hand on his chest to keep him in place. "Stay here. Miss Calliope, there's a Wyatt Kent here. Says he's supposed to meet with you."

"Oh, that's right. It's okay, Beth. I'm expecting him."

Beth tossed a thumb over her shoulder. "Go on back. You're in my way."

"Go on back where?"

"Straight down the hall, then turn right. All the way to the end."

Wyatt nodded and dodged a bunch of giggling little girls on his way. They were a few years younger than his eight-year-old niece, Zoey, but they were all dressed in pink—Zoey's favorite color.

Most of the kids must have gone home by now. With the exception of a few stragglers dashing by him on his way down the hall, the place had gone quiet. He found the room Beth had directed him to. It was fairly small and completely empty.

A playroom, it was stuffed with overflowing bookshelves and toys and tables and a giant castle.

He stood in the middle of the room, figuring Calliope had stepped out.

Until he heard a rustling in the castle, then a groan. He turned around and saw one very attractive, jeans–clad butt attempting to back out of the castle opening.

"I swear if my butt gets any bigger I'm not going to be able to clean the toys out of this thing and we'll need to get a bigger castle."

He disagreed. She had a great ass.

She flung toys over her shoulder while Wyatt stood there, feeling sort of inept.

"You need some help there?"

She stilled, her head jerked up and she bumped it against the opening. "Ow. Dammit." She rubbed the wild curls on top of her head, then backed all the way out and sat on the floor, adjusted the tortoiseshell glasses that had ridden down the bridge of her very cute nose.

"Wyatt. I thought you were Beth. You're not Beth."

"No, I'm not."

"Sorry. I was cleaning up in here." She pushed off her knees and stood, adjusting her shirt over some very full breasts and grinned at him. "I'm so glad you're here. Let's go to my office where it's a little less insane."

The last time Wyatt had seen Calliope Andrews, he'd still been married to her older sister Cassandra, and Calliope had been—hell, in college? Maybe nineteen or twenty, at most, was his guess. She'd been chubby, her hair a corkscrew of untamed brown curls, and she'd worn really ugly glasses. In short, she'd been a hot mess.

He followed her down the hall, watching the way her hips moved when she walked.

"Here we are." She opened the door and led him into a small office. Her desk sat next to the window and there were a couple chairs on either side. He took one and she sat across from him instead of at her desk.

She still wore glasses and her hair was still curly and she was still hot, all right. But she wasn't a mess at all. Calliope had grown up. It had to have been six years or so at least since he'd seen her last. She'd lost the baby fat, was curvy in all the right places, and her glasses made her eyes look like sparkling emeralds.

God, she was gorgeous.

But she wasn't at all like Cassandra, who'd been tall, slender and blonde.

And the devil in disguise.

"Thank you for taking on this project, Wyatt."

"No one else had the time."

She quirked a brow, then grinned again. "So you're stuck with me, then?"

"I didn't say that."

"You didn't have to." She laughed and didn't seem at all offended. "I know this is probably hard for you, seeing as how you've managed to avoid me since I came to town."

"I haven't avoided you."

"Yes, you have. But it's okay. I understand why. You're not very fond of my sister, and you think we're exactly alike." She patted his hand. "But trust me, I'm nothing like Cassie."

He blinked, not sure he understood anything that had happened so far. He figured the two of them would dance around the topic of Cassandra, and here Calliope had said her name, torn open the wounds, making them bleed fresh, like it had happened yester...

"Wyatt. Wyatt." She snapped her fingers. "You okay?"

"I'm fine." He stood. "Let's go see where you want this addition."

"Sure." She stood, too. "Surely you're over her by now, aren't you? I mean, it's been three years. She's not worth mourning over for that long."

Calliope opened the door to her office and walked down the same hallway they'd come from.

Her saying it that way made him feel foolish for feeling closed up and angry for three damn years over a woman who'd only cared about herself.

"You are over her, aren't you?"

God, she was persistent. "Yeah. Over her."

"Good. Because I want us to be friends."

He stopped in the middle of the hall. "What?"

She stopped, too, turning and dipping her head back to look into his eyes.

Damn she had pretty eyes. Pretty hair. And she smelled good, too. He couldn't figure out what she smelled like. Something that made him want to swipe his tongue across her neck.

His jeans tightened. It had been a long damn time since that had happened. He didn't trust women, tried to stay away from them.

And he sure as hell planned to stay away from Calliope.

"Wyatt. Are you drunk? Did you stop at the bar after work?"

"What?" He looked down at her. She must have been saying something, because her lips quirked.

"I've been talking. You're not listening. Want to do this another day?"

"No." He didn't want to do it at all. "Show me what you want."

She paused, her cheeks turning pink. "Sure. This way."

They went into the room where the castle was. "I want the

addition off this room, to extend the play area so I can separate the kids by age group. Younger kids in here, older kids in the new room."

Finally, something to distract him from Calliope, from the way she looked, the way she smelled, the things—people—she reminded him of. He took out his tape measure and started making some notes based on what she wanted, which was a room a little larger than the one they stood in, with ample storage space.

Nothing fancy. Doable. Easy enough. He'd bring in some extra labor to help, and he'd be out of there. Calliope stayed quiet while he wrote down materials and labor needed to get the job done. He turned to her. Looked at her. And all the memories came flooding back.

He couldn't do this.

"Wyatt. I know I was kidding you about getting over things and doing this job, but if you're seriously having second thoughts, I know there's this other company I looked up that can handle it. The Johnson Brothers?"

That did it.

Kent Construction was a family-owned business and had been since their father and grandfather had started up the company over fifty years ago. They'd had a stronghold on Deer Lake with very little competition.

The Johnsons were a new outfit who'd been leeching into their territory for the past few years, stealing business away from them. Wyatt didn't mind competition, but he didn't like the Johnson brothers. They weren't local, their workmanship was shoddy, they cut corners and used inferior products. And he hated losing to them.

It was only a single-room addition. How long could it take? A month, six weeks at most.

He could suck it up and deal for six weeks. And even if he

couldn't, he wasn't about to give a job away—an easy job he could handle.

"I don't know what you're talking about. I'll go back to the office, write up an estimate and have it delivered to you tomorrow."

She cocked her head to the side. "Won't you bring it by so we can get the contract signed? I'd like to get started on this as soon as possible." She raised her hands out to her sides. "As you can tell we've outgrown the space and really need the extra room here."

He inhaled, let it out. "Fine. I'll deliver it in the morning and bring a contract with me."

There was that grin again. She had dimples. Awfully cute.

No. She wasn't cute. Not at all. Nothing about her was cute. Or sexy.

"I gotta go." He turned and fled the room.

"Okay." She skirted in front of him. "Here, let's go out the front door."

Once again he was forced to trail behind her, giving him a great view of her ass.

Calliope was the first woman he'd noticed—really ogled, as a matter of fact—in a long time.

That sent danger and warning signals flashing in his head. *Say no. Walk away. Don't do this job.*

But he'd be damned if he was going to lose another job to those asshole Johnsons. How much danger could he be in with Calliope Andrews? She owned a day care center. She would be busy all day. So would he. They'd barely run into each other, right?

She opened the door and stood with her hand on the door knob, the other pushing up her glasses.

"Thanks for coming by, Wyatt. I'll see you tomorrow."

"See ya."

He hurried out the front door and hadn't even realized he'd been holding his breath until he reached the sidewalk. He turned back to look at the door.

Calliope was still there. She waved at him.

Like an idiot he waved to her, then snatched his hand back and shoved it in his jacket pocket.

He was not going to be nice. He didn't have to be. All he had to do was his job.

And nothing more.

CHAPTER TWO

Calliope finished cleaning up the playroom, then went into her office to shut down the computer.

That was when she saw Wyatt's clipboard.

Oh, no. He'd need that if he was going to do her estimate. She picked up the phone, intending to call his office, then laid it back down.

She was on her way out the door anyway, and the offices of Kent Construction were a few miles away. She'd drop it off on her way home.

So maybe his office wasn't exactly on her way home, since she only lived a couple blocks from the day care center, but she didn't mind going out of her way to deliver his clipboard.

And maybe she might want to see him again tonight.

And maybe she might still have a crush on him.

But crush or not, this was business, and it had to come first. She needed the addition to the day care center and she needed Wyatt focused on giving her that estimate.

She climbed into her car and headed toward his offices, remembering how it had been all those years ago.

She'd been more than a little bit in love—or at least lust—with Wyatt since she was fifteen years old and her older sister Cassandra had dragged him over to the house to meet their parents. When he'd walked through the door, she'd been sitting at the kitchen table doing her homework. She'd looked up, saw him and her breath had stopped.

Wyatt had been twenty-three back then—and gorgeous. And then Cassie had walked in and slipped her hand in Wyatt's and all Calliope's hopes were dashed. Cassie had been taken with Wyatt's lean good looks, his dark hair and blue eyes. And why wouldn't she? Every girl in Deer Lake wanted him, and Cassie loved competition—loved to win. She'd won Wyatt, though Calliope had been certain Cassie had never loved Wyatt. She'd only wanted him because every other girl in town had wanted him, too. Once Cassie had him, she paraded him around town like a prize possession.

Cassie was beautiful, with her dark blond hair that fell straight and sleek to her waist, and a killer body that she honed for hours at the gym. And she was so smart, had gone to college and gotten her business degree, then gone to work for one of the top real-estate firms in town, eventually branching out to start her own company. Real estate and construction—Cassie and Wyatt's businesses had even meshed.

They'd really been the perfect couple.

But the two of them hadn't been the perfect couple at all, and it had broken Calliope's heart to see both of them so unhappy. Sometimes things don't work out. They were better apart than together. Cassie had moved on, but for some reason, Wyatt seemed to hold a grudge.

But the past was the past and she'd hoped Wyatt was over it by now. Nobody was worth pining over for three years—not even her sister.

She pulled up to the offices. Wyatt's truck wasn't there.

Huh. She got out anyway and went to the front door, tried to open it, but it was locked up tight. She peered through the glass. It was dark.

Maybe he decided he'd come in early in the morning to do the bid. She shrugged and got back into her car, deciding she'd come back in the morning and bring him the clipboard.

On her way back down Central, she spotted his truck parked in front of Stokey's bar.

Oh. That's where he was. She'd drop off the clipboard to him there. She parked and went inside, blinking to adjust her eyes to the darkness.

She wasn't much of a drinker, so she'd never been in Stokey's before. There wasn't a whole lot of atmosphere to the place. Dim lighting, bottles of alcohol stocked behind a very dark wood bar. There was a pool table off to one side, a dart board on the opposite wall and a couple televisions scattered about showing various sporting events.

There were only a handful of people inside—all men. Then again it was a Tuesday and not even seven-thirty yet. Maybe the big crowds didn't show up until later.

The men who were present stopped what they were doing to give her the once-over as she made her way to the bar.

Wyatt had a beer in hand, his focus on one of the televisions mounted behind the bar. She climbed onto the barstool next to his.

"Hey there."

Nothing. He didn't even acknowledge her. Then again, the television was turned up pretty loud, so maybe he hadn't heard her.

"Wyatt, you forgot your clipboard."

He finally turned his head, then frowned. "Calliope. What are you doing in here?"

She slid the clipboard across the bar to him, then smiled at him. "Your clipboard. You left it at the center. Thought you might need it to work up those numbers for me."

He looked at her like he had no idea who she was. Then he gave her a quick nod. "Yeah, right. Thanks."

He used to be so full of life. He'd laugh and his face would light up when he smiled. Her toes curled remembering what he looked like when he smiled.

"You want something to drink?"

She shifted her gaze to the bartender, a heavyset guy with male pattern baldness.

"Oh. Uh. You know, I don't know." She turned to Wyatt. "What should I have?"

Wyatt stared at her. "How should I know?"

"Well, I don't really drink that often, so I'm not the best judge of what's good. What do you suggest?"

Wyatt raised his bottle to his lips. "Beer."

She nodded and looked at the bartender. "I'll have a beer."

The bartender flipped the top off the bottle and slid it to her. She reached into her purse for the money and paid him, leaving an extra dollar for a tip. Then she slid around on the stool to check out what was going on while she took a long swallow of the beer, shuddering at the taste.

Soda would be better, but this would have to do.

She slipped off the barstool and walked over to the pool table to watch the two guys play. She'd never played pool, either, though there'd been a table at her dorm in college.

The cool people played. She'd never been one of the cool people. Now that she was a single adult, she should learn to do cool things instead of always being wrapped up with work.

One of the guys—a burly, halfway-decent-looking type wearing jeans and a plaid shirt, shifted his gaze to hers and grinned at her. "Want to take me on, honey?"

"Oh, I've never played before. Can you teach me?"

He took his shot and straightened, grabbed his beer and

came over to stand beside her while his partner took a shot. "Honey, I can teach you anything you want to know."

"Great. Then I'd love to learn how to play."

They finished up their game, and the guy—who introduced himself as Joey Johnson—put the balls in the triangular thing. He called it "racking the balls". Once they were all set, he put the white ball in front of them.

"Now we break," he said, leaning forward with the pool cue.

She watched as he shot the white ball toward all the other balls. They scattered, some falling into the holes around the table.

"We'll play simple eight ball," Joey said. "I'm solid, you're stripes. I shoot until I miss. Then it's your turn to get your ball into the pockets."

"Seems simple enough."

Except Joey didn't miss very often. He put four of his balls in one of the pockets before she had a chance.

Of course that meant she'd gotten to watch his technique. It seemed easy enough. She bent over the table and tried to hold her pool cue the same way he did.

She wasn't very coordinated, though, and couldn't quite remember the hand positioning.

Joey laughed. "Here, let me help you."

He aligned his body next to hers, his pelvis shoving up behind her.

She might be naive about pool, but she wasn't dumb about men. Joey was hitting on her in the most basic of ways, and wasn't subtle about it at all.

He could teach her to play pool, but she wouldn't be going home with him tonight.

"Just do it so it's comfortable for you." He put the cue in

her hands, showed her the proper positioning. And that wasn't the only positioning he showed her.

Really? Sometimes men were so obvious.

Her gaze drifted over to Wyatt, who had swiveled around on his barstool and glared daggers at them.

He looked upset. At her.

She rolled her eyes.

And sometimes men were just plain dumb.

She straightened, smiled at Joey. "I think I've got the hang of it now, and if you shove your—" she looked down at his crotch "—assets at me again, I'm going to knee you in the balls. Understood?"

His eyes widened, then he grinned. "Loud and clear."

Now that they had that straight, she took her shot. And amazing thing, the ball fell into the pocket. She let out a loud whoop and the guys around her cheered and high-fived her.

She might yet get the hang of this game.

Wyatt watched Calliope play pool. She wasn't very good at it, but maybe it was an act to gather an entourage of men who were all too eager to help her out.

Within a half hour there were six guys hanging on her. And who wouldn't? She had a great ass, perfect breasts and the kind of hips a man wanted to grab on to and never let go. She looked you straight in the eye and smiled—a lot. And her laugh—damn, her laugh made his balls tighten. Deep and throaty, and she threw her head back and let it go for all she was worth.

Cassandra had always been subtle. She only had to enter a room and the men would come running. And she loved the attention. She barely noticed Wyatt was in the room once the guys swarmed around her.

He guessed the sisters were alike in that respect.

Except after two games, Calliope put the pool cue down, waved goodbye to the guys she'd collected and headed toward him.

She slid back onto the barstool and signaled the bartender. "Another beer?"

"No, thank you. How about a diet soda?"

She turned to Wyatt. "You don't play pool?"

"I play."

"Why didn't you join us?"

"I don't hang out with the Johnson brothers."

She quirked a brow. "Why not?"

"They're competitors."

She thanked the bartender for the soda and dug into her bag for money.

"I've got this. Add it to my tab, Bill."

"Thanks." She turned back and took a sip from the straw. "So because you and the Johnson brothers compete in business, you can't be friendly?"

"Not with those guys."

"Huh. Why not?"

He turned his head and gave her a look. "Because they're assholes."

She snorted. "Seemed like nice enough guys to me."

"I'm sure you'd think that."

"What does that mean?"

He faced ahead again. "Nothing."

"You're very irritable, Wyatt. Did you have a rough day?"

Calliope—unlike her sister—wasn't subtle at all. "No, I didn't have a rough day. And I'm not irritable. I'd like to be left alone."

"Being alone just makes you lonely. And that's not good for anybody. Is this what you do every night?"

Now he was forced to look at her again. "What?"

"Do you come here every night by yourself?"

Mostly. "Sometimes."

"And do what? Drink alone?"

She had him pegged. He didn't like it. "Why do you care?"

"I've always cared about you. You should get out and have some fun, not sit in this dark place and brood. You're like Heathcliff. Or the Beast from *Beauty and the Beast*." She laid her hand on his thigh. It made him want to groan. He didn't want to think about her being a woman—and a very attractive, sexy woman, at that. He wanted her to go away.

"Who's Heathcliff? And the Beast? Thanks a lot."

"I told you. Brooding. And really? Heathcliff? *Wuthering Heights?* Surely you've read that."

"Heard of the book. Never read it."

She leaned an elbow against the bar and put her lips around the straw, sucking up soda. His brain immediately registered *lips* and *suck* and there went the quivering in his balls again. She had a great mouth—a full bottom lip made to be tugged on.

Dammit.

He pulled out a couple bills and paid his bar tab, then grabbed his clipboard. "I gotta go."

He headed for the door. She followed.

"Yeah, I probably should, too. 6:00 a.m. comes awfully early. Thanks for buying me a drink."

"It was just a soda, Calliope."

It was dark outside. She zipped up her jacket and turned to him, gracing him with her beautiful smile again. "Still, you didn't have to and I really appreciate it."

Cassandra had never thanked him for anything. She'd always expected men to do things for her—buy her things, hold the door open for her, worship her.

He walked Calliope to her car. She grabbed her keys out of her bag, opened the door and quirked her lips up at him.

A man could get lost in a smile like that. There was something so guileless and innocent about it.

She laid her hand on his arm, then surprised the hell out of him by stepping in and wrapping her arms around him to hug him. The warmth of her seeped through his jacket, and every part of him that was a man felt every curve of her body as she pressed against him.

It was a brief hug, likely nothing more than something friendly. She pulled back and said, "I'll see you tomorrow, then. Good night, Wyatt."

His breath caught in his throat. "Yeah. Good night."

He went to his truck and climbed in, laying the clipboard next to him while he watched Calliope pull out of the parking lot.

He could still feel every part of her body that had touched his, could still smell the faint scent of vanilla.

He shouldn't have taken this job.

CHAPTER THREE

Tori brought the bid by the next morning. She explained that Wyatt had to finish up a project on another site. Calliope signed off on the bid and Tori told her they'd start on it right away, but it would likely be a while because they couldn't do anything until they filed the permits and the cement floor was poured.

It took a week for the whole permit and cement thing, and through it all she didn't see Wyatt again. He'd sent a cement crew out to lay the foundation, and then trucks came to drop off materials. Tori had called saying Wyatt would start the project today.

Not that she'd been counting the days until she saw him or anything.

Not that she'd spent any time thinking about that ridiculously impulsive urge to hug him that night a week ago outside the bar.

What had she been thinking? They were about to enter into a business relationship. And she might be a touchy-feely type of person, and maybe she did hug just about every person on the planet, from her kids at the center to their parents and everyone who worked for her, but that didn't mean she had to go and hug Wyatt.

But oh, he'd been a solid wall of muscle, his body a hot

furnace of steel that she wanted to climb onto and never let go of, once again reminding her of how incredibly lucky her sister had been.

He hadn't hugged her back—not that she'd given him any time to. As soon as she realized what a bad move that had been, she'd taken a step back and said good-night. He hadn't looked at her like she'd grown two heads or anything, but he hadn't exactly been swept away and put his arms around her, either.

Then again, she wasn't swayed by rejection. Wyatt had a big gaping hole in his heart from the way his marriage had ended, and it was about time he healed. She figured she was the right person to help him with that. The fact he'd been married to her sister didn't factor into her way of thinking.

And she'd been doing a lot of thinking about Wyatt, so while she was in her office doing financials, she heard the trucks pull up. She grabbed her jacket and walked outside.

Wyatt was there along with two other guys. She stayed out of sight and watched as he directed his employees.

If she thought he was gorgeous before, seeing him strip off his jacket and strap on a tool belt nearly made her knees buckle. There was something about a man who worked with his hands that was downright devastating to a woman's libido—or at least *her* libido.

She walked over to him, and just seeing him put a giant smile on her face.

It was already noisy, his two laborers setting up the frame with hammer and nails. Wyatt was inside the small trailer he'd brought with him hitched to his truck. She stepped inside, knocking on the open door as she entered.

"Hey."

He straightened, turned to her, frowned. "What are you doing here?"

"Checking in to say hello. How's it going?"

"It's not going at all yet since we're just getting started."

He was good at pushing women away. Tori had told her he hadn't dated at all since the divorce. It was time to put a stop to that.

"If you or the guys need anything, come on in to the center and the staff or I will fix you right up. There's coffee or soda or—"

"We have everything we need right here."

"Okay. I'll let you get to work."

He didn't say anything, so she stepped out of the trailer and got back to doing her job. Other than listening to drilling and hammering, she mentally tuned him out. Kids were excellent for that. They commanded your attention and didn't let you think of anything but them. By the time the last kid and the last of her employees left the center, it was six-thirty. She figured Wyatt and his crew would be long gone by then, but she was curious how much work they'd gotten done in a day, so she put on her jacket, closed and locked the doors and set the alarm, then headed around the corner to see what had been done.

It was dark, but the streetlight shed enough light on the project. They'd made a good start on the framing. She was impressed.

And Wyatt's truck was still parked on the street, a light on inside the trailer. She went over and knocked on the door. No answer at first, then Wyatt opened the door, his typical frown on his face.

"What do you want?"

She stepped up and came inside. "I thought I'd stop by to take a look. You did a great job today."

"Thanks."

He stood there, arms folded. She skirted around him to see what he was working on at the table. "Are these the blueprints for the room?"

He sighed. "Yes."

She leaned over the table. "Looks complicated." She lifted her gaze to his. "I could never figure this out."

His gaze met hers. "It's not that hard. Look. This is the frame of the room. This is electrical…"

He outlined everything in the blueprint for her, not that she was paying attention. She was close to him and he smelled like sawdust and sweat, a lethal combination. She leaned closer and breathed him in, her shoulder brushing against his.

"Calliope."

"Yeah."

"What are you doing?"

Fantasizing. "Trying to get a closer look. My prescription is old and I probably need to see an eye doctor to get new glasses, but I haven't had time." She bent closer to the blueprints—actually shifting closer to Wyatt.

"Any closer and you're going to be on top of my desk."

Wouldn't that be fun? She wondered what Wyatt would do if she climbed on there? Would it give him ideas? She wished she had something sexier on—like a dress—instead of jeans covered in spilled chocolate milk and a sweatshirt baby Ryan had spit up on. Not an alluring ensemble at all.

Still, she wasn't about to give up on him. She had her jacket zipped up to hide the spit-up and it was dark enough he might not notice the milk stain.

She turned around and leaned against the desk.

"Wyatt, do you ever date?"

His eyes widened. "What?"

"Do you ever date? You know…women?"

Wyatt damn near swallowed his tongue. Where the hell had that come from? He'd thought she'd left and he could spend an hour or so going over the blueprints to make sure they were on track with this project. But then Calliope knocked on the

door of the trailer, forced herself inside and then threw herself all over his blueprints, practically draping her body over
him. Her scent drove him crazy. He was sure if he'd walk her
through the outline of the project she'd be satisfied and leave.

Instead, her curls brushed his cheek, and her hip nudged
his, and then she flipped around and leaned against his table,
making him think thoughts he had no business thinking, like
bending her over his drafting table.

Her green eyes mesmerized him, and then she asked him
if he ever dated?

She was driving him out of his mind and it was only the
first day of the project.

"Calliope…"

"No, really. I know we haven't seen each other in a long
time, but you don't seem very happy."

"Calliope, you need to leave."

She didn't look like she was going anywhere. She crossed
her arms under her breasts. "Have you been out with anyone
since you and Cassie divorced?"

"That's none of your business."

"That means no. Why not? It's been three years."

"Don't you have somewhere you need to be?"

"No. Why, do you?"

He wished he did.

"If you don't, we could go out."

He had no idea what to make of this woman. She was like
a bulldozer. "What?"

"You know, go out. That thing you do when you're single."

"I know what it means. Are you asking me out?"

"Well, I wasn't, but sure. Would you like to go out with
me?" She wasn't teasing or playing a game with him. She was
honest to God asking him on a date. And she was beautiful
and made his palms sweat and she was Cassandra's sister and
no way in hell was he going anywhere near her.

"No."

He figured it would crush her. Instead, she cocked a brow, brushed an errant curl away from her cheek and continued to stand firm. "Why not?"

"You know why not."

She took a step forward. He took one back, but the trailer was small and there wasn't much room. He bumped the wall. She moved forward again and he was reminded of playing checkers with his brothers. He was backed into a corner with no place to go, and if he moved, he was going to be jumped by his opponent.

He suddenly couldn't remember why that was such a bad idea, especially when Calliope moved into him, tilted her head back and stared him down with her deep green eyes.

"I can't believe a big tough guy like you is afraid of a little thing like me, Wyatt." Then she stepped back, her gaze traveling halfway down and staring at the part of him she had no business staring at. When she lifted her gaze again, she grinned.

"I know you have balls in there. Why don't you try and find them? When you do, it's your turn to come ask me out."

She stepped out of the trailer and shut the door behind her.

Wyatt had never been so confused, confounded and downright irritated with a woman in his entire life.

No balls, huh? A man didn't take an insult like that from a woman.

He'd show her balls.

No, he wouldn't. He wasn't about to show Calliope anything, especially not his balls. If he was smart, he'd ignore her completely. She was his client, he'd been hired to do a job, and that was all he should do.

But no balls? He couldn't let that one go.

No way in hell.

CHAPTER FOUR

"You told him he had no balls?"

Tori tilted her head back and laughed, making heads turn all around them.

Ensconced in the booth at Lodge by the Lake, their favorite outskirts-of-town restaurant, Calliope and Tori ate their dinner and had their weekly gossip and catch-up session.

"I did tell him that."

Tori scooped up a forkful of pasta and slid it between her lips. A couple guys at the bar near their booth watched every bite Tori took. It always amused Calliope because Tori was gorgeous, with her flaming red hair and killer body. Men flocked to her, and Tori was immune. It was like she never even noticed men looking at her. Likely because she had the hots for Brody Kent, though Tori would never admit to it. She wasn't sure why Tori wasn't going all out for Brody. He was cover-of-a-magazine gorgeous, lean and sexy, and the two of them had combustible chemistry.

"So what did Wyatt say?" Tori asked.

"Nothing, because I never gave him the chance to respond. I just walked out of the trailer. That was four days ago and he and I haven't spoken a word to each other since."

Tori leaned back and took a long swallow of raspberry iced tea. "He's avoiding you."

Calliope nodded. "Like you wouldn't believe. He doesn't come inside the center at all, and whenever I pop outside to check on the progress of the addition, he ducks inside the trailer as if I caught him naked or something."

"That's great," Tori said. "You've got him on the run now. He must really like you. If he didn't care, he'd tell you to kiss his ass, or even worse, he'd ignore you, shrug his shoulders and go about his business. You've got him rattled, girl."

Calliope pushed her plate to the side and sipped her soda. "I'd like to think so. The man is simply too uptight for his own good."

"Don't I know it. I'm the one who has to work with him every day. He needs to get laid in the worst way."

Calliope sighed. "I'd love to be the one to take care of that for him."

"I have no idea why anyone would want to poke that bear. Get him all riled up and who knows what could happen."

Calliope knew exactly what. Her fantasies ran amok with the possibilities. "I can only imagine. If he hasn't had a woman since my sister, he's got all this pent-up passion inside just ready to explode."

"I hope you know what you're doing."

Calliope grinned. "No clue, but won't it be fun?"

After dinner and girl talk, Calliope and Tori parted ways. It was still early and the weather continued to be unseasonably warm, so Calliope took a drive around the lake.

And, okay, maybe she was checking to see if Wyatt was home, since his house was near the restaurant. She drove by his house, the one he'd built for him and Cassandra.

Technically this could be classified as stalking, but what

the hell. It wasn't like she was going to knock on his door. She loved his house.

It was a beautiful place nestled at the foot of the hills, surrounded by lush forest and the lake off to the left of the house. He'd built the house for him and Cassandra thinking they'd never have to move again. A two-story, it was big, rustic and gorgeous, with blue-and-gray trim and white gables.

Cassandra hated the house. She'd said it was too big, too remote. She hated the woods that backed up to the house, claimed it would draw wildlife.

Well, duh. That was the idea. Calliope could imagine watching deer while sitting on the back porch drinking coffee. How awesome would that be?

Their marriage had ended before the house had been finished. Wyatt had completed it anyway and moved in. She was surprised he hadn't sold the place. It was kind of big for one person.

She'd never known two people more wrong for each other. But both had been so stubborn and determined to make it work. That relationship had *failure* stamped on it from the get go. They'd wanted different things out of life, but Cassie had wanted Wyatt, and Wyatt had been head over heels in love with Cassie, so they'd both been blind.

His truck was parked in the driveway, and the garage door was open. Wyatt was in the garage, and since he'd looked up when she drove by, there was no sense in pretending he hadn't seen her. She pulled in behind his truck and got out.

He was under the hood of a pretty sweet muscle car—a Chevelle, maybe? It was some kind of Chevy. It was beaten up and had seen better days, but shades of its former glory could still be seen in the parts Wyatt was restoring. She didn't know a whole lot about cars, but she knew a great engine when she saw it. He'd already dropped that in and was working on sanding a fender, his body once again sweaty, greasy and smelling like motor oil.

What a turn-on.

"This is nice. Is it yours?"

"No, I stole it. I work part-time for a chop shop."

She leaned against the wall of the garage. "You've got a bit of the smartass in you, Wyatt."

He lifted the safety glasses from his eyes and glared at her. "You stalking me, Calliope?"

"Maybe a little. You've been avoiding me."

"Thank God you finally noticed." He grabbed his can of beer and emptied it in three swallows.

Undeterred, she followed him into the house.

For a big place, it was ridiculously devoid of furniture. Sofa and chair in the living room, big-screen television and that was it. Small kitchen table with two chairs. Everything looked garage-sale quality.

He went into the kitchen and grabbed another beer. Just one.

"I'd love one. Thanks for offering."

He frowned, then grabbed another and handed it to her.

"Thanks." She popped the top off her beer, waiting to see if he'd head back out in the garage. He didn't, instead took a couple long swallows and leaned against the counter, so she grabbed a stool at the bar and opened her beer, sipped and swiveled around to take a look at the house.

It was stunning despite the lack of furniture. High ceilings with natural wood beams. Tile and pale wood floors. Rustic, charming, and though it needed a few rugs and some decent furniture, it looked as though it had been made with a man's handcrafted expertise—someone who had taken their time and used a keen eye for detail, from the carefully constructed stone fireplace to the cornice at the bottom of the staircase.

She swiveled back around to find Wyatt staring at her.

"The house is amazing, Wyatt. Can I see all of it?"

"Why?"

"Because if it's anything like the family room, it takes my breath away."

Wyatt didn't want Calliope to like the house. He didn't want to show her the house. But dammit, something inside him made him push off the counter and start walking.

She followed silently, murmuring her appreciation as they went.

Somewhere along the way she'd shed her coat. She wore a sweater that clung to her body, outlining her spectacular breasts, and jeans that looked like they'd been painted on. He was going to try really hard not to notice that, though he supposed it was already too late.

Concentrate on the house. She only wanted to see the house. Quick tour and she'd be out of there.

Only it wasn't a quick tour, because she'd pause occasionally to run her fingers along the wainscoting, an exposed beam or a doorknob—small touches he'd put some thought or effort into that Cassandra had never noticed.

Never appreciated.

Calliope noticed. Appreciated.

Something inside him clenched as she paused at the stairs and inspected the way the wood wrapped around itself. It had taken him weeks to do that staircase. He'd wanted something elegant, yet sturdy, something beautiful that Cassandra would appreciate, yet stairs that would stand the test of time—and maybe a houseful of kids.

Cassandra had blown right by the stairs and never said a word.

"It's like music," Calliope whispered, her fingers a light

caress over the wood. Her gaze met his, and her lips lifted. "It's amazing, Wyatt. You must have spent months on this."

He didn't know what to say, so he turned away and headed up, listening to the sound of her feet behind him.

The master bedroom was the only place he'd spent any money on, furniture-wise, since by the time he'd finished the house he and Cassandra were already divorced. He'd bought a big bed since he was a big guy, a double thick mattress and he'd made the headboard and footboard himself, grinding out his anger and frustration by creating the scrolled patterns in the wood.

Calliope leaned over and traced the pattern with her fingertips.

"This is beautiful. And the bed is so big." She turned to him and arched a brow. "For your harem of women?"

"Funny."

She wandered into the bathroom and gasped. "Oh my God. I'm moving in tonight and living in your bathroom."

He couldn't resist the smile as he entered the doorway and leaned against it.

"A tub made for four people. With whirlpool jets. And that decadent shower—Wyatt, that's just dirty and sexy. I want to get naked and get in there right now."

She was making his dick hard with that kind of talk and the corresponding visuals. He could already imagine her naked, the jets from all four showerheads spraying her, steam enveloping them both as he put his hands and his mouth all over her body...

Yeah. That train of thought had to stop. He turned around and left the room and started some complex algebra so his hard-on would go away.

He breathed in and out as he reached the top of the stairway.

"I always wanted to live in a big house," she said, grasping the railing in the sitting area at the top of the stairs. "I used to pretend I was a commoner—which I was, of course. That I was forced into servitude, but someday I'd meet a prince and he'd fall madly in love with me and carry me away to his huge castle where we'd marry and have children and live happily ever after."

When he didn't say anything, she turned to him and laughed, then pushed her glasses up the bridge of her nose. "I was a big fan of *Cinderella*."

"Obviously."

"And of course you've seen the house I grew up in. It wasn't exactly a castle."

Yeah, he had seen the house. It was a two-bedroom, about a thousand square feet. Small, built in the fifties. Calliope's parents still lived in the same house they bought when they were first married—the house her grandparents used to own.

"My mom and dad never had a lot of money, but we had love and a sense of family. It was always enough."

"For you, maybe." Not for Cassandra. She'd always bitched about wanting to get away from that cracker-box house, how much she'd hated it and how confined she'd felt living there. He'd often wondered if she spent so much time at his house—and with him—more as an escape than because she really cared about him.

He wondered about a lot of things. Like why he'd built this huge house with everything Cassandra could have wanted—and she'd hated it anyway.

Calliope must have sensed his thoughts, because she laid her hand on his arm. "You can't change the past, Wyatt. You have to let it go."

"Yeah, well, it won't let go of me."

She pushed off the railing and moved in front of him.

"Maybe you don't distract yourself enough. Put something in your head besides my big sister."

"Like what? Her little sister? That's a little too close to home for me."

She tilted her head back, and instead of anger he saw the same bright-eyed smile she always wore.

"You need to separate me from Cassandra. I'm not her."

No, she wasn't. Cassandra always pouted. She was never happy, was always moody and the slightest thing would set her off.

Wyatt had been nothing but rude to Calliope. So far, she'd been nothing but sweet to him.

He brushed his fingers across her cheek. "You can't be real."

She inhaled, her breasts rising. "I am real. And it's about damn time you noticed me."

"Oh, I've noticed you plenty."

Her lips curved. "Have you? How?"

"I notice you're driving me crazy."

"Again. How?"

The invitation was obvious. One step and she'd be in his arms. He wanted to taste her so badly he licked his lips. Her gaze drifted to his mouth, then back to meet his eyes. The tightening in his jeans was almost unbearable.

It had been a really long damn time since he'd been with a woman. Hell, since he'd kissed a woman or touched one.

This woman in particular made him crazy.

And she was the wrong woman.

He took a step back instead of forward. "I need to get back to the car."

He caught the flicker of disappointment before she replaced it with a smile. He'd hurt her and he hadn't meant to. But he couldn't be what she wanted. He wasn't the man for her. She needed someone with an open heart, someone who'd appreciate her and be able to love her. Someone who wasn't damaged and bitter.

That wasn't him.

"Calliope."

"It's okay. I need to get home anyway."

They headed downstairs. She grabbed her jacket from the counter and slid into it. If he were a gentleman he would have helped her with it.

He didn't feel much like a gentleman right now, and if he got too close to her she wouldn't be leaving his house tonight. He'd have her naked and in that shower so fast her head would spin. And after he worked out some of the boiling tension tightening his insides, he'd never see her again.

Yeah, not the right guy for her.

He adjusted his jeans and followed her out into the garage. She turned around to face him, and he took that step back again.

She noticed, and her lips curved.

"I'll see you later."

It wasn't until she got into her car and pulled out of his driveway that he realized he'd been holding his breath. He wasn't sure if it was because he wanted her to be gone, or because he was waiting for her to turn around and come back.

He exhaled on a curse, then dragged his fingers through his hair and turned to face the car. He picked up the sandpaper, determined to take out his sexual frustration on the fender.

CHAPTER FIVE

The weather turned abruptly, their strange late-November warmth obliterated by dark clouds and sharp wind that seemed to cut right through thick layers of clothing and heavy coats. The threat of snow hung in the air, and Calliope wondered how much work would be done on the addition before the bad weather moved in.

Wyatt and his guys had the framing finished, and had spent the past few days putting the roof on. Once that was done, the sheetrock would be next. Calliope hoped they'd get it all completed before it started to snow.

She'd already had to relocate the kids' playroom to another section so Wyatt could cut the hole in the existing wall to make the doorway, and for safety's sake the existing playroom was off-limits until the project was completed. That meant they were crammed in like sardines in the other playroom. Not too bad when the weather was warmer and her staff could take the kids outside to run off some of that pent-up energy. Once it snowed, though, they'd all be stuck indoors together.

She wasn't looking forward to that.

Marcy was sick today, which meant Calliope was in charge of the three-year-olds. She had them out in the play yard right now, a perfect location to let her watch Wyatt and his guys as they put up drywall.

The wind was blustery. She pulled her hat down to cover her eyes. The kids bounced around and squealed with joy. She was freezing. Wind was blowing out of the north and seemed to cut right through her jeans.

Where had that nice touch of sixty-degree weather gone? She wanted that back. Didn't seem to bother Wyatt, though, who worked on the roof in a short-sleeved shirt. Just the thought of it added goose bumps to her goose bumps.

She wished she had the time to lean over the fence and watch him, but not only did she have to keep her eyes on the kids, he and his guys almost had the roof finished and would be going inside soon, so she'd lose sight of him.

Too bad. She did enjoy looking at him.

"Miss Calliope, Jeffrey won't share the teeter-totter with me."

She glanced down at Lawrence's freckled face and smiled. "He won't, huh?"

Lawrence shook his head.

She slipped her hand in his. "Let's go see about that, shall we?"

Wyatt took a long swallow from his jug of water, trying not to watch Calliope with the kids.

It was hard not to be utterly taken in by the way she corralled a group of fifteen toddlers who couldn't be more than three or four years old. The kids were rambunctious, screaming and running wild on the playground. Yet when she bent down and called a couple of them over, she had their rapt attention. She didn't raise her voice, always smiled—like she did with him.

And she played with them. She didn't stand around and supervise. She ran around the yard with them, she climbed on the equipment, and she squealed as loud as they did. When they tackled her and she fell, she laughed, then got up and chased them until they were giggling.

He'd bet they'd all take great naps today.

Calliope obviously loved her work. Though it didn't appear to be work to her. It was clear she loved the kids, that it was more than a job to her.

Night and day difference from her sister. Cassandra had treated children like they all had communicable diseases. She'd wanted nothing to do with them, though he hadn't known that when they'd gotten married.

They'd wanted so many different things. How could he have not seen it?

Enough. He pushed Cassandra away, which was getting easier than it used to be.

He was going to have to go inside the center to start work from the existing playroom into the newly constructed doorway, which meant avoiding Calliope wasn't going to be an option.

He rang the bell at the front door. Beth the Bouncer, as he'd gotten used to calling her, opened the door and glared at him.

"I need to get to the playroom."

She opened the door. "Stay on the plastic runner so you don't spread that dust all over the floors."

He found himself smiling at her brusque tone. It reminded him of himself. "Yes, ma'am."

Kids were stuffed into the entryway, and stopped to gape at him.

"Who are you?" one little boy asked. He had dark curly hair and green eyes, with glasses. If Calliope had a son he'd probably look just like that.

He squatted down. "I'm Wyatt. I'm building a new room on to this place."

"You have hammers and stuff?"

"I do."

A little girl came up beside him. "You're dirty. Miss Beth will make you wash up before you come inside."

Wyatt lifted his gaze to Beth, who fought a smirk.

"And you'd better clean off your shoes, too," another little boy said.

"Miss Calliope doesn't care if you're dirty. She likes dirt."

"She gets dirty, too. She even plays in the mud with us."

A lot of giggles, then they ran off, his novelty wearing off. He straightened and walked down the hall. He caught sight of Calliope in another room with a handful of kids. She was on the floor playing with blocks. She looked up, pushed her glasses up, smiled and waved at him.

He couldn't help the smile that curved his lips or the involuntary wave back.

Or the warmth that filled him at seeing the way her eyes lit up when she saw him.

So she was Cassandra's sister. So what? She was obviously attracted to him, and God knew he wanted her in a way that defied all logic or reason.

Then again, was it illogical or unreasonable to want to be with a woman who was positive, bubbly, friendly and obviously loved kids? Wasn't Calliope the kind of woman he'd wanted all along, before he'd been seduced by the dazzling beauty of her sister?

Was that what he was afraid of—that the apple didn't fall far from the tree? She didn't seem at all like Cassandra—a one-eighty from her sister, in fact. Cassandra wouldn't be caught dead with muddy handprints on her jeans, or chalk on her face. She wouldn't spend five minutes of her day sitting on the floor coloring or reading a book to a bunch of three-year-olds. Getting dirty hadn't been on Cassandra's list of fun things to do at all.

He'd like to get dirty with Calliope. The thought of it had him hard and sweating, despite the dropping temperatures.

He'd let fear and failure rule him for so long he'd forgotten all the fundamentals. Like how to treat a woman. How to ask someone out on a date. How to let attraction take over and just go with it.

Why couldn't Calliope be a woman he'd met at random? That would make this a lot easier, because every time he looked at her, he made the connection to Cassandra, and then the big bad of his past kept rushing back to him.

Which was all in his head and not in reality. Calliope had nothing to do with the failure of his marriage. Maybe it was time to separate the sisters, think of Calliope as an individual and give himself a freakin' break.

But first he had to work. He focused his attention on the sheetrock and let Calliope slide to the background for a while.

Hours later, his crew had gone home and he was still in the center when he decided to call it quits for the night. The sheetrock had been finished. His crew had put up tarp on the outside to make sure any bad weather wouldn't ruin the work they'd done.

Wyatt walked into the adjoining room on his way out the door, stopping dead at the window.

It was dark outside—and snowing like crazy. From his guess, there was a foot on the ground already. He grabbed his phone. 8:00 p.m. No wonder his stomach had been growling.

Damn, where had his head been, and why hadn't Calliope come to tell him she needed to close up the center?

He saw a light on in her office so headed there.

Her back was turned as she studied her computer, furiously clacking the keys.

"You're still here."

She jumped, then swiveled in her chair. "Wyatt, you scared me to death. It was so quiet in here, and I saw you were still working after everyone left, so I decided to leave you alone."

He leaned against the doorjamb. "You could have said something to me."

She shrugged and pushed her glasses up the bridge of her nose. "I had reports to do anyway. I didn't mind working late."

"There's a foot of snow on the ground."

Her eyes widened. "Really?" She got up and swiveled open the blinds in her office. "Wow. I knew it looked like it might snow earlier. Had no idea it was going to come down so hard so fast."

Now was his chance to not be an asshole for once. "Have you eaten?"

She lifted up a package of half-eaten peanut butter crackers. "A snack. How about you?"

"No."

"You're probably ready to get out of here then. I've locked the front door with the keys. I'll let you out." She grabbed the keys.

"You aren't leaving?"

She stopped in front of him at the doorway. "Yes, but I need to shut the computer down and grab my stuff."

"I'll wait."

"Are you sure?"

"I'll wait. Go shut down and grab your coat."

"Okay. Thanks." She went back to her desk, bent over her computer. He enjoyed the view of her butt as she did. She folded her crackers, slid them into the drawer and grabbed her coat, bag and keys.

"I need to turn off some lights around here, then I'll be ready."

He followed her around as she turned off the lights, checked doors to be sure they were locked and went to the front door. He grabbed her coat and held it out for her this time. She gave him a look as she slid her arms into it.

"Better zip it up. Winds are howling."

She did, offering him up a smile. "Thanks."

"Don't you have a hat and gloves?"

"Yes. In my car."

He shook his head, threw on his coat, then slipped his knit cap over her head and handed her his gloves. "Put those on."

She looked down at the gloves, then at him. "But what about you?"

He cracked a smile. "I'm a pretty tough guy. I think I can handle it."

Wyatt was being nice to her? That was a change. Calliope didn't know what had come over him, but she wasn't going to question this rare gift of him in a good mood.

She slipped the gloves on, giggling as they flopped in her hands since they were three sizes too big for her. She squeezed her fingers in them to keep them on while Wyatt pulled the door open.

The wind slammed them hard, tossing snow inside and knocking Calliope against him. He put his hand against her back to steady her.

"Wow, that's some storm," she said.

Wyatt took her keys, pulled the door shut and locked it, then put his arm around her and helped her down the stairs. She really wished she'd brought her boots in from the car, but she hadn't expected an epic snowstorm. Now, snow slid into her socks and tennis shoes and she shivered.

It was hard to walk—at least for her. Wyatt had work boots on and had no problem. He grabbed her arm and led her to the street where her small car was buried.

She looked at the car. "Well, this will take some work. I have a shovel in the trunk."

"You aren't driving. We'll take my truck."

Snow had already covered his hair. It was coming down so fast she couldn't even see, and she wasn't about to argue with him. He led her over to the side street where his truck was parked. The effort to get there exhausted her. By the time he opened up the side door and helped her get in, her jeans and feet were soaked and freezing and she was shivering so hard her teeth chattered.

He turned on the truck's engine and hit the heaters full blast, then went back outside with a scraper to clean off the windows while she stayed inside. Her feet and ankles stung from the cold.

She should have handed him his hat and gloves back. The temperatures had dropped outside and he was doing the work bare-handed and without a hat. He must be freezing.

He climbed back in and looked at her. "Put your seatbelt on."

She did, noting his red hands. "You should have taken my gloves."

"I'm fine. I'm used to working outside in all kinds of weather."

He put the car in gear and pulled carefully away from the curb. The truck tried to fishtail, but Wyatt controlled it. The roads were hazardous, the snow thick and coming down so hard that even the windshield wipers on full blast couldn't clear the whiteout conditions enough to see clearly.

Calliope sat quietly and let Wyatt concentrate on the road. He made the right turn and headed down the narrow street. She was glad her house was only a couple blocks from the center, and even making it that far was treacherous driving.

There were no other cars on the road. This was a bad storm. He pulled into her driveway and she was glad it wasn't uphill.

"Got your keys ready?" he asked when he turned the engine off.

She'd already tugged the gloves off and handed them back to Wyatt. "In my hand."

Wyatt snagged the keys from her. "I'll open the door. You put the gloves back on. And don't get out of the car until I come over to your side to get you. You don't have boots on."

"You're coming in with me, aren't you? The roads are really bad out there."

He gave her one of those "You're kidding me, right?" looks that guys gave women sometimes when women thought men couldn't do something—like climb a mountain. "My truck is four-wheel drive. I can make it."

But she'd still worry like crazy about him being on the road. "I'll make soup."

"You're on."

She grinned and waited for him to come around and open the door for her, instantly shivering again as the cold blast of air, sleet and snow smacked her body. They made a mad dash for her front door—as much of a dash as two people could make in snow that deep. Wyatt unlocked the door and they rushed inside. He pushed the door shut and locked it.

She shuddered against the cold and stripped off the hat and her coat, then toed out of her soaked tennis shoes. "I need to change clothes."

Wyatt stood on her front hall rug and did his best impression of a snowman. "I'm just going to stand here and defrost."

She laughed. "You are not. Take your coat off and come into the kitchen. After I change clothes I'll make us some coffee and get started on that soup."

She ran into her bedroom and pulled off her wet clothes,

grabbed some sweats and dry socks, then made a quick stop in the bathroom to check herself in the mirror.

Oh, ugh. She cleaned the wet spots off her glasses, but otherwise there wasn't much hope for her wet hair, and she didn't think Wyatt would appreciate her taking the time to shower and put on some makeup. He likely wanted some coffee and homemade soup, not a glamour girl.

She fluffed her wet curls as best as she could, stuck her feet into slippers and went into the kitchen.

She inhaled when she walked in. "I smell coffee."

"I raided your cabinets and made myself at home."

Her stomach flipped in a decidedly warm way. "I'm glad. Sorry it took me so long."

"It didn't. I don't think you need to wait on me when I'm perfectly capable of making a pot of coffee."

He poured her a cup. She reached into the fridge. "Cream?"

"Yeah."

"How about sugar?"

"No, thanks."

She grabbed the sugar bowl on the kitchen table and scooped a spoonful into her cup, stirred and watched him.

There were never men in her kitchen. She dated on occasion, but never invited them home and sure as hell didn't have them in her kitchen making coffee for her.

Seeing Wyatt, his tall, lean body relaxing against her counters, was a little disconcerting. He was so big and her kitchen was small.

And speaking of the kitchen…

She took a swallow of coffee, then set it aside. "Let me get started on that soup I promised."

"You don't have to do that."

She bent down to grab her soup pot and grinned up at him. "Sure I do. I'm starving." She put the pot on her stove, then went to the freezer to dig out the chicken stock she was so glad she had on hand.

She put the container in the microwave to defrost, then opened the refrigerator, also happy she'd gone to the grocery store yesterday.

"What can I do to help?"

"How are you with a knife?"

He went to the sink and rolled up his sleeves to wash his hands. "Expert."

"Good." She laid celery and carrots on the cutting board. "Start slicing."

While he got busy with that, she tossed the chicken in the stock, added a little garlic and ginger and a few more spices. Soon the soup was bubbly and thick and she put a loaf of bread in the oven to heat up, then added the carrots and celery Wyatt had sliced.

She had a few minutes to rest while the soup simmered and the bread cooked, so she refilled her coffee. Wyatt was sitting at her table, one she'd found at a garage sale.

"You rent this house?" he asked.

She shook her head. "No, I'm a homeowner."

He arched a brow. "Really. This and the day care center."

"Well, this place is tiny. Only a one-bedroom. But it's a house and it's what I wanted when I moved here."

"Why not an apartment? I mean, you're young and single. I would think a condo or apartment would suit you better."

"That's just pissing money away every month."

He laughed. "A lot of young people do that."

She took a sip of coffee. "You make it sound like I'm sixteen and you're my dad. I'm twenty-six and I wanted the investment. I bought this little cracker box of a house because it was all I could afford. When my grandmother died and left half her money to me, I knew exactly what I wanted to do with it—invest it in the day care center.

"But I also wanted a house. I didn't want to throw money away every month on an apartment. I found this place. It was so small, but what else did I need? I'm single, have no kids, no husband, no boyfriend. So as an initial investment it was perfect."

He was staring at her with that unfathomable expression on his face that told her nothing of what he was thinking.

"What?"

"You surprise me."

She turned to stir the soup. "Yeah? In what way?"

"I always think of you as being a kid. But you're not. You're all grown-up."

"I've been a grown-up for a long time now, Wyatt. Maybe it's past time you realized that."

"Yeah, I guess it is."

She felt his gaze on her, but didn't turn around. He could just simmer on what she'd said.

The soup and bread were ready, so she served it up and they ate, drank, and what was most surprising of all—they actually talked.

Wyatt told her about the progress on the room addition at the center, as well as other ongoing projects their construction company had going. She could tell he really loved his family business, even though his brothers seemed to irritate him.

"I understand familial relationships," she said as they moved from the kitchen to her living room after they finished eating. She had poured them a snifter of her favorite winter naughty indulgence—brandy. Maybe she could get him drunk and take advantage of him. "Families can test you under the best circumstances, but underneath I know you love your brothers."

He nodded and swirled the brandy around the glass. "They

try my patience—I'm sure on purpose at least half the time. Brody likes to tease and Ethan eggs him on. The two of them gang up on me."

"Most likely to irritate you on purpose because you're so naturally cranky."

He tilted the glass in her direction. "People who throw those kinds of words at me generally live to regret them."

She leaned back against the sofa and grinned at him. "Good thing I know your bark is way worse than your bite."

"Are you sure about that? I haven't bitten you—yet."

Whoa. Where had that come from? It had been a bonafide sexual come-on, and Calliope nearly self-combusted right there. Heat flared through every part of her. The whole room seemed to go up in flames, or maybe that was just her, and likely because of the way Wyatt's gaze burned into her. Her nipples tightened and everything that was female in her shouted for joy.

Usually never at a loss for words, she had no idea what to say.

Wyatt downed the brandy, then stood. "Well, I should go."

She shot off the sofa. "What? Are you insane? There's two feet of snow out there. You're not going anywhere tonight."

He arched a brow. "You thinking of holding me prisoner here?"

"I might if you come up with another dumbass idea, like trying to drive in that."

"It'll still be there tomorrow morning, Calliope."

"By tomorrow the road crews will have been out all night, spreading salt and plowing. The streets will be in more decent shape than they are right now. What if you get stuck getting back home? It's not like you'll have an easy time getting a tow tonight. I'm sure there are a lot of cars getting stuck."

He gave her a dubious look. "We don't live in a major city.

I can call Roger. He owns one of the two wreckers in town to give me a pull."

She crossed her arms. "Or you can use some common sense and not be one of those idiots on the road tonight."

"I think you're trying to keep me here for your own nefarious purposes."

She laughed. "Yeah, all one hundred thirty pounds of me, plotting devious things against all—" she looked him over "—two-ten of you?"

"Two-twenty-five."

"So you're nearly twice my weight. I'm sure I could pounce on you and take you down."

She saw his jaw clench.

"You could try."

"I could, couldn't I?"

It sure was warm in here, and the sexual innuendos were flying around the room like crazed bats. She supposed she could cut to the chase, but it sure would be nice if Wyatt came after her for a change. She was tired of being the one doing the chasing.

He finally settled back down on the sofa. "I'd rather you stop calling me an idiot."

"Since you're sitting and obviously staying, I'll refrain from further insults as to your state of mind." She grabbed his empty glass. "How about a refill?"

"Got any beer? That shit's too sweet."

"Sure." She refilled her glass while she was in there, handed him the beer and slid back onto the sofa, pulling her legs up behind her.

"Would you like to watch television?"

"Not much of a TV watcher."

"Neither am I."

He studied her. She pushed her glasses up.

"What do you do at night?" he asked.

"I read. I'm usually so exhausted by the time I get home, I eat dinner, take a hot bath and soak for a while, then curl up with a good book and generally pass out early."

"Kids are exhausting, huh?"

She laughed. "They can be."

"What made you decide to open a day care center?"

"That's easy. I love children. Always have, ever since I got my first babysitting job as a teenager. I knew then that I wanted to do something with kids."

Something flickered in his eyes. "Why not become a teacher?"

"I do have a degree in early childhood education, thought about becoming a teacher, but the little ones wrap me around their fingers and don't let go. I worked at a lot of day care centers while I was in college, and my career naturally progressed in this direction. I apprenticed under a director near my college, and worked as a director at one in Nebraska for a couple years. When the opportunity came up to buy out Miss Bettie, I leaped on it because I could own my own business, and it gave me a chance to come home."

"It's a lot of work."

She nodded. "It is, but it's so rewarding. The staff is amazing, and I feel like I'm doing something important. I can't imagine how worried these parents are, having to leave their little ones while they go off to work. I like to think I can ease their minds a little, knowing their babies are being well taken care of."

He took a long swallow of beer. She liked watching the way his throat worked, liked the beard stubble on his jaw, wondered what that would feel like on her face—and other parts of her body.

Again, that abrupt flash of heat scored her from the inside out.

She really should stop thinking of sex, especially sex with Wyatt. Especially when Wyatt sat less than a foot away from her. His fear that she might pounce on him? Not too far from the truth.

He laid his empty beer can on the table. She got up.

"I'll get you another."

He grabbed her hand. "I know where your fridge is. I can get myself another beer if I want one. You don't have to wait on me."

"I don't mind."

He released her hand and she hurried into the kitchen. What she really needed was a minute or two to catch her breath. She opened the refrigerator, letting the cool air bathe her face. She took a deep breath to calm down her riotous libido.

Geez, Calliope. You aren't sixteen anymore. Get a grip.

She stood, closed the door and turned around, then gasped when she found Wyatt standing right there.

"What are you doing here?" she asked.

"Wondering what the hell you're doing. Hell of a time to take inventory of the fridge, don't you think?"

"Oh. Uh. That wasn't what I was doing."

He placed his palm on the refrigerator door, right next to her shoulder. "Yeah? What were you doing?"

"Looking for this, of course." She handed him the beer.

He took it from her. "You're a little odd, Calliope."

"I prefer quirky." She skirted around him and headed back into the living room, conscious of him right on her heels.

Wasn't this what she wanted? Him going after her?

So why was she suddenly so skittish?

Likely because she was out of practice. It wasn't like she had a parade of men chasing after her. Going after Wyatt was one thing, because she was pretty sure he wasn't going to take the bait.

Now that he seemed interested? Yeah, that was another story.

He was a lot of man. Could she handle him?

She blew out a breath and stared at the brandy.

"Calliope."

She lifted her gaze to his. "Yes?"

"Would you like me to take off?"

She shook her head. "No. I don't want you to leave."

"This is uncomfortable for you. For me, too."

Damn. She'd screwed it up. She'd hesitated. But she wasn't a quitter. She leaned forward. "I'm not used to having men over."

"Ever?"

"Uh…no." She'd never brought a guy to her house. It was too…intimate. Of course she'd had sex at college, and there had been Steve's apartment. Then there was that one time at the motel with Bobby. But no, she'd never brought a man here. She'd never had a long-term relationship because no guy had been…keepable.

"So you're a virgin."

Her head shot up. "I am not."

His lips quirked. "Yeah, I can tell you're full of experience." He got up and went into the kitchen.

Irritated now, she followed. "You can't tell anything about my…experience."

He tossed his empty beer can in the trash, then turned to face her. "Honey, you're like a lamb facing down a wolf."

She quirked a brow. "And you're the big bad wolf, I suppose?"

He grinned. "You got it."

"You think I can't handle you?"

"I know you can't handle me."

"Try me."

He laughed and moved past her. "I don't think so."

Now she was pissed. He was treating her like a child. "You prefer more experienced women."

"I don't want any woman."

"You lie. Ever since we met up again you've been dancing around your attraction to me. But because I'm Cassie's sister, you've held back because you've got some screwed-up notion that we're one and the same."

He looked her up and down, his gaze raking over her body. "Calliope, you are nothing like Cassandra. Not in appearance, not in actions, not in any way."

She knew how he felt about Cassie. It wasn't an insult.

"So you've given up trying to compare me to my sister."

He held up his hands. "Throwing the white flag on that one. You win."

Her lips curved. "I don't know about that, Wyatt. Seems to me we both win. So why not take what you want—what we both want—and quit fighting it?"

Her heart pounded as she stood in the middle of the room, her hands on her hips. Only a few feet of distance separated them, but she wasn't going to cross that distance. If he wanted her—and she knew damn well he did—he was going to have to bridge the gap.

He stared her down. He was mad, whether at her or himself she didn't know. Frankly, she didn't care. It was now or never because she wouldn't ask him again.

He came to her in two fast strides and jerked her into his arms.

And then he hesitated, his lips just inches from hers.

Don't walk away. Not again.

His gaze bored into hers and she nearly melted to the floorboards. She knew from the smoldering look in his eyes that he wasn't walking away this time. When his mouth came down on hers, the first contact of his lips stole her breath.

She went up in flames and her body exploded in a wild-fire of heat.

CHAPTER SIX

There was nothing gentle about this kiss. This was no sweet seduction. It was a full-on siege. Wyatt wrapped his arms around her, one hand gravitating to her butt to draw her against his erection. Calliope shuddered at the feel of him, so hard and ready as he plundered her lips. He slid his tongue inside and she moaned, arched against him, slid her hand in his hair and held on while his tongue played with hers.

She was lightheaded as sensations pounded at her. The softness of his lips warred with the scrape of his beard against her face and the steely hardness of his body as he moved against her. And when he cupped her breast, his thumb brushing her nipple, she whimpered at the sheer pleasure of it.

He pulled his mouth from hers, his eyes dark and full of hunger.

"Say no."

She blinked. "What?"

"Tell me to go."

"No."

He backed away. She grabbed his arms. "That's not what I meant. Don't go."

He raked his fingers through his hair. "If I don't leave now, I'm not leaving until morning."

She was panting, her breasts painfully full, her sex throbbing with need for him, and he wanted to have this discussion now?

"That's the general idea, Wyatt."

"If I stay tonight, I'm sleeping in your bed. With you."

She resisted the urge to suggest they likely wouldn't be sleeping much, instead stayed silent, her chest heaving with the force of her breaths. "Can we get back to the kissing part? I really like the way you kiss me."

"I just wanted you to be sure."

"I'm sure. And thanks. Now kiss me."

The smile he gave her was the kind any sane woman would call dangerous. He pulled her glasses off and set them down, put his hand on the nape of her neck and drew her close.

He hovered, his lips just an inch from hers. "You make me crazy, Calliope."

She palmed his chest. "Trust me. The feeling is mutual."

And then their lips touched again, and it was like a burst of fireworks. Wow, he really could kiss. Wyatt was formidable, no doubt about that. Her toes curled, her legs felt like jelly, and she was damn glad he had all that muscle in his frame to hold her up, because she sank against him, sighing against his lips as he overpowered her with his sheer masculinity. She breathed him in, the scent of outdoors, brandy and beer mingling together.

When he lifted her in his arms—and she was no light-weight—she felt small and feminine, and decided she liked that sensation.

He moved down the hall and bent to open her bedroom door, found the light switch and flipped it on, then settled her in the middle of her bed, coming down on top of her, his mouth taking hers again in a kiss that made her writhe with impatience. She wanted clothes off, needed to feel his bare skin against hers. She reached between them, pulling at his shirt.

He lifted, straddling her, and unbuttoned his shirt. She laid her hands on his thighs and watched as he pulled the flannel shirt off and the T-shirt underneath, leaving his torso bare.

She sucked in a breath. Wide shoulders, well-muscled chest and arms, and flat, washboard abs, not from time spent at the gym, she imagined, but from honest-to-God labor. She snaked her hands along his stomach and farther down, where a soft line of hair disappeared into his jeans. She reached for his belt buckle but he snatched her hands away and placed them on the bed.

"But you're not naked yet."

"I'll get there." He lifted her sweatshirt over her stomach, leaned down and pressed a kiss to her belly.

His lips on her skin were just as flame-inducing as his kisses. She wondered if spontaneous combustion was possible. She'd really hate to set him on fire, especially before they had sex. But seeing his mouth on her stomach as he gradually lifted her shirt and mapped his way north made her heart pound so hard she was sure he could hear it. She knew he had to feel it, because it ricocheted throughout her body.

"Lift," he said, and she arched enough so he could pull the shirt over her head.

His lips curved, and he laid his hand over one of her breasts, covered only by the flimsy, discount-store-purchased bra. Dammit, if she'd known she was going to have sex with Wyatt tonight she'd have put her more expensive lingerie on. She made a mental note to drag out the hot lingerie, so she'd be prepared for future events. And there would be future events, because every touch of his fingers and hands to her body was like she'd never been touched before. Her nipples peaked and hardened while she panted like the woman in heat she was. He brushed a thumb over the bra and she arched against him.

"Tell me what you want."

She lifted her gaze to his, saw the intensity, the hunger and need there. Yup. He was going to set her on fire before the night was over. "I want your hands and your mouth on me."

He reached under her and lifted her, undid the clasp in an instant and drew the straps down her shoulders, then laid her back down. He stared at her, not moving to touch her.

"You're beautiful, Calliope."

A heated flush spread over her body as he continued to look down on her like she was some goddess or something. She'd never thought herself particularly breathtaking, but she wasn't hideous, either. She was pretty in an average sort of way. She kept her body in shape—God knew running after kids burned a lot of calories. But her sister was the real beauty in the family, and Wyatt had been married to her.

Yet as his gaze burned into hers and she saw the lust in his eyes, the pure male appreciation, she knew then he wasn't comparing her to Cassandra. The desire he felt was for her.

She reached up and swept her hand across his jaw, tingling at the sensation of his beard tickling her palm.

"I think you're pretty hot, too, Wyatt."

He cupped her breast, then bent and took a nipple in his mouth. She sighed at the sheer pleasure of it, watched as he sucked her nipple, licked it, teased it with his tongue. Sensation shot south and she bit down on her lip to keep from whimpering. It had been an embarrassingly long time since she'd been with a guy.

Boys, really. That's what they'd been, while Wyatt was a man. A man who knew his way around a woman's body. A man with infinite patience. This wasn't about quickly stripping her clothes off so he could get right to the action. He worshipped her body, licking her nipples, teasing her into an absolute frenzy of passion until she was mindless, breathless and writhing without shame.

And when she thought she couldn't take any more, he kissed her, so deeply and passionately she forgot all about getting right to the action. She lost herself in the taste of him, the different textures of his face. She reached up to touch the softness of his lips, the scratchiness along his jawline, and the silkiness of his hair as she threaded her fingers through the strands to hold on for dear life while he fondled her breasts and kissed her until she lost all sense of time.

Only then did he caress his fingers along her ribs and stomach and make his way to her jeans, releasing the button effortlessly and drawing the zipper down in a way she found ridiculously sexy.

He didn't even bother taking her jeans off, just dove his hand inside and cupped the center of her, drawing out a low moan she couldn't contain. She was hot, wet and ready—had been for weeks now. She strained, lifted against his touch, meeting his gaze as release found her and he took her mouth, absorbing her cries.

He held her as she settled, then her jeans came off, her panties, and he moved down her body, put his mouth on her and amped her up all over again.

She'd never known a man like him before, so eager to please when she knew it had been a long time for him, too. But she lost herself in what he was doing to her, and after he gave her a second climax, she was limp.

When he climbed off the bed and shucked his jeans and boxer briefs, she rolled over on her side and sucked in her lower lip between her teeth, studying the utter beauty of his body. She rolled over and pulled a box of condoms out of the nightstand.

He arched a brow. "Have men coming and going regularly?"

She laughed. "Ha. Never. But I was hopeful about you so I figured I should be prepared."

He put his hand on his hips, and lord, he was magnificent. Powerful, hard and beautiful. She pulled a condom out of the box and he put it on, came to her and nudged her legs apart.

He stilled, watching her as he fit his cock inside her.

It was perfect, this moment everything she could have imagined as he filled her, swelling inside her. They fit together in so many ways, especially like this.

This time she didn't hold back, whimpering at the sheer pleasure of every sensation, every movement.

He brushed her hair away from her face, kissed her jaw, her nose, her mouth, then took her lips in a deep kiss as he moved within her. She wrapped her legs around him and lifted.

They strained together, murmured and kissed as passion ignited between them. Hands clasped, Calliope gave as much as Wyatt did, knowing this might be her only chance to show him what he meant to her—how much this moment meant as the tensions they both held united. He drove within her, relentless in his pursuit of her pleasure. She didn't think she was capable of it, but as he ground against her, refusing to give up until she did, she finally broke on a harsh cry, and he went with her, slipping his hand underneath her to tilt her close while he shuddered and buried his face in her neck.

She stroked his back and his hair, unable to believe this had really happened. When he rolled to the side he pulled her with him, adjusting her so her back was against him.

She wondered if he'd feel awkward. Wyatt was so quiet, but he kissed the back of her head, caressed her arm and cupped her breast in a lazy, playful way that made her smile.

He didn't speak—she knew he wouldn't—so she knew she'd have to be the one to break the silence.

"Well. That was pretty good."

His hand stilled. "Pretty good?"

"Yeah. For a first time and all."

He rolled her onto her back and she grinned at him.

"Not funny."

She laughed. "I thought it was. Wyatt, you nearly killed me. I came three times. I don't think it gets much better than that."

She knew he fought it, but his lips curved in that supremely male satisfied way. "It's still early. Trust me. It gets better."

He leaned over and kissed her, and she sighed, shocked to realize she was ready to go again.

It was going to be a long night.

Wyatt left Calliope's house early the next morning before the sun came up.

She was on her stomach on the bed, buried under the blankets. Her face was flushed, her curls spread all over the pillow.

He'd never seen anything more beautiful.

She'd looked warm. He knew she would be. He could have shucked his clothes and climbed in the bed with her, woken her up by making love to her again.

Instead, he'd gotten dressed and left the house as quiet as he could so he wouldn't wake her.

More like so he wouldn't have to talk to her. Face her. Have that inevitable conversation about how this could never happen again.

Once had been bad enough. Though they hadn't really done it once, had they? More like three times.

He started the truck and let it warm up while he cleaned off all the snow. A couple feet on the ground at least. Damn good snowfall, but the salt trucks and plows had been busy last night so the roads looked passable. He should make it just fine, though he doubted any of the businesses would be open today, including Calliope's day care center.

He climbed in the truck and eased it away from the curb. It pulled right off the frozen snow mound and into the street without a problem.

The main roads were even better than the side streets. He should stop at the office, see if anyone made it in, but he decided he needed to go home, take a shower, grab something to eat.

He should have left her a note.

Nah. He wasn't a note kind of guy. She'd figure it out. She was smart. Though it was rude to just leave.

Then again, she should be used to him being rude.

After all, she'd been nice enough to invite him in last night. She'd fed him. Hell, she'd slept with him.

And he'd just walked out on her this morning.

That made him an asshole. The kind of guy he'd been before. The kind of guy who'd been married to Cassandra.

Maybe he should stop being that kind of guy.

By the time he pulled into his garage at home, he'd decided too much introspection wasn't good for him. It didn't come out in his favor. He brewed some coffee and sat at the kitchen table, looking out at the piles of snow in his backyard, and wondering what the hell he was going to do with his day.

Right now he could be in bed with Calliope.

Instead, he was home.

Alone.

There was something inherently fucked about his decision-making.

CHAPTER SEVEN

Calliope blew an errant hair away from her face as she cleaned up one of the playrooms while the one-year-olds slumbered during nap time. The day care center had only been closed one day, and the kids obviously had snow fever, because they were all rambunctious and full of energy today. She was certain the parents were all happy to be back at work today and leave their wild little charges with her. The worst thing was the playground outside was still covered in snow, so they would have to deal with having the kids inside all day long.

Along with Wyatt and his men, who were working away inside the room addition.

He'd been gone yesterday by the time she woke. Normally a light sleeper, she must have been half-dead not to hear him dress and leave her house. Then again, they'd stayed up almost all night, and it wasn't like they'd been leisurely playing cards. She blushed as she remembered exactly what they'd been doing all night long.

He'd greeted her with a nod this morning, back to his usual gruff demeanor.

Yeah, that wasn't going to fly. She had a few things to say to him at the end of the day today. She was no mouse or doormat who would stand idly by and be treated this way.

She counted down the hours until the final child and the last of her employees left. Wyatt stayed behind after his two men headed out the door. She smiled at both of them, wished them a good-night, then locked the door behind them and headed into the new addition, determined to have a serious conversation about how you treat a woman after you've spent a night worshipping her body.

The existing playroom door was closed so none of the kids would wander in there. She opened the door at the same time Wyatt did.

He looked down at her. Frowned.

"Everyone gone?" he asked.

"Yes."

"About time." He moved her out of the room, away from the wind coming in from the addition, and closed the door. He backed her against the hallway wall and pressed his body to hers. "I've been waiting all damn day for this."

He slammed his mouth down on hers, obliterating all the righteous anger she'd worked up since he'd left her house yesterday. The kiss was dark and passionate and needy and made heat coil low in her belly. She melted against him, but then laid her palms on his chest and gave him a gentle push.

He drew back, his lips moist from their kiss. She wanted to grab his hair and pull him back, but she resisted.

"What was that all about?" she asked.

"The kiss?"

"Yes."

His gaze drifted to her mouth. "I've been thinking about it all day. Yesterday, too."

"You could have been with me yesterday, instead of sneaking out of my house while I was still asleep."

"Yeah, about that. I'm sorry. I shouldn't have left like that.

It was stupid and inconsiderate. And I should have called, but once I left I felt like an ass, so I just…didn't."

This was new. An apology? "Okay."

He palmed the wall next to her head. "Look, Calliope. I'm not very good at this."

"This?"

"Relationships. Women. Dealing with them. I'll try to do better, but I'm probably not going to be good at it. You should know that going in, so you can change your mind if you want."

Her lips curved. As an apology, it kind of sucked, but it was honest. She couldn't ask for more. "It's okay, Wyatt. I understand."

He cocked a brow. "That's it? I'm forgiven?"

"That's it."

"You're too easy."

She laughed. "Not the best thing to say to a woman."

He laid his forehead against hers. "Shit. I told you I wasn't good at this."

She framed his face with her hands. "No, you aren't, but if you're honest with me, I can deal with everything else. Besides, you're a great kisser, and that forgives a lot of sins."

"Yeah?" He leaned in closer, grabbed the loops on her jeans and directed her toward her office.

When they got in there, he pushed her against the wall again, pulled off her glasses and tucked them in his pocket.

She might be old-fashioned, but she had to admit she dug his caveman moves.

"Oh, yeah."

He brushed his lips across hers, his breath a warm caress as he teased his tongue along her bottom lip, then went in for the kill, sliding his arm around her to draw her against him. He brought his mouth full force against hers, and kissed her until she forgot all about yesterday. All she thought of was right now, and the fact they were alone and the door was firmly locked.

And when he dropped to the floor, pulling her on top of him, she went willingly, eager to pick up where they'd left off the night before.

"This is kind of wicked," she said as he swept her hair away from her face.

"Never done it at work before?"

She snorted. "I work at a day care center. I don't get many hot guys hitting on me here."

He popped the button on her jeans and drew the zipper down. "That's too bad. They should be lining up at the door."

Now he was making up for fumbling his words earlier. She felt warm all over, though maybe that was due to him rolling her over and touching her. He took off her tennis shoes and slid her jeans and panties down her legs.

By the time he'd removed her sweatshirt and bra, and gotten rid of his own clothes, she started to giggle. He frowned at her.

"This is no laughing matter," he said.

"I've never been naked at work before."

He grabbed a condom from the pocket of his jeans. "You should try it more often."

She rolled over on her side. "Oh? You make a habit of it?"

"Yeah. I wander around jobsites naked all the time. You haven't seen me on the news?"

She grabbed his shoulder. "Careful, Wyatt, or I might think you have a sense of humor."

"Don't worry. It doesn't come around all that often." He pulled her back on top of him and reached for her breasts, and all humor fled as she tilted her head back and lost herself in the magic of his hands.

Wyatt hadn't meant to start this. All he'd wanted to do was

talk to Calliope tonight, to get her alone so he could apologize for acting like an ass and running out on her yesterday. But seeing her as she opened the door, fury and irritation instead of hurt in her eyes, had primed the pump and made him forget everything he intended to say to her.

Anger had lit up her face, put a bright spot of color on her cheeks and made her eyes come to life. The only thing he'd thought about then was kissing her and getting his hands on her.

Okay, so maybe those were the only things he'd thought about since he left her house yesterday.

But now she sat on top of him naked. He didn't know if he'd ever seen anything more beautiful than her body, lush and flushed pink with arousal as she tilted her head back while he thumbed and teased her nipples.

She rolled against him, causing him no end of agony—the pleasurable kind. Buried inside her, he connected with her in the most primal way, reaching up to pull her against him, to take a nipple into his mouth, to touch her on a basic level so she'd feel what he felt.

He loved the way she responded, the way she looked at him so he knew she was as connected as he was. She gripped his shoulders as she rode him, as she raised and lowered on him, and when she climaxed, she kept that connection, digging her nails into him, her eyes widening as she tightened around him. He cupped his hand around the nape of her neck and flew with her, losing himself in her depths.

A part of him wasn't ready for this—this bond he felt with her. The last time he'd felt this attached to a woman had been Cassandra. And that hadn't ended well.

Calliope was like a hurricane—wild and turbulent. He wasn't sure he could handle her, but he wanted to see what she threw at him, and right now he just couldn't resist her. She was beautiful, a little scary, and he couldn't walk away.

"I'm hungry," she said, pushing up to look down at him. "You like pizza?"

He grinned up at her. "Sounds good."

"How about Rizzoni's?"

"How about we go to your place and order delivery? Fewer clothes involved that way."

She arched a brow. "Naked pizza eating could be dangerous."

"I live on the edge."

She climbed off him and started grabbing her clothes. "You're on, but hurry. Sex makes me hungry."

He grabbed his jeans. "I'll be sure to order an extra-large pizza, then. You're going to need it."

CHAPTER EIGHT

"The party is scheduled for the sixteenth," Tori said, handing out the information sheet along with the menu.

Staff meetings at Kent Construction were his least favorite thing, but business had to be conducted. Discussing the annual holiday party was something he'd rather Tori handle. As the office manager, she dealt with the day-to-day running of the business, as well as all the financials. He'd much rather just get out there and work with his hands.

Unfortunately, when Tori called a meeting, you showed up. She might be only in her twenties, but she was formidable. When she bellowed, you came running or you'd never hear the end of it.

Wyatt took the information sheet and scanned it. "I assume there'll be meat at this party."

She rolled her eyes at him. "No. We're serving celery and carrots. Our clients like rabbit food."

"Har."

"We're having roast beef, chicken and pasta. There'll be hors d'oeuvres and an open bar, though I twitched at the open bar thing."

"We can handle it," Brody said.

"You say that now. Wait until you have to write the check. It's the holiday season. People like to drink."

"You like to drink, too, you lush," Brody teased. "Will I have to throw you over my shoulder and drive you home again this year?"

Tori glared at him. "That was one stinkin' year. And I had just turned twenty-one. It's never happened since so I'd appreciate it if you'd never mention it again."

Wyatt's lips twitched.

"I saw that, Wyatt," Tori said, as if she had eyes in the back of her head. "Don't you dare smile."

"I don't smile. You know that. I'm the bad-tempered one."

Tori swiveled in her chair, narrowed her gaze at him. "You're almost in a good mood. What the hell is wrong with you?"

Ethan rolled his chair closer to Wyatt, inspecting him like he had ticks or something. "There is something different about you. What's up?"

"I know what it is." Brody leaned back and crossed his arms. "He's getting laid."

"What?" Tori's eyes widened. "How come I don't know about this?"

"You mean I know something you don't? What the hell, Tor? You having an off week?"

"Shut up, Brody." Tori narrowed her gaze on Wyatt. "What's going on?"

Shit. He knew he should have gone straight to the day care center this morning and bugged out of this meeting. "Nothing's going on, and if it was it would be none of your business."

"So he is getting laid." Ethan grinned. "Who is it?"

"Oh. I know who it is," Tori said. "And why she hasn't said anything to me is a subject I'll be taking up with her very soon."

"Who is it?" Brody asked.

Tori didn't say anything, just gave Wyatt a knowing smile.

"Oh," Ethan said. "It's Calliope Andrews."

Wyatt winced.

"Wow. Keeping it in the family, aren't you?" Brody asked.

"Shut up, Brody," Tori said. "This is none of our business. Let's move on with the meeting."

"Hey, you started it. Now we're going to take the ball and run like hell." Ethan nudged him with an elbow. "So…is one sister—"

Wyatt shot Ethan a look. "Don't go there. I mean it, Ethan."

Ethan kicked his chair back and raised his hands. "Hey, I was joking with you."

Brody leaned toward Tori. "A little sensitive, isn't he?"

"I'm not fucking deaf, you idiot."

"I mean it, Brody," Tori said. "You need to leave this alone. This is Wyatt and Calliope's business. Not ours."

Ethan shrugged. "Who am I going to tell? Besides Riley, of course. And she's out of town."

"It's not a big deal."

"Do you like her?" Brody asked.

Tori stared at him. He knew Tori and Calliope were friends. He'd have to be careful what he said. "Again, none of your business."

He knew this was going to be a problem, that once word got out he was seeing his ex-wife's sister people would start talking. He could trust his brothers and Tori…but other people? He didn't want to deal with the gossip. The talk after the divorce had been bad. And since he hadn't bothered to say anything, people had made up their own minds about what had happened between him and Cassandra. None of it had been true.

People could think whatever the hell they wanted to think,

but he didn't want them talking shit about Calliope. It was best they didn't know about the two of them.

If he was smart he'd put an end to it now before things got out of hand, before people found out.

They finished the meeting and Wyatt grabbed his stuff. Brody stopped him.

"Hey."

He turned to his brother. "What?"

"You know we were teasing you in there. If you want to see Calliope, that's your business."

Wyatt nodded.

"If anyone's entitled to a life and some fun, Wyatt, it's you. And if that's with Calliope, then go for it."

"It's not that simple. She's Cassandra's sister."

"So? If she's the one you want…"

"Again, not that simple."

"Why? You worried about what people will think, what they'll say?"

He didn't say anything.

Brody frowned. "Screw that. We're behind you. Family sticks together and we'll kick anyone's ass who has something to say about it. Calliope's cool. And damn, man, you're the most relaxed I've seen you in years. It's about time you went out and had some fun. If she's the reason behind it, then don't let anyone stop you."

He nodded. "I'll think about it. Thanks."

He headed out the door and climbed in his truck, tossed his gear to the passenger seat.

Maybe Brody was right. Maybe he was worried too much.

Then again, he knew what small-town gossip was like. He knew his family would rally around him. It wasn't himself he was worried about. Anything people had to say, any whispers and innuendos were water off a duck's back to him. He'd heard it all after his divorce.

But Calliope was building a business. She dealt with families with small children. Rumors and gossip could hurt her and her business.

And that he wouldn't tolerate.

Calliope stood and laid her hands at the small of her back, stretching out her tight muscles.

What an interminably long day. She was glad it was Friday and the week was over. All she wanted was a hot bath, a good meal and her man. And a massage by said man. She wondered if she could convince Wyatt to give her a back rub. Maybe she could use her feminine wiles to wrangle a back rub out of him.

Or, she could just get naked. That should convince him.

Then again, they hadn't made official plans for tonight, or for the weekend. She'd assumed they'd see each other. He'd come over to her place or she'd gone to his after work almost every night for the past two weeks.

He and the other guys had left the addition about an hour ago, so she assumed she'd find him in the trailer doing some paperwork. She locked up the center and headed that way, frowning when she saw all the lights out in the trailer. She pulled on the door. It was locked.

Huh. She walked around to the front of the trailer and didn't see his truck.

He'd left. Without saying anything to her.

Okay, so maybe he'd had an emergency and didn't have time to tell her about it. She hoped everything was okay.

She drove home, tossed her coat and purse on the sofa and grabbed her phone, dialing his number as she kicked her shoes off.

He answered on the third ring.

"Hi," he said.

"Is everything all right?"

"Yeah. Why wouldn't it be?"

"I looked for you after I closed for the day. I thought you might be in the trailer but you had already left."

"Yeah. Cut out on time for a change. Had to head back to the office."

"Oh, okay." She took a seat at the kitchen table. "So what are your plans for tonight?"

"I thought I'd work on the car."

"Oh." She heard the definite brush-off signals in his tone of voice. "What about tomorrow? There's a new movie out I'm dying to see."

"I don't think so. I have a few things I need to catch up on."

Pain and irritation swirled around in her empty stomach, making her nauseous.

"Sure. I understand. I'll see you on Monday, then."

"Okay. See you."

She clicked off the phone and slid it across the table, angry with Wyatt, and with herself.

No. Not with herself. Definitely with him. They had a relationship. They'd been together every day for three weeks. That allowed her to make assumptions. He'd been happy, dammit. He couldn't just make an about turn and suddenly blow her off without an explanation.

An explanation she deserved.

She went into the bathroom and took a shower, washing off the day and some of her annoyance with it. By the time she'd dried her hair, she had the phone to her ear and Tori on the line.

"Are you busy tonight?" she asked.

"I was going to do a home pedicure. It doesn't get more exciting than that."

Calliope laughed, which was exactly what she needed. "How about a girl's night out?"

"Sounds fabulous," Tori said. "What do you have in mind?"

"Food and lots of margaritas."

"Bingo. I'm so game for that."

They made plans to meet at one of their favorite Mexican restaurants in town. She put on makeup, dressed in a pair of her tightest jeans, put on high-heeled boots, then slid into a sexy silk top instead of her day care center sweatshirts.

Tonight, she intended to party.

El Partido was a popular restaurant, especially on the weekends. In a small town, entertainment was limited. You went out to eat, you hit a bar, or you went to the movies. Though there was also bowling and ice-skating if you were in the mood for those activities.

Calliope was in the mood to drink, and she knew Tori was always game for a fun night on the town. They started out with a top-shelf margarita, settled in at the bar and waited for their name to be called for their table. Judging by the long line out front, it could be a while.

"I haven't seen you in like…forever," Tori said, her long earrings grazing her neck as she twisted her barstool around while juggling the oversize drink. "I've missed you."

"I've missed you, too. I'm sorry we haven't gotten together. I've been busy."

Tori lifted her brows. "Yeah? Busy doing what? Or should I ask…whom?"

"What do you know, or what do you think you know?"

Tori gave an innocent bat of her lashes. "I just know Wyatt has been a lot less grumpy lately. He even smiled. He might have cracked a joke. We thought the world was ending."

Calliope's lips curved. "Well, good for him."

"And you're saying his good mood over the past few weeks has nothing to do with you."

Calliope shrugged. "I'm not responsible for his moods."

"Uh, oh. He's pissed you off. What did he do?"

"Nothing. He's not responsible for my mood, either."

"What a crock. Tell me everything."

She did, starting with the first night and every night since.

Tori leaned an arm against the bar and sipped her margarita, her expression changing as the story went on. By the time Calliope finished, Tori was frowning.

"What an ass."

"He has a right to his space."

"Bullshit. He sees you every night, and then suddenly blows you off with no explanation other than working on his car and some vague 'other stuff to do'? No. There's something else going on."

"He's not seeing anyone else. It practically took an act of Congress for him to have sex with me."

Tori snorted and signaled for a refill on their drinks. "Isn't that the truth? That man had a serious dry spell going. Hence his three-year bad mood. Thank God you came along and ended that."

"Yeah."

"So how's the sex?"

"Tori!"

Tori straightened in her seat. "What? I want to know how the sex is. Wyatt's gorgeous. Virile. Studly."

Calliope took the fresh margarita from the bartender and licked a spot of salt from the rim. "Yum."

"The drink or the man?"

She smiled. "Both."

"So he's good, right?"

"I wouldn't be sitting here pissed off at him if he wasn't."

"That's what I figured. I always knew he had some deep, smoldering sexuality simmering under the surface of that testy exterior."

"I'm surprised you even notice given the hots you have for Brody."

"I do not have the hots for Brody. At. All."

"You. Lie."

"First, I work for him. Second, I've known him since I was like…sixteen. Third…"

Calliope waited while Tori tried to come up with another objection.

Instead, Tori took a drink and Calliope laughed at her.

"What?"

"Why haven't you ever done anything about it?"

"About what?"

"Brody."

Tori rolled her eyes, then set her drink down and fiddled with the bracelets on her arm. "I am never doing Brody. We are not meant to be. The man gets on my last nerve. He's egotistical, loud, annoying, teases me too much and already has way too many women in this town who think the sun rises and sets on his perfect abs and great ass."

"And you're not one of them."

"Hell, no. I am not a member of the Brody Kent fan club. Besides, we're not here to talk about me. Nice try in deflecting, though. What are you going to do about Wyatt?"

"Nothing. I can't make him want to be with me."

"No, you can't. But why the sudden brakes on your relationship?"

"Maybe it's run its course."

"After a few weeks?" Tori shook her head. "I don't think so. There's something else, and you need to talk to him to figure out what it is."

"I don't want to talk to him. I want to drink my margarita, hang out with you, then have a giant enchilada."

"I think you'd rather have Wyatt's giant enchilada."

Calliope nearly choked on her drink. "Oh, my God, Tori. Don't do that to me when I'm drinking."

Tori grinned. "Just here to state the facts, my friend."

Calliope thought about what Tori had said all through drinks and dinner.

She wasn't a quitter, wasn't one to sit back and let things happen. Maybe all this togetherness had been too much too fast for Wyatt, but if so, she needed to hear that from him, not some flimsy excuse about stuff and cars. She'd told him from the very beginning the only thing she wanted from him in this relationship was honesty.

So she gave him the weekend to do whatever "stuff" he had to do. Monday morning he walked right past her office without dipping his head in, looking to see if she was in there or even trying to find her the entire day.

Yeah, something was definitely up.

If the relationship had run its course and he wanted to be done with it, then he owed it to her to have a face-to-face conversation with her and tell her.

So at the end of the workday, she stood at the entrance to her office while her staff shuffled the kids out the door to their parents. She waved to the other guys who were working on the room addition, and when Wyatt grabbed his tools on his way out the door, she stopped him.

"Wyatt. Can I see you in my office for a minute?"

"Kind of busy here, Calliope."

"Whatever you're busy with will have to wait. This is important."

He paused, looking toward the front door as if he considered a mad dash for freedom. "I'm dirty and full of dust. How about we do this in my trailer?"

"Fine. Let me lock up in here and I'll meet you there."

He nodded and walked out.

As soon as her staff left, she locked the door and headed over to his trailer. For a brief second as she rounded the corner she wondered if he would take off without talking to her, but he wasn't that much of a coward. The light was on in the trailer. She opened the door and walked in. Wyatt was in there going over blueprints on the drafting table. He looked up, but didn't smile.

"What's going on?" he asked.

She leaned against the opposite wall. "Why don't you tell me what's going on?"

"Huh?"

"Things between us were great, and then suddenly you backed off. I want to know why."

"Calliope…"

"Don't." She pushed off the wall, came to the table and laid her hands on it. "All I want is the straight truth, Wyatt."

He looked down at the blueprints, then back up at her. She saw sadness and pain in his eyes and her heart squeezed.

"I don't want anyone to hurt you."

"What?"

"You started talking about going out, and you deserve that. But you know people are going to talk."

That wasn't at all what she expected to hear. He was protecting her? "Talk about what? That you were once married to Cassie and now you're dating me?"

"Yeah."

She rolled her eyes and slid her hand over his. "Wyatt. I don't care what anyone has to say about that."

"You know as well as I do it's the kind of thing that will

get small-town gossip going. It doesn't bother me at all. I don't give a shit what people say. But you have a reputation to maintain. This could hurt you."

She snorted. "A reputation? Am I some kind of saint in this town?"

"You run a day care center. You can't be seen with me."

"Oh, for the love of chocolate chip cookies. That's the dumbest thing I've ever heard." She moved in between him and table and palmed his face. "I want to be with you. In public. People can say whatever they want, gossip all they want about it. I'd be proud to be with you. If they care that you were married to my sister, that's their problem, not mine."

She saw the worry on his face.

"You know what they're going to say, all the things they're going to say."

"Let them," she said. "I won't be listening."

"What about the people who bring their kids to you?"

"If they're bothered by it, they're not the right kind of people. It's not going to hurt my business." She swept her hand along his jaw, tingling at the scratch of his beard. "But I love that you were worried for me. Thank you."

"I don't want to hurt you, Calliope. I'm trying not to be that guy anymore."

She tilted her head to the side. "That guy?"

"Never mind. It's not important. Look. I'm sorry. I warned you I wasn't any good at this."

She laughed. "You're only going to get so many free passes at using that as an excuse. If you want to be in a relationship, you have to work on your communication skills."

He wrapped his arms around her and tugged her close. "I'm not much of a talker. I'm more of a doer."

This is what she'd missed over the weekend. The rush of

heat, the sudden flame of desire he could draw out of her with one touch.

"A doer, huh?"

"Yeah."

She looked over her shoulder. Her butt rested on the blueprints. "You know, I've had this fantasy about your trailer and this drafting table ever since the first time I walked in here."

She felt the hard ridge of his erection as he pushed her against the table. "Do tell."

"It has something to do with you bending me over it."

He flipped her around so fast she was dizzy, his hands roaming over her breasts, her back, her butt. "I like the way you think, Calliope."

"Good. Then shut up. More doing, less talking."

CHAPTER NINE

Wyatt watched the people around them as he escorted Calliope to their table at McCluskey's Restaurant. He intended to shoot visual daggers at anyone who gave Calliope even a sidelong glance.

So far they'd gone to a movie, eaten at her favorite Mexican restaurant, and gone out with Ethan, his wife, Riley, and their daughter, Zoey, since Riley was back in town after doing a recording session. As soon as Riley heard he was dating Calliope, she insisted on meeting her, so Ethan had suggested they all go out to dinner.

All this going out was wearing on him. Wyatt had spent so much of the past few years as a recluse he had lost the ability to be social. Fortunately Calliope was social enough for the both of them. She and Riley had talked for hours, and of course since Calliope loved kids she'd engaged Zoey in conversation, too. He and Ethan had kicked back and talked work while the three girls laughed together, talked fashion and music and the latest kid stuff.

Calliope was just damned…perfect.

He was in love with her, which scared the shit out of him.

The last time he'd fallen in love with a woman it hadn't ended so well for him. And this was Cassandra's sister. He couldn't imagine what her parents would think of all this. They weren't too fond of him because of what had gone down the first time. He didn't think they'd be overjoyed at the prospect of having him back in the family again.

"Wyatt."

He lifted his gaze to Calliope, who, along with the waitress he hadn't noticed standing at their table, gave him a look of expectation.

"What?"

"What would you like to drink, sir?"

"Oh. Iced tea would be great."

"Thanks, Rachel," Calliope said, then turned back to Wyatt after the waitress bounded off. "Where is your head tonight?"

"Sorry. Was thinking about work stuff." Or proposing to Calliope.

And where the hell had that come from?

He knew where it had come from. He was tired of being alone. Calliope had filled a void in his life he hadn't realized had been there. She was everything he'd ever wanted in a woman. She was full of life and laughter, she loved kids, and she didn't put up with his crap. She wanted the same things he did, so what the hell was he waiting for, other than it was all too familiar, family-wise?

It was too soon. He wasn't ready. He had no idea how she felt. What the hell was he thinking?

"Wyatt."

He lifted his gaze. "What?"

She tilted her head toward Rachel, their waitress again. "Sir, what would you like to order?"

Shit. He did a quick scan of the menu, ordered a steak and handed her the menu.

"Are you even here tonight?" Calliope asked.

"Sorry. A lot on my mind."

She reached for his hand. "Would you like to talk about it?"

"No." Hell, no.

"Well, there's something I want to talk to you about."

"Okay." This time he was determined to pay attention.

"The holidays are approaching, you know."

He lifted his lips and took a sip of tea. "Yeah, I have a calendar."

"Smartass. Anyway, I was wondering if you'd be willing to come over to my parents' house. They're having an open house this weekend."

He swallowed. Talk about tuning into his train of thought. "I don't know, Calliope. I'm not exactly their favorite person after Cassandra."

"I don't agree. They don't hold a grudge. Anyway, there're more."

"It gets worse?"

"I don't know if you'd call it worse. But I think if you and I are going to go anywhere with our relationship, there are some issues you need to put to rest."

He didn't like where this was going. "Go on."

"Cassie's coming home for the holidays."

And the train just jumped the tracks. "No."

"Hear me out on this."

"No. She and I have nothing to say to each other. Everything was said between our attorneys."

She squeezed his hand. "See? That's the problem. Neither of you had closure."

He pulled his hand away. "I had plenty of closure."

"Wyatt."

"Calliope. No. I don't want to talk about this anymore. I have nothing to say to Cassandra that hasn't already been said. I don't want to see her again, or talk to her again. Ever."

She opened her mouth to argue, but the waitress brought

their drinks. Maybe she could tell by the look on his face, but she didn't bring up the topic again, at least until they left the restaurant and went back to his place.

They were curled up on the sofa together and she was un-buttoning his shirt, a slow seduction that was too damn slow in his opinion. He was more than ready to get to the good stuff, like her gorgeous naked body, with him inside her, hope-fully rocking her world.

"What if you and I end up having…let's say a long-term relationship."

Fun halted. He took a deep breath. "Okay. Let's say we do."

"Eventually you're going to have to see my parents, come over to my house, hang out at holidays and birthdays and stuff."

He turned to face her. "My relationship is with you. Not with your family any more than your relationship is with my family. I care about you. Just you."

"But that isn't the way it works and you know it. You're trying to be simplistic and putting the two of us in a bubble. I don't want it to work that way, and I don't think you do, ei-ther. I like your family. I want our future to include *our* fami-lies—providing, of course, we have a future together. Do you want us to have a future together?"

He inhaled, let it out. "This is complicated."

"It doesn't have to be. You're making it that way by shov-ing this giant obstacle between us."

"Cassandra."

"Yes. And she doesn't have to be there. If you'd—"

He put his fingers to her lips. "I don't want my ex-wife in our lives, and I sure as hell don't want her between us right now. I don't want to talk about her or think about her. What I want right now is to kiss you." He put his mouth where his fingers had been. He much preferred kissing her to talking.

When she leaned against him, he felt her surrender. She curled her hand around his neck and moaned against him. He'd won this battle.

But it was a temporary reprieve. This wasn't over, but he was content to let it go for now. All he wanted was this moment, and to have Calliope in his arms, to feel the softness of her body as she moved against him.

He reached behind her to the zipper of the incredibly sexy dress she'd worn to dinner. All he could think about was getting the dress off her. He dragged the zipper down, then drew the dress off her shoulders. She wore a black silk bra that made him hold his breath because her breasts nearly spilled over the top.

"Wow."

She grinned and pushed her glasses up.

Damn, she was one sexy woman. She slid off his lap, unhooked her bra then shimmied out of her panties. "You know what I really wish we could do?"

"If it has anything to do with sex, your wish is granted."

"Good. Because I want to take a shower."

He liked the direction of her thoughts. They made his dick pound hard against his jeans. He stood, scooped her up in his arms and carried her up the stairs, depositing her on the floor in the bathroom. He turned the shower on while he removed his clothes, loving the way Calliope watched him as he undressed. He was hard and aching by the time he pulled her inside the oversize shower.

"I told you the first time I came here that this shower gave me naughty thoughts," she said.

"And I want to hear all about them."

"Four showerheads? It's a woman's dream, in more ways than one." She stepped under one of the sprays, not at all self-conscious about her hair getting wet or her makeup running down her face. One of the things he loved about her.

Wyatt stood back and watched the water stream in rivers down her gorgeous body as she slicked her hair back.

He moved in and put his arms around her to tug her against him, let her feel what she did to him. She reached between them to stroke him, agonizing him with slow, careful movements that made him clench his jaw.

He pushed her against the wall and lifted her arms over her head, held them there with his hand while he used the other to roam over her body. Water poured over them both, steam shadowing them and making the temperature rise as his body heated to unbearable. He bent and took a nipple, licked it then sucked it between his lips. Her moans of pleasure and the way she rocked her hips toward him were an invitation for more.

He wanted more, so he straightened and cupped her sex, watching her eyes as he rocked his hand against her, found the tight nub and rolled it between his fingers and took her where she wanted to go. She gasped, her eyes widening when she came.

He grabbed the condom he'd laid on top of the shower and put it on, then pushed her legs apart and entered her. She held on to his shoulders as he thrust into her again and again, his passion as hot as the water and steam pouring over them.

She dug her nails into him. "More," she said, her voice a whisper, a sensual command.

He gave her more, and she tightened around him, then convulsed, and he shattered, wrapping his arm around her and lifting her. He took her mouth as the maelstrom of sensation wrecked him, left his legs shaking so hard he had to grab the top of the shower to hold them both steady.

He set her down easy, kissing her lips and her throat, stroking her hair while she threaded her fingers through his hair.

Neither one of them said anything. What they'd done, what they'd shared, had said enough.

They dried off and climbed into his big bed, but only used a quarter of the space because he tugged her close against him. She pulled his arm around her and he realized he liked having her here in his house. In his bed. In his life.

He'd do anything to keep her here.

Except the one thing he knew she wanted.

That, he couldn't—wouldn't do.

"I have a problem, and I need some advice."

Tori tossed her oversize bag on Calliope's desk. "You've come to the right person."

Wyatt had a meeting with his brothers at a potential new job site, so he'd left early. Tori had agreed to pop over after work, so now that the day care center was closed, she and Tori had some quiet time to talk.

She'd let a week go by. Things with Wyatt were almost perfect. They were together all the time, and even though the room addition project was a couple days from being completed, she knew the two of them would continue to be together after it was finished. But still, things weren't quite whole between them, and she knew why. It nagged at her, refusing to go away.

Tori took a seat in the chair across from Calliope's desk.

"It's about Wyatt."

Tori smirked. "I figured. What's the problem? Is he being grouchy again?"

"No. Well, not really. He's...uncooperative about a particular subject."

"What subject is that?"

"His ex-wife."

Tori's eyes widened. "You do realize that subject is off-limits. None of us ever bring up the ex. I know she's your sister and all, but, honey, that marriage did not end well."

"I know." She pushed back from her desk and stood, looking out at the streetlights and cars passing by. She turned to face Tori. "The scars of that marriage are holding him back. It's holding us back. He can't let it go."

"Ugly things were said between the two of them. I wasn't privy to it all, but from what I heard, it was a bitter divorce."

"Yes, it was. Mistakes were made on both sides and they walked away without closure. Without forgiveness. Without talking to each other. They need that closure now. Without it, I don't think Wyatt will ever be able to move on with a clear conscience."

"And you want him to be able to move on. With you."

She nodded.

"Honey, you know I love you. But some things—some people—can't be fixed."

"I don't want to fix him. I want him to be happy."

"Doesn't he seem happy? With you?"

"Yes and no. I feel like there will always be a wall between us."

"Meaning Cassie."

"Yes. He needs to get past her, really let her go, before he can ever be truly happy."

"You do realize this could be a deal breaker for him."

Calliope nodded. "I know. But I love him, and I know that on the surface he's happy with me, but Cassandra will always be between us. Which means I have to try. And if that means he walks away from me, then I guess we were never meant to be."

Tori stood, came over and hugged her. "So what do you want to do?"

"I have an idea."

"That Wyatt won't like."

"He'll hate it. He'll be angry with me."

"And you need my help to make it happen."

"Yes."

Tori nodded. "You know I love you both. So what can I do?"

CHAPTER TEN

Wyatt hated parties. It required more socializing, and God knew he'd done enough socializing the past couple months to last him a lifetime.

But it was part of what they did for business, and the annual Kent Construction holiday party included inviting their clients. Treating clients to a night of fun, dinner and dancing was good for their business. So he'd suck it up, put on a smile and a suit, and down enough whiskey so he could numb the pain.

At least this year he'd have Calliope by his side, so he wouldn't have to huddle in a corner with some drunken businessman he'd have to end up driving home at the end of the night.

Trying not to strangle on his tie, he pulled into Calliope's driveway and got out, went to her front door and rang the bell.

"It's open," he heard her holler. He opened the door.

"How do you know I'm not some serial killer?" he said as he walked in. "Lock your damn door, woman."

"There are no serial killers in this town," she said from the bedroom.

"I'm sure the last person to be killed by a serial killer in a small town thought that, too."

"Fine. I'll have a key made for you and I'll start locking the front door."

She came out, and he forgot all about the lecture he was going to give her about locking the door.

Dressed in a black dress that swept across the tops of her knees, her shoulders were bare, the dress sparkled, clung to her amazing breasts and every curve of her body. Long silver earrings hung from her ears, her hair was swept up and into some kind of sparkly clip, curls dangling down her back. She even wore different glasses, black ones with tiny crystals on the side. Sexy as hell. Her shoes made her legs look miles long and all he could think about was getting her out of that dress later on tonight.

"I can't breathe, Calliope."

She frowned and walked toward him. "What's wrong?"

"You're so goddamned stunning you take my breath away."

She paused, and her lips curved. "Really?"

"Yeah." He came to her, lifted her hand in his and pressed a kiss to it. "I'm going to make every man at the party jealous."

"Stop."

"No. You're truly beautiful. I'm a very lucky man."

She grinned. "Thank you." She adjusted his tie. "You look so handsome in a suit. Black suits you. We make a fine couple."

"Thanks. I'm uncomfortable."

"Suck it up, hot stuff. It's only for one night."

"You ready?"

She inhaled, let it out, and he couldn't help watching the rise of her breasts.

"You keep looking at me like that and we won't make it to your party tonight."

"And that would be a bad thing…how?"

She laughed. "I'll get my coat."

★ ★ ★

Calliope's stomach was twisted up in knots. The venue was beautiful. She found Tori and told her she'd done a fantastic job.

"Thank you." Tori squeezed her hand. "We have so many people here tonight. I'm so nervous."

"Don't be. This is amazing."

Tori took a sip of champagne and looked around. "We have such a great turnout. I'm glad we booked on a Friday night. I think people were ready to party, let loose before the holidays."

"And you look gorgeous." Tori's flaming red hair was in an updo, with tendrils framing her creamy face. She wore diamond studs in her ears, and a knockout, tight-fitting red dress that showcased all her assets. "Has Brody seen you yet?"

"Brody who?"

Calliope laughed. "Deny all you want, but that is an impress-a-man dress."

"How do you know it isn't for Jimmy Redding of Redding Tools?"

Calliope snorted. "If you had the hots for Jimmy Redding I'd already know about it."

Tori shrugged. "I'm on duty tonight, making sure our guests have a great time."

Calliope saw Brody frown in Tori's direction, and head their way.

"We'll see what Brody has to say, since he's coming at you like a runaway freight train."

Tori turned. "Huh. Oh, look, there's Jimmy Redding now. Gotta go."

Tori skirted away in a hurry. Calliope had no idea what kind of game Tori was playing with Brody, but from the steaming-mad look on Brody's face, she'd guess that game was going to reach a conclusion soon.

Calliope dug her phone out of her purse, then palmed her stomach to calm the nervous jitters.

This had to work. If it didn't, her relationship with Wyatt would be in serious jeopardy.

She spotted Ethan and Riley along with Ethan's parents, so headed over there to say hello. Riley looked gorgeous in a pale cream dress, her hair cascading down her shoulders.

"I love a good party," Riley said. "And these aren't the industry type of parties I'm always stuck going to. Small-town parties are always the best."

"You didn't always think so," Ethan said, sliding his arm around her waist.

She leaned her head against Ethan's shoulder. "I'm reformed now. I might have to be on the road a lot, but there's nothing better than coming home."

Calliope grinned. Ethan and Riley had gone through a lot to be together. Seeing them so happy together now gave her hope.

"Calliope," Stacy Kent said, taking her hands. "It's so wonderful to see you here."

"Thank you, Stacy. It's nice to be here."

Stacy looped her arm in Calliope's after Ethan and Riley moved off. "Can I say thank you?"

"Why?"

"For giving life back to my son. He hasn't had much of one since the divorce. Until you."

Calliope smiled. "Can I tell you a secret?"

"Of course."

"I'm head over heels in love with your son."

Stacy hugged her. "He's very lucky to have someone like you."

Obviously Wyatt's mom had no problem with her being

Cassie's sister. That was one Kent in her corner, at least. Her fingers were crossed this was going to work out.

She'd made a calculated decision. A tough one. One that might blow up in her face and cost her the man she'd fallen madly, hopelessly, irrevocably in love with.

But she didn't see any way around it, because this needed to be done. Not only for Wyatt and her, but for her sister, whom she loved.

It was time to bury the past, forgive the sins and move on. She just had to get Wyatt on board.

The evening passed with little fanfare. There was food, drinks were plentiful and Wyatt seemed to be having a great time. He wasn't drinking a lot—mostly water, so that was good. She didn't need him drunk and difficult to deal with. This night was going to be tough enough as it was.

She pulled her phone out, judging the time. She wandered around the party, saw Tori and Brody in a dark corner engaged in a heated discussion. Tori's hands were flailing like they always did when she was pissed off. Brody towered over her, his voice raised. Calliope wondered if she should go over and intercede, see if Tori needed any help, but then Brody jerked Tori into his arms and planted one seriously hot kiss on her.

Uh. Wow. That was some kiss. Tori didn't seem to be fighting it, either. In fact, she grabbed the lapels of Brody's jacket and tugged him closer. Calliope pivoted and walked the other way, her lips lifting in a wide smile.

Go, Tori.

Intending to find her own hot kisser, she searched the crowd, found Wyatt engaged in conversation with a few of his clients. She slid her arm through his. He looked down and grinned at her, then excused himself from the conversation.

He pulled her into his arms and kissed her, making her entire body swirl with warmth and emotion. A little over a month ago he wouldn't have even wanted to be seen with her. Now he was kissing her in public. Not only in public, but surrounded by his family and friends.

That was some serious progress.

"People are watching us, you know."

He brushed his lips across hers again. "Don't care. Let them watch. You're mine and I want everyone to know it."

Her stomach tightened. She didn't want to lose Wyatt over this. "I like being yours."

"Let's dance."

He dragged her out on the dance floor and pulled her into his arms. The music was slow and his body was all muscle. They fit together perfectly.

Other couples were out there, but Calliope didn't notice. All she saw was Wyatt, the way he looked at her, as if she was the only woman in the world for him.

She wanted to be the only woman in the world for him. That's why she was doing this tonight.

It was now or never. "I hope you don't mind, but I have a surprise for you later."

His brows lifted. "I hope it has something to do with you and me finding a private room somewhere so I can see what you're wearing under that dress."

She let out a soft laugh. "Yes, there's that, too. But there's another surprise. After the party's over."

He cocked a brow. "I can't wait."

They finished the dance and Wyatt pressed his lips to hers. He hovered, as if he wanted to say something, but one of his clients came up and the moment was broken.

"Go ahead," she said. "We'll catch up later."

He wandered off and she tried to find Tori, who seemed to have disappeared. So had Brody.

Interesting.

Maybe the two of them went off to have their own private holiday party.

If they had, it was about time.

She ran into Ethan and Riley.

"Have you seen Tori?"

Riley looked around. "No, I haven't as a matter of fact."

"I was looking for Brody earlier," Ethan said. "I can't find him."

"You don't think—" Riley's eyes widened. "Did the two of them run off to some dark corner together?"

Calliope refused to answer that one, but Ethan and Riley put two and two together and grinned at each other.

"I guess I can stop trying to hunt down my brother," Ethan said with a knowing smile.

Calliope had no idea what was going on with Tori and Brody, but she hoped whatever it was, it was a good thing and nothing bad.

The party wound down and guests had begun to leave. By midnight, the place was empty. Still no sign of Tori and Brody. Wyatt's parents had already gone home, and Ethan and Riley had to go pick up Zoey from the babysitter.

Which meant she and Wyatt were the last ones standing. She made the call. It was now or never.

"You ready to head out?" Wyatt asked.

"Not yet. I need you to follow me."

His lips curled. "Are you planning to drag me to some dark corner for sex?"

She laughed. "Uh. Not exactly."

She took his hand and led him out of the main ballroom. Her heart pounded and her pulse began to race. Her legs felt weak and she pondered calling a halt to this whole thing, but as soon as they reached the lobby, she was standing right there, right on time.

Cassandra had always been punctual.

She had left a party of her own at the hotel next door, promising Calliope she'd show up.

Wyatt's hand tightened in hers. He stopped, looked at Cassie, then down at her.

"Why? After I told you no, why? You have no business interfering in my life."

She saw the hurt and anger on his face, but lifted her chin.

"I have every right to interfere in your life. I'm in love with you. I want you to be happy, and as long as this animosity lingers between you and Cassie, you'll never be free."

He turned, started to walk away, but she grabbed his hand. "Wyatt, don't. Don't walk away. Not this time."

"I asked you not to do this. I trusted you. The last time I trusted a woman she screwed me over. I guess it runs in the family, doesn't it?"

His words were like a stab in the heart, but she knew it was just his fear talking. She refused to let him push her away. Instead, she was determined to stand and fight.

"Grow up and act like a man, Wyatt. Once you do you'll realize I'm the best damn thing that's ever happened in your life—a life you'll never be able to wholly live until you let go of the past." She pointed down the hall at her sister. "That's your past. I'm your future. Pull your head out of your ass and figure out what you want. A life of regret and anger, or a life with me."

She turned and walked away.

Wyatt had never been more furious about anything in his entire life. Not even when things had been at their worst with Cassandra had he felt as betrayed as he did right now.

He'd asked Calliope to stay out of it, not to put him and Cassandra together.

He'd trusted Calliope to honor his wishes, yet there Cassandra was, the nightmare of his past.

Fuck a Christmas turkey. What the hell was he supposed to do now?

Cassandra didn't look any happier about this than he did. In fact, she looked downright miserable. Not angry. Miserable.

Shit.

He'd never wanted to see her again, talk to her again, think about her again, but all he'd been doing for the past three years was think about every goddamn thing that had gone wrong in their marriage. And he'd done a lot of blaming—mostly blaming Cassandra for his failures.

Maybe Calliope was right, and it was time to talk it out. If he and Cassandra could have a civil conversation that lasted five minutes.

He strolled toward her, and she came toward him, looking as wary as he felt.

She was still as beautiful as he remembered—even more so, her long blond hair straight and pulled back into a ponytail. She wore heels, some fancy black coat and a party dress.

"You come from a party?" he asked as they stopped a couple feet from each other.

"Real-estate event, yes. A holiday party, like yours."

"How's business?"

"Good. I hear yours is going very well."

"It is."

"Wyatt. Is there someplace less…busy…where we could talk?"

He raked his fingers through his hair. "Yeah." He led her through the lobby and into one of the private ballrooms that wasn't having an event tonight, flipped on the lights and pulled up a chair at a dressed-up table that was set up for some luncheon tomorrow.

She slipped off her coat and he grabbed a chair, straddling it to face her.

"It's been a long time," she finally said.

"Yeah."

Neither of them said anything for a while. Wyatt didn't know where to start, what to say. For years he'd thought of nothing but the words he'd say to her if he ever saw her again. Angry words. Hurtful words. Now, seeing her, she looked small, vulnerable, not the pit viper he'd conjured up in his head all these years.

"Calliope forced me to come here," Cassandra finally said. "She browbeat me, said the two of us left things…open. That there was so much animosity between us, neither of us could move on with our lives until we had closure."

"She's good at pushing people into doing what they don't want to do."

Cassandra laughed. "She's pushy. Always has been."

"I love that about her," he said, then lifted his gaze.

"It's okay. I know you two have been seeing each other for a while. It's all right, Wyatt. I think it's well past time we both move on, don't you?"

"Yeah."

"You two are a good fit. You and I never were."

"You're right about that," he said, and found himself falling into conversation with her easier than he thought he would. "I fell in love with the prettiest girl in town. I put you on a pedestal, and projected everything I wanted out of life on to you, expecting you to toe the line. I was blind to the fact the things I wanted weren't the same things you wanted."

For the first time, she smiled. "I did the same thing. You were the boy all the girls in town wanted, so I set my sights on you. Then I thought I could turn you into the man I wanted you to be, but you were never that man. I was wrong to try and change you."

"So we both screwed up."

She laughed then. "We should have never gotten married. We were never right for each other."

"I'm sorry I hurt you."

Her eyes glistened with tears. "I'm sorry, too."

This wasn't what he expected. She wasn't what he expected. All these years, he'd had an image of her in his head, and she wasn't that person at all.

"Are you happy now?" he asked.

"I am. I'm getting there. I love my job, and where I live. I'm seeing someone who treats me well, and we do want the same things. I've learned to be honest about what I want—and what I don't want. I have learned from my mistakes."

He inhaled, let out a long breath. "Yeah, I'm still learning, obviously."

She laid her hand over his. "Do you really love my sister?"

"Yes."

"No hesitation. I like that." She stood. "I love her, too. She's perfect for you."

He needed to ask, needed to know. "Does that hurt you, that I'm in love with Calliope?"

She paused, tilted her head. "Not at all. I think maybe we're both moving on, don't you think?"

"I think so." They both stood and he helped her with her coat. "I'm sorry for the pain."

She hugged him, and he realized he felt nothing. No anger, no bitterness, nothing at all.

She turned around and smiled at him. "I wish you happiness, Wyatt. And I'm so glad Calliope forced us into this. I hope we can work on being friends someday. Maybe even… in-laws?"

He smiled back at her and walked her out.

Now he needed to go find Calliope, because he had a few more apologies to make, this time to the woman who really had his heart.

CHAPTER ELEVEN

Calliope paced on the back steps of the hotel, switching from angry to hurt back to angry again, then tossing in worry and angst for good measure.

Her stomach was a ball of knots. She could use her best friend and a tall margarita right now, but Tori was otherwise occupied somewhere with Brody. She made a mental note to call her tomorrow for a full recap of what that kiss had been all about.

She was going to give Wyatt another half hour—mainly because she was freezing her ass off out here—but also because he needed to cool off and so did she before they talked again.

"You didn't leave."

Her head shot up at the sound of his voice. He was standing at the top of the stairs.

"You're not wearing a jacket," she said.

"What?"

"It's freezing out here. Where's your coat?"

"Inside."

"Then let's go inside before you freeze to death."

"Calliope. Aren't you mad at me?"

"Furious. But I don't want you to get sick and it's cold out here. I'll yell at you inside."

He shook his head and helped her up the stairs and inside.

"Where would you like me to yell at you?"

He punched the elevator button and they rode up in silence to the penthouse floor. She noted the floor, but otherwise stayed silent, figuring she'd have plenty to say when they got to wherever they were going.

When he pulled out a key card and slid it into the penthouse suite's door, she turned to him. "Really?"

"Yeah. Figured we'd live it up tonight."

"Huh." He pushed the door open and held it while she walked in. When he flipped the switch, she resisted the urge to gasp.

The room was opulent. She'd always wondered about the penthouse suite at this hotel. Now she didn't have to wonder anymore. It was lavish, decorated in creams and blacks, with marble flooring, floor-to-ceiling windows and more square footage than her entire house.

"Would you like a drink?"

"No, thank you," she said, pulling off her coat and laying it over a chair. As she rubbed her chilled hands together, she walked to the window, surveying her entire town in one sweep. Beautiful.

But she wasn't here to enjoy the view, so she turned to face him.

"I know I meddled, that you asked me not to contact Cassie and have the two of you meet. But here's the problem, Wyatt. I love you. And you're never going to be whole until the past is firmly in the past where it belongs. And maybe I don't do things the right way all the time, but I'll always have your back. I'll always want what's best for you. So you know what? What's best for you is me."

"You're right."

She pause her train of thought. "What?"

"You're right. About all of it. I did need to talk to Cassandra. We both needed to exorcise the past. We both did things that were wrong, but I was the worst. I had it in my head that she was the enemy, and all this time I carried this giant grudge. She wasn't the enemy. She was just the wrong woman for me."

"You talked to her."

"Yes. It's over for good now. We mended fences."

Some of the tension dissolved and she dropped her shoulders. "Oh. Well, I'm glad. Better now?"

He came toward her. "A lot better. I feel light now, Calliope. Like a weight was lifted off me."

She nodded. "Good."

He picked up her hands, slid his thumbs over them. "The past is gone now. All I want to think about is the future. The only person in my future is you."

Her heart squeezed.

"I love you, Calliope."

"I love you too, Wyatt."

"I'm sorry for what I said earlier. I'm probably going to say I'm sorry a lot over the next fifty or sixty years, so get used to it."

Her heart did a little song and dance, fluttering in her chest. "Okay."

He dropped to his knee. "I want to marry you. I want to have kids with you. A lot of kids. I want you to move into my big house that you fell in love with, and raise those kids with me there. I like dogs. Do you like dogs?"

She swiped at the tears that rolled down her cheeks. "I love dogs."

"Good. Will you marry me?"

"Yes. Of course. Yes."

He stood and pulled her into his arms, kissed her in that way that never failed to make her feel a little bit faint.

"I love you, Wyatt. I want to marry you. I want to make babies with you—FYI, as soon as humanly possible. I want as many dogs as you can tolerate underfoot—kids too, for that matter. I'm yours."

He smoothed his hand over her hair, her face, her lips. "You are the rarest gift. I'm a very lucky man to have found you, and it isn't even Christmas yet."

She gave him a wicked smile. "No, but you might be getting your gift early. Wait 'til you see what I'm wearing under this dress."

He reached for the zipper in back of the dress and pulled it down. "Now that's a challenge I accept."

Her skin broke out in goose bumps, her body flaming to his touch. Her dress unzipped, he drew it off her shoulders and let it pool at her feet. She stepped out of it, and Wyatt's eyes widened.

"Merry Christmas to me," he said, his eyes roaming appreciatively over her body.

She'd splurged on a fire-engine-red, lace-and-satin thong with a matching demi-bra that barely contained her breasts. With her shoes still on, she knew she looked like a wicked temptress. She felt like one. And when she dropped to her knees to undo Wyatt's belt buckle, he let out a litany of curses that only served to drive her arousal to danger levels.

He kicked off his shoes while she unzipped and removed his pants and boxer briefs, then took his shaft in her hand and stroked it before taking him in her mouth to show him how much she loved every part of him.

He tangled his fingers in her hair, removing the clip she'd put her hair up with earlier. He wound his hand around her hair and held her while she engulfed him, taking him in deep, until he let out a low groan and pulled her to a standing position and swept her into his arms.

"When I come, it's going to be inside you."

"Without a condom," she said as he laid her on the bed.

"You would risk me knocking you up before we're married?" he asked, his expression one of mock horror.

She laughed. "Well, I am still on the pill, but you did catch the ASAP part of my speech about kids, didn't you?"

He drew her panties off, his eyes gleaming with heated desire. "Yeah, ASAP works for me, too. In more ways than one."

He crawled between her legs, spread them and put his mouth on her. She bit down on her lip to keep from screaming as he used his tongue to take her right to the peak, and then over. When he moved up her body and entered her, he cupped her butt, lifted her against him and took her right to the edge again with slow and easy strokes.

"I love you," he whispered as he brushed his lips across hers, using his mouth and his body to take her so close she thought she'd die from the sweet pleasure of it.

She rubbed her palm against the quickly growing stubble of his beard. "I love you, too." She wrapped her legs around him and brought him home, and when they both came together, she couldn't think of a more perfect way to cement their love.

After, he held her against him and she listened to the sound of his heart beating against her ear.

"You really want kids right away?" he asked.

She lifted her head and turned over onto her belly to look at him. "I do. Do you want to wait?"

"No. I've waited my whole life for you. For this. I want to get married right away. How soon can you do that thing that women do?"

She arched a brow. "That thing that women do?"

"You know. The whole putting together a wedding thing."

She laughed. "Oh. I don't know. Six months?"

"So I have to wait six months to get you pregnant?"

"Hey, pregnant brides are the new black, you know."

"Huh?"

"In other words, knock me up, stud. I'm ready."

He rolled her over onto her back. "Have I ever mentioned I take direction really well?"

"Now who's the rare gift?" she asked with a laugh.

But that laughter turned into something else as he kissed her, and they got down to the business of making their future.

★ ★ ★ ★ ★

IT'S NOT CHRISTMAS WITHOUT YOU

HelenKay Dimon

To Melissa Thomas-Van Gundy
for stepping in during national disasters,
fighting fires, getting your doctorate and
conserving our nation's forests, but mostly for being
a dear friend who helped me survive high school.

HELENKAY DIMON

Bestselling and award-winning author HelenKay Dimon spent twelve years in the most unromantic career ever—divorce lawyer. After dedicating all of that effort to helping people terminate relationships, she is thrilled to deal in happy endings and write romance novels for a living. Her books have been featured in *Cosmopolitan* magazine and on E! Online. Even better, she hasn't had to buy panty hose in four years.

HelenKay loves hearing from her readers. You can visit her at her website, www.helenkaydimon.com, or at her Facebook page, www.facebook.com/helenkaydimon, or follow her on Twitter at twitter.com/helenkaydimon.

CHAPTER ONE

Carrie Anders loved Christmas. The lights, the cookies, the holiday spirit, the cookies, the carols…the cookies. She'd spent every holiday of the last twenty-six years in Holloway, West Virginia, the small town a few miles from the Maryland border where she grew up and her parents and brother still lived. She planned on breaking her streak by staying in Washington, D.C., this year.

No big family dinner. No week off. Just one day at home in her tiny apartment before heading back to her shift at the museum. Though she loved the job, the idea of working over the holidays made her grumpy to the point of sneering. But keeping busy meant keeping her mind off the man she missed more each day instead of less.

That whole absence-makes-the-heart-grow-fonder thing? Yeah, that wasn't her experience. Not if the constant dull ache in her chest was an indication. After months away from home, and him, she still felt the pull. She'd read all about eternal longing in books and thought it sounded dramatic. Now she lived it.

She'd be in a meeting or even brushing her teeth and her mind would wander back to the man who'd grabbed her heart when he was still a long-haired boy driving a muscle car.

Good thing her mom had shipped two tins of sugar cookies for early holiday taste testing. They took her mind off everything else...for a second or two. Only broken edges remained, but Carrie kept eating. She may even have licked her finger then crunched it against the crumbs for a snack.

Rather than mope in a sea of cookie dust and dwell on that whole broken-heart thing, she buttoned her peacoat and went downstairs for some fresh Sunday air. Standing in the lobby of her apartment building, she stared at the empty lot across the street. Make that the formerly empty lot.

The corner at the end of the Whitehurst Freeway that separated the Foggy Bottom area of Washington, D.C., from its wealthy neighbor Georgetown now housed what looked like a misplaced forest. Hundreds of soon-to-be Christmas trees lined the small strip of grass usually reserved for resident dog walking. Something about the combination of dog poo and Christmas trees fit with her feelings about the holiday this year.

A string of white lights clipped to beams outlined the space in a square. A building about the size of a shed sat at the end closest to the street. As she watched, a man grabbed the trees from the stacks one-by-one and staked them upright.

Despite the chill and last night's dusting of snow, he wore faded blue jeans and a half-tucked-in flannel shirt. His only nod to the weather was the combination of work boots and gloves, and those likely had more to do with the way he was throwing six-foot trees around than the icy air.

It was the first week of December. She'd been counting down the days until the lot opened because, by God, she'd have a tree even if she had to move her couch into the hallway to fit the tree in her five-hundred-square-foot apartment.

But it looked like she'd have to wait a few more hours until the lot was up and running. Maybe she'd grab a coffee and...

Her gaze went back to the guy and an unexpected heat

rolled through her. Broad shoulders and a waist trim enough to make the hem of his shirt hang away from his body. The rip in his decade-old jeans right under his left butt cheek. The slight flap to the pocket where the thread lost its battle with time.

Oh, yeah. She knew that ass. Knew all of him, actually. Brown hair that brushed against his eyebrows, bright blue eyes and a stubborn streak to rival the obstinance of two eighty-year-old coal miners engaged in a political argument.

Austin Thomas. High school love, ex-boyfriend of six months who refused to stay ex, and the reason for the constant ache around her heart.

Her sneakers slipped against the slick sidewalk as she stumbled her way into a perfect furious stalk. Excitement and anger warred inside her with each breath. She tamped down on the white light of happiness that bloomed in her stomach just from seeing him and let the darker side of her emotions fuel her steps.

Five feet away, Austin spun around and shot her his best I've-been-waiting-for-you smile. The same one guaranteed to make her panties hit the floor and her common sense pack for vacation.

Oh, no. Not this time.

"What are you doing here?" She almost hated to look into his eyes because they possessed the super power of turning her witless.

"Working."

"No."

He peeled off his gloves and tucked them in his back pocket. "No?"

"You're not supposed to be here." He got West Virginia in the breakup and she got D.C. She'd never said the parameters out loud, but she shouldn't have to. Austin was an avowed city-hater. "We broke up."

"Yeah, you've mentioned that."

They'd been on-and-off since high school. Separate colleges led them to date other people. When they both landed back home in Holloway more than three years ago, the comfortable pattern of hanging out turned into dating and sex and finally something much deeper. Then the offer from the National Museum of Women in the Arts came and she had to choose between the life she never believed she wanted and the one she spent years dreaming about.

"This time was for good." She played with the coat button right at her stomach, sliding her fingers over the plastic until she accidentally twisted it off.

"You said that a year ago, then we kept dating. You said it again six months ago when you left Holloway. You wrote me a note that time explaining why. You even emailed to confirm I received it." He cleared his throat. "Very organized of you, by the way."

Admittedly, the email may have been overkill, but she had to keep saying they were over or neither of them would believe it. Ten minutes together and they fell into old patterns of hanging out and laughing on the couch then finding a soft bed, which explained why she'd put a full state between them this time around. A woman couldn't be too careful when it came to the one man who made her forget everything else.

"If you remember what happened between us and how we're over and all, why are you here?" she asked.

"This is a lucrative spot for selling trees."

He actually delivered the line with a straight face. Carrie rolled her eyes anyway.

"You're trying to tell me you schlepped all the trees and equipment from the farm for a few extra bucks?" When he tried to talk over her, she held up a finger. "That you walked away from the nursery and your work, and just so happened to end up in the lot across from my apartment."

He smiled until the dimple she loved so much appeared in his cheek. "Uh, how about I say yes and leave it at that."

"No." She waved her finger at him this time. "That whole adorable thing you do, with your head falling to the side while you flash me a big smile and rock back on your heels, isn't going to work this time."

If possible, he got even cuter. "I can live with that since we've established you still think I'm hot."

"I said adorable."

"I'm pretty sure I heard the word *hot*."

He somehow managed to be hot and adorable and totally infuriating. He reminded her of the simple things she enjoyed in life, like fresh lemonade in summer and diving into the frigid lake at the first sign of spring. Like snowball fights and sipping hot chocolate while sitting with her feet on his lap and watching football, which usually included screaming at the television.

Loving him, enjoying time with him, getting all hot for him—those had never been a problem. But shifting into adulthood and balancing what she wanted to achieve with how hard he fought to keep everything the same had proven impossible until walking away became her only option.

"What you're not hearing, Austin, is the 'we're over' theme."

He exhaled in that my-life-is-so-difficult way men locked in verbal battle with women did so well. "Because you want to live and work here instead of back home?"

"In part."

"What's the rest?"

To figure out who she was separate from him and the safety of the life she'd always known. To follow her dream of working in a big museum instead of a small regional one. To keep from looking back with regret five, ten or twenty years from now. To keep from seeing the regret and pain that danced in her mother's eyes mirrored in her own one day.

The list exhausted her. "Haven't we been through this?"

"You said I didn't appreciate your career."

That argument had gone on for two days, so she was sure she'd said more than that. "Talk about selective memory."

"Do you still love me?"

He didn't move but his presence closed in around her. This was what always happened. Her feelings for him overwhelmed her resolve and next thing she knew she was doubting her choices and looking at her clothes scattered all over the floor. She'd never been a slave to her hormones. She'd walked away from a guy in college who cheated on her and went a year without any physical contact when no one interested her. But something about Austin weakened her resolve to the point of breaking. She'd once tricked her brain into thinking she could enjoy sleeping with him while keeping a wall of protection around her heart. Now she knew better.

This time he physically moved. A hand brushed over her arm as he stepped in closer. "Well, Carrie. Do you?"

"How I feel about you isn't really the point." And her weakness for him wasn't a question. She had to push him out of her memory to survive the days without him.

He treated her to a half snort, half guffaw sort of thing. "Uh, yeah. It is. It's all that matters."

He was a good man and determined enough to wait her out. He'd all but told her that when she walked away six months ago. She didn't want to hurt him and being close to him all but guaranteed that. "Go home, Austin."

"I'm good here."

She slipped around him, heading for the coffee she now needed in an extra-large size. A stray thought had her turning back to face him. "Where are you staying while you're in town?"

"You offering me your bed?"

"No."

"Couch?"

"Still no."

He shrugged. "I won't take it personally."

"Austin—"

He waved a hand in the air. "No, it's okay. I'll be fine."

Carrie ignored the non-answer and got back to walking. She made it the whole way across the street without looking back. The heat of his stare burned into her back, but she shoved her hands in her pockets and kept going. As she rounded her building and ducked out of sight, her mind crashed and her steps faltered. She slammed her back against the brick wall on the far side of the complex and forced her brain to focus.

This can't be happening. A sharp breath rushed out of her, taking the last of her energy with it.

"I can't do this again," she whispered, ignoring the worried stares of two older women as they passed.

She had bigger problems than looking like a crazy person. She depended on the distance from Austin to stay strong in her resolve. He hadn't contacted her since the initial flurry right after she'd left Holloway. Every day she resisted calling his home number during work hours just to hear the sound of his voice on the answering machine. But the potency of the live version of Austin crashed through her control.

She wanted him to change, to want her back without quietly pushing her to give up her dreams. She didn't want to be charmed and she definitely didn't want to love him. Now she had to figure out how to make her heart listen.

CHAPTER TWO

They'd made contact. Yeah, Carrie was half yelling at the time, but Austin still considered it progress of sorts.

"That went well." Spence shut the door to the makeshift office and joined his brother in watching Carrie practically run from the lot.

"It's a start."

"Were we listening to the same conversation?"

Austin tore his gaze away from her ass and tugged his gloves back on. He'd waited months to see her again. He could hold out a few more days to touch her. "She thinks I don't appreciate the things she cares about."

"Whatever that means."

Spence could identify plant species, had handpicked every choice in their hothouses and on the sales floor, and could classify every tree on the three hundred acres they owned along with their father. But women? Not his area of expertise.

Since the brothers lived together on the top two floors of the farmhouse in Holloway whose bottom floor served as the business office for Thomas Nurseries, Austin had a front-row seat to the parade of women Spence slept with then showed the door. The guy didn't do commitment. He barely did overnights.

Austin tried to explain his position anyway. "Carrie is big on the boyfriend support thing."

"Aren't all women?"

The man had a point. "I guess that's why you run away from them so fast."

A sea of red crept up Spence's neck to his cheeks. "When did we start talking about my love life?"

That topic needed months of dissecting and a therapist. Austin wasn't touching it. "My point is I know Carrie's issues and can handle them."

Spence snorted as he dropped down on the step to the office. "Since she's living here and you're living two hours away, you might want to work on the way you handle things."

"And since one of us actually needs to work so we can sell trees and make money, can you hand me that?" Austin pointed to the pocket knife on the ground next to Spence's foot.

"I have a job. Landscaping, running a family business." He kicked the closed knife in Austin's direction. "Any of this sound familiar?"

"Mitch is handling everything back home with the business while I take care of my problem with his sister here."

"And you think I don't get women." Spence muttered something about idiots.

"Meaning?"

"You have more than a problem with Carrie. You have a full-blown disaster."

As Carrie's brother, Mitch was the one member of the Anders family Austin could read and depend on not to pack up the car and run. When Mitch had let it slip his sister might be dating as part of her new city life, fury had burned through Austin. He'd almost ripped down the trees on the back ten of their property with his bare hands.

Then Mitch said something about Carrie not coming home

for the holidays and Austin funneled all his anger into action. He'd been waiting for her to realize she missed him and return to Holloway on her own. But, damn, women could be stubborn, especially this one. This coming-to-her-senses thing was taking her forever.

Her lack of a reaction left him with few options. After all, a guy had to have some pride. Racing after a woman and begging her to come back carried the stink of desperation. Not his style. Yeah, he missed her like hell, but he was not about to lick her shoes and cry like some neutered stooge.

Visiting her now was a totally different thing. Not lame at all, or so he kept insisting in his head. The plan was simple. He'd remind her of what she was missing. Seeing him might jumpstart something. Get the clock moving again. Unless he went bankrupt first. The amount of money he'd had to pay to get the permit for this site made his head pound. The cash came out of his pocket because he couldn't ask his brother and Mitch to front it. But when Carrie returned home and got settled it would be worth it.

"If she calls the cops on you for stalking, you're on your own." Spence jumped to his feet and reached for the nearest tree. "I don't have extra money for bail, so don't ask."

"I'm not stalking."

"You crossed state lines to hunt her down then set up shop outside of her window." Spence shook his head. "What would you call it?"

Austin had to admit pieces sounded bad when Spence laid them out like that. "She's hiding. If she were really over me, she wouldn't do everything she could to keep from seeing me. She'd meet me head-on."

"Your logic is nuts."

No, he'd worked it all out in his head and it made sense. "Her pride is in the way. Once I get around that we're good."

"Now you sound like an egotistical prick."

Austin's confidence took a kick but he didn't even flinch. "I'm being realistic."

"If that were true I'd be at home right now."

"Look, this will only take a few days then you can get back to the nursery." Austin had to believe that was true. If he entertained the idea of life going on as it had since she left… well, it couldn't happen. It was that simple.

"She broke up with you," Spence said, as if he read his brother's mind.

"Yeah, I got that."

"Several times. I'm not even talking about this time. There was that month when you were in college and she still was in high school. Then that other—"

"Are you done?"

Thanks to Carrie his family had joined in on drilling the breakup point home. But he knew what they didn't. That they'd never really separated, not until she picked up and moved here. Even then she stared right at him and begged him to go with her. Instead of asking her stay or saying anything, he told her to leave if she had to and then fell into a drinking stupor when she actually listened and did it. Spence held the trunk of a five-foot pine and shot Austin one of those annoying older-brother looks. "The woman isn't exactly being subtle here. That has me wondering how slow you are."

When it came to Carrie, glacial. "She wants to be with me."

"She's hiding it well."

"She needs to get the D.C. thing out of her system then we can get back to where we were before."

"You mean before she took off."

"Don't make me kick your ass out here on the street where everyone can see you cry like a little girl."

"Just saying love is making you stupid."

Austin dropped the branch and let the tree he was holding fall back to the ground. "She ran because she was scared, not because we're over."

"Does she know that?"

"Give me one week."

Spence snorted. "I already bet Mitch you'd be back in two weeks, all alone, so I'll spot you an extra one."

"Thanks for the support, man."

"I love Carrie. I think you're great when you're actually together. Hell, I did a dance when she moved into your bedroom for those few months after Dad claimed the caretaker's cottage as his new residence." Spence shook his head. "And speaking of Dad, he keeps asking who's going to take over the farm and nursery operation when he's gone."

The comment knocked Austin mentally off stride. Dad had been grooming them ever since he insisted they major in environmental science and business if they wanted to have jobs to come home to after college. "Other than us?"

"He's on the hunt for grandchildren and told me twice to get serious 'because thirty is long enough to fuck around'— yeah, he said that."

The rough-edged voice played in Austin's head and he laughed. "I can almost hear him."

"I'd throw you a damn party if you could get Carrie down the aisle. Would take some of the pressure off me."

Since that was the plan, Austin didn't argue. "Happy to help whenever I can."

"Bottom line is no one is cheering harder for you than me." Spence's words tumbled to a halt. He stood there, staring off into the distance for a full thirty seconds before turning back to Austin. "I just think you're missing the signals here. I'd rather see you go back home and find someone who's not going to rip you apart."

"I'm fine."

"Yeah, well, I'm the one who fished you out of the ten-day bar binge after she left six months ago. The one who had to call Dad when everything went to shit."

Every day of those lost two weeks fell into a mental black hole. Austin remembered the beginning and turning to a bottle of scotch before working his way through a case. He drank at home and at work. He'd stayed in the town's only bar until it closed and waited in desperation until it opened again the next day.

Losing her had carved out a piece of him the liquor couldn't fill, though God knew he tried. If he were a different guy, and if he'd listened to Spence's advice back then, he would have screwed his way out of his anger over Carrie's decision to go. Let a long line of faceless women wash away her memory. Instead he'd turned to the bottle.

Or he had until he ran the tractor into the property's pond and sank it to the bottom. It didn't matter that he was twenty-eight and a grown man, or that he worked in a dangerous occupation, spending most of the day at the top of trees. He drank for ten solid days and kicked around in a haze for four more before that. But on that last drunken day, with his car keys in his hand, he headed toward his truck. Only a flash of common sense sent him to the barn instead. He saw the tractor and decided it would be brilliant to race it all over their land, saving him from hurting someone else.

He'd never driven drunk in his life, not even as a teenager. Thought people who did were irresponsible jackasses. But for a few seconds as an adult who should have known better, he'd toyed with the idea. The reality of how close he'd come to screwing up and taking his truck on a public road in that spaced-out state scared the shit out of him. And opening his eyes in the hospital to see the disappointment written all over his dad's face pulled Austin back from the edge of stupidity.

"Man, I promised you before. That's not going to happen ever again." His voice cracked on the words. He'd made a vow and he would not break it.

Spence's white-knuckle grip on the tree didn't let up. "It was fucked up. That's all I'm saying."

"I'm not arguing. That's why I've kept my drinking to an occasional beer since and limit even that to the house." And when he did, three pairs of eyes watched him. Even Mitch joined in.

For weeks after the accident Austin would find his office at the nursery a bit too perfect. Straight stacks of paper and unlocked file drawers. As the business manager, Mitch had a vested interest in conducting alcohol sweeps. When Austin assured Mitch he wasn't an alcoholic and made a promise to refrain from drinking in return for Carrie never hearing about those days, the covert searches ended.

"Ever tempted to lose control like again?" The tree shook in Spence's hand.

"No."

"That was a quick response."

"I don't need to think about it."

"It's just that…" Spence kicked the turf under his feet as his gaze turned down.

"I get it." Austin wrapped a hand around his brother's biceps. "I do."

He'd put them through hell and done a number on his body. Even now he'd head to the fridge during a game and all conversation would cease. It was like a collective breath holding until he returned with a soda.

"Despite all that other shit, I want this to work for you," Spence said.

Part of Austin wondered if his brother blamed Carrie for the death spiral. Austin refused to go there. He shouldered the guilt alone. He'd ordered the drinks and stumbled down that driveway. He had no one to blame for his stupidity but him. But he wasn't sure Spence saw it that way. "Is that why you agreed to come with me? A combination of babysitting and support?"

"You'd do it for me."

"Then you need to know I'm not leaving until she agrees to come home."

Spence shook his head. "You better work on your skills because I'd give you a D so far."

"Hey, I'm just getting started."

Nine hours and three cups of coffee later Carrie sat at her desk and tried not to stare outside. It wasn't her fault the window behind her computer monitor had a clear view of the tree lot across the street. Well, it did if she slouched down, ducked her head a little and peeked in the space between her clock and her pen holder. She also had to squint a bit, but she didn't have any trouble making out Austin as he walked around under the lights.

The slow stride of his legs. The confident way he stood with his shoulders back and his hands tucked into his back pockets. He talked and the broad smile never left his lips. She had to guess at that last part, but knowing him the smile was guaranteed. He buzzed around the lot, greeting all the customers and shifting trees from piles to cars without resting.

She'd missed so much about him. She could watch him work for hours, listen to his deep voice forever.

But she had other priorities now, ones he refused to appreciate and share. Despite long hours, the piles of work never seemed to go down. She glanced at the open file in front of her. She had to finalize the museum's summer education programs and get the contracts out to the artists and instructors who would fill the calendar. Too much procrastination and the deadlines stacked up. She had to get the agreements out, get the pamphlets printed and set up the advertising. The museum depended on the extra income, along with donations and grants, to pay for special exhibits.

Yeah, no pressure.

The black ink blurred on the pages in front of her. She rubbed her eyes, hoping to jumpstart her concentration. But her gaze wandered back outside and her stomach flip-flopped.

He was determined now, chasing her here and staying close, but how long would it last? She'd given him the chance months ago to come with her and live out her dream, and he told her to go alone. Being here now could be a mix of ego and loneliness, and she didn't want a part of either.

He had work and a life two hours away. From what she'd witnessed that morning, he didn't seem one inch closer to accepting the part of her life he didn't understand. He thought he could wait her out and believed he was being so subtle with his plan. About as subtle as being hit in the head with a brick.

But he *was* here. All six irresistible feet of him. And the months apart hadn't done anything to put out the fire inside that burned without end for him. She knew the sad drill. He wouldn't change, would get sick of waiting, would leave and her heartache would spike all over again. Her only choice was to ride this out and not believe in the show.

He hadn't changed and she wasn't ready to come home on his terms. That left little room for compromise. Not that he even understood the word.

She eyed her cell phone. Four calls to her scheming brother for an explanation about his role in this mess and all had gone to voice mail. Mitch was hiding. The coward. She'd see how he liked it if she called every hour until he answered.

She picked up the phone and her finger hesitated over the camera icon. She clicked. Her photos scrolled until she found the one she wanted, the one she stared at almost every day. Austin in his safety harness, what looked like miles above the ground in a tree.

She traced the outline of his body and smiled as she remembered that spring day. He sang some stupid made-up song off-tune as he shimmied up there. The carefree act eased her jumping nerves and made her forget about the danger, which had been exactly his plan. But that's what he failed to get. She accepted this side of him. She just wished he would do the same for her.

CHAPTER THREE

Spence finished locking up the trees on the right side of the lot before wiping his hands on his pants. "She never came back today."

"Thanks for highlighting the obvious." As if Austin needed that newsflash.

On one level he knew just seeing him wouldn't be enough to make Carrie realize she'd made a mistake and come running back to him...but a guy could fantasize. God knew he did that a lot when it came to her.

He dragged a net over the last tree on his side and dropped to his knee to rope the wire around the trunk then clicked the lock. Since he didn't plan on sleeping outside in the cold, he had to make sure he secured everything for the night. The two guards walking the outline of the lot would take care of the rest.

With the final close-up work done, he stood up and glanced at Carrie's apartment building. He hadn't been inside and had no idea which window belonged to her, but the restlessness kicking in his gut over the last few months wound down. Being close to her helped ease the anxiety pounding through him. She hadn't taken him back, but she would. He just needed time to convince her.

"It's not too late to cut our losses and get back home." Hope echoed in Spence's voice as he took up a position standing next to his brother.

Austin shot down that line of thinking before it took hold. "This is only the first day."

"I'm not convinced the rest of the days are going to go any better."

He treated Spence to a side-scowl. "You're not great with the brotherly support thing."

"How about this?" Spence turned around, blocking Austin's view of the building. "Why don't you go up to her apartment, apologize for being a giant ass and end this torture?"

"She needs romance."

Spence's eyes widened. "What the hell are you talking about?"

"Women like that shit." It made Austin's head pound, but a guy had to take a hit now and then to make his woman happy. Maybe this was the price he had to pay for being so flippant when she asked him to move to D.C. with her.

Spence folded his arms across his chest. "Define romance."

"Yeah, that's where my plan gets fuzzy."

"That's what I thought."

Austin ignored his brother's smirk and stayed on topic. "She thinks I don't care. I need to show her I do."

Spence threw his head back and laughed. "Priceless."

Yeah, his brother was going to die if he kept this up. "What?"

"Seeing you knocked on your ass by a woman." Spence shook his head, adding a tsk-tsking sound as he did. "After months of having every eligible woman, and some not-so-eligible, in Holloway knock at your door, now you're getting the cold shoulder."

"Do you want to be knocked on *your* ass?"

"I wish Mitch was here to see this. He's your best friend.

He really should have a front-row seat." Spence pulled his cell phone out of his back pocket.

Austin grabbed Spence's arm. "Press any button and you die."

"What, this?" Spence shook his phone. "I was looking up *romance* for you on the internet. Trying to help."

"I got this covered." Or Austin vowed he would once he spent all night thinking about formulating a plan.

Something or someone thumped against her front door early the next morning. At the sound, Carrie jumped and a black smudge of mascara slashed across her cheek.

"What the hell?" A glance at the small clock on her bathroom counter told her it wasn't seven yet.

After barely sleeping and hours of trying to kick the image of Austin's ridiculously handsome face out of her head, she'd showered and gotten as far as drying her hair and throwing on a robe before the thud. Thanks to the scare, the makeup application was a bust and would need a second attempt.

But first, the door. She wiped off the smear and dropped the tube into the sink. Stepping into the entry, she cursed under her breath and generally worked her nerves into a full-blown fury as she went. There were twenty apartments on her floor and if someone had wandered to the wrong door she'd scream. She glanced through the peephole and her planned unreasonable explode-on-a-stranger rage fizzled. A whirring mix of anxiety and unwanted hope spun around in her belly. The sound of whistling hit her a second later.

No, no, no.

She'd thought about Austin nonstop and now he appeared at her door and…she was a dead woman. No way would her shaky control withstand this. Staring at him through the safety of a window and from six floors up last night made her twitchy enough. Smelling him, seeing him, hearing him, being inches away from touching him. It was all too much.

To keep from bending, she focused on her frustration over his stubbornness. He pretended to listen to her talk about her job but he didn't really hear her. The anger at his refusal to see her as more than the woman who'd always been there for him washed over her. She let it fuel her until it pounded in her ears.

She threw open the door and glared. "How do you know where I live?"

"Uh, hello?"

How the man could look so yummy so early in the morning was a mystery. Hair ruffled from the air and a chill on his skin that swept over her from two feet away. The faded jeans and checkered shirt hanging open over a gray tee added to the scruffy, just-out-of-bed look that never failed to make her jaw drop.

She ended the visual tour with a practiced frown. "You can't possibly expect a warm welcome at this time in the morning."

"It's seven."

"Your point?"

He executed the perfect eye roll. "I've been up for two hours."

"You're not normal." Her gaze bounced down to his hands and she wondered how she'd missed the two cups of what looked like coffee and a white bag of something in the carrier.

The man knew how to get to her. She'd once joked about how a woman could forgive a lot for a man who brought her breakfast. She was trying to weasel a coffee run out of him at the time.

"You've enjoyed my early rising in the past," he said.

She bit down on her lip to keep from laughing at his dumb joke and the sexy smile that followed. "You haven't explained how you found me."

"We come from a town of, like, ten people. They lined up to tell me how to find you."

Traitors. "So, Mitch squealed. That would explain why he won't answer my calls."

"Your brother has to work with me." When she snorted, Austin talked louder. "Then there's the part where I threatened to kill him if he didn't spill."

"I'm going to smack the crap out of him when I see him again." She stood back and opened her arm to usher Austin out of the hallway. "Come in before we give the neighbors a show that will get me evicted."

"In that robe? I'd be willing."

Her skin warmed everywhere his gaze touched. She grabbed her lapels and gathered them in her clenched fist to stop that sort of thing. "I wasn't expecting company."

"I'm not complaining."

Her all but naked and his gaze traveling down her front spelled *disaster.* "I'll go get dressed."

Before she could shuffle off to the bedroom and lock the door behind her, he raised his hands. The move put the goodies he brought at eye level. "Are you sure you don't want to try these first?"

The smell of deep roast filled her senses. Hot man and hot coffee. Who could resist that combination?

"What's in the bag?"

"A cinnamon-swirl pound cake to go with your grande nonfat vanilla latte." He shook the bag as he spoke.

The evil coffee pimp remembered her usual order. "Lucky guess."

He walked into her kitchen and went to the silverware drawer as if he'd been in the apartment a hundred times. "You tricked me into a caffeine run almost every morning in Holloway once that joint opened the next town over."

"Tricked?"

"Maybe I should say bribed with sex and the promise of football tickets."

She leaned in the doorway and fell into the gentle rhythm of their comfortable conversation. "A gentleman wouldn't mention my methods."

"A gentleman wouldn't have jumped on the deal, but I did. On the deal. On you. All of it."

She eased up on the grip on her robe as she watched his lean fingers work on the lid and empty what looked like three pink packets into his coffee. And people accused her of having a sugar addiction.

"Those were good times," she said as the pictures played in her mind.

"But your mother's cinnamon rolls are better than anything I've been able to get in a store." He opened the bag and peeked inside.

"And more fattening."

He frowned. "Not a big concern for you."

Sweet talker. Carrie wasn't the weight-obsessed type but a healthy weight in Holloway was a good ten pounds heavier than an expected weight for the high-heeled, big-checkbook crowd she moved with at work.

"Every woman worries about her weight. Mine leveled out when I left Mom's kitchen." The daily hour on the treadmill also helped.

He dropped a slab of cake on the piece of wax paper stuck underneath it and slid it to the edge of the counter closest to her. "You have to miss those special meals. That woman can cook."

A skill she did not pass on to her daughter, not that Austin ever complained. Carrie had loved him for many things. His willingness to put up with her crappy meat loaf without gagging was one of them. He'd insisted she was getting better with each meal she made. She was just grateful she hadn't accidentally poisoned them.

"When will you try them again?" he asked.

Carrie picked up her breakfast but stopped in mid-chomp. "What?"

"When are you coming home to visit your family?" He took a sip of coffee and eyed her over the cup.

"Now you sound like Mom."

"She misses you."

Carrie threw the cake on the counter as the acid in her stomach bubbled. "Don't do that. Don't use family guilt to lure me back to Holloway."

"Fine." He pushed off from where he leaned against her stove and started toward her. "How about this? I miss you."

The words she'd longed to hear. The same ones that cut through her, bringing both pain and joy. Her heart spun but the knot in her stomach tightened.

"Austin…" She held up both hands in a halfhearted attempt to fend him off.

When he wrapped his fingers around her wrists and carried her wrists to the back of his neck, she didn't fight him. His scent washed over her senses, lighting every cell on fire. She smelled the cool outdoors on his skin, that subtle mix of pine and soap with a touch of fresh firewood.

The soft strands of his fine hair slid through her fingers as her body melted into his. The robe, his clothes, it all faded away. In her head, her soft skin smoothed over his rough edges.

His mouth danced in a trail from her ear and down her throat. Her heartbeat spiked in response.

"Am I supposed to pretend like I don't miss you? No way could I pull a lie that big off." His husky voice rumbled against her bare skin.

"You're not even supposed to be here."

"But I am." He blew the words across her lips.

She didn't know how much she'd wanted his mouth on hers until his tongue swept across her lips. The kiss started out achingly slow, brushing from one end to the other, until his mouth covered hers and her body sparked to life.

Demanding and hot, he kissed her until the breath left her lungs and her fingers dug into his shoulders. When he slid his hands down her back and pressed her deeper against him, waves of need crashed over her.

A groan escaped her lips, snapping her back to reality. In a flash, the roaring in her ears stopped and the sounds of life returned. The sharp clack of her kitchen clock beat out the minutes as she pulled back first emotionally, then physically.

She nudged his shoulders. "Austin, stop."

He did, just as she knew he would. He was rock solid and never used force, except for that one time she'd found the two ties he owned and asked him to go all he-man on her.

In slow motion, his arms slid against her sides until his hands dropped to her hips. "You okay?"

Stupid and half-dizzy from kissing him. Other than that, terrible. When a woman got knocked off her feet from the touch of a guy's lips, she wanted the feeling all the time. Knowing this was a temporary thing filled her with a flulike weakness that reached into her bones.

She cleared her throat. "Of course."

"Should I apologize?"

She stared into eyes the color of a cloudless summer day. "Are you sorry?"

"No."

She waited for the slap of regret to hit her but it never came. She could at least have this moment. Savor it. "Me, either."

His hands clenched into fists against her as if he was forcing his fingers not to hold on too tight. "Then?"

Stepping out of his arms was like ripping a strip of skin off an inch at a time. She almost screamed in pain as she left the warm circle of his body.

"I have to go to work."

He nodded. "Ah, yes. The museum."

Sadness crawled over her. She felt it spread until it infected everything. "I don't want to fight with you about this."

"Makes two of us."

"I know my career means nothing to you."

"Oh, Carrie. Come on." He threw his head back and stared at the ceiling. "That's not fair."

"This is my dream job. A position at a prestigious museum, mixing with people in the art world. Being close to masterpieces and seeing works some people will only ever experience in a textbook." When he finally gave her eye contact again, she poured all her intensity into the words to get him to understand. "I get to live them, to stand there, feeling the artist's emotions wash over me."

"Okay."

The air rushed out of her, taking her last bit of hope along with it. She'd struggled to find a new way to make him understand and failed again. "Forget it."

She'd left Holloway specifically to avoid scenes like this. She would explain and he would close down. He didn't say it, but she knew he viewed working in a museum as a hobby she would outgrow. That she'd fall into line and come rushing home again.

Rather than fight, she headed for the bedroom. This was her turf and she could abandon the fight if she needed, and with her emotions so close to the surface she needed to.

"Hey, wait a second." With a gentle tug, he turned her

around until they faced each other again. "All I said was okay and you're running."

"Austin, come on. This part of my life doesn't mean anything to you. You've never spent even one second getting to know what the work means to me."

"It's your world, not mine. I don't sit and talk about tree climbing with you."

She laid a hand against his chest and felt the steady thump of his heart beneath her fingers. "Do you really think it's the same thing?"

"Isn't it?"

"Okay, look. I can't do this. I have responsibilities and I have to get to them." She stepped back and fought the urge to run.

He exhaled, blowing a warm breath across her cheek. "Don't use that excuse. Talk to me."

These discussions never got them anywhere. They went around in circles, throwing out the same accusations and arguments. The spark between them hadn't died but it wasn't enough to hold them together, either.

He had to leave before she lost it.

"Thanks for the coffee, but for the future, I don't need a wake-up call. I bought a latte maker when I moved in here." She kissed him on the cheek and reached out for the wall behind her to keep from sliding to the floor.

"Mary Cassatt."

Everything inside her froze. It took all her strength to turn her head and look at him. "What?"

"Right now you're in charge of a lecture series surrounding the Mary Cassatt exhibit at the National Museum of Women in the Arts."

"How did you—"

He picked up his coffee cup off the counter. "I haven't spent more than ten minutes in a museum in my life. A discussion about art makes me look for a pen to stab in my eye sockets. Honestly, I'd rather watch soccer than hear anything about an artist ever, which should tell you something since I find soccer pretty boring."

Without even trying he listed some of the stumbling blocks between them. "See, that's what—"

"But it matters to you, so I made it a priority to know something about it."

The words slashed against her. "Since when?"

"Since you walked out and I realized I'd do anything to get you back." The flatness of his voice matched the bleak despair in his eyes.

"Austin."

He pointed toward the kitchen. "There's a salad at the bottom of the bag. From the look of you, you've been skipping lunch. Maybe that's a city thing, but you're beautiful without some damn diet. Eat."

Then he was gone and the hollowness in her stomach enveloped her.

CHAPTER FOUR

Carrie made it the whole way to the next evening before seeing Austin. Not that she was hunting him down or anything. Not that their talk yesterday ran through her mind all damn day until she had to give her cell to her intern to keep from calling him. She only skipped the gym and headed straight for the lot after work to check out the tree supply. Yep. That was her story.

Bundled in her coat and wearing the oh-so-sexy combination of a conservative navy skirt and white sneakers, she crossed the side street, dodged around a car that had been illegally parked near the building for two days, and passed under the string of white lights outlining the tree lot.

A group of people gathered around Austin. Being six feet, he towered over most as he laughed and smiled and generally wooed them with a story about a bobcat and tractor. His enthusiasm was infectious. When he laughed, her insides warmed.

His rapt audience smiled and clapped… Wait, audience? Make that his posse of women.

Over the steady thrum of traffic, Carrie scanned the lot in search of men other than the Thomas brothers and couldn't find one. Funny how all the women in the neighborhood congregated at this lot. Who knew there even were this many twenty-something women in the area?

"Little Carrie Anders." Spence gave his welcome from right behind her left shoulder.

The richness of his voice flooded her with an unexpected kick of longing. Something about him, seeing the brothers together, made her miss home.

"Spence."

"Good to see you, babe." He followed up the greeting with a strangling brother hug then set her away from him.

"Austin dragged you into this crazy plan, too?" The idea made her smile since Spence wasn't exactly the romantic type.

He groaned. "You'd think I'd be smarter than to get wrapped up in his mess."

"I've never been called a mess before."

Spence winked. "But you are a very lovely mess."

"Is Mitch hiding around here somewhere?"

"No, your brother is the real smart one in this scenario. He and my dad are running the place at home while we're here…" Spence swallowed his smile.

"Checking on me?"

"Let's go ahead and say it that way since it makes Austin seem more like a concerned boyfriend than a crazed stalker."

She let the label pass. No need to throw "ex" around. "Austin is determined but not a stalker."

"I'm happy you think so. That will save a lot on lawyer fees."

She had to laugh at that. Austin had many faults. She was tempted to make a list, but stalking was not one of them. He'd never hurt her or force her. Drive her crazy? Now that was a different story.

Carrie's good mood faded when she spied a woman hanging on his arm as he pointed to a tree. Carrie tore her gaze away from the big flirtation scene. She'd broken it off with Austin. That meant he could date, she could date…but surely he could see through that woman's fake laugh and even faker boobs.

Spence shifted his weight. The move put his body right in her line of sight. Since peeking around him seemed a bit over the top, Carrie stayed put.

"I'm just hoping Dad doesn't burn down the place by accident while we're gone," Spence said.

Carrie wondered if the comment amounted to another attempt to guilt her home. When he stared at her with those blue eyes so like his brother's and an expression somewhere between amusement and horror, she decided he was imagining what the office would look like when he returned.

Karl Thomas had raised two teen boys on his own. Picking up and vacuuming weren't exactly his priorities. He hadn't changed much now that Spence and Austin were adults, but his business success couldn't be questioned. He'd taken an overgrown piece of property and turned it into a thriving business that supported numerous employees and served four states.

Landscapers, designers, homeowners and fellow business folks came to Thomas Nurseries for help. Add in Austin's specialty as an arborist in managing the health and stability of plants and trees, and his contracts with the state, utility companies and the U.S. Forest Service, and they had everything from simple gardening to arboriculture to botany covered.

"Your dad ran the farm and business without you for years, so I'm thinking he can handle a few days," she said.

"You think Austin only plans to be here for a few days?"

Her stomach did a bounce against the hard ground. "Uh, yeah. I assumed this was a short-term offensive strike."

"You're kidding."

"So, weeks?"

Spence shook his head. "Either way, Dad's history is not as comforting to me as you might think."

A lot could change in six months, including someone's health. That thought sent panic spinning inside her. "Is he okay?"

Spence waved off her concerns. "Exactly the same. Ornery, driven and now, damn my luck, demanding a grandkid."

A laugh bubbled up before she could control it. "From you?"

"I'm capable."

"Of producing one or raising one?"

The area around Spence's mouth turned green. "Now that I think about it, neither. I'll keep practicing the method where I don't produce one."

"Probably wise."

Horns honked as three more women crossed the street on their way to the lot. No sneakers in this group. One had bare legs and four-inch heels. Carrie almost laughed. Yeah, those were perfect for this weather. The woman would have hypothermia in an hour if she didn't find some socks.

"You guys seem to be doing well." Carrie tried to block the grumbling she felt from sneaking into her voice.

"I gotta hand it to Austin. He's had a steady stream of customers all day." Spence crossed his arms over his chest and rocked back on his heels. "Apparently women like him. Who the hell knew?"

"I can think of a few people."

Spence leaned in as if telling a big secret. "I swear one woman has already bought two trees."

Well, wasn't that just terrific. "How festive of her."

"He should be done in a second. I know you're not used to being the one waiting, but Austin doesn't take long to close a deal."

"Okay." She turned Spence's words over in her mind. "Wait. What does that mean?"

A woman tugged on Spence's arm and he shot her that flirty Thomas smile before turning his focus back to Carrie. "I have to handle this."

It seemed handling women was a Thomas male specialty all of a sudden.

Austin steered the handsy woman with the low-cut sweater to a display of six-foot Douglas firs and snuck away. He'd hear her throaty giggle in his sleep. He could appreciate women of all sizes and types but this one freaked him out. So did the way she looked twenty years old from a distance and at least fifty close up.

Then there was the ass tap. He could have done without that. He didn't exactly run from her now, but he did double-time his retreat just in case those fingernails came out again.

The one woman he wouldn't mind touching his ass stood near the office shed. He wondered if Carrie realized she tapped her foot hard enough to create a divot in the frozen ground. Two seconds ago she'd been smiling and laughing with Spence. Now she had that unfocused look that meant she was thinking. Austin knew it probably also meant he'd done something wrong.

No need to pretend not to see her since he'd traveled to D.C. to find her. She knew the score and hard-to-get wasn't his thing. That was a woman trick. A smart man let himself get caught. He waved as he walked but dropped his hand when she didn't return the greeting.

Oh, boy.

Despite yesterday's big kiss, he kept the greeting professional. "Are you looking for a tree?"

"I better since you'll be sold out soon."

He glanced at the mound of trees stacked around the lot. "How do you figure that?"

"You have nonstop interest around here."

"Apparently the residents of D.C. like nice trees." He didn't even know what they were talking about anymore. She seemed a bit on edge for a discussion about future firewood.

"Like her?" Carrie's attention focused over his shoulder.

He turned and saw the handsy customer standing at the edge of the tree display and staring him down. "I'm not sure she's here for a tree."

Carrie shot him a men-are-so-dumb look. "Gee, really?"

That flat tone usually meant he'd done something stupid and male and he had about ten minutes to figure it out before she went all Medusa on him. "Why do I think I'm in trouble?"

"She gave you her number." Carrie nodded at his closed hand.

He opened it, palm up, and showed her the paper ball inside. "It's for the sales receipt."

The excuse was lame but no way was he going down for this. He hadn't done anything wrong except separate from the woman without shoving her away and hurting her, which hadn't been that easy since she all but wrapped her legs around him.

Carrie fingered the ball of paper but didn't say anything. He flipped her hand over and dropped the paper in her palm. To keep her from giving it back, he wrapped her fingers around it. "You can't possibly believe I'm interested in anyone else."

Yesterday's kiss burned through him. Holding Carrie broke through his control and had him wanting more. He'd used Mitch's emergency key last night after the lot closed to get in her apartment building but stopped short of knocking on her door. He could hear Spence's voice in his head and realized just showing up might actually cross the line to stalking.

Austin wanted to be invited in this time. Into her apartment, her life and her bed. That required the right balance of pushing and letting her lead.

Here he was figuring out his timing and the perfect touch and she thought he was making the moves on someone else. Man, for a smart woman she didn't always look at the clues and come to the obvious conclusion.

"Is this the plan?" The wind whipped up, taking Carrie's hair. She tucked it behind her ear before he could do it for her.

He wasn't sure how to answer or even what the question was, so he went with his usual response to rough conversations. "Excuse me?"

"Do you want to make me jealous?"

A breath held in his chest, scraping his insides raw. "Are you saying I still can?"

"Yeah, that's what I thought." She spun around, sliding as she went and marched away from him.

"Wait up." He'd about reached his end with her running. There had to be another way for her to deal with her issues. "Man, you get all prickly then run faster than any woman I've ever met."

"Good thing you're so popular. You can find another woman in no time." She started out shouting but lowered her voice when he pulled even with her.

He stopped her with a hand on her elbow. "To be clear, I've never flirted to make you jealous. Ever. I'm not dead. I can appreciate a pretty woman, and I might look now and then, but my hands don't wander, and you know that. Blame my dad for the example if you want, but fidelity is a big thing with me."

"We're not dating." The words stayed sharp but her voice lacked punch.

Still, they slashed through him with the brutal rip of a knife. "I disagree."

"You can see anyone you want."

Permission. That was just great. "I only want you."

"I don't… Are you…?" She nibbled on her bottom lip. "You're saying you haven't seen anyone else in six months?"

"Right."

Her eyes widened and he knew why. He didn't exactly lack in the sex-drive department. Nothing about their time together had been tame or G-rated. He hated being without her and had slept with her every chance he got, sex and actual sleep, over the years.

She shook her head. "I never asked you to refrain."

"I know."

"Then why did you?"

Her wide eyes told him she didn't know. She frustrated the crap out of him. "Because I'm not an animal."

She sighed as her head fell to the side. "I'm serious, Austin."

In the past he would have evaded the conversation, made a joke and moved on. Seeing Carrie now, every inch of her aware and engaged in his words, he didn't hide. "My mother has been gone for fifteen years and I've never seen my dad date another woman. When I started having sex and realized how good it was, I couldn't believe Dad was denying himself. I figured he had to be sneaking out and meeting someone."

A small smile played on Carrie's lips. "Was he?"

"Not that I could tell. I once asked him why he didn't move on and he told me he was a married man."

Carrie's eyes bulged at that one. "But your mom left."

Austin lifted Carrie's hand and brought it to his lips. "That changed who she was, not the promises he made. In his mind, he had an obligation to be a faithful married man."

Carrie brushed her palm over Austin's cheek. "You're a healthy male with needs and smile that attracts women from miles around. I don't expect you to deny yourself."

"You really want me sleeping with other women?" Her body bucked as if he'd hit her. The flinch gave him hope. "Yeah, that's what I thought. The idea of you with anyone else makes me crazed."

"I haven't…I mean, I'm not." She cleared her throat. "Not yet."

Relief plowed through him hard enough to knock him on his love-struck ass. Somehow, he kept his body upright and his voice even. "Mitch said you were dating."

"He was probably trying to make you nuts."

Austin tugged her even closer. "It worked."

"You should get back to work." She whispered the words just inches from his mouth.

The ground shifted. Not in a shattering earthquake type of way. This amounted to a tiny tremor, but Austin felt the subtle move all around him. The conversation provided an opening, a way in and back to her. Now he had to figure out how to use it without scaring the crap out of her.

"Why don't you go get changed and come back and look for a tree for real this time." He'd use Christmas or anything else he could think of to win her over and keep her close.

With a small kiss on his chin, she stepped out of his hold. "For both our sakes I better go home and stay there."

"Are you sure?" When she nodded he took a risk and asked the question playing in his mind. "Will you come back another time?"

She hesitated until he wiggled his eyebrows at her and she laughed. "Okay, fine."

"I'll be waiting."

"Not tonight. Tomorrow, and I'll bring you guys dinner."

He held a hand to his chest. "You know the way to a man's heart. Wait, you're not cooking are you?"

"Funny. And I'm taking care of your stomach. You're on your own with your heart."

He watched her walk away and thought about how wrong she was.

CHAPTER FIVE

This time Carrie came to the lot prepared for the cold weather and a duo of hungry men. She wore jeans and boots and her warmest scarf, the maroon one her mother had made for Christmas last year.

You could take a girl out of West Virginia but that didn't mean she'd lose her mind and forget how to dress for snow.

As usual, the lot buzzed with endless activity, most of it female. Both Spence and Austin worked the crowd, showing off trees and tying the precious purchases to the roofs of cars. They collected money as if it didn't matter, keeping all the focus on the clients.

Their dad had taught them that trick. She'd seen him do it a million times. Focus on the person in front of him as if there was no one else in the world.

Good thing she'd brought the thermos because this could be a long wait. She opened the shed door and heard the low rumble of voices. Not just voices, the familiar sound of football play-by-play.

"Leave it to Austin to find a rebroadcast of the West Virginia game on the radio."

Shaking her head, she set the bag of plastic containers down on the makeshift office's desk, along with the coffee and soup.

She'd almost made it back out when Austin stepped inside, bringing a gust of frigid air with him.

"Only a true fan would have the repeat game on when he can't be in the room to listen to it." She leaned over and fiddled with the knob on the side.

"Hey, what are you doing there?"

"Turning it off?"

His eyes grew wide in mock horror. "Rebroadcast or not, touching that dial would be a criminal offense."

"I'll settle for turning it down." And she did before he could yell about it. "Go Mountaineers."

"Could use more enthusiasm since they lose this one to Pittsburgh, but better." He blew on his gloved hands. "It's going to snow."

"You could always tell."

"Not sure if it's my innate ability to read the signs or the fact it started coming down a second ago."

She leaned in and glanced out the big window that overlooked the lot. "Ah, brilliant."

White flecks filled the near-black sky and landed on the tree branches. She inhaled and even through the walls could pick out the refreshing scent of pine, the same smell she associated with Holloway and hayrides and hours of racing around outside once the school cancellation announcement came across the crawl on the bottom of the television screen.

If she closed her eyes she could blink her way back to the wooded acres surrounding Austin's house and relive the last winter she spent there. The nights so deadly quiet except for the soft rustle of branches and slick click of icy snow as it fell and piled in feet-high stacks.

Austin slid a thigh onto the desk and studied her. "What are you thinking about?"

"Why?"

"You're smiling."

The memory filled her with the same comfort as a cozy blanket on a cold night. "Trudging through the snow until I could barely lift my leg and was so tired I almost fell over. Impromptu snowball fights and the rumbling sound of the snow blower."

"You're kind of making me hot."

She coughed out a laugh and kept going until she doubled over and her stomach ached. When she opened her eyes again, he was at her side with that soft expression of amusement on his sexy mouth.

He slipped an arm around her shoulders and pulled her body tight to his. "You okay there?"

"You make me smile."

His hand tightened on her arm. "Good to know."

"Everything about you tempts me."

"Then I'll stay quiet to keep from messing this moment up."

She turned in his arms, settling in and resting her palms against his chest. "You know this isn't about you or my feelings for you, right? It's never been a matter of being unsure about those."

He just stared at her.

She rested her forehead against his. "You can talk, you know."

A long breath escaped his chest and blew across her cheek. She could feel every last inch of him tense under her fingertips.

"Gotta be honest. The breakup feels like it's about me. I'm the one you left. That you keep leaving."

The sadness in those blue eyes zapped her strength and left her weak and shaking. She searched for the right words to shift the blame back to her where it belonged.

Fancy explanations and big psychology words filled her

brain. She pushed it all out and went with the simple truth. "I don't want to be my mother."

His eyes narrowed but his hands kept up their soothing brush against her back. "I don't get it."

"Mitch and I have known for a few years that we're the reason she stayed in West Virginia, with my dad. In the family."

"I still don't—"

Carrie pressed a finger against Austin's lips. "She wanted out. Still wants out."

"Maybe you're being hard on her? She may not be perfect but she's a hell of a mom. Always there for you no matter what."

With Austin's fractured family background, having a mom who managed to hang around and stuck it out likely seemed damn near perfect. His life made her explanation even harder. "She's there in body only."

Austin, always so sure with his words, stumbled and stammered until he finally got a sentence out. "She can cook a meal for fifty people without blinking. She came to every event for you and Mitch, and stayed up for the end of every date when I brought you home like she was a member of the kissing police or something."

"Baking and sewing, yeah, she taught herself all of it because her mother told her that's what good wives did." And Carrie's mother had refused to pass on any of the kitchen wisdom. Whether on purpose or not wasn't clear, but the list of supposed wifely virtues skipped right over Carrie.

Austin put a hand under her chin and lifted her gaze to his. "I'm lost."

She fought to bring back the memory she'd worked so hard to trample and erase. "She wanted to be a journalist. To see the world. The job at that dinky penny saver is as close as she got to roaming in search of stories that mattered to her."

"You're making a leap from your mother's college major and current hobby to a life of dissatisfaction."

Carrie wished that were true. She'd give anything for Austin to be right...but he wasn't. "I lived it. Saw how desperation and disappointment could eat away at a person until there was nothing left. No dreams or hope."

The way her mom sat at one end of the dinner table and stared down to the other end with eyes filled with anger. A misplaced comment about how there was nothing left for her or a harsh joke about how Carrie's father ruined everything. Jokes her father never joined in.

Her parents didn't have an easy give-and-take or even a steady comfort. They laughed and smiled, but never while in the same room together. The separate beds and separate bedrooms amounted to more than a hint about their coexistence. They tolerated each other and nothing else.

"Did she tell you all of this?" Austin asked in a low voice as his thumb traced the outline of Carrie's lower lip.

"She never planned to get married. She got pregnant. Mitch's birth certificate gave that part and his real birthday away. The diary we found in the attic when we cleaned it out for her to make a sewing room told us the rest." The words were burned on her brain until they blurred in front of her.

"Damn."

"She settled on a life she didn't want and has spent forever being bitter about it."

"Have you asked her about the diary and what it means?" The doubt in his words came through. He all but shouted his denial.

"I don't have to. I can see it in everything she does. She gave up her dreams and regrets her choices."

Austin's hands fell from her sides. "And we're not just talking about her right now."

Carrie's heart thundered. She was surprised it didn't pound right out of her chest. "No."

"You're afraid the same thing will happen to you."

All the pressure and all those fears bubbled up to the surface. "I can't look back twenty years from now and hate myself, and you, for not at least trying the life I've always wanted."

Everything boiled down to those simple statements. Imagining a life where she hated Austin and their kids for all they stole from her? She couldn't do it. Couldn't risk it.

"Hey." Spence stuck his head in the door. The red nose and cheeks either meant he'd reached ice-cube level or the fury inside him spiked his temperature.

From his severe frown, she wasn't sure she wanted to know. "Do you need something?"

"Sorry to break up the lovefest, but we have about a thousand people out here wanting trees." Spence focused all of his intensity on Austin. "I think I spied a bus of gawking women waiting for a sighting of you, so let's go."

Austin didn't look at his brother. "I need a second."

Spence stepped inside and closed the door behind him, trapping them all in the small space. "You're not getting me here, little brother. If you don't get out here I am going to kill you. Probably with one of our Christmas trees."

That time Austin broke eye contact with Carrie and turned to Spence. "We'll be right out."

"You'll go now while I take two seconds to warm up."

Before Austin blew up, she put a hand on his forearm and nodded. "We're okay. Go."

He grumbled something about wishing he was an only child and stomped out of the shed. He slammed the door on his way. As if they needed another sign of his anger.

"Grumpy, isn't he?" Spence smiled as he dug into the bag she brought.

Amazing how all that outrage disappeared as soon as Spence found the food and Austin got pushed into the cold. Carrie shook her head in reluctant respect over Spence's calculating plan. "That outrage thing was fake?"

"The threat and forcing him out of here? Yeah." Spence held up the thermos and shook it. "Soup?"

"Chicken noodle."

"Homemade?"

"Only if you want to be poisoned."

"Still a fine chef, I see."

She refused to spend one second feeling guilty. Finding pre-prepared dinners in the upscale grocery stores in town was not a hardship. "I can order with the best of them."

Spence poured a cup and then blew on it. It took another few seconds for him to stop eyeing up the food and look at her again. "What?"

"Your brother is not happy with you."

Spence's eyebrow lifted. "Are we sure I'm the problem?"

"He didn't threaten to kill me."

"Actually, I did the threatening, but if you're worried you go out there and help him."

Realizing she wasn't going to win this argument, or any Thomas argument for that matter, she pulled her gloves back on and headed for the door. She stopped right before she opened it. "May I ask you something?"

"Anything."

"Where are you two staying while you're in D.C.?"

"Spent one night in a total dive off New York Avenue and are lucky to still be alive. The rats had claimed the shower, so we went without." Closing his eyes, he took a long and savoring drink of the soup. "Now we're staying in the basement of a guy Austin knows from the Forest Service. He's in the middle of a divorce and needs the cash."

Sounded like more money Austin couldn't afford to spend. "It's an odd arrangement for grown men."

"Austin will do anything for you." Spence toasted her with the thermos cup. "Even if it means sharing a ratty old sofa bed with me. Way I look at it, you both owe me."

CHAPTER SIX

Austin watched Carrie walk around the lot the next evening. The lights danced against her hair as she studied the branches and dodged the icy patches in the grass.

Unlike some other ladies looking at trees, Carrie wore her sturdy West Virginia weather gear and had her hands tucked into her jacket pockets. She had the unapproachable and un-interested thing down, but he knew the warmth blooming under all those layers. The blank expression didn't fool him.

"This is the fifth day in a row she's been here. I guess you are irresistible." Spence looked Austin up and down then scoffed. "You hide it well."

"She must not be sold on my charm either since she's still fighting me so hard."

"Did I miss something? Because when I walked in on you guys yesterday in the trailer you were all over each other."

What Austin wouldn't give to be over her, under her, next to her. He'd take any part of her at this point. Any sign that he had a shot and wasn't wasting his time. "Hardly."

"More action than I'm getting."

Austin wasn't touching that. He had more important things to worry about than his brother's temporarily derailed sex life.

"She's afraid she's going to end up like her mother, resenting her life because she didn't go out and see the world."

"Are you serious?"

"Unfortunately."

"So, she's picking the world over you. Interesting." Spence covered his laugh with a fake cough.

"Happy you're amused."

"It's all a bit New Age for my taste. City folks tend to make easy things difficult. I'm convinced they like the stress."

Austin agreed. Tiptoeing around Carrie's moods took a lot of energy. He found the whole game they were playing a nuisance, but a supportive boyfriend kept that kind of thing to himself if he ever wanted sex again. And he did.

"She just needs to experience some of what's out here then she can come home," he said.

"Do you know how condescending that sounds?"

"I'm telling the truth."

Spence shook his head. "I see an idiotic plan in your future."

"She's seeing the world now. It's just a matter of her realizing D.C. is not that much different from home and giving in."

Austin replayed the comment in his head right after he said it. Even he had to admit the words sounded stupid all strung together like that. He'd all but been chest-pounding. Not his finest moment to be sure.

"Have you looked around?" Spence pointed around the lot, twice stopped on a blonde hovering near the office steps.

"What?"

"The woman." Spence adjusted his aim. "Not that one. I mean Carrie."

"I have no idea what you're talking about."

"It's not just about the traffic and the tall buildings. This place is different. I'm betting that museum she works in is a step up from the crappy tourist gallery she worked at in Harper's Ferry."

All good points. Since he didn't have a good response, Austin decided to ignore them.

Spence shook his head. "You're still clueless."

"I agree." Carrie snuck up on them and shouldered her way between them.

Austin almost launched into a half apology, half explanation until he saw the smile on her face. Whatever she overheard hadn't ticked her off. Got lucky for once. "You don't even know what Spence is talking about."

She handed her coffee cup to Spence after he stared at it without blinking for what felt like a half hour. Folding her hands in front of her, she smiled. "I heard the word *clueless* and assumed he meant you."

Austin made a face and pretended to be offended, even though they all had enough experience with each other to know it would take a hell of a lot more than that. "That's harsh."

Spence took a sip then closed his eyes in a look of appreciation seldom reserved for caffeine. "I think she's reading you about right."

As far as Austin was concerned there was one person too many in this discussion. He pointed at the one who needed to leave. "Spence, go away."

"Subtle."

"I could have dumped the coffee on you instead."

"I'm going to take this drink and see if the lovely lady over there needs my help." With that Spence made a direct line for the woman with the low-cut shirt and a jacket better suited for a cruise ship than winter.

Carrie rolled her eyes while Spence dropped his best line. "Some things never change."

Austin wished he could make that true. "You find the right Christmas tree yet?"

"Still looking."

The stalling had to be a good sign. She'd stared at the same three trees for days. The process shouldn't be that hard. You went out, picked a tree and dragged it home. Anything more bordered on obsession.

He hoped he was the real reason for her sudden lack of decision-making abilities.

"Carrie? Is that you?" A guy in his midthirties with a wide smile and strangely unmoving hair despite the wind appeared in front of them.

Austin hated the guy on sight. Hated everything. The shoes, the key ring he kept spinning on his finger. Everything.

"Shawn." A smile replaced the shock on Carrie's face. "What are you doing here?"

"My sister lives nearby and was raving about this lot." He took her hand and didn't seem all that inclined to let go.

Austin's fingers inched toward his pocket knife.

"I bet." She waved her arm. "Apparently all the women love this lot."

"And you?" the guy asked.

"I live right there." Carrie finally broke off the touching with the guy and pointed at her building.

Little did he know how close he came to getting that hair messed up, along with a few other body parts.

Austin stopped plotting his attack and held out his hand. "And I'm her boyfriend."

She rolled her eyes. "Ex."

"That's up for debate."

"Austin is a friend from my hometown."

Carrie rushed in with that explanation a little too quickly for Austin's liking. "Really? That's what you're calling me?"

This Shawn guy ignored the conversation and pretended Austin wasn't even there. "It's nice to see you outside of work. I didn't know you even owned blue jeans. I've only ever seen you in a skirt."

Austin decided right then there was something wrong with the men in this town. That line? Jesus.

He folded his arms over his chest and leaned against Carrie. "That is some amazing flirting right there."

"Austin, stop."

Shawn finally focused on the other man in the conversation. "Excuse me?"

Carrie put her hand on Austin's arm...and pinched. "He's being difficult."

"For any specific reason?" Shawn asked.

"It's his personality."

When she almost drew blood , Austin pulled his arm out of her grasp. "Some women find me charming."

She frowned at him. "Not at the moment."

Shawn's gaze traveled between them before settling on Carrie. "Want to help me look for a tree?"

"I don't think that's good idea."

"Go ahead. Don't let me stop you." This could work. Good ole Shawn might be just the person Austin needed to shake up Carrie.

She wanted to live a little. Fine. She could do it with Austin right there beside her. Let her look at the guy with the curly blond hair and the all-over Art Garfunkel look and do an up-close-and-personal comparison.

Her eyes narrowed to you-are-so-dead territory. "What are you up to?"

Shawn's mouth fell open. It moved a few times before any words came out. "Is there a problem here?"

"Depends." Austin shifted his weight until most of his body was in front of hers. "Are you looking for a date?"

Poor Shawn blinked about fifty times. "With you?"

Now there was a misfire. "With Carrie here."

She tugged on Austin's arm until he faced her. "What are you doing?"

"I'll be there, too."

"When?"

"With you two." It was as if she didn't know him at all. As if he'd actually set her up with some other dude. No fucking way.

She started tapping her foot and that was never a good sign. "Then how is that a date?"

"Consider it a get-to-know-you thing."

"I know you just fine already." She leaned in, putting her mouth right next to his ear. "And, for the record, you're hovering on that stalker line."

He viewed this as a practical way to prove a point. "Really?"

"If I say yes, will you stop?"

Shawn stuck his head between them. "Do you two need to talk alone for a second?"

"Friday, tomorrow, at that Italian place around the corner." Austin almost choked on the words, but in his brain he knew this was right. "You and Carrie."

Shawn's smile grew until his face resembled a perfect target. "That sounds great."

"I didn't say yes," she reminded them.

"Technically, he didn't ask anything. I did it for him." Austin cuffed Shawn on the shoulder, not as hard as he wanted to but harder than he needed to. "You have to step up there, man."

"I'm, ah, not even sure what's happening."

Austin felt a little bad about the other guy's sudden stutter.

He gave off the put-together vibe and in less than five minutes had fallen apart.

"We're having dinner with Carrie. Tomorrow at seven." Austin glanced at his watch but had no idea why.

The smile on Shawn's face lit up his eyes. Then his face froze. "Wait. Did you say we?"

She nodded. "Believe it or not he did."

Austin took Shawn's shock as a good sign the plan might work. "Yes."

Shawn coughed twice before he spit any words out. "I thought you meant me and Carrie."

Wrong answer. Austin debated whether to let the guy live long enough to have dinner. "That's not going to happen."

Carrie sighed. "Anyone want to ask me?"

Austin shot Shawn a man-to-man look. "She's just nervous. Hasn't dated in a while."

"I'm getting a headache," she mumbled.

"You're supposed to say that at the end of the date to get rid of Shawn here."

"Austin, stop." Her voice echoed across the lot. More than a few patrons glanced over to see what was happening.

Shawn didn't wait around for the plans to fall apart. "Maybe I should go. I can call you tomorrow."

Austin wanted to let Shawn leave but the comment begged for another question. "Don't you two work together?"

"She's at a conference out of the office tomorrow," Shawn explained.

Austin already lost interest in the explanation. He'd planted the seed, so as far as he was concerned Shawn could leave now. "Sounds like a waste of a day."

"Not at all. It's about the foreign market for lithographs and—"

Looked like the guy was hunkering down for a painful art

lesson of some sort. The hands and mouth were moving, so Austin cut him off before his head exploded. "You already lost me."

Shawn stopped moving around. "I didn't really say anything yet."

"He means he's bored." Carrie didn't smile but Austin could hear it in her voice.

"Who doesn't like art?" Shawn asked as if the idea was un-American.

She hitched her thumb in Austin's direction. "Him."

He nodded. "Me."

Shawn's hands started flying through the air again. "But civilizations use—"

Austin shook his head and felt a kick of satisfaction when the motion alone stopped Shawn from saying anything else. "Nope. Still don't want the lecture. Save that for the big date."

"Right. See you tomorrow, Carrie." Shawn's smile faded when he faced Austin. "Nice meeting you."

The guy was off. He waited for the light before crossing the empty street, but he never looked back.

So much for Shawn coming to this part of town for a tree.

"I don't think he meant that about it being nice to meet me," Austin said.

Carrie stared after her friend, or whatever the hell he was. "Is there a reason you're acting like my pimp?"

Austin knew he should wince at that comment but he ignored it instead. Seemed safer. "You wanted to experience life before you came back to Holloway."

"When did I say that?"

"I'm helping."

She tapped his forehead. "You're insane."

"Not the first time you've accused me of that."

"You do realize you just set me up on a date with another man."

The words made Austin's back teeth slam together. He thought of the whole thing as an experiment. Tagging it as a real date would make Austin the biggest idiot in town. For now, he wasn't ready to wear that honor. "You're forgetting I'll be there."

She snorted. "How in the world could I forget that?"

"Shawn is not your type."

"What are you talking about? We work together and have the same interests. Shawn is nice and hasn't shown a serial killer side so far."

If Mitch knew her low-level dating criteria he'd probably hide her in a shed in Holloway until she turned sixty. "Is that your only test for seeing someone?"

"I'm saying on paper Shawn is perfect for me."

Since she almost yawned when she said it, Austin knew she didn't believe her theory any more than he did. "In real life he comes off as a douche. And he's got that springy hair thing going on."

"Care to tell me why?"

"I guess he was born with the hair. Hate to think he did something to make it look like that on purpose."

She talked right over Austin. "I mean, why are you doing all of this?"

He debated telling her the truth and gave in. He'd waited so long. All he wanted was her home by Christmas. Then they could make plans for next year. "You need a guy who challenges you. Who you can't push around. Sitting there, with the two of us, you'll see that you'd walk all over that guy."

"It sounds like you just called me a bitch without actually saying the word."

Austin kept his mouth flat as he held up his hands. "Whoa."

"This is dangerous. You don't know what could happen. Maybe I'll fall for him instead of you."

"Unlikely."

"You're so confident?"

He was until she used his ego for toilet paper. "I know you."

"If this works out with Shawn you'll have no one to blame but yourself."

Now she was just messing with him. Austin shoved the Carrie-plus-Shawn possibility out of his head as fast as it came in. "Answer one question. Does the idea of that guy kissing you make your heart beat like crazy?"

She actually made a face. She quickly hid it, but it was too late. "We haven't—"

"I'll take that as a no."

"You're awful sure of your appeal."

"I'm sure of us. Of this." Before she could pull away, he leaned in and pressed his mouth over hers. His hands settled on her waist as his lips crossed and caressed.

Heat, need, pulse-pounding want. It all rushed up on him. As soon as the kiss started he had to pull back or risk dragging her across the street to her apartment. Six months was a long time. As far as he was concerned, he deserved a damn medal.

But since he was determined to have her understand she meant more to him than a temporary bed partner, he dropped his hands. Unable to fully break the contact, he rested his cheek against hers and felt her smile.

"You're breaking the hearts of all the women on the lot," she said.

As if he gave a damn about any other woman.

"The hammering you feel?" Right there, just inches apart, he placed her palm over his heart. "You do that to me."

He dropped a quick kiss on her lips because he didn't trust his body for more. "Remember that at date time."

CHAPTER SEVEN

The next day at the conference Carrie rounded the corner with her head down and mind lost in an article about Interpol's Stolen Artwork Database and smacked right into something. Papers flew and her ankle turned. Swearing before she could control it, she put her hands out and hit biceps.

When her eyes focused again, she saw an aqua tie. Following it up, she met Shawn's shocked gaze. "Uh, hi?"

"Are you okay?" Concern showed on every inch of his face right before he bent down to pick up her scattered papers.

In his midthirties, he was smart and charming and objectively good-looking for a guy with hair resembling a sponge. But he barely registered on her hot-o-meter. In fact, she wasn't attracted to him at all and worried Austin's scheme would backfire by making Shawn think there could be something between them. She didn't want to hurt Shawn, though the idea of injuring Austin sounded good right about now.

"Carrie, did I do something to you when we hit? Can you talk?"

Where Austin knew she could split and stack wood with no trouble, Shawn acted as if she were made of glass.

His response made her want to poke fun at the situation. "The headache will pass in a month or so."

All of the color left his face. "I'm so sorry."

"It was a joke." One Austin would have gotten but flew right over Shawn's head.

"What?"

Time for a change in topic. "You didn't tell me you were signed up for today's conference."

"I'm here to see you."

That got her to let go of him and take a good step back. "Why?"

"Yesterday."

She let out a long groan but only inside her head. "Yeah, about that."

"I wasn't expecting that sort of greeting."

Probably because he wasn't a crazy person. "Not surprising."

"It was, well, weird."

Poor guy sounded traumatized from Austin's bizarre behavior. She sure was. "Austin has a strange sense of humor."

"Was his display supposed to be funny?"

"Good question. I think he was trying to prove a point."

"You're dating him."

This was where the definitions got tricky. Present tense. Past tense. She could be clearer if there was a tense that stood for *sometimes.*

She shifted from one foot to the other as she weighed her words. "We've gone out over the years. He still lives in West Virginia."

Shawn lowered his voice as a group of conference attendees, all with shiny name badges, walked down the other side of the hall. "But he's in D.C. now."

"Confusing, isn't it?" From the way Shawn's eyebrows snapped together she could tell it was. "Look, forget about tonight."

"We should go to dinner."

She was going to strangle Austin. Might even use her favorite scarf to do it. "You're a very nice man, but—"

"Not that. I mean all of us."

"Excuse me?"

"Your boyfriend—"

"Ex."

"—wants you to go. He clearly wants to make a point." Shawn shrugged. "My suggestion is that we play this out to see what he really has in mind."

Well, well, well. Look at Shawn being all conniving. She liked it. "You'd be willing to go through heaven knows what for me?"

Shawn laughed. "You think I'd miss this?"

"It is kind of frightening to think what Austin has brewing." She could only imagine what went on in that messed-up head of his.

"And if we're wrong and his intentions are good—"

"Doubtful."

"We can have a nice dinner." When she started to say something, Shawn stopped her. "As friends only."

She held out her hand. "You have a deal."

Shawn smiled. "And I think we should get there a half hour early. See if walking in after the supposed date has started knocks your man off stride."

Carrie frowned at how right the "your man" description felt. Despite all the craziness and cluelessness, with every word Austin wormed his way deeper into her heart. She should be furious with his interference in her life, but when she tried to dredge up some fury and write him off as a stalker type, she couldn't. She knew he'd never hurt her and would leave if she insisted. She just couldn't find the words or the will to order him gone.

"That could be interesting." And by that she meant nuts.

"I'm counting on this being the most entertaining date of my life."

She feared it would be.

Austin buttoned his shirt over a clean gray tee. He kept shifting the small mirror on the office wall to get a good look at his teeth. Hard to impress a woman with food in your teeth.

Spence let the door close with a bang when he came in. "What kind of idiot sends his girlfriend on a date with another guy?"

"Your quick-thinking brother, and this isn't really a date. I'm going to be there."

"I hope this kind of stupid isn't in the genes."

Since he forgot a comb, Austin used his fingers. It wasn't as if Carrie expected him to show up in a tux. "This is the perfect solution."

"Are you sure because it sounds pretty damn dumb."

"She's not interested in this other guy." She'd barely looked at Shawn in the lot yesterday. Austin knew that was because she was too busy glaring at him, but that fact didn't support his argument, so Austin kept it quiet.

"Yet."

The word hung out there just long enough to make Austin twitchy. "Shawn is not her type."

"This is the same guy who works with her and shares her interest in the art world, are we talking about that guy?"

Austin took a second to analyze those facts then discarded them because they didn't fit in with his plan. "She needs something else. We'll both be sitting there and she can compare. Seeing us both she'll realize whatever else she wants to change about her life, she wants to keep me."

Spence sat on the edge of the desk. He wore his usual big

brother I-know-better expression. "Have you taken a good look at her lately? The suits and the job. She fits here."

"For now."

Spence whispered something that sounded suspiciously like "dumb bastard" under his breath. "Does she know that all of this so-called romancing you're doing is aimed at bringing her back to Holloway rather than accepting her job and coming up with a compromise?"

Compromise. Carrie used that word a lot before she left home. She hadn't said it since. He got that she liked her job, but he wanted her to need him more.

"I have to go or I'll be late."

"Hold on a second." Spence hesitated as if turning the situation over in his mind. "You'll be chaperoning this date and I'll be working the lot alone?"

Austin waited for the full truth to hit his brother. "Yes."

"On the Friday night, two weeks before Christmas. The busiest time for people to buy trees." The longer he talked, the slower Spence's pace got until a beat of silence separated each word.

"I'm still going with yes."

Spence stood up, hands on his hips and ready for battle. "Will you be saying yes when I throw you in traffic?"

Knowing the argument was coming, Austin had worked out a contingency plan. Not a great one, but a workable one. "The security guys can help you for a few hours until I get back."

"Hours? As in more than one?"

"I won't be long."

Spence pointed out the window at the guard circling the lot and eyeing up the potential customers as if they were terrorists waiting to attack. "That one has a neck the size of a utility pole."

Which was exactly why Austin hired him. "Then he should be able to lift trees onto cars without getting a hernia."

"You're paying them to watch the lot and make sure our inventory isn't stolen while we sleep. Another bill you're fronting, by the way." When Austin stepped toward the door, Spence shifted and blocked any attempt at a speedy exit. "Did you rob a bank and not tell me?"

Austin wasn't touching that question. He'd cleaned out a hefty portion of his savings. Between the engagement ring and the D.C. trip, it was a good thing he didn't have to put a down payment on a house anytime soon. "Carrie is worth it."

"I'm not arguing with that."

He'd tried joking and explaining and failed. This time Austin went with the simple bottom line. "I need to do this."

"What you need is meds."

"Probably true but I'll settle for convincing her to come home with me."

Spence exhaled in a sound weighed down by the burden of being the older brother. "I'm betting it won't be that easy."

"Nothing ever is for us."

"You know she left more than twenty minutes ago, right?"

"*What?*"

"Figured you'd missed that." Spence opened the door. "Try not to be arrested."

Austin was still stunned by Carrie getting the drop on him and leaving early. "I can't promise that."

CHAPTER EIGHT

They made it to the end of the salad course before Austin wandered in. He walked over, waved off most of the waitstaff and did not stop until he hit the side of their table.

Austin shot Shawn one of those hard-to-read smiles that could go either way—furious or happy. "Did we change the time and no one told me?"

To his credit, Shawn shrugged off a threat, implied or otherwise. "Carrie and I decided to start without you."

"Fair enough." Austin's shoulders visibly relaxed. "How are we doing?"

Since this likely meant the end of the rational part of the evening, Carrie dragged the napkin off her lap and folded it on the edge of the table. "Before or after this minute?"

"Funny."

"Shouldn't you be working?"

"Spence can handle it, and I promised I'd join you, so here I am." Austin turned around and in five seconds sweet-talked the table next to them out of their extra chair. Dumping it in the small space next to her, he sat down and scanned the table. "What is everyone eating?"

"I ordered the halibut," Shawn said, sounding calm despite the arrival of Hurricane Austin.

Shawn's acting skills impressed Carrie. Austin had been there only for a few minutes and she had to fight off the urge to roll her eyes about a hundred times already. She had no idea how far Austin intended to go with this, but she knew she'd only be able to take so much.

"Fish?" Austin made a face. "I don't have to look at the menu and can tell you Carrie ordered something with four legs."

Not that her meat-and-potato ways were a big secret. "Yes, but I'm hoping they remove those before they put the meat on the plate and serve dinner."

"You don't like fish? I would have thought you were a fisherman." Shawn leaned back in his chair, clearly enjoying the byplay.

"Why?" Austin asked.

"Because you're from West Virginia. I assumed you fish and hunt." Shawn's gaze went to her. "Is that offensive?"

Austin took a sip of her water before waving the waiter over. "Being from West Virginia?"

"My comment placing you as an outdoors type."

"Outdoors type?" Austin let out with a *hmpf.* "Been called a lot of things before but never that."

"Austin likes to pretend he's a country hick, but he's actually smart." She looked him up and down and frowned as she did, just to let him know her patience with his acting was waning. "Well, usually. And a college graduate with a whole bunch of certifications for his work."

Austin nodded. "Took the refrigerator off the porch long ago."

"Not married to your sister?" Shawn's burst of laughter died out when no one joined him.

"Oh, no, Shawn. I can make fun of West Virginia." Austin used her water glass to point but his voice stayed light.

"You can't. You have to be from there to get away with the hick jokes."

Shawn cleared his throat. "Right. Sorry."

The waiter appeared at the table with another place setting. "Are you joining the table, sir?"

"Actually, there were supposed to be three chairs from the start," Austin said.

"My mistake," Carrie mumbled so only he could hear.

"Well played." He winked at her before turning back to the waiter. "Yes. I'd like my own water and whatever she's having."

The waiter's fake smile fumbled. "Your meal may take a bit longer than theirs."

"That's okay. I don't plan on eating it anyway."

The waiter's eyes narrowed. "Sir?"

"It's fine." Carrie let the poor man go before Austin drove him over the edge then she turned to the cause of most of the evening's difficulties. "I'd remind you this is a date."

Austin reached into the bread basket and rummaged around, ignoring the bran roll and heading right for the white-flour option. "I know. I set you two crazy kids up. With a third, of course."

"Dates usually mean two people," she said, not caring at all about the date. Austin might have a point to make, but so did she.

"Not in West Virginia," Austin said.

Shawn just looked confused. Had the whole eyebrows-pulled-together thing going on. "Pardon?"

This time she did roll her eyes. "The stereotypes about our home state are bad enough without you adding to them."

"Like the whole people living on farms and men swinging from trees?" Austin slathered butter on his roll and popped a strip into his mouth.

She wondered what else to try since eye rolling clearly wasn't working. "Are you done?"

"Do you climb, Austin?" Shawn asked.

"Climb what?"

Shawn's face went blank. "I don't—"

Just when she thought the evening couldn't get stranger. "I think Shawn means hike."

"Ah. I thought you meant trees." After spreading most of the remaining butter on his last piece of roll, Austin put it on the small plate in front of him.

"You really climb trees?"

"It's my job."

Shawn threw back his head and laughed. People at the table next to them stared. When no one joined in this time, either, he immediately sobered. "Wait, you're not kidding?"

"Have the shoes with the spikes in them to prove it."

Austin made the job sound simple. She knew differently. He risked his life because he thrived outdoors and had a love of nature in his blood. Another love passed on from his father. She'd never been anything but proud of Austin's work and his dedication to it. He didn't let fear or weather or anything else stand in the way of doing a job. She envied his laserlike focus.

"Austin is an arborist. He checks the health and placement of trees. He often works with the utility company, sometimes with government entities and private landowners."

"Interesting." Shawn shifted in his seat and leaned in with that just-between-men look. "I do some high adventure activities myself."

Carrie debated leaving the men alone to fight this out. They didn't need her. Not with all the testosterone pumping around them.

"At the museum?" Austin asked, managing to sound serious as he did.

"On the weekends. Kayaking and hiking, that sort of thing."

One of Austin's eyebrows lifted. "I'm impressed."

"There's a group of us that goes out with a guide."

The brow dropped. "Not as impressed now."

"We go through training."

"That sounds safe."

Between the sarcasm and clanking of glasses, she had just about enough. "Austin."

He didn't ask "what did I do" but it was there in his expression. "What? Safe is a good thing."

If Shawn was offended by the macho display or circular conversation, he didn't show it. He stayed engaged. "You prefer things a bit more risky, I take it."

"Some things. Other things I want consistent and sure." Austin's voice dipped low and husky as he talked.

The tone licked at her. She swallowed a few times, trying to break the sudden clog in her throat. "Are we still talking about climbing?"

The corner of his mouth kicked up. "No."

"Maybe I should leave." Shawn mumbled his comment but was already standing up.

"Sit." She pointed at the chair and didn't stop until Shawn dropped back down. Then she turned to Austin. "Why did you really set this up? Other than the thing about me sitting with both of you and coming to some revelation."

"Thought I could help break the ice." Austin nodded in Shawn's general direction. "Help a guy out."

"I do really need to use the restroom," Shawn said.

Austin made a tsk-tsking sound. "Let the man get up, Carrie."

She didn't know if Shawn was being honest or just matchmaking, and she didn't have the energy to figure it out. "Fine."

Austin waited until Shawn was out of hearing range to talk. "The rolls are pretty good."

When he reached for another one, she pushed his arm against the table and held it there. "This isn't a date."

"Maybe you're not trying hard enough."

"You're not getting it. I'm not seeing anyone else because I don't want to, not because I haven't had the opportunity."

He flipped his wrist and slipped his fingers through hers. "That should tell you something."

The warmth of his hand against hers made her sigh. "It's my choice."

"And?" He rubbed his thumb against the back of her hand.

Her nerves jumped around with each sweep of his finger. "Whatever point you're trying to make, whatever you think this scene will prove, I don't think it's working. Shawn and I are friends and will only ever be friends."

Austin lifted their joint hands to his lips. His words vibrated against her fingers as he spoke. "Because you're not interested."

She tried to drag air into her lungs and nothing happened. It was as if she couldn't catch her breath. "Right."

He traced the back of her hands with his lips. "You're not interested in anyone right now."

She was interested in the man touching her to the point she couldn't swallow. "Exactly."

"Except me."

"We broke up." The usual heat she put behind the words just wouldn't come.

"You left for what I'm hoping was a temporary period of time. As far as I'm concerned, we're still dating."

"You never give up, do you?"

"Not when it comes to you." He glanced across the room. "Shawn is coming back."

Austin placed a soft kiss against the back of her hand then

down on her wrist. When he let go and sat back, it took all her control not to grab for him.

"Austin, I—"

"If you want a real date when this is over, text me," he said.

The possibilities floated through her mind. Kissing him, touching him, making love with him. Reality closed in on her from every angle. She wanted this. Wanted all the closeness and laughter, all the warmth and security he brought into her life.

Six months and her feelings for him hadn't changed one bit. She hadn't moved even an inch in a new direction. Was not one step closer to getting over him.

She shook her head more at the direction of her thoughts than at Austin. "This is so dangerous."

"Doing nothing is dangerous because it means standing still. This is right. We're right. We always have been and no job or long drive between us on the highway is going to change that." He stood up and nodded as their third date partner returned. "Shawn, welcome back."

His gaze traveled between Carrie and Austin and back again. "What's going on?"

"I'm leaving," Austin said.

The words ricocheted through her, wounding every space they hit. "You are?"

He stared at her with an intensity that shook her. "Call me if you need me."

CHAPTER NINE

An hour later, Austin thought about breaking down the door to Carrie's apartment. Waiting for her call nearly had killed him. He'd paced the lot and loaded trees onto cars in a zombielike state. He might even have sold a tree for a buck. He couldn't remember and really didn't care.

When she finally texted, he'd sprinted across the street. Ignoring the car that almost knocked him off his feet and Spence's yelling, he raced with only one thought in mind—getting to Carrie as quickly as possible.

Much more of that out-of-control behavior and someone might call the police. If the running and jumping didn't do it, the way he was banging on Carrie's door with the side of his fist might cause the neighbors to call 911.

The door flew open and Carrie stood there wearing the same skirt from dinner and her shirt now untucked. And nothing else. The blazer and shoes were gone. He got a peek at bare feet and pink toenails before she snapped her fingers and brought his gaze back to her face.

She shot him her usual are-you-out-of-your-mind look. "You have to give a woman five seconds to walk across her apartment before acting like an uncaged animal and banging like that."

"It's a small apartment." The defense made sense to him but her frown deepened.

"I wanted to change."

He wanted her naked and counted down the seconds until he could get her there. A man could only take so much. "Didn't have to for me."

He swept her inside and kicked the door shut behind him. A second later he had her pinned to the wall with her hands beside her head and his lips on hers. Rather than tame the beast inside him, Austin let him loose.

He kissed her with all the pent-up longing inside him. Hot and long, deep and intense. His mouth crossed hers over and over, first soft and then hard.

By the time he lifted his head, his breath came out in harsh pants. "I missed you so much."

He whispered the confession against her mouth before moving to her neck and that delicious spot at the base of her throat. When she opened her legs, he moved between them and pushed her tighter against the wall. With a sharp intake of breath, she dropped her head to the side, giving him greater access and he took it. He nibbled his way across her collarbone, with soft bites and smooth kisses.

Her head rolled against the wall while small half breaths, half moans played on her lips. "We need to set out some rules."

"Uh-huh." He reached the top of her shirt and nudged it aside with his nose.

One of her hands slipped into his hair. "Austin."

"Later." When she inched her foot up his calf, tangling her toes in the material, he caught her under her knee and tugged her leg higher on his hip. The move pushed her skirt right to danger territory. Taking advantage, he shifted his lower half and rubbed his erection against her panties. Her heat radiated through his jeans as he stretched his body over hers.

"Yes." Her fingers went to his shoulders and shoved and pulled.

He stepped back and let his jacket drop to the floor. Fingernails scratched through his shirt just before a cool blow of air brushed against his skin. Desperate to feel her hands all over him, he signaled his brain to move. His mouth left her skin only long enough to shrug off both shirts.

Then his chest was bare and her hands smoothed over his muscles. "We need to keep this in perspective."

He had no idea what she was saying. The words blurred in his head as the heat thumped around them. He wanted her clothes off with skin against skin.

"We can talk after." His hands moved to her shirt. Fingers shook as he struggled to free the tiny white buttons from their holdings. "I promise."

He bent down and pressed a line of kisses over the skin he'd exposed. The creamy softness of the tops of her breasts. The peppery scent of her skin from the bath set he gave her for her last birthday. It all spun around him until the last of his control snapped.

He bent down and slipped her other leg around his waist, balancing her weight between the wall and his hips. Without any effort, he pulled back, taking her with him. He lifted her and felt her slim arms wrap around his neck. She pressed kisses across his jaw until she found his mouth again.

Knocked backward by the force of her kiss, he stopped. Standing in the middle of her family room with his heart hammering, he held her. His hands flexed on her bare thighs as his tongue slipped into her hot mouth.

After a few seconds, she swept the tip of her tongue over his lips. "Bedroom."

She didn't have to ask twice. He'd have a heart attack if he didn't get inside her soon. Six months without her, thinking about her and remembering, kept him in a near-constant state of arousal. Even when he'd wanted to hate her, the need for her broke through.

"Austin." She placed her palms on his cheeks. "Walk. Now."

"Right."

Easing his fingers under the elastic of her panties, he touched her. He felt her wetness as her hot breath blew across his ear.

He walked faster. His erection brushed against her panties with each step. When he hit the doorway to her bedroom, his arms shook. He could hold her forever. This was about tunneling under her clothes, stripping her bare and kissing every inch of her.

When his knees hit the bed, he turned and sat down. She straddled him with her knees pressing against his thighs. Her shirt hit the floor a second later.

With a click, he had her bra open. Sliding the straps down her arms, he unveiled her breasts. Round with tight nipples, pale and perfect for his hands. He caressed her with his hands and mouth, licking his way until he found her nipple.

"Now." She tugged on his hair until he lifted his head. "You're right, we can go slow later."

His mouth covered hers as his hands pushed her skirt to her waist. He flipped her to the mattress, pressing her back deep into the comforter as his fingers tunneled under her panties to the very heat of her.

With his lips on her breasts and fingers sliding inside her, he managed to lift his head. "Back pocket."

Her cloudy eyes didn't clear. "What?"

"Condoms."

Her hands reached around him then they were on him. Her palms smoothed over his erection right before the buttons on his jeans slipped open. One by one, the tension pulling at his erection eased. When she got to the last one, he fell into her hand.

Fingers wrapped around his length and his brain exploded. He tried to count backward from a hundred and couldn't remember a single number. The slickness on his fingers said she was ready. The thumping in his erection let him know he was.

She'd asked for fast and was about to get it.

Balancing on one elbow, he reached down and peeled off her panties. He got the scrap of material down to her knees before she kicked it off. Then he was on top of her, his erection right at her opening. The rip registered in his brain right before her hands rolled the condom over him.

The final touch of her fingertips touched off the wildness inside him. Settling between her legs, he slowly slipped inside her, savoring the pressure as she closed around him. Filling her caused her mouth to drop open. Pulling in and out had her grabbing the covers next to her hips.

Instead of setting a steady rhythm and wooing her, he poured all of his desire into her. He pumped, shifting his hips and feeling her muscles squeeze and tighten around him. The room filled with the sounds and smells of their lovemaking. Breathing pushed out of him on a guttural groan.

Every bone in his body pulled tight to the point of snapping. The tension spiraled in his stomach then moved lower. He went faster. Deeper.

When she let out a harsh exhale and her fingernails dug into the mattress, he pressed forward one last time. That was all it took. Dark spots burst in his head as his hips moved without any message from his brain.

Her head fell back and his bent forward. Their bodies shook and tightened…and then let go.

His last rational thought was that it was about time this happened again.

★ ★ ★

Carrie burrowed deeper into Austin's side. He was naked. She was naked. She hadn't seen clothes or any room other than her bedroom for hours.

It was somewhere around three and he'd made love to her with his hands and mouth and body until every inch of her tingled. Years after their first time together, his stamina hadn't waned. His expertise increased but his need didn't seem to diminish.

And she loved him just as much as she ever had. More maybe.

If she were honest, she'd admit she never stopped. She loved him when she left and even more when he showed up in D.C. Having a man put his life and work on hold for you was pretty damn sexy.

Getting him to accept her life promised to take longer. She knew his visit signaled the end of his patience. He viewed her career as a whim she needed to exorcise.

She wanted to be offended, indignant, but part of her knew he didn't understand. He'd known what he wanted to be from the time he was a kid. His father groomed him for it. What Austin didn't get was that she felt the same way about working in a prestigious museum.

If she could just show him…

She smiled as she poked him in the side. "Austin."

He came awake in a rush. He jackknifed into a sitting position and held his hands up as if ready to fight off whomever was about to launch an attack. "What is it?"

"I want you to come to a party."

The tension didn't ease across his shoulders. He didn't lower his hands, either. "Is that code for something?"

She slipped her arms around his stomach and placed a kiss

on his impressive shoulder. By the second kiss, his firm stance melted and his body fell against hers.

"Sorry I scared you," she said.

"More like put me on my guard, but you can wake me up in bed anytime."

She pressed him back on the bed. Not a surprise he didn't put up a fight. The man enjoyed being naked.

But she wanted his attention. Was suddenly desperate for him to understand and agree. "There's a party at my museum at the beginning of the week. A fancy holiday party."

"Okay." He made the word into about eleven syllables.

"I want you to be my date." She tucked her hair behind her ear. "A real date. Not a Shawn date."

"At the museum." Austin said the words nice and slow as if he needed to taste them before committing.

"Yes."

The hand that had been brushing up and down her arm fell to the bed. "Is this a test of some kind?"

She wanted to say no but she had to admit in a way it sort of was. An unfair one, maybe, but a chance for her to show him something that meant so much to her.

"You don't have to look at the paintings. You just have to be there with me."

A huge smile slashed across his face. "Well, why didn't you say so?"

She bit her bottom lip. "Remember this is a big party."

"You might want to stop trying to sell it since you're going the other way now."

"Is that a yes?"

He turned until he lay facing her. "Baby, I can't think of a place you could go where I wouldn't follow."

"You need to wear a tux or at least a fancy suit."

He stopped in the middle of rolling her to her back. "Probably a good thing you waited to tell me that until after I said yes."

"I'm not stupid."

"But you are sexy." Her back hit the mattress and he loomed over her. "And awake. I'm pretty happy about that last part."

That familiar revving started deep in her stomach. The thought he might touch her again so soon was enough to kick her breathing into high gear. "Noticed that, did you?"

"I say we put this thing where we're both awake to good use."

Then he lowered his head and she forgot about anything but him.

CHAPTER TEN

Carrie stood by the bar temporarily set up in the museum's Great Hall and waited. Her sleeveless royal-blue dress fell soft around her and dusted the floor. She knew the rich velvet showed off her curves and hugged her body in all the right places. The sparkly broach, hiding her cleavage, gave her just a touch of bling for the festive night. It also caught the light from the three elaborate chandeliers hanging from the ceiling right above her.

She'd picked the dress for the party long before she knew Austin had come to town. It just so happened to be his favorite color on her. Total coincidence. Just like it was a coincidence the color filled her closet.

Right.

The museum's towering entry looked like a magical fairyland filled with rows of tiny white lights and beautiful trees placed in baskets tied with holiday ribbon. A plush red carpet lay over the marble inlaid floor. Garland ran up the grand staircase that rose from each side of the large entry room and met at a landing on the second floor mezzanine. People weaved in and out of the bright poinsettias arranged on each step.

Visitors, dignitaries, patrons and artists walked along the open floor above while she nursed her drink. She'd been waiting for Austin for fifteen minutes and wondering if this plan would backfire. She'd hoped to show him her world and how he could fit in it, but he had to actually show up for her clever campaign to work.

"Hello."

A fresh drink appeared in front of her. She turned around and smiled at Shawn.

Wrong man.

"You look very dapper." She straightened his tie then stepped back. "How are you doing?"

"I'm impressed."

She took the glass and deposited her other one on the tray of a passing server. "With what?"

"The room." Shawn waved his hand in front of them. "As special events coordinator, most of the work fell to you."

"It was a matter of calling and hiring people." She also did a lot of ordering around and worrying the big party would be a bust.

If no one came or her boss turned out to be dissatisfied, Carrie's new job could end during her year-long probation period. Her task was simple. She had to top last year's event under the old coordinator everyone raved about and still professed to miss, yet do it for less money thanks to the failing economy.

Plus Carrie had to lure everyone in town to this party as opposed to one of the thousand other holiday parties being thrown across town. That meant her party had to sound more appealing than a get-together at the Kennedy Center and numerous embassy open houses. And she did it all while juggling her feelings for Austin.

Yeah, just a regular day at the office for Carrie Anders.

"The accountant in me is grateful you came in on budget," Shawn said.

Carrie eyed an artist as he made a broad gesture and spilled white wine on the famous staircase. "The night's not over yet."

"I'm surprised you're alone over here," Shawn said.

"I needed a breather after saying hello to everyone I needed to welcome, but I doubt the moment of quiet will last for long. Someone will stumble by any second and want something."

"I meant surprised Austin left you all alone while he's on the other side of the room." Shawn motioned toward the front door. "He strikes me as a bit more possessive than that."

This time she was the one who spilled wine. Brushing drops off her dress, she scanned the room. "What?"

"There."

She followed Shawn's nod to Austin. He stood right by the entry steps. And, lordy, he was in a tux. Her dreams would never be the same.

Nothing could have prepared her for the sight of Austin in a crisp white shirt and coal-black tuxedo. Combed hair, the right shoes and no work gloves, yet he didn't seem out of place. In fact, he was talking with her boss, Mrs. Alesandra Harper-Cunningham, a woman with several dead husbands and a house full of diamonds to go with her many names. She'd grown up in a manor house in the Virginia country-side and attended every expensive school from kindergarten through graduate degree. She radiated grace and old money.

She also talked with a pseudo-British accent and hated any-one outside of her social circle, so not exactly Austin's type. Heck, the woman wasn't Carrie's type. But Alesandra had taken a chance on Carrie despite her limited experience and lack of a graduate degree. Carrie didn't understand why she got the chance but would always be grateful for the opportunity.

The fact Alesandra laughed at whatever Austin said would take longer to analyze. The older woman put her hand to her chest then her mouth. Giggled like a flirty schoolgirl.

Then she waved to Carrie. Actually, put up her hand and wiggled her fingers like she was the queen or something.

Carrie blinked but the picture didn't change. "What the heck?"

Shawn let out a low whistle. "Don't see that every day."

"He charmed her." Carrie watched it but didn't believe it. Oh, she knew Austin could win most people over. Her boss was just not a normal person. Alesandra moved in that realm of people blessed with power and prestige thanks to rich parents. Talking about anything other than art and horses didn't suit her, and those happened to be two of Austin's least favorite subjects.

"I guess we found someone who thinks he's funny," Shawn said.

"That is a terrifying thought."

As she said the words, Austin looked up and snagged her gaze. He treated her to a half bow then leaned down to listen to whatever her boss whispered in his ear. After a few nods, he kissed the older woman's hand and started down the steps, leaving her flushed and smiling.

Carrie waited to wake up. This had to be a dream.

"Good evening." Shawn held out his hand to Austin and they shook.

But Austin's gaze never left Carrie. "You look stunning. Like, I-can't-find-the-words stunning."

"Thank you." She couldn't really say much else over the dryness in her mouth, so she went with that.

"I especially like the color."

If he wanted to think she dressed for him…well, she couldn't really deny it with a clear conscience, so she let the comment drop. "Where did you find the tux on short notice? You could have worn a suit."

"If you pay a high enough amount to the rental place, they'll get it done same day." Austin leaned in and kissed her cheek before turning back to Shawn. "I see you recovered from your date with Carrie."

"It was the date with you that's taking longer to overcome."

Austin smiled. "Nicely done, Shawn."

"I was about to say the same to you." Shawn offered Austin a drink.

His smile faltered as he waved off the glass. "You lost me."

"Mrs. Harper–Cunningham. The old crone isn't known for small talk."

They all glanced over at the woman in question. She now wore her usual puckered frown. With arms crossed over her thick stomach, she shook her head at some unsuspecting board member.

"Now, that's the Alesandra I know," Carrie said.

"I wouldn't talk negatively about her. She loves you," Austin said.

Carrie snorted.

"She told me how impressed she is with your work ethic and enthusiasm. She's very satisfied she discovered you, and that's a direct quote, by the way." Pride filled Austin's voice.

The fact he heard the compliments, that Alesandra even said them, stunned Carrie. When she crashed back to earth she had to concentrate to keep from jumping around.

She wasn't the weepy type, but that almost did it. She put in long hours and did whatever anyone asked so she would be viewed as indispensable. If the museum needed to cut costs, she didn't want to be considered extra overhead.

But praise? Alesandra didn't give much of that and to know she said it to Austin made Carrie want to raise her fists and shout hooray. She was desperate for him to get it, see it. For him to want to share moments like these with her.

"She seems to think you were born for this career," Austin said.

Something in his tone grabbed Carrie's attention. "How did she know we even knew each other?"

"She asked who I was, demanded really, and I told her."

"What exactly did you say?"

Austin didn't hesitate. "I'm your boyfriend."

Shawn laughed. "She'll have engagement announcements out within the week."

"Works for me." Austin shrugged as Carrie frowned. "What? It does."

The conversation around them buzzed as the room hummed with activity and music pumped through speakers hidden in plants. Still, Carrie didn't move. Even her heartbeat slowed as she stood there and stared at Austin.

He sounded so serious, so ready to commit. Despite months apart and all the arguments about work and leaving, his voice didn't waver and neither did his eye contact. She had no idea where that wealth of determination came from—a father who demanded excellence or maybe from a mother who didn't bother to stick around through the uncertain times. Either way, Austin stood there now making what appeared to be a vow and it nearly drove her to her knees.

Shawn broke the silence. "Well, hold up your glasses and we'll toast Carrie's accomplishment."

Austin dragged his gaze away from her and smiled at the other man. "Winning over the lady with multiple names?"

"No, this party. Carrie organized it. Did everything."

"You did?"

The sudden flatness to Austin's voice tugged at her. She downplayed her hard work until she knew the reason for the change. "It's part of my job."

"She's making it sound easy, but it's not. She works long

hours, negotiates for big exhibits and has set up an artists' workshop series for young women." Shawn grabbed three glasses of champagne off the tray offered by the waiter and passed them out. "To Carrie."

"To Carrie." Austin held the glass, swirled the liquid around, but didn't drink it.

"I'm off to mingle with board members." Shawn waved to someone behind them. "Good to have you here tonight, Austin."

"Thanks." He put the glass on the edge of the bar.

They both watched Shawn light up as he talked with a group of men in matching tuxedos. Austin's gaze stayed too long, as if he was looking but not seeing.

The hope drained right out of her again. For a second there she'd hovered on the edge of something spectacular but Austin's sudden mood change brought her crashing back down. "You don't have to pretend."

Austin finally faced her again. "About what?"

"You couldn't even toast my job, Austin. I know you hate it."

Confusion fell over his bright eyes. "It's not that."

"Then what is it?"

They stood there not talking. People passed and said hello. The music swelled as it reached the chorus. Just when she couldn't take the blank stare, he opened his mouth. When he closed it again without saying a word she seriously considered walking away.

"Maybe we can talk about this later." He nodded at the banner introducing the Cassatt exhibit and featuring one of her better known paintings. "I thought you'd show me her work."

"You can't be serious."

"I am."

She refused to be derailed, not even by a new chance to

show him her world, not when the topic was so important. "Tell me."

He didn't pretend confusion. Instead, he leaned one elbow on the bar. The move brought his face even with hers. "I'm not drinking."

After all that preparation she expected a different answer. "What?"

"No alcohol."

Something nibbled at the edge of her conscience. She remembered emails with odd comments and her brother's sharp insistence that everything was fine and she should stay in D.C. The minor accident with the tractor. The memory of the lack of beer at the trailer on the tree lot.

The pieces sat there just out of reach but she couldn't bring them together. She needed Austin to trust her enough to do it for her. "I don't get it."

"I've stopped drinking."

No, that didn't make sense. With three guys living alone without a woman's influence the family always had beer in the fridge and a full bar. She couldn't remember a time when Austin didn't have alcohol available to him. It was normal to his father who thought the drinking age was a waste of time.

Austin didn't drink to excess often, but he went out with friends and could throw back a lot of beer at a party, especially if a football game was on. He wasn't a mean drunk, or really even a drunk at all. For him it was a social event and he got quiet and thoughtful, which is why it never bothered her.

"Since when?" she asked.

He looked at his hands, at the ground, at everything and everyone but her. "A few months."

The pieces shifted in her mind and landed in a clearer picture. "Six?"

"That's about right." He cleared his throat and glanced up. "What's upstairs?"

"Austin, please. Just say it."

He pressed a hand to her elbow and steered her to the doorway on the far right side of the room. People came in and out of the exhibit hall, but he'd pulled her out of the main flow of traffic. "I don't really want to do this now."

"I think we have to."

He sucked his bottom lip between his teeth then let it go. "I was drinking too much and stopped."

"Six months ago."

"Yes."

"After I left."

He hesitated before nodding.

The newly formed picture horrified her. "The accident on your property."

His mouth dropped open. "How do you know about that? I swore Mitch and Dad and everyone else to secrecy. Even the police stayed out of it since I wasn't driving a car and hadn't gone on a public road."

"And your cousin is a policeman."

"I took the classes and stopped drinking. I'm not getting special treatment." He shook his head. "I still don't understand how it all got back to you. I'm not exactly the first guy in Holloway to get drunk and in trouble. It wasn't big news or shouldn't have been."

"As you pointed out before, we come from a small town. News travels, even the type you want to hide. Especially that type."

He swore under his breath. "Gotta love that."

Memories flooded back to her. She'd paced her floor for hours as she waited for Mitch to call her back. The time between finding out about the accident and hearing Austin was uninjured except for a concussion stretched until she'd thought she'd scream.

She'd threatened to get in the car and drive home, but Mitch begged her not to. He convinced her it would send Austin the wrong message so soon after she left. Reluctantly, she'd agreed. Now she knew the people she loved had hidden the truth from her. Probably one of those for-her-own good things, but it sure didn't feel like it.

"I got emails and that touched off a telephone chain. Mitch promised me it was minor and you were fine." The explanation sounded so hollow. She knew if she'd been hurt, Austin would have walked barefoot to her across snow-filled fields if he had to.

"See, no problem." Austin's smile didn't reach his eyes.

"You started drinking too much because of me." Guilt overwhelmed her. It ran right over her until every muscle in her body ached from the weight of it.

"No." His sharp response echoed off the marble. "I was drinking because of me. The blame is all mine."

"You have to be furious with me for putting you in that place." She tried to think of a way to work around this betrayal, to make it up to him, but she couldn't come up with a thing. She was right to leave, but she would have rushed right back if she knew he strayed into danger territory. That's what you did for someone you loved, and stubborn or not, she'd loved him for as long as she could remember.

"No, Carrie. Don't take this on."

"How can you not blame me?" She nearly choked from it.

"You were here and—" His voice dropped off. When he talked again a husky gruffness moved into his tone. "You clearly belong here."

Panic whizzed through her, knocking the guilt into second place. "What are you saying?"

"I think we've had enough secret telling for one night. We're here to party with people with hyphenated names. To celebrate what you created here tonight."

"I don't care about work right now."

"Well, I do. This is your big night and we're not missing it." He slipped his hand down and grabbed hers. "Show me the museum."

CHAPTER ELEVEN

Austin sat on the edge of Carrie's bed wearing only his tux pants and his shirt open to his waist and hanging loose. With his elbows balanced on his knees, he rubbed her blue dress between his hands. Just remembering how he'd unzipped it hours ago after a night of partying had his gaze skipping to her head on the pillow.

Taking her to bed had been his only thought when they got back to the apartment. He'd blocked out the truth and flashes of common sense in the rush to get her naked. To make love to her one last time.

Now unwanted thoughts tumbled through his mind as he tried to deal with the memory of the huge smile on her face as she walked around the museum. He'd spent most of the night trying not to stare at his watch and hoping for a reason to cut out early. She thrived, talking and smiling and not caring if the person in front of her was an artist or a dignitary.

She fit there.

After trying to manipulate her and win her over, and doing a whole bunch of dumb male shit to get his way, he finally understood. She wanted to be in D.C. This wasn't about him saying the right thing or about him at all. Her, the museum, it all made sense. He was the piece that didn't fit.

Tonight's crowd moved in a world very different from his own. Lots of money and strange concerns about what people did for a living. He shook his head, thinking the question "where do you vacation?" would stick with him for a long time. He "vacationed" for an hour before bed each night. Weeks in Europe didn't appeal to him and who the hell had the time and money for that crap?

Even with all the questions about him tonight he'd never spent one minute wishing he had more money or a different life. He certainly didn't see people with multiple names and their own tuxes as better than him. That didn't mean he belonged here. But she did and that changed everything.

Carrie shifted her legs under the sheets and threw an arm over his empty side of the mattress. When her fingers hit only sheets, she sat up with the comforter pulled tight against her chest.

She brushed her hair off her face and blinked a few times, as if trying to adjust to the dark room. "Austin?"

"Right here."

She reached over and clicked the light on low. "It's the middle of the night."

"Quarter to five."

"Like I said." She threw him a sexy smile as she tapped the ruffled pillow. "Come back to bed."

"I have to get to the lot." He had to pack up and end this.

He rubbed his hand against his chest to try to ease the burning underneath. No matter how hard he pressed, the stabbing pain under his ribs wouldn't let up.

"Are you okay?" she asked with a voice filled with concern.

He heard the rustling of sheets and felt the mattress dip right before her arms wrapped around his neck. Her mouth landed on his ear and her hair fell over his shoulder.

His body jumped to life right before the pain ran down his arm and seeped into every bone. "I owe you an apology."

She breathed in deep then bit down gently on his earlobe. "I like the sound of that."

His hand smoothed over the soft skin of her arm. "I convinced myself working in a city museum was some sort of dream you'd get over."

She froze for a second before caressing him again. "I know."

He finally turned his head and brushed his lips over hers. "Really?"

"Subtlety is not your best attribute."

"It was egotistical bullshit. Like you didn't know what you wanted and I did." He shook his head. "I should have seen it and not pushed."

"Your scheme started out rocky, but I'm happy you're here now."

Her silky hair tickled his chest. He wove his fingers through it, loving the feel of the strands against his skin. "I was a dick. You should have kicked my sorry butt back to Holloway a week ago."

"But it's such a cute butt." She gave him a loud, smacking kiss on the cheek. Then she grabbed his arm and swung in front of him and got a good look at his face. Her smile disappeared a second later. "Something really is wrong. What is it?"

"You love your job."

She shifted to his lap, letting her legs fall over his and her hand rest against his bare stomach. "That's a good thing."

For her. Not so much for them. "You tried to tell me but I didn't listen. I'm listening now. I'm not trying to con you or figure out how to get my way. I'm really listening."

"I believe you." She kissed him then, short and almost painful in its sweetness.

"Sorry it took so long for me to get it."

She shook her head. "The timing doesn't matter. What I've wanted is for you to understand that I have this professional side, these dreams that need nurturing. I didn't want you to dismiss or minimize what was so important to me."

"I did all those things." Regret washed over him like a river. "I messed up in a big, stupid guy way."

"That's over now. You came here for me and went with me tonight. A woman likes that sort of dedication." She tapped a finger against his nose.

Her light tone and happy mood made every word he uttered even harder. The syllables stuck in his throat as he tried to push them out.

She acted as if they'd made some breakthrough when they'd really reached the end. All he assumed about her motives and needs was wrong. She didn't need Holloway or family or even him. She got by fine in D.C. on her own.

That reality kicked him in the gut and kept kicking. He'd always loved her independence and strength. She never backed down from a fight with him. She never hid and cried. She faced him head-on with a feistiness that made him hot.

But he knew what happened when a woman craved something bigger, something better, than the man who slept beside her. She'd leave and run. He'd already lived that story. His mother taught him that hard lesson when she cut out and never bothered to call. Carrie had been warning him she saw a dead future like her mother's if she didn't explore now. He didn't believe the theory then but now he did.

The sharp pain ripped through his chest. He had to close his eyes and clench his jaw to keep from shouting.

"Austin?" Panic showed in her wide eyes and played in the shock in her voice as she shoved his shirt aside and ran her hands over him. "Are you hurt?"

"I'm fine." Dying inside, but fine on the outside.

"You're pale. Maybe you've been outside in the cold too much." When he frowned, more words rushed out of her. "I know you're an outside guy, but you are a man. You can get sick like regular humans."

"I wanted to be enough for you."

There, he'd said it. She acted like she was on the verge of calling an ambulance or giving him mouth-to-mouth, and he spilled his big secret. He couldn't imagine what else could go wrong.

She definitely heard his big admission because her hands froze still wrapped in his shirt. "What?"

This was the last conversation he wanted to have with her. It should have meant something that he'd never have to do it again, but it didn't. "I wanted to mean more than the job."

"You do."

He didn't. Any idiot could see that. She walked away from him not the job offer. He made her choose but he'd kept thinking he could find the right words to change her mind back.

He'd run through the options in his head so many times. There were ways to make the distance work. Not perfect ways, but options. Holloway and her apartment sat two hours apart. Not an impossible gap to bridge.

But distance wasn't their issue. She wanted something and it wasn't him. Yeah, she loved him and liked being with him. He knew that wasn't enough. *Thanks again, Mother, for that hard lesson.*

"Since Spence covered for me last night, I need to be on the lot first this morning and do all the crap jobs." Austin shifted her off his lap and stood up.

She stopped him from walking away by grabbing on to the ends of his shirt. "You've changed. There's something else going on here."

He sure as hell had. "Just an early riser."

"Austin."

He leaned down and kissed her, letting his lips linger over hers. When he lifted his head he could barely speak. "I love you."

The sweet smile matched the sudden wetness of her eyes. "I love you, too."

The pain inside him ran rampant now, shredding everything it touched. "I can't remember a time when I didn't love you."

Her eyes got all soft. "You know how to steal a girl's heart."

"I will always love you. No matter what or how many years pass."

She brushed the back of her fingers over his cheek. "I believe you."

He turned his head and kissed her palm. "Go back to bed."

When she got up again, he'd be gone.

Austin's bedroom scene played on Carrie's mind all day. She'd tried texting him and calling, but he didn't respond. After all that racing after her, all those plans and the plotting, he seemed to being playing hard to get. Not exactly his style and not her favorite game. And she planned to tell him that.

Playing on the goodwill from the successful party, she was able to sneak away from work early. She got to the lot shortly before two. The crowds had thinned, which was to be expected for the middle of the work week even if Christmas was only three days away.

Spence stepped in front of her, peeling off his gloves as he did. "For the record, you've been here thirteen days in a row and haven't bought a tree."

"I'm still deciding."

He slapped his gloves against his thigh. "Do it quick since this is my last day here."

"What are you talking about?" She noticed his usual smile had been replaced with dark circles under his eyes and the urge to laugh at his joke passed.

"I'm packing up so I'm home and settled in by Christmas Eve."

All the lightness washed out of her. She'd been so happy last night, this morning. Now anxiety churned hard enough in her stomach to make her worry about losing her breakfast.

"Where's Austin?"

Spence looked past her. "He took the first batch of trees and some supplies home."

"He didn't tell me that."

"Far as I can tell he only made the decision this morning."

"Is he coming back?" She grabbed Spence's arms and squeezed until he looked at her. "Answer me."

"I'll admit I'm confused here. I thought you wanted him to give up and go away."

Her breathing roared in her ears. "I want him with me. That was the point of last night."

"Interesting."

Spence's man-of-few-words thing was ticking her off. He had to see that she teetered on the edge here. "What is so damn interesting?"

"Well, seems Austin learned something different from your evening." Spence's hard eyes softened as he peeled her fingers off his arms. "He's already on the way home, Carrie. He plans on staying there."

No, no, no. "What?"

"You won."

"How can you say that?" Spence's words were too awful for her to answer in anything more than a whisper.

"You told him—"

She willed him to understand. "That was days ago. Not now."

"Look, he gets it. At least, he finally did. Your life is here. His is there."

The pounding in her head threatened to pummel her into the ground. "I love him."

"You're not the first woman to love him and leave him."

"Who—" The words cut off as soon as the answer blew into her brain. "Your mom?"

"I wanted you two to make it. I really did. I think of you as a sister. Always have. And believe me, he's going to be a piece of shit for months over this." The words were rusty, as if it hurt Spence to say them.

"You're worried he's going to drink again." She piled that concern on top of all the others racing through her mind.

Spence's eyebrow lifted. "You know about that?"

"I do now."

"Don't think about it. I'll take care of him." He kissed her cheek then turned away. "You go live your life."

"What if I want a life with Austin?" She shouted the question.

Spence didn't answer at first. He stood there with his back to her. "This time you'll have to do the chasing."

"What does that mean?"

He eyed her over his shoulder. "I think you know."

She somehow got across the street and back to her apartment. She didn't remember taking the steps or walking through the snow but her damp hair told her she did. Her body had gone numb and her mind spun in so many directions that she couldn't grab on to a thought and hold it. After fumbling with her key, she got the door open.

The lights caught her attention first. There, right in front of her window, was the perfect four-foot tree. Full and bright green with a fresh pine scent that filled her apartment, wrapped in those tiny white star lights she loved so much.

Her feet echoed on the hardwood floor as she moved across the room, not quite sure what she was seeing. Her fingers traced the familiar red ball with her name on it in script. She saw the angel Austin bought her years ago and the doves her mom had crafted. Every ornament that meant something to her hung on the tree.

Carrie knew the truth then. Her mother had refused to part with them, but Austin got them away from her.

Austin. Her gaze went to the folded white card sticking out of the branches. She'd recognize his bold print anywhere.

I hope your dreams come true. Merry Christmas.

She turned the card over, hoping for something. No claims of love and nothing else. Not even a signature.

Life sparked back into her body. Fury did that to a woman. If the man thought he was going to dump her at Christmas and make it all better with a beautiful tree, he was dead wrong. And good thing he did leave because if she got her hands on him right now, he might just be dead.

She just hoped the party she'd put together was good enough to earn her another day off. Because she had some unfinished business in Holloway.

CHAPTER TWELVE

Austin stood at the far end of the property and let the snow dance all around him. Big wet flakes stuck to his jacket and coated his hair as it piled around his feet. Still, he didn't move. His focus centered on the sway of the trees and peaceful sounds of the thick woods.

It was noon on Christmas Eve but the puffy gray clouds shut out all the light until the day resembled early evening. He kicked the snow off his boots only to see it accumulate again. The weather folks predicted nine more inches by Christmas morning. Good thing he planned to stay right here, on his land and away from people, for days. Maybe months. And he didn't rule out the possibility of years. He wouldn't be the first old guy in Holloway fumbling around his house and talking to himself.

He'd been home two days without any word from Carrie. Not that he expected or deserved one, but he thought maybe the tree would at least get a thank-you and maybe an agreement about how they could stay away from each other for the sake of the people they cared about.

He wasn't interested in her friendship and didn't think he could stand being near her and not touching her. But Mitch had been his best friend since high school. They played football together and worked every day in the same office. Engaging in open warfare with his sister could mean losing both of them, and Austin couldn't stand that possibility.

The engine rattle of the old truck they kept for farm errands sounded behind him on the rock-and-mud trail. Not a surprise. Spence had said something about hunting him down after an hour. Since everything would soon be slick and impassable except by utility vehicles, it made sense the rescue party headed out. Spence sometimes took the big brother thing too seriously.

Not that Austin was looking for brotherly bonding. The icy wind fit his mood. Wrapped in a thick jacket, he felt nothing. He hadn't experienced a single sensation since the morning he left Carrie. He functioned, brushed his teeth and walked around, but the dark emptiness inside him refused to go away.

The truck stopped a good ten feet behind him. Austin waited for the slam of a door and Spence's yelling. The man had no idea how to coax and convince. He went right to threatening. Any other time Austin would appreciate the concern. Not now.

He turned around to wave Spence off. Then he saw her. Carrie, sitting in the front seat, leaning over the steering wheel and staring at him through the soft thwack of the windshield wipers.

He shook his head. When her image refused to leave his brain, he closed his eyes. Opening them again, he saw the door open and a woman's boot slide out of the car.

She jumped into the snow from the high seat, wearing those tight jeans and the puffy jacket he loved so much. Something about the outfit reminded him of the easier times together on the farm, back before the rest of the world invaded.

"I've got a question for you." She didn't wait for him to talk.

"What kind of a man makes love to a woman then leaves her the next morning without even saying goodbye?"

"I wrote you a note." He said the words without thinking.

They made her snort. "That was a Christmas card, the kind of thing you'd send your great aunt or a business associate. Not the appropriate way to communicate with your girlfriend."

His mind rejected the word. He still couldn't believe she even stood in front of him. "My what?"

"I expect an apology." She lifted her hand from where it was tucked in her back pocket and pointed at him. "And a good one. Not the 'mistakes were made' boy type. Like, down on your knees begging my forgiveness. Even then I plan to make you grovel a bit."

None of this made sense. He'd finally set her free and yet she stood four feet away. "Why are you here?"

"Why do you think?"

He finally looked at her. Really looked. Behind all the bluster and the rosy cheeks, he saw wariness. Her usual spunk took a backseat to something else. The drawn face, the flat lips. He recognized the signs of a person who was barely existing because that's all he had done since leaving her.

"If you had stuck around we could have talked this out." She took two steps forward.

He fought the urge to keep space between them. "We've done that a million times. You said what you wanted and I finally listened."

"Leave it to you to start paying attention at the wrong moment."

Was she smiling? "I don't understand."

"Obviously."

She took that final step to eliminate the gap between them. This close he could reach out and touch her hair. He clenched his hands at his sides to keep that from happening.

"I told you I wanted to take the museum job because I didn't want to end up like my mom, all disenchanted and full of regrets."

That familiar pain throbbed in his chest. What he'd feared was a heart attack was really heart break. Seeing Carrie and reliving it all…he couldn't take it.

"I can't do this with you again. I admitted I messed up and now I'm trying to give you the space you asked for. You deserve at least that much." He barely had the strength to talk. And seeing her there on his turf pushed the last hold on his control right to the brink.

When he would have preserved what little was left of his dignity and turned away, she put her hands on his chest. "You're only half-right."

"You lost me." Hell, he could barely concentrate with her standing so close.

"When I gave you that explanation about Mom, I missed something very important about us."

Between the layers of clothes and gloves, the weight of her hands pressed into him. "What?"

"While I was busy worrying about becoming my mom, something else was happening. Something just as strong and emotionally devastating. You were convinced I was becoming *your* mom." Sadness filled her eyes. "I'm sorry I didn't see it before now. I knew all about your past but I didn't take a second to think it through and realize how you saw our relationship."

He refused to be a victim of his past. His mother left and he moved on. His dad filled all the roles, made everything right. "I took my mother out of my life a long time ago."

"But not out of your heart." Carrie took her glove off and slowly unzipped his jacket just far enough to slip her hand inside. The warmth seeped right into his heart. "What she did to you shaped you. She hurt you and even now you pretend not to grieve."

"I'm a grown man."

"And you see me reaching for something and are convinced I'll pick that dream over you and leave."

"You did." He wanted to call back the words as soon as they slid out.

"And it was the right decision but not the whole decision."

As gently as possible, he touched her hand and pulled it away from him. The harsh rip of the zipper sounded through the woods as he dressed again, creating at least a symbolic barrier. "Okay, I have to go."

"Listen to me." Carrie laid her hands against his cheeks. The bare palms flat against his cold skin. "This time I'm the one fighting for us."

That's all he ever wanted, for her to care as much as he did. "Okay."

"I brought you to that party because I needed you to see me as a whole person and understand the place my work has in my life."

"I get it." The truth had slammed into him like a body blow and he still hadn't recovered from it.

"But you don't see that there's a place for everything. That the job is what I do, but you are part of who I am. The best part. I didn't even realize I was bumping along, going from home to work and blocking out everything else, until you swooped into D.C. and found me."

This time he let her see the need inside, let it seep out of him. "I was desperate to see you again."

"I thought we were finally on the same wavelength and you ran."

An unexpected rush of heat returned to his body, forcing him to defend his actions. "I didn't run."

"You left me, which is okay because it was your turn."

"Meaning?"

"I left you several times, all for the right reasons, but still in the wrong way. I apologize because I now know how much it sucks." She stretched up and rubbed her cheek against his. "I'm so sorry. Please know that even as I fought you I never stopped loving you and wanting us to find a way back to each other."

He wanted to believe, to give life to the flicker of hope inside him, but she didn't understand. He needed her to know he'd given her the room she begged for. "I didn't leave D.C. to punish you. I was setting you free."

"I don't want to be free from you."

His breath hiccupped in his lungs. "You don't?"

"We can figure out the distance and keep two places."

Hope burst to life inside him. "We'll go back and forth. I can find some work in the D.C. area and you can come to Holloway on the weekends. I don't even care if I do all of the commuting." God, he just wanted a chance to prove to her they could make it work.

She nodded as she pulled his face closer. "It's not perfect, but we'll figure it out and come up with something long-term. I know we can. The logistics were never the issue. Respecting and trusting each other were. It took us until now to get there."

Doubts crept in, pushing out everything else. He'd lived with them for years but never mentioned them. With the door open he had to drag them out and face them. "What happens when you want the job or a life in D.C. more? I want to lie and tell you I could become a city boy, but we both know that's not me. For a short time, but not forever."

"Listen to me." She placed a soft kiss on his mouth. "I have loved you since I turned fifteen and I had a crush on my big brother's best friend long before that."

The words washed over him, drowning out every bad memory.

He wrapped his arms around her narrow waist and pulled her body in tight against his. "Good to know."

"You're the one I come home to, the reason I get up and keep moving. The museum is a job and I don't plan to give it up because I've wanted it for so long and am actually good at it, which is a nice combination. But if I have to fight for something in my life, I pick you. I'll fight for you."

Relief and happiness soared through him. She smiled and all the darkness brightened. She brushed her finger over his lips and his insides jumped to life.

But she had to know he had some ground rules. If they were moving forward, they were doing it at warp speed. "I'm not doing the dating thing again. We've practiced long enough. If we're making the commitment, we need to make it."

"Are you proposing?" The way her eyes lit up suggested she was pretty thrilled by the idea. "You better not be, because I need a ring and a full apology first for your dumb decision to scamper away from D.C. like that."

"Scamper?" A guy had to draw the line somewhere. That word seemed like a safe place to call a halt.

"I'm still waiting for the apology."

Part of him wasn't sorry. They needed the shock as a couple. If he hadn't walked away they might still be going round and round and never moving, all those doubts festering.

Not that he was going to tell her that. "I should never have left you."

She snorted. "Damn straight."

He pressed his forehead against hers. "I was an idiot."

"Yep."

His fingers plowed into her hair as his lips traveled over the bridge of her nose to her cheeks. "I was devastated because I looked around and thought you didn't need me."

"Idiot." There was no heat behind the word. Instead, her head fell to the side and her hand went to the back of his neck to pull him down for a hot kiss, this one longer with a touch more heat.

After what felt like forever, he pulled back and stared into those deep brown eyes. "But when I told you I'd love you forever, I meant it. Now and always. In West Virginia or Minnesota. I just need to know you'll always come home to me."

Tears formed in the corner of her eyes. "Oh, Austin."

He couldn't be derailed. He had to get it all out because once he stopped talking he'd find other things to do with his mouth. "And you need to promise that if you're tempted to take your life somewhere else, you'll give me the chance to come with you."

"My home is wherever you are. Always. My heart begins and ends with you."

He'd been dying to hear those words his whole adult life. To thank her for giving him everything, for loving him and trusting him, he treated her to another lingering kiss, this one filled with the promise of the loving to come.

After, he brought her hand to his mouth and kissed each finger. "I have another present for you."

"The tree was pretty spectacular."

"Are you kidding? Your inability to pick one off that damn lot was the only thing that gave me hope."

She shrugged but her eyes sparkled with mischief. "I'm particular."

"You were scoping me out."

"Guilty. You do look hot in blue jeans."

"I knew it."

Without warning, she jumped up, wrapping her legs around his waist. "Now tell me about this other gift."

He caught her, only stumbling a second from the surprise launch. Then his arms came around her and the whole world tilted right again. "It's a tiny box that I've had for months."

Her eyes widened until they took up most of her face. "Let me see."

"You can have it tomorrow. Christmas Day." That was the perfect day to start building a new family. He'd propose then take her upstairs to celebrate.

She actually stuck out her lower lip. "I want it now."

"I'll make you a deal. You can have me now."

She peeked around his shoulders. "The truck does have a big front seat. We could consider it a pre-holiday gift."

As far as he was concerned, their future could start right now. "What are we waiting for?"

★ ★ ★ ★ ★

MISTLETOE AND MARGARITAS

Shannon Stacey

SHANNON STACEY

New York Times and *USA TODAY* bestselling author Shannon Stacey liv
with her husband and two sons in New England, where her two favori
activities are writing stories of happily ever after and riding her four-wheele
From May to November, the Stacey family spends their weekends on the
ATVs, making loads of muddy laundry to keep Shannon busy when she
not at her computer. She prefers writing to doing laundry, however, ar
considers herself lucky she got to be an author when she grew up.

You can contact Shannon through her website, www.shannonstacey.com,
where she maintains an almost daily blog, visit her on Twitter at
twitter.com/shannonstacey or on her Facebook page, www.facebook.com
shannonstacey.authorpage, or email her at shannon@shannonstacey.com.

CHAPTER ONE

When Justin McCormick was fourteen, a dirt-bike crash had put him in the hospital for two weeks, but even three broken bones and a concussion hadn't hurt as much as loving his best friend's widow did now.

And yet, here he was, parking his truck next to her geriatric Volvo and walking up the exterior staircase to the apartment over her landlord's garage, just like he'd gotten back on that dirt bike. Knowing there was a chance he'd get banged up again, but willing to take the risk.

Unlike with the dirt bike, though, there wasn't any chance about it. Justin *knew* he'd get banged up again every time he showed up on Claire's doorstep. He knew it would hurt, but even if he didn't have an empty Dunkin' Donuts bag full of crumpled-up receipts he had to drop off with her, he would have stopped by. He always did. Because they were *buddies*. Instead of weakening after Brendan's accident, their friendship had only gotten stronger.

Claire opened her apartment door to him just as he reached for the knob, her pale blue eyes alive with excitement and her long, blond ponytail swinging as he flashed her the friendly smile he'd been perfecting since the day they met. A friendly smile so perfect, in fact, Claire had never guessed—through two years of dating Brendan and three years of marriage and two years of widowhood—how Justin felt about her.

"You brought me doughnuts?"

"Receipts." He handed her the bag and laughed when she scowled at the contents.

"Work *disguised* as doughnuts? That's just mean." She walked over to the corner of her apartment that served as her office and tossed the bag on her desk. "I should give Moxie your sandwich."

The massive tortoiseshell cat in question wound between his feet, pausing to head-butt his shin before Justin picked her up and scratched between her ears. "You don't even like doughnuts that much."

"I like them more than I like handfuls of filthy, torn receipts you've scrounged from under the seat of your truck."

"Watch it or I'll start to think bookkeeping's not your true calling."

"Of course it is." She gave him a smile that would have struck him dumb if he hadn't have so much experience resisting it. "There are only so many jobs I can do in sweatpants."

He set Moxie on the couch and moved toward the kitchen in search of the food Claire had said would be waiting. The only thing she did better than keep books for local small-potato contractors was cook.

Since he'd warned her this would be a quick stop, Claire had thrown together some sandwiches. But they were thin-sliced honey ham with Swiss cheese on homemade whole wheat with butter and spicy mustard, just the way he liked it.

She knew how he liked everything and most of the time knew what he was thinking before he even said it out loud, but she didn't know how much he loved her. It puzzled him sometimes. He couldn't see how, unless she was refusing to see it. Maybe she did know, but she'd never feel the same and the pretense preserved their friendship.

While dumping some chips onto her paper plate, Claire looked at him and asked, "How are things going with…Trish, was it?"

"Yeah, Trish. But we broke it off a few days ago."

"You mean *you* broke it off." The look she gave him was a familiar one, full of womanly disgust. "What was wrong with her?"

She wasn't you. "It wasn't going anywhere. I did us both a favor."

When she reached over and touched his arm, it took all of his willpower not to pull away. "At the rate you're going, you'll run out of fish in the sea, you know."

She was a touchy-feely kind of person, always touching his hand or grabbing his arm or resting her hand on his shoulder, with no idea how agonizing it was for him. He felt the warmth of her palm through his shirt and he ached to feel it against his bare skin.

"We still on for Friday?" he asked, even though he'd told himself earlier in the day he was going to tell her he couldn't make it.

"Yeah. Since my only niece is turning three, I can't back out."

"Do you mind if we take my truck so I can stop and have the tires changed? Since we'll be going through Manchester anyway."

"That's fine, but if you're driving, I'm paying for the gas. Pizza tonight?"

"Yeah." Tuesday night was always pizza night. Pizza and pool at the local pizza house on the night least likely to have a bunch of kids running around. It had been a tradition forever—just Justin and Brendan in the beginning. "I have to pick up the contract for plowing that new plaza, so I'll swing in and pick you up."

Taking a bite of her sandwich, she stretched her legs out under the table. Her ankle brushed his, but she didn't pull it back. She just rested it there, comfortably and without any clue it was slowly killing him inside.

He had to cut her loose.

Not totally, maybe, but he needed to put some distance between them. He'd been telling himself that for months, as her natural humor and joy for life gradually overwhelmed her grief and she became more like the Claire he'd known—and loved—for years.

No matter how often he told himself to distance himself, though, he couldn't bring himself to do it. The thought of not having Claire in his life anymore hurt. And the question he couldn't answer was whether living without her or continuing to live as her best friend hurt more.

Nothing made Claire want to bust out the butt-wiggle dance like snowflake graphics dancing across the weather forecast grid portion of the evening news. The snowflakes were a couple of days away and they weren't going to amount to much, but it was a start.

Snow meant plowing and plowing meant she'd get to see more of Justin. He was a roofer by trade but, like a lot of guys whose work crapped out during the winter months, he plowed snow to make up the difference. Since his house was in the middle of nowhere and most of his client base was in town, he'd crash on her couch for power naps between plow runs. And, if she didn't have any work backing up on her desk, she'd ride along and keep him company while he cleared driveways and parking lots.

Now that the procrastinators had gotten their last-minute

roof fixes and her customers weren't quite ready to start freaking out about taxes yet, there was a window of several weeks where they could play a little harder than they worked and she intended to take advantage of it. Starting with pizza and pool tonight.

First, she had to get some work done, though. Starting with the new bakery that had managed to make a horror show out of their books in less than two months of business by deluding themselves about their accounting abilities. Shaking her head and muttering under her breath, with frequent breaks to explain to Moxie yet again why she couldn't lie on top of the papers, kept her busy for several hours and she only stopped because it was almost five o'clock and every Tuesday at five, Penny stopped by.

Penny Danvers' dad owned a plumbing outfit that employed Penny's three older brothers, as well as a few other guys. Penny worked in the office, answering the phone and handling most of the paperwork, and she could keep basic books and balance the checkbook, but payroll was beyond her. So every Tuesday she dropped off the information and on Thursday afternoon she picked up the checks.

Right on time, Penny knocked twice and let herself in. She was a very tall brunette who practically crackled with energy and, while Claire had considered her a friend for years, she could be exhausting.

As always, Penny dropped the folder of timesheets onto the desk and then wandered over to drool over the framed photos of Justin Claire kept on the bookshelf. "When are you going to take pity on me and hook me up with him?"

"When I don't like you anymore and want to see you curled up in front of a Meg Ryan movie, bawling into a pint of Ben & Jerry's."

"You're so sure he's going to break my heart. How do you know I'm not *the one?*"

"Justin doesn't have a *one*. He has many and I don't want you to be one of them."

Penny turned and gave her a speculative look. "Or maybe you want to keep him for yourself."

A blush heated Claire's face and she looked down at the papers on her desk while shaking her head, hoping her hair would hide her pink cheeks. "Don't be stupid. He's my best friend."

"So?"

"He was Brendan's best friend."

"So?"

"So…" So what? "It would be weird."

"What's weird about it? You already know you're compatible in almost every way. Why would sex be any different?"

Sex. With Justin.

Her body tingled like an extremity that had fallen asleep and was waking up in a blaze of pins and needles. And that's all it was, she told herself. Her sex drive's sudden fixation on Justin was just its way of letting her know it was ready for a man again, even if her heart wasn't.

She forced herself to laugh and look straight at Penny. "For somebody who wants to be hooked up with him, you're awfully pushy about me sleeping with him."

She shrugged one shoulder. "I don't necessarily want to keep him. Just play with him for a while. But I'd deprive myself of the toe-curling pleasure of multiple orgasms to see you happy, because I'm a good friend that way."

This time Claire's laugh was genuine. "Gee, thanks. What makes you think sex with Justin would be toe-curling and multiorgasmic?"

Not that it mattered, of course, since she wasn't going to

have sex with her best friend, toe-curling or otherwise. There was too much between them and the only thing she'd end up with when the alleged multiple orgasms were over was no best friend.

"The guys with commitment issues are usually the best in bed," Penny said, and Claire wondered if she spoke from experience or if she'd read it in a magazine. "They have a lot of experience with a lot of different styles on a lot of different models, if you know what I mean."

She didn't even want to think about that. "You've known him longer than I have, anyway. Why do you need me to hook you up?"

"We travel in different circles. Always have."

Penny was the reason she'd met Brendan and Justin in the first place. Claire and Penny's senior year at UNH, they'd ended up roommates and friends. One weekend, Claire had gone home with her instead of heading to her parents' and they'd gone to a party. A few minutes with Brendan had been all it took.

Since Penny was giving her a funny look—like maybe she thought Claire wanting Justin all to herself wasn't just a joke—she decided to wrap it up. "The checks will be ready by the usual time Thursday."

Once Penny was gone, Claire straightened her desk and fed Moxie. Then she did a little housekeeping and her thoughts turned to Justin.

She couldn't quite put her finger on what it was, but something was definitely wrong with him. Even though they were practically best friends, she suspected he was hiding something from her. And whatever that something was, it probably wasn't very good.

He'd be there any second to pick her up, so she slid her driver's license and debit card into her back pocket and clipped her cell phone to one front pocket while dropping her keys into the other. She'd wait to pull on her favorite fleece pullover until he pulled into the driveway.

On her way through the apartment, she paused as usual and looked at the row of photos sitting atop her bookshelf—the ones Penny had been looking at—her gazing coming to rest on the silver frame just to the left of her formal wedding portrait.

It was a double frame, holding two 5x7 photos side by side. On the left was a picture of Brendan and Justin standing in front of the elementary school on their first day of fourth grade. Both of them grinned at Brendan's mom, who'd held the camera, obviously excited to be embarking on a grand new school year together.

The photo on the right, taken at her reception, was her favorite picture of the two guys together. They both looked outrageously handsome in their tuxes—both tall and athletic, but Brendan was blond and fair-skinned, while Justin had darker hair and the tanned complexion of a man who worked outdoors. She'd looked at the photo a hundred or more times since Brendan died.

This time, though, her gaze lingered on his best friend. The photographer had captured them laughing and Justin's honey-brown eyes practically sparkled out at her from the frame.

She'd been noticing his eyes a lot lately. The warmth in them when he looked at her. The something—almost sadness—in them when she caught him watching her. And he watched her a lot.

No, she wasn't sure what was up with him, but she had to admit—even if only to herself—that she watched him a lot, too.

It was a natural thing, she told herself. With a little over two years for her heart to come to grips with Brendan's death, her body was awakening again. She missed sex and Justin was a very good-looking guy. It was only natural she'd sometimes wonder what it would be like if he touched her—or so she tried to convince herself.

She jumped when the chime on her cell phone alerted her to a new text, as if she'd been caught doing something wrong. Grabbing her sweatshirt, she pulled up the message as she locked her door behind her.

Here.

She rolled her eyes and slid the phone back into its holster. Justin hated texting. He claimed his hands were too big and his fingertips too calloused for the small buttons, but she loved his hands. They were the working hands of a capable man, strong and rough, and for a few seconds she found herself wondering what they would feel like against her soft, naked skin. Then she shove the errant, confusing image away and went down the stairs to the driveway.

He smiled at her as she climbed up into his truck and pulled the door closed. "Hey. We might need two pizzas. I've been thinking about it all afternoon."

While she'd been thinking about him. "If we get two, you can have mushrooms on yours and we'll both have leftovers for supper tomorrow."

The smile spread into a grin. "You might have leftovers. I'm starving."

He used his mirrors to back down her driveway, but to see down the busy main road, he twisted his body to look out the back window of the truck, resting his arm across the back of the seat. He'd done it a hundred times, but this time she was aware of how close his fingertips were to brushing her shoulder. This time she had the urge to shove his pile of paperwork and business cards and supply house slips onto the floor and slide to the middle seat, into the shelter of his arm.

She didn't, though. Instead she looked out her window and cursed Penny for putting the thought in her head.

Justin had a slice of pizza in one hand, a pool cue in the other, and was trash-talking Claire's shot when the Rutledges walked through the front door. Brendan's parents saw him immediately through the big window to the game room and he felt the same quick flash of shame he'd felt every time he saw them since Brendan had introduced them to Claire. Then he smiled and waved with the hand holding the pizza.

Claire turned to see who he was waving at and he didn't miss the way her face lit up. There had been no in-law drama surrounding the Smith-Rutledge wedding since the families had hit it off almost as well as Claire and Brendan. It was storybook, really. Except the ending. The ending had sucked.

"I forgot Tuesday was pool night," Judy Rutledge said as she and Phil turned the corner into the game room.

Claire kissed them each on the cheek, then it was Justin's turn to get a kiss from Judy and a handshake from Phil. They'd been like second parents to him since they'd moved to town the summer before Brendan and Justin started fourth grade and struck up a friendship. The Rutledges had a family room, two televisions, a never-ending supply of freshly baked cookies and no time limit on video games, so the boys had hung out there a lot more than at the McCormick house. Justin's mom worked a lot of hours at her hair salon and was just as happy to have her only child out of her hair as much as possible.

"All ready for Christmas?" Phil asked, because that was the usual conversation opener two and a half weeks before the big day.

"No," Justin and Claire said together.

Claire laughed. "I'm going to get a Christmas tree on Saturday and I'll probably get around to shopping next week. Maybe."

Judy shook her head. "I expect to see you both Christmas Eve."

"Wouldn't miss it," Justin said. That was the plan. An appearance at the Rutledge family Christmas Eve party, then he and Claire at her place, watching *National Lampoon's Christmas Vacation*. It was a tradition.

The Rutledges went to order their takeout and since Chris Jones was just walking in, Claire handed her pool cue to him and went to sit with Judy and Phil while they waited.

Chris had youth and a pretty face on his side, but not much in the way of book smarts. And his work ethic was a little iffy at best, too, which Justin knew since he employed the kid off and on during the summer. When Chris's beer and video-game money ran low, he'd help out on a roof or two, then take off again.

"Must be about time for you to head north," Justin said. In the winter Chris worked and lived at one of the fancy resorts because an almost freakish natural ability to teach rich people to ski was another thing he had on his side.

"Monday. But for the fifteenth, I managed to score a few hours off in the middle of the day. You in?"

"Hell, yeah." That was the day the gates were officially opened on the snowmobile trails. "A few hours is better than nothing. I'll text you when I get there and we can head out."

"So you get with that yet?" Chris asked, and Justin realized he'd been watching Claire through the window as she laughed at something Judy said.

He forced his attention back to the pool table. "I told you, it's not like that."

"I don't know what the problem is. She's hot and you hang out more than a married couple."

"We're friends, Chris. It's possible for a man and a hot woman to be friends without having sex." It wasn't easy, but it was possible.

Judy and Phil poked their heads in to say goodbye when their food was ready and Justin gave Chris a warning look behind Claire's back. That subject was closed, at least as far as the other guy was concerned. It was never closed in Justin's mind.

"Who won?" Claire asked, grabbing another slice of pizza from the tray.

"Me," Chris said. "Smoked him, actually. His mind must have been on something else."

Since her back wasn't turned, he couldn't send another glare in Chris's direction, so he concentrated on keeping his expression neutral. "I let you win. Figured your ego could use the boost."

"Whatever, dude. Claire, you in?"

"Rack 'em up."

Since watching the two of them play really meant watching Claire bend over the table to line up her shots, Justin lined some quarters up along the edge of the pinball game and set about taking out his frustrations on the metal ball. The action was loud and fast and just what he needed to distract himself from the game behind him.

Until Claire moved up beside him to watch and he smelled the slightly tropical scent of her soap and shampoo and imagined he could feel the warmth of her body standing so close to his and the metal ball went down the chute with an electronic flushing sound of failure.

"Good timing," she said. "I just kicked his ass, so you're up again."

"Be right there." He picked up the quarters he hadn't used

and shoved them back into his pocket, taking the opportunity to adjust the crotch of his jeans.

Time to have another talk with himself about cutting back on the time he spent with Claire. Tomorrow.

CHAPTER TWO

It was still dark when Claire woke feeling flushed, a little breathless and a lot confused.

She dreamed about sex a lot, which was probably normal considering she was a twenty-eight-year-old woman who hadn't had the real thing in two years. But this was the first time the dream had been so deliciously potent and the imaginary sex so mind-blowingly good she'd awakened with her body aching for more.

Which wasn't good because it also happened to be the first time she'd dreamed about having sex with Justin. That couldn't be a coincidence.

Moxie, sensing she was awake, strolled up the bed to bump heads with her, but Claire rolled onto her stomach and buried her face in the pillow. She'd just had the best sex of her life. Too bad it wasn't real. And it was with the one person she shouldn't be thinking about having sex with.

Everybody knew the quickest way for a man and a woman to ruin a friendship was to have sex.

Moxie mewed plaintively, kneading Claire's shoulder, and she sighed. Five-thirty or not, it was time to get up. If she went back to sleep she might have imaginary sex with her best friend again and her nerves said once was enough.

"It's Penny's fault," she muttered to the cat as she sat up. "She planted these thoughts in my head."

She started the coffeepot brewing and hit the bathroom, but the shaky, off-kilter feeling didn't fade. The first cup and the early-morning news didn't help, nor did Moxie nudging her, wanting to know what was wrong. She wasn't so far gone she was going to try to explain being blindsided by an erotic dream about her best friend to her cat.

Maybe she *didn't* want to have sex with Justin. Maybe it was her body's less-than-subtle way of telling her it was time to wade back into the dating pool. Actually, her body wanted her to cannonball off the diving board, but her heart wasn't up to more than dipping her toes into the shallow end.

She realized she was twisting her wedding band around on her finger and forced herself to stop. Nobody wanted to explore even the shallow end of the dating pool with a woman wearing a wedding ring. Well, not any guy worth dating, anyway.

Maybe it was time to take it off and put it away. Quick and painless.

Or it would have been if the band didn't hang up on her knuckle. Dish soap didn't do it. Butter didn't help. When even a liberal application of olive oil didn't budge the ring, she leaned against the counter, tears running down her cheeks unchecked because her hand were so gunked up she couldn't wipe her eyes.

Maybe it was a sign. If she couldn't get the wedding band off, she didn't have to think about dating again. She laughed through the tears and Moxie, who'd been watching her with disdainful interest, retreated to the back of the couch.

"It's not a sign," she said out loud. "It's all those potato chips I ate watching *The Biggest Loser.*"

After ten minutes with her hand stuck between two baggies of crushed ice and another dousing with olive oil, she was able to work the ring over her knuckle.

Claire set it, slimy and glistening, on the counter while she washed her hands. Even though winter was setting in, she'd spent a lot of autumn outside and the white circle of flesh was stark against the tan that had yet to fade. When her hands were clean, she washed the ring and then rubbed it dry.

Brendan's wedding ring was on her dresser, in a small wooden box covered in tiny shells—a Cape Cod honeymoon souvenir so tacky they'd *had* to have it. She opened the lid and took out the gold band that was identical to hers, except larger. It had gotten hung up on his knuckle during the ceremony, though potato chips probably weren't to blame. They hadn't had to resort to begging hand lotion from a guest, though Justin had told her in a low voice to spit on it. Instead she'd shoved, Brendan winced and they all laughed about it at the reception.

She had vague memories of being asked if she wanted it left on Brendan for burial, but she hadn't been able to part with it. For a long time she'd worn it on a chain around her neck, but she wasn't a necklace person and when the time came that she was annoyed by it more than comforted, she'd put it away.

Now she dropped both rings into the box and, after sucking in a deep breath, closed the lid and waited to feel different. Maybe lighter or more free or…something.

But all she felt was a little hollow. And she wasn't suddenly hit with an urge to sign up for an online dating service. All she could do was hope that one small step would be enough to satisfy her subconscious and put an end to the deliciously naughty dreams about Justin.

A few minutes later, her phone rang and she almost spilled her second cup of coffee down the front of her T-shirt. To make matters worse, Justin's name was flashing at her from the caller ID window. Praying her voice sounded close to normal, she answered, "Hello?"

"You awake?"

"No. I answer the phone in my sleep."

"Smartass. Just wanted to see if you'd be up to leaving earlier than we'd planned. If you're awake."

"I've been up since five-thirty, thank you very much."

He laughed. "You? Did the smoke alarms go off or what?"

"Very funny." She couldn't very well tell him she'd been awakened by exceptionally good sex with him. "We don't have to be at my parents' until two."

"I'm going to buy breakfast. I don't know how long it'll take to get my tires changed, and I still need to pick up a gift for Nicole."

"She's turning three and my parents probably bought out the toy store. You don't need to bring a gift."

"Can't go to a birthday party without a gift. Then I feel guilty taking a second piece of cake."

Claire laughed, letting his easygoing normalcy chase away the last of the lingering weirdness. "Fine. What time do you want to leave?"

"I'll pick you up at eight?"

"Sounds good." She hung up the phone, feeling better. It was just a stupid dream.

Justin noticed it right away—the soft ring of pale skin where the gold band had been—and his heart turned over in his chest like a sluggish engine on a sub-zero morning.

He knew he should say something—like maybe *hello*—but he was frozen, watching that tan-free ring of skin as she zipped her coat, and the only coherent thought in his head was *what the hell does it mean?*

Five years ago, he'd watched Brendan slip that wedding

band onto Claire's finger and he'd never seen her without it since. It had served as an unmistakable, highly visible reminder she was Brendan's wife and now it was gone.

"You feel okay?"

No, he didn't. His pulse was racing. His palms were sweaty. And the chronic ache that was his constant companion had flared into a throbbing pain.

She was ready to move on.

"Justin? Hello?"

"Yeah. Sure. You ready?"

Without waiting for an answer, he turned and went back down the stairs, needing to put some distance between them. It didn't do any good, of course, since she was going with him and a few minutes later Claire and her naked ring finger were sitting next to him in the suddenly claustrophobic cab of his truck.

Having a girl for a best friend was challenging enough. They didn't have the upper-body strength to help a guy change out an engine. They cried during movies. They needed blenders and umbrellas for their drinks instead of just a cold bottle of beer. Hell, he'd even bought a box of tampons once. Claire had been sick and thank God she'd texted him a picture of the right box or he'd still be standing in the girl aisle because, holy crap, women had options.

But having the girl you were half—or more—in love with as a best friend was a special kind of hell. He'd endured it well enough so far, but there was no way he was going to sit on her bed and watch her dig through her closet for something to wear on a first date. He didn't want to watch her sigh over a text from some guy. And no way in hell was he going to giggle over the morning-after *details* if she invited the asshole up for "drinks."

"What's got you so pissed off?"

"What makes you think I'm pissed?"

"Oh, how about the fact you're strangling the steering wheel? Or that your eyebrows are practically touching over your nose? Or the fact you just burned off half your tires in my landlord's driveway pulling out?"

He made a conscious effort to relax his grip on the wheel, but faking even a half-assed smile was out of the question. "It's nothing. Rough day."

"It's eight o'clock."

"Fine. Rough morning."

"You sounded fine on the phone earlier."

She wasn't going to let it go until he gave her something. "Hot water heater's crapping out on me. Cold showers aren't a happy way to start the day."

It was only half a lie, since he'd taken more than his fair share of cold showers. The falsehood, of course, was that it was the hot water heater's fault.

By the time they'd hit their favorite diner for breakfast and had his tires changed, he was finding his footing again. Except for when that band of pale skin caught his eye, which was a problem since she used her hands a lot when she talked.

They were in the toy store, looking at shelves of preschool board games, when Claire crossed her arms and sighed. "Just say it, Justin."

"Okay. Nicole's three. Why can't I just buy her a doll? No pieces to lose."

"Fine. Buy her a doll, even though she asked for games. And that's not what I'm talking about. I lost count of the times I've caught you staring at my hand about two hours ago. Just say it."

"You took your wedding ring off."

She looked at him like she was expecting more, but he didn't know what else to say. It was a big deal for her and, even though she didn't love him the way she'd loved Brendan, he knew he was important to her. What he said mattered.

"It doesn't mean I'm going to forget him," she said in a quiet voice.

"I know that."

"And nobody's ever going to take his place in my heart."

Oh, he knew that, too. "I'm not upset you took it off, Claire. It's just different, so it catches my eye. Makes me think about him, you know?"

Tears welled up in her eyes, but she was doing her best to blink them back as she nodded. "I know. Me, too."

"One of the things he loved most about you is the way you're always happy about things. He'd want you to, you know…move on. Be happy…and stuff." Justin wanted it for her, too. Just not with some other guy. Especially the *and stuff* part.

She laughed and swiped at a stray tear with the heel of her ringless hand. "You're not the best with words, but you're a really good friend, you know."

Great. That's what he was shooting for. Really good friend. He held his arms open. "You better? Need me to hug you so you can wipe your face on my shirt?"

"No, I'm good," she said, and he hid the disappointment. "Let's get something for Nicole and get out of here or we'll be late."

Justin found a stuffed cat that looked exactly like Moxie and, even though it wasn't a board game, he decided Nicole would like that. Then, according to Claire, he had to pick out a card. And a gift bag. And bows.

By the time they pulled into the Smiths' driveway, Justin was beat. All he wanted was a steak, a beer and a game on the flat screen. What he got was a houseful of people, a wound-up little birthday girl with a horde of wound-up friends, and

Debbie Smith—who noticed immediately her daughter had taken off her wedding ring.

He was hiding in the kitchen, pretending to look for more paper cups, when Mrs. Smith walked in. "Oh, Justin. I was wondering where you'd gone to."

"Looking for paper cups."

"Hiding." She laughed when he blushed. "We'll hide together. When Kelly asked me if they could have Nic's party here because I have more room, I should have asked how many of Nic's playdate friends she was going to invite. And at two o'clock on a Friday afternoon!"

"You should make Mr. Smith take you for a nice dinner after everybody leaves. Have a drink. Or two."

"Trust me, I'll be telling the waiter to leave the bottle." She pulled out a stool at the kitchen bar and perched herself on it. "How's Claire doing?"

Since he knew she'd noticed the lack of gold on her daughter's finger, he didn't bother hedging. "I think she's a little wobbly today, but she's good. It was just time, I guess."

The smile she gave him was warm and sincere. "I don't know how she would have gotten through this without you, Justin. If only everybody could be blessed with a friend like you."

He gave her a return smile he hoped showed nothing of the guilt eating away at his gut and thanked his lucky stars when one of the moms flew into the kitchen looking for a roll of paper towels.

Her now three-year-old niece was one of the people Claire loved most in the world, but she wanted out. Badly.

Watching her sister, Kelly, and her brother-in-law fussing over their daughter and her little friends did nothing but remind her she and Brendan were going to start trying for a baby as soon as they signed on their new house. She kept try-ing to fidget with her wedding ring, only to find bare skin. And Justin was nowhere in sight. Not the most fun she'd ever had at a party.

"Ohmigod, you took your ring off!"

Claire curled her left hand inside her right and cursed her-self for picking this day of all days to take that particular step. "Gee, Kelly, I'm not sure they heard you next door."

"Sorry." Her sister plopped down on the couch next to her. "So does this mean you're thinking about dating again?"

"No." As she said it, Justin emerged from kitchen and she watched him as he scanned the room until his gaze found hers. Then he smiled and she rolled her eyes at him.

"What does he think about it?" Kelly asked.

"He just wants me to be happy…and stuff." Claire smiled, remembering his awkwardness in the toy store.

"I bet he does."

She turned to look at her sister. "What do you mean?"

"Nothing." And there was the fake innocent face Kelly did so well. "Hey, J.J., watch out for that—crap."

A herd of adults converged on the shattered vase, shooing kids away from the broken glass, and Claire laughed when Justin slid into the seat Kelly had vacated in a hurry.

"Not that I'm not having a great time but how much lon-ger?"

"Maybe ten minutes. After they clean up this mess, but be-fore some kid makes the next one."

It was closer to forty minutes before they were able to sneak goodbyes in and make their escape. They both buckled their seat belts with a sigh of relief and then Justin pulled out of the driveway and took a right.

Claire closed her eyes and tried to tell herself it was no big deal. Turning right led to the back roads that led to Dunkin'

Donuts, where Justin would grab a coffee. Then that back road led into a bigger back road which led back to home. A road that went right by the house she couldn't bear to look at.

She'd been so excited about signing the papers for their dream home she'd called Brendan three times in the span of a half hour the day of the closing. To ask if he was on his way. To tell him to hurry up. He'd laughed at her and told her she was worse than a little kid on Christmas morning. Then he'd told her he loved her and he wouldn't be late.

The State Police said speed was definitely a factor in the accident that turned Brendan's Camry—and Claire's life— upside down. The roads were slippery and he'd been driving too fast for the conditions. Because he'd loved her and he'd promised he wouldn't be late.

She'd walked away from the house. Walked away from everything and everybody as she sank into a black pit of despair and guilt she couldn't kick her way free of.

It was Justin who'd taken her hand and wouldn't let her drown. Justin who'd refused to accept that it was her fault Brendan was dead and who'd washed her face with a cold washcloth when she cried so hard she threw up. He'd told her over and over it was an accident until she finally started believing it herself. And he didn't leave her side until she agreed to drag herself out of her apartment and go out with him for some cheeseburger therapy.

They'd come out of those dark days better friends than they'd ever been and not a day went by she wasn't thankful she had Justin in her life. And she was thankful enough today she decided not to stand in his way if he wanted a coffee.

She felt the truck pulling off the road and opened her eyes just as he jerked the wheel around and did a U-turn in the road. "What are you doing?"

"With all those kids, I didn't get a chance to take a leak before we left and I'll never make it to Dunkin' Donuts. I'll stop at the gas station up the street and I can grab a coffee there, too, before we jump on the highway."

He'd remembered and now he was lying. She thought she should call him on it—tell him it was okay and it was just a house. But she'd had just about enough for today, so she let him get away with it.

When the day came she *did* go looking for another man, she hoped she could find one as good as Justin. Only without the whole *best friend* thing.

CHAPTER THREE

Having the garage door open let in the morning chill, but it let out the four-stroke exhaust as Justin revved the engine of his snowmobile, warming it up so he could transfer it to the trailer for the riding season. When he could sneak a free day, all he had to do was hook the trailer up to the truck and drive to a trailhead.

Once he'd loaded his machine up, he pulled back the cover on the sled in the back corner of his garage. It wouldn't go on the trailer and the registration sticker was long expired, but Justin set the choke and fired it up anyway.

It was Brendan's sled and he couldn't bring himself to sell it, but he couldn't let it sit and gather dust, either. So he kept it covered, did the maintenance it really didn't need and ran the engine every so often. Now, listening to his best friend's pride and joy, he wondered if it was time to let it go. If Claire could take off her wedding ring, he could pass the sled on to a new owner.

He'd have to talk to her about it, of course. Technically, she owned it. But she had no interest in snowmobiling and, since her apartment didn't come with any garage space, she'd asked Justin to hold on to it. So that's what he'd done.

The cell phone vibrated in his pocket, so he hit the kill

switch on the sled and pulled it out, thankful for any distraction right now. He smiled at the name on the screen and flipped the phone open. "Hi, Mom."

"Hi, sweetie. Are you busy?"

"Never too busy for you. Where are you?"

"I don't know. Del, where are we?" Justin heard the low rumble of his father's voice. "He says we're about four hours away from Branson, Missouri. We're going to spend a few days there and then head down to Texas."

"You guys don't even like country music," he said as he put a red thumbtack into Branson on the huge map hung on the garage wall. Then he took a fine-tipped permanent marker and wrote in the date.

"I know, but your father heard there's a Ripley's Believe It or Not Museum there, so off we go."

That had been their motto—Off We Go—since they'd sold the house to Justin, bought an RV and hit the road a year and a half before. After decades of hard work and accumulating stuff, they'd made the decision to have the mother of all yard sales, gave away what was left over and became nomads.

At the time, Justin had been sharing an apartment with a guy he didn't like and that was so small most of his stuff was still at his parents'. Since he didn't seem any closer to finding a wife or starting a family, buying the house he'd grown up in seemed like a good idea. And they'd given him a helluva deal on it, too.

"How's Claire?" his mother asked as he walked through the mudroom that connected the garage to the kitchen.

"She's good. I'm taking her to get her Christmas tree in a while."

"Give her our best, of course. Anything else interesting going on? The house okay?"

"Everything's fine, Ma. I can't think of anything that's changed since the last time I talked to you."

Except Claire's newly bare ring finger, of course, but he was trying to convince himself it didn't mean anything and therefore wasn't newsworthy.

"Your father's pulling into a gas station and you know how he is. He makes me turn off the cell phone while he pumps gas, even when I stay in the RV."

"Better safe than sorry." He rolled his eyes, thankful she couldn't see him do it. "Tell Dad I said hi and I love you both."

"We love you, too, sweetie. I'll talk to you soon."

After they hung up, he dropped a couple slices of bread into the toaster, then smeared the popped toast with peanut butter. He'd need the protein to survive Christmas tree shopping with Claire. Her taste in decorations ran to *Better Homes and Gardens*. Her budget and her apartment didn't.

If there was one thing he knew for sure, it was that the first tree she tried to buy would be at least eight feet tall.

Claire took one look at the Douglas fir and fell in love. "This is my Christmas tree."

"No, it's not." Justin nudged her, but she planted her feet. "Keep walking."

"What's the matter with this one?"

"It's too big."

"There's no such thing as a too-big Christmas tree."

He eyeballed the fir, then shook his head. "Even trimmed up, this is at least an eight-foot tree."

"I have an eight-foot ceiling." She folded her arms, determined to be stubborn about it, but he laughed at her.

"You have sloped ceilings. The only place it's eight feet is smack dab in the center of the living room."

"Then I'll put it there."

"And when you call me because you couldn't tether it and Moxie pulled it over swinging from the branches, I'll laugh before I hang up on you."

"But—"

"Keep walking, Rutledge."

"Maybe I could tether it—"

"No, you can't tether it to the ceiling."

"Grinch," Claire muttered. After a final, mournful glance at the Christmas tree of her dreams, she kept walking.

After fifteen minutes, he'd vetoed several more trees and Claire's holiday mood was slipping like a thirty-year-old transmission. "What's the matter with this one?"

"When you touched it, half the needles fell off. It must have been cut in an earlier batch because it's not going to last and you'll end up with lights hanging off naked branches."

She flicked one of the branches and watched the needles flit to the ground, hating when he was right. "So my friend Penny was asking about you."

"Not interested."

That was as far as she usually would have taken it, but she hated the way his expression closed off and felt an urge to poke at him a little. Plus, maybe if he was seeing a friend of hers she'd stop having decidedly nonplatonic thoughts about him. "You could ask her to Cal's Christmas party tonight. It's last-minute, but pretty casual."

"You're going with me to Cal's. Like always."

And he'd crash on her couch, like always. The problem was the fact she didn't always have hot, sweaty dreams about him. She didn't always toss and turn thinking thoughts she had no business thinking about him.

"Whatever," she said. "I told her I liked her too much to hook her up with you, anyway."

He turned to scowl at her. "What's that supposed to mean?"

"I like Penny. Why would I set her up with a guy that's going to take her out a few times and then dump her?"

"What makes you think I'd do that?"

"It's what you always do."

"That's a pretty rotten thing to say."

"It's the truth, and you know it."

He turned his back on her, then walked to a stand of four-foot trees, which made her sigh. She knew he was being practical—he did practical so well—but these trees weren't going to be gracing the pages of magazines any time soon. "This one's good."

What it lacked in height, the tree made up for with full, symmetrical branches and needles that didn't scatter when she breathed on them. "At least I won't need a stepladder to put the star on top."

"That's the spirit."

Leaving the lot attendant to wrap the tree in netting, Claire and Justin made their way through the crowd to the cashier at the back of the lot. Pinned to the stack of wooden crates serving as a makeshift stand for the cash box were sprigs of mistletoe bound by red string. On impulse, Claire grabbed one and added it to her total.

"What's that for?" Justin demanded as she shoved her change in her pocket.

"It's mistletoe."

"I know what it is. Why did you buy it?"

"Because it's a Christmas decoration and because it's fun. Same reason you have a snow globe with a picture of your snowmobile in it."

"I have a snow globe with a picture of my sled in it because you gave it to me last Christmas. And I don't kiss a girl every time I shake it and make the snow fly. You're supposed to kiss somebody under the mistletoe."

That was true, which meant she really needed to have a talk with her subconscious. First sex dreams and now an excuse to kiss a guy in her apartment. "I thought it would look cute. Stop overanalyzing my impulse buy."

"Who are you planning to kiss?"

"Moxie," she snapped, just to shut him up.

They found her wrapped tree and, after showing the attendant her receipt, she took the light end—careful not to bend the top branch where the star would rest—and Justin took the heavier base end and they carried it to his truck. He probably could have just swung the thing over his shoulder and carried it alone, but she liked to at least pretend to do her share. He took the heavy end again to carry it up the stairs to her apartment and then helped her center it in the stand she already had waiting.

When he started working on tethering the tree to the wall, necessary thanks to Christmas trees bringing out Moxie's inner kitten, Claire went to the kitchen to wash the sap off her hands. Unfortunately, the kitchen was more of an area than an actual room, which meant she could see him from the sink. Tethering the tree required a lot of leaning and stretching and the leaning and stretching kept making his T-shirt ride up, and she wondered how she'd never noticed how incredibly sexy the small of his back was.

And now that she was looking, that exposed strip of skin wasn't the only thing sexy about him. There was the way he filled out his blue jeans. The way his broad shoulders moved under his T-shirt. The way his hair curled just a little at the base of his neck because he was overdue for a haircut. And when he turned and grinned at her, she went ahead and mentally penciled that in at the top of the list.

"Moxie would need a chainsaw to take this sucker down now."

She tried, as a rule, never to compare Brendan and Justin, other than a natural curiosity at times as to how two such opposite men had been best friends for almost their entire lives.

Justin was worn jeans and faded T-shirts, usually with a hole at the back of the collar where the tag sometimes stuck out because rather than grab the hem, he took off his shirts by grabbing the back of the neck, bunching the fabric and hauling it over his head. If she needed a repair done, Justin would load the supplies in his truck, show up and get it done in exchange for food and all the iced tea she could pour. He liked country music and liked to watch movies at home, where he could pop the button on his jeans and put his feet on the coffee table.

Brendan was khakis and button-down shirts. He listened to classic rock and loved going to the movie theater to experience films the way the directors intended him to. If a repair needed doing, he would call somebody to fix it, write the check and then take Claire out someplace on the town so the construction wouldn't bother her.

Such different guys with an unbreakable bond. And they both meant everything to her.

"You want me to hang that mistletoe?"

"No, thanks. I'll hang it somewhere later." If he hung it, then he'd end up standing under it and she might be tempted to kiss him.

"This is the part where you offer me food," he reminded her.

"We'll be at Cal's party in a few hours and there's always tables of food."

"The keywords being *in a few hours.*"

She rolled her eyes and pulled open the refrigerator. "I don't have much. Haven't worked up the ambition to go grocery shopping in a while. Deli meat. A leftover chicken breast. It was a little dry the first time around, so I don't think a microwave is going to help it any. I could slice it thin, maybe. Make a sandwich with lots of mayo."

"You got any chocolate pudding?" His voice so close to her ear made her jump.

He was standing behind her, looking over her shoulder. With one hand on the open door and the other braced on the fridge itself, she was trapped by his body and awareness of it crackled through her like an August wildfire.

It had to be that stupid dream, she told herself. Now that she knew her body was thinking about sex again, she was fabricating desire where it didn't exist. She didn't feel that way about Justin.

He moved closer, trying to see around her, and when his hip bumped hers, it took every ounce of self-control she had not to react. Okay, so maybe she felt that way about Justin a *little*. But it would pass. As long as he didn't catch on, things wouldn't get weird and eventually her body would find somebody else to lust after.

She hoped.

"Next right," Justin told the cab driver, who put on his turn signal and slowed the car. Then he sent a quick text to Claire to let her know they'd arrived.

Neither of them were big drinkers, but the booze flowed freely at Cal's Christmas parties and Justin would have at least a couple of beers and Claire would have some kind of sparkly, fruity drink. Before Brendan's accident, he would have risked it, telling himself two drinks was nothing. But, even though alcohol wasn't a factor in the accident, Justin had been the one to visit the impound and collect any personal items from the mangled wreck that had been Brendan's car. Since then, he did what he could to make sure his family wouldn't have to do the same.

When the cab was in Park, Justin got out and walked around to open Claire's door for her just in time to see her making her way carefully down the staircase in red high heels he'd never seen before. And, holy crap, her legs. He'd seen her legs before. Kicking around in shorts and flip-flops. Hell, he'd even seen them at the beach a time or two, when she wore nothing but a modest, one-piece suit.

But they looked different tonight. He'd never seen her long, curved-just-right legs going on for what looked like forever, from her short black skirt to those red high-heeled shoes that would make any hot-blooded male instantly hard just because they were red high-heeled shoes.

"You ready?" she asked, and he realized he'd watched those amazing legs walk right up to him and stop.

"Aren't you cold?" he asked, thinking maybe being concerned for her health would sound like a legitimate excuse for the staring.

She hesitated, looking like she was going to say something but changed her mind. Then she shook her head. "Not really."

"The dress code for Cal's party's pretty casual."

"So I felt like dressing up a little." Her hair was up in some sparkly red clip thing and she had on just enough makeup to keep his gaze bouncing between her gorgeous eyes and a mouth just begging to be kissed.

As she walked past him to get into the cab and he closed her door for her, he thought about that mouth and those legs and those shoes and swore softly, but very earnestly, under his breath. She looked like a woman who was hoping to find a man.

What the hell was he supposed to do if she found one? He

wasn't sure he had the willpower to watch her leave with some other guy.

Especially once he was in the cab and those legs were in his peripheral vision. The skirt wasn't indecent by any means, but it had ridden up and when she shifted in her seat, he got a painfully delicious glimpse of her smooth, pale inner thigh. He turned his head to look out the window and was thankful it was only a ten-minute drive to the small resort hosting the party.

Cal Reading was a builder who specialized in building overpriced custom homes for people with way too much money and he threw one hell of a Christmas party every year. Justin's invite was thanks to the occasional roof he'd do if the regular Reading Builders roofing crew was held up on a big job. Claire worked with a lot of the outfit's subcontractors and Cal appreciated how well she coordinated with his big-city accountant.

They both knew pretty much everybody in the big banquet room, so it wasn't long before they'd gone their separate ways, each with a drink in hand. It was only when he heard her laughter over the crowd and the music that he realized the men really outnumbered the women in the room. By a lot. And too many of them didn't appear to have women to leave with.

No wonder Claire was practically surrounded. Okay, maybe not surrounded, but there were a few guys who seemed to be orbiting her like they were just looking for an opening to land their lunar modules. And the shimmery, flowing red blouse that matched her shoes and hugged her curves wasn't helping any.

"Hey, Justin." A woman slid up next to him at the cash bar and it took him a few seconds to place her. She ran the contractor desk at the local home-improvement store and he was pretty sure her name was Jen. Usually she had a name tag on pinned to her work vest, but tonight her dark hair was teased and hairsprayed to what looked like its breaking point and her V-neck sweater was a little more V-necked than it should have been.

"Hey, how's it going?"

"Not bad. Running empty, though." She set an empty glass on the counter and waved to the bartender.

"Next one's on me," Justin said, because he wasn't sure if she was fishing for him to buy her a drink or not, but he thought she might be. It seemed the polite thing to do, plus she always took good care of him at the store, so he pulled out his wallet.

Jen was smiling at him over the rim of a fresh rum and Coke, when it belatedly dawned on him she might be looking for some extra-curricular company, so he looked around the room until he spotted Claire again.

This time, she wasn't laughing at something one of her clingy male satellites had said. She was looking at him. Or rather, she was looking at Jen. And she looked annoyed, which wasn't like her. Then a tall plumber who'd once screwed up one of Justin's roofs with a bad venting job walked up and handed her a glass of something red, and she smiled up at him.

"I think you have to have a claim on the lady before you can beat the crap out of the guy hitting on her," Jen said and he scowled at her, which made her laugh. "Don't bother denying it. You looked like you were mentally ripping his head off his shoulders."

"He hacked up a roof I did once."

"And then he bought a drink for the woman you arrived with."

"We're just friends."

"Sure. Hey, I see somebody I want to say hi to. Thanks for the drink."

"No problem. See you around." He took a sip of his beer and looked around for somebody—anybody but Claire—to talk to, and spotted a few guys he knew standing around in the corner shooting the bull.

On his way over, he caught sight of Claire through the corner of his eye. She was still talking to the idiot plumber, but she was watching Justin. And her expression looked a lot like Jen's expression before she caught on she wasn't holding his interest, but he told himself it was just his imagination.

Just friends. That was all they were.

CHAPTER FOUR

Claire sipped at her cranberry margarita—a lovely and potent holiday concoction of tequila, orange-flavored liqueur, and cranberry and lime juices—and watched Justin over the rim of her glass. She wasn't sober anymore, but she wasn't drunk, either. She'd hit that sweet spot of inebriation where she could check out the man's ass and not feel weird about it.

And what an ass it was. Every woman in the room had checked it out, even the ones who'd had to be sneaky about it because they hadn't come to the party alone.

Claire hadn't come alone. And she wouldn't be going home alone, either. The hot ass in the tight jeans would be leaving with her, since Justin intended to crash on her couch, as he always had in the past.

Warm and flushed and basking in a mild alcoholic glow, she watched Justin laugh at something one of the other guys said and thought about how, a few hours from then, he'd be stretched out on her sofa in his sweatpants and the Bruins T-shirt that always rode up in his sleep and exposed his abs. And then, because her hormones and the margaritas had lit a fire in her belly, she thought about him stretched out on her bed, minus the sweats and T-shirt.

He turned at that exact moment and caught her staring.

Or devouring him with her eyes, as the case may be. Judging by the way his eyebrows rose and a soft flush of pink crept up his neck, whatever look she was giving him wasn't one he'd seen her give him before.

Without breaking eye contact, he took a long swig of beer and she realized he was giving her a look *she* hadn't seen from him before, either. Hot. Hungry. The kind of look a man gave a woman when he was considering his chances of getting naked with her and hoping they were good.

She gave him the wrap-it-up signal and he smiled at her over his bottle. He extricated himself from the conversation and then pulled out his phone to call for a cab. And as he made his way over to her while saying a goodbye here and there, she tried not to think about the fact they were going home together. Which they'd done before, of course. Quite often. But not after exchanging sizzling glances over the tops of their drinks.

He did most of the talking on the ride home, telling her a funny story about a drywaller accidentally closing a homeowner's Chihuahua up in the wall, but she was barely listening. And when they got home, she unlocked her door and picked up Moxie to get her welcome-home love in a daze. Not an alcoholic daze, but a daze caused by the now undeniable fact she really, *really* wanted to have sex. With Justin.

When Moxie squirmed in her arms, Claire set her down and found herself with nothing to do but stand in the middle of the living room and look at Justin. Who was looking right back at her.

He shook his head, even though she hadn't said anything out loud. "You should go to bed."

Oh, she intended to. The question was whether or not she was going alone. Sleep wasn't going to happen. Not with dreamed images of his hands on her filling her head while her body trembled for his touch. She wanted to feel him against her. Not fleeting nocturnal imaginings, but hot and hard and real.

"Jesus, Claire, stop looking at me like that," he said in a low, rough voice she wanted saying naughty things against her ear.

"I'm a little bit drunk."

"So am I, which is why you need to stop looking at me like that and go to bed."

"Or…" She paused to catch her bottom lip between her teeth, which was a nervous habit rather than intentionally sexy, but she saw his jaw tighten.

"There's no *or*. Go sleep it off."

"But you're standing under the mistletoe." Kind of. Close enough, anyway.

"You told me it was just a fun decoration. Go. To. Bed."

She didn't think—just acted. Standing on her tiptoes, she pressed her mouth to Justin's.

His body stiffened and his lips were unyielding against hers. The butterflies of delicious anticipation turned to stone, dropping like lead weights in her stomach as she realized what she'd done.

She pulled away, turning so she didn't have to look at his face, while desperately scrambling for words to fix what she'd done—words that could salvage the most important relationship in her life.

Then Justin swore viciously under his breath and she gasped as he spun her back to face him. Before she could even read his expression, he slid his hand behind her neck and hauled her against his body.

His kiss was hard and punishing and she surrendered to it completely. When she wrapped her arms around his neck, he moaned quietly against her mouth and she knew she wouldn't be going to bed alone. But then, just as suddenly, he ended the kiss and tried to take a step back.

"God, Claire. Go to bed before we do something you'll regret in the morning."

Instead she moved closer and pressed her palms to his stomach because she didn't miss the fact he didn't think *he'd* regret it in the morning. His abs tightened as he sucked in a breath and she slid her hands to his hips. When he did nothing but stand there frozen with his hands fisted at his sides, she gathered up the bottom of his shirt until she could get her fingers under it. She wanted skin.

"Claire." She ignored him, busy as she was exploring the hard expanse of his chest, but he grabbed her wrists through the fabric. "Claire, listen to me."

"I don't want to."

"Because you know what I'm going to say."

He might have her wrists, but she could still slide her fingertips over his skin. "Are you going to say you're not attracted to me?"

"Uh…no." His heart was thumping under her fingers and his quickened pulse made her brave.

"Are you going to say you don't want to make love to me?"

"I do want to make love to you, but—"

She kissed him again before he could finish the thought. He'd already said everything she needed to hear. It was a few long, seemingly endless seconds before his lips parted under hers and he gave in to the kiss.

They managed to make it to her bedroom before the clothes came off, but it wasn't quick enough for Claire. It had been such a long time and she wanted him and seeing him strip off his boxer briefs as she unhooked her bra just made it so much worse.

"You're so beautiful," he said as he picked Moxie up off

the bed and set her on the floor. She gave him a disdainful mewl before walking out of the room with her tail held high.

Claire was going to close the door to make sure she didn't come back, but Justin took her hand to pull her onto the bed and she forgot all about the cat.

He took his sweet time getting down to business, stroking every part of her that ached to be stroked and stopping a lot to kiss her as if she was the oxygen he needed to breathe and he was starving for air.

She'd probably seen him shirtless a hundred times, climbing a ladder with a bundle of roofing shingles over his shoulder, but looking was nowhere near as good as touching and she touched him a lot. His muscles were hard under her fingertips and his skin was warm and...God, how she'd missed this.

"I hope you're ready, Claire, because you are so hot and I've been watching you all night and I can't not do this now."

She smiled at the desperation in his eyes and lifted her head to kiss him, nipping at his lower lip before she let him go. "I am *so* ready."

She heard the crinkle of a condom wrapper as he sat back on his heels and she closed her eyes, stretching like a cat on a sunny windowsill. She hadn't felt so good in...a long time, and she savored the loose, languid feeling in her muscles. She could get used to this again.

Justin's mouth closing over her nipple made her jump and she opened her eyes to find him smiling down at her. She ran her heels up over his calves, letting him settle between her thighs. She gasped as he slowly filled her, lifting her hips as he pressed deep.

She ran her hands over his shoulders and back, feeling the fine sheen of sweat coating his muscles. "Justin..."

"God, you feel amazing."

She wanted to say more—something about how he felt

pretty damn amazing, too—but he was quickening his pace and she couldn't breathe and it was all she could do not to scream his name.

The orgasm hit her and maybe she did scream then. She didn't know. Didn't care. All she knew was that her body was screaming *yes yes yes* like Meg Ryan in that movie and she didn't want it to stop.

When it did stop, Justin collapsed on top of her and panted against her neck, she sucked in a deep breath and held it for a long second before letting it back out. Oh, yes, she'd wanted that. *Needed* that.

And once he made a quick trip to the bathroom and returned to wrap himself around her—after fighting Moxie for the pillow once she deemed it safe to enter the bedroom again—she drifted off to sleep with a silly smile on her face.

Justin opened his eyes just long enough to register where he was and focus on the empty pillow beside him, and then closed them again. Shit. He was in Claire's bed.

Brendan's bed.

"Son of a bitch," he muttered, even as memories of the night before played through his mind like an X-rated slideshow. It had been nothing short of amazing and he wanted to do it again. As soon as possible. Now would be good, though from the mouthwatering aromas drifting into the bedroom, she was already up and working on breakfast.

After rolling onto his back, he stretched his arms up over his head and opened his eyes again. He'd been in her bedroom before and remembering that made him realize he hadn't *technically* spent the night in Brendan's bed. A few months after the accident, Claire had gotten rid of their queen-sized bed and replaced it with a double. When he'd shown up to help her set it up, she'd explained she wanted the extra space in the room. To his eye, the difference wasn't worth the effort and he suspected she'd been hit by a need to be rid of the bed they'd shared.

He jerked sideways and almost fell off the bed when something furry brushed his armpit. "Jesus, Moxie! Meow or something before you do that."

The cat headbutted him in the chin a few times before jumping off the bed. When she squeezed through the slightly open door, it opened wider and let in the mouthwatering aroma of a good, old-fashioned breakfast. With bacon.

As good as it smelled, he hoped it wasn't ready to go on the table yet because he needed a few more minutes before he could face what they'd done. What *he'd* done.

"Ten minutes," she yelled from the kitchen.

He didn't have to wonder how she knew he was up. If there was a sleeping human to be found, her cat wouldn't be budged from his or her side. As soon as Moxie left the bedroom, she knew he was awake.

Thankfully, he managed to slip from the bedroom into the bathroom without having to make eye contact, since she was busy at the stove. He shaved and showered, pulling a set of clean clothes from "his" shelf in her linen closet. He crashed on her couch often enough so it make sense for him to keep some stuff there, but it was a one-bedroom and they couldn't very well share a dresser drawer. That would be weird.

Like sleeping together.

He put off facing the music as long as he could, even taking an exceptionally long time brushing his teeth, but when she banged on the door and told him breakfast was on the table, he finished up and took a deep breath before opening the door.

She didn't look any different. The hair he'd buried his face in only hours before was piled on top of her head in a messy knot. She'd thrown on a T-shirt and sweatpants, along with the clunky, sheepskin-lined slippers he'd bought her for Christmas last year. The garage under her apartment wasn't heated, so the floor tended to be cold. As she set two mugs of coffee on the table, he watched her and, no, she didn't look any different than the last time she'd done it.

But everything *was* different because now he *knew*. He knew what it felt like to hold her. He knew what her body felt like under his and what her long legs felt like wrapped around his hips. And he didn't know if he'd ever get to feel it again.

And he already wanted to.

Since she already had everything on the table, he took his seat and dug in. They'd burned more than a few calories before falling asleep. But, hungry as he was, he wasn't so intent on his breakfast he missed the fact she was avoiding eye contact. In his experience, when a woman you'd spent the night with wouldn't look you in the eye, she either had a bellyful of regret or you sucked in the sack. Or so he'd heard.

"I guess I should thank you."

He paused with a forkful of home fries halfway to his mouth. That was an odd thing to say. "Thank me for what?"

"You know...for last night."

"Then I have to thank you, too, because it was mutually amazing. I think. I...hope." Before he'd been sure it had been just as good for her as it had been for him, but now he was sitting across from a woman who didn't look like she'd had her socks knocked off between the sheets.

"It was!" She said it a little too quickly for his taste. "It was definitely amazing. And that's why I said thank you."

"Okay. You're welcome, I guess." He couldn't shake the feeling he was missing something in this conversation.

"It meant a lot to me to...test the waters, so to speak, with a guy I trust so much." She took a deep breath and smiled at him. "You're a good friend."

Oh, hell no. He was…what? A test drive to make sure all her parts were in working order before she went on a *real* date? "Tell me you didn't just say that."

"You *are* a good friend." She looked confused. "You're my *best* friend."

"If you want a buddy, get a golden retriever," he muttered, and then he shoved the home fries into his mouth to shut himself up.

Claire dropped her fork onto her plate with a clatter. "I knew it. This is why friends shouldn't have sex. Now it's going to be weird."

"No, you thanking me like I gave you a tire and lube job so you can go on a road trip is making it weird." As he watched her expression change to one of restrained amusement, he replayed his words in his mind and groaned. "You know what I mean."

"Lube job isn't the sexiest euphemism I've ever heard," she said, her voice heavy with suppressed laughter. "But you did give me one helluva tune-up."

He laughed and then shook his head. "Wiseass."

With amusement written all over her face, Claire dug into her breakfast, so he followed suit. But, as the food slowly disappeared, the tension grew thick again.

Pretty soon it would be time for him to go and he had no idea where they stood. Was she even expecting him to go or was he supposed to spend the day with her? And, if he went, did he kiss her goodbye?

The only thing he knew for sure was that he'd made one hell of a mess of things.

He was swallowing the last bite of his veggie omelet when she said softly, "Did I wreck everything? Is it going to *stay* weird now?"

"You didn't wreck anything." Except maybe *him,* since there was something that sounded a lot like regret in her voice.

"I haven't been with anybody since Brendan." She wouldn't look at him, concentrating instead on moving a mushroom around her plate. "I just wanted to… I just… I shouldn't have put you in that position."

"Hey, that happened to be my favorite position."

She rewarded him with a laugh, but it was a quick one and then she grew serious again. "I mean it. You were Brendan's best friend. You're *my* best friend. It was wrong of me to throw myself at you because I was a little lonely at night. Your friendship means everything to me and I just hope I didn't screw it up."

He forced himself to look her straight in the eye. "Our friendship means more to me than anything, Claire. You know that. And I shouldn't have let it happen. You were my buddy's girl and that makes you off-limits. It won't ever happen again."

"Let's chalk it up to too much to drink." She was full of crap and they both knew it. He'd seen her drunk before and she was nowhere near plastered last night. And neither was he. "Forget it ever happened."

Forget what was seared into his very soul? Not freakin' likely. He suspected when he was ninety years old and couldn't remember where he'd left his teeth, he'd still remember the jolt of her blue eyes looking into his and the whisper of his name on her lips as he moved inside her. "Forget whatever happened?"

She grinned and the world felt mostly okay again.

By the time they'd cleaned up the breakfast dishes and put everything away, the awkwardness between them was almost gone. She went on and on about Christmas and shopping and what she wanted to buy for Nicole now that she was old enough to really get a kick out of the holiday. He said the

Shannon Stacey 373

right words in the appropriate places, but his mind refused to concentrate on the mostly one-sided conversation.

He'd managed to royally put the screws to himself this time, and there was no way out of it.

If he walked away from her, she'd not only be hurt, but she'd probably blame herself for not going to bed—alone—when he told her to. He couldn't bring himself to do that to her. But if wanting her and not being able to have her was hard before, now it was going to be downright torture. Now he'd know without a doubt what he'd be missing.

He'd deal with it, though, for Claire's sake. Even if it killed him.

CHAPTER FIVE

Claire was doing nothing much but alternating between staring at the row of photos on her bookshelf and glaring at the stupid sprig of mistletoe when Penny showed up Tuesday afternoon with the timecards for payroll. She stood in the kitchen to take off her snowy coat and boots, but did a double take when she saw Claire.

"The Sandman delete you from his GPS or what?"

Always nice to know the lack of sleep was *that* visible on her face. "Rough couple of nights, I guess."

"It's really coming down out there."

Which meant Justin would be out plowing and he hadn't called her. Maybe it was because he knew she had a standing appointment with Penny. Or maybe it was because, since Sunday, he'd had more time to think about the night they'd spent together and he was putting some distance between them.

She knew all *she* had done was think about it. Mostly while she was supposed to be sleeping. At the time, she'd tried to chalk it up to a raging case of libido neglect meeting being dosed with a steady flow of cranberry margaritas, but she was going to have to face facts. Any guy who knew his way around the female body *wouldn't* do. The need that was building all over again and making her toss and turn at night was definitely Justin-specific.

"I can't stay and chat today," Penny said. "Dentist. But call me later if you want to talk. You look like you need a shoulder. Or a drink."

"Last thing I need is a drink."

That got Penny's attention and she looked at her watch. "You have three minutes to tell me what alcohol made you do. And who it made you do it with."

She didn't need three minutes. She didn't even need three seconds. "I got waylaid by a migraine, that's all. And alcohol doesn't help."

Penny would probably be hurt to know Claire was lying to her, but she didn't think Justin wanted their business to become the latest fertilizer for the town grapevine. And neither did she.

"No offense, Claire, but that's boring as hell. You need to go out and have a good time." She shoved her feet back into her boots. "How's the migraine now?"

"Better. Just need to catch up on my sleep now."

She tried, after Penny left. Curling up on the couch with Moxie, Claire tried to nap, but she could see the snowflakes falling outside the window and they made her think of Justin. Then she heard the big state plow truck go by and made herself close her eyes.

If the town and the state were out plowing, so was Justin and she couldn't stop herself from wondering if he'd stop by, looking for food—since he wouldn't make pool and pizza night—or a power nap. Or maybe some company if he hadn't been lying about their friendship still being solid.

It was dusk when she woke to Moxie knitting her claws in her sweatshirt and the sound of somebody rummaging around in her fridge. For a long moment she just lay there, soaking up the normalcy. Then Moxie jumped down and sauntered over to figure-eight her way around Justin's ankles and she knew the jig was up.

"I stopped at that deli you like and got a couple of turkey bulkies and a bucket of German potato salad. Are you out of mustard?"

"There's a new one in the cabinet." She sat up and tried to rub the lingering sleep from her eyes. "You should have called. I would have had everything ready."

"By the time I thought of it, I was almost here."

She went into the bathroom and when she emerged, he had everything spread out on the table so all she had to do was sit. "Has the snow let up any?"

"It's winding down. After I eat, I'll probably make another quick pass for clients who have to get in or out before eight o'clock or so tomorrow morning and I'll do the rest then."

She nodded and took a bite of her bulky, shuddering a little as he drizzled mustard over the top of his potato salad.

Justin paused with his first forkful halfway to his mouth, looking at her. "You gonna ride with me tonight?"

"Sure." There, that was casual and to the point. Not even a hint of the insane relief she felt at this small sign they were back on track.

And that was good, even if the track was going to have a few more potholes in it than it had before. All she had to do was pretend she'd forgotten the night they'd spent together and never thought about how amazing and wonderful the sex had been between them.

If she lied to herself—and to him—long enough, maybe someday it would become the truth.

She smelled so good. Even as Justin tried to concentrate on not hitting Mrs. Wilson's car while backdragging the plow to clear the snow from behind it, he was aware of how delicious Claire smelled. Which, of course, led him directly back to those thoughts about how good she tasted he'd sworn he wasn't going to think anymore.

"How was opening day?" she asked, and it took him a few seconds to clear his head and realize she was talking about snowmobiling.

"It was good. Chris and I put on about sixty miles. Not a lot, but they're still getting the trails in shape and it was a good shakedown run." Mrs. Wilson's driveway was done, so he raised the plow and pulled out onto the road to head to the next place.

"That's good." She was staring out the side window and he wondered what she was thinking about. "Is Brendan's snowmobile still in your garage?"

That answered that. "Yeah."

"I was thinking about learning how to drive it. Maybe go out with you sometimes."

He laughed and nudged her arm with his elbow. "You? Out in the woods in the freezing cold?"

"I might like it."

"Or you might whine."

She turned away from the window to slap at him. "I don't whine."

When he grabbed her wrist to keep her from hitting him, it seemed like the most natural thing in the world to slide his hand down and interlock his fingers with hers. She didn't pull away and he rested their joined hands on the seat between them.

"If you really want to ride, I'll teach you," he said. "But Brendan's machine's too much for you. If you're serious, I'll take it and trade it in for something more your speed."

"Would that bother you? Letting it go, I mean."

He could see her watching his profile through the corner of his eyes, so he shrugged like it was no big deal. "It's just a sled, Claire. I started it up the other day and was thinking it was a damn shame, the way it just sits there."

"You love snowmobiling more than anything," she said softly. "I'd like to do that with you."

He squeezed her fingers. "I'll call the shop and see what kind of deal they'll give me."

Then he had to let her go, needing both hands to navigate down the dirt road that led to the Swenson house. The town did a half-ass job of plowing the road, but they didn't touch the driveways. Harry Swenson lived in the last house on the road, isolated from his neighbors. He worked nights, so he'd already left. Justin would give it a quick swipe to make it easier for him to get home.

While he worked, she went back to staring out her window, which worried him. She was usually a chatterbox while they were out plowing, to the point he'd sometimes regret taking her because she wouldn't shut up.

"What are you thinking about?" he asked her, putting the truck in Park and killing the headlights so he could give her his full attention.

"Kissing you again," she said to the window.

He was surprised the windows didn't fog up from the rush of heat that washed over him. "You pro or con?"

"I'm still afraid it'll ruin our friendship in the long run."

"I hate to say it, but having it between us all the time like the big, horny elephant in the room isn't doing it any favors, either."

"So what are we going to do about it?"

What he *should* do was put the truck in gear, put his foot on the gas and drop her off—alone—at her apartment. What he did instead was shove a whole bunch of crap onto the passenger side floor and then take her hand to tug her over to his side of the truck. "What do *you* think we should do about it?"

"Maybe we just need to…get it out of our systems."

There was no way that was ever going to happen. "We could just play it by ear."

Since she was already kicking off her boots, he figured she was okay with that idea. "Can anybody see us?"

"No." It was getting warm in the truck all of a sudden, so he reached out and slid the fan controls down to low. So what if the windows fogged up? As a matter of fact, he was hoping they would.

She kissed him, long and slow and sweet, while their elbows bumped into things because she was trying to shimmy out of her jeans and he was trying to get a condom from his wallet in the back pocket of his.

"Slow down," he whispered against her mouth.

"Can't. Don't want to. I need you, Justin."

He didn't need to be told twice. Once he got his wallet free, he lifted his hips enough to drag his jeans down and covered himself with the condom. Then she covered him with *her* and the windows steamed like a sauna.

"I've been thinking about this since the night of the Christmas party," she said, her breath against his cheek as she moved slowly, stroking him.

He'd been thinking about it a lot longer than that, but it wasn't the time for *that* discussion. Not when she was moving up and down like that, making him forget…whatever it was keeping them from doing this all the damn time. It wasn't going to last long and then he'd probably remember, but for now all he knew was the feel of her body, her breasts in his hands and her mouth against his.

He felt her body tensing and he wanted to slow her down, but she was in control and she quickened the pace until he thought he'd explode. She dug her nails into his shoulders as she came and, with a groan, he let himself go.

It was a few hot, breathless minutes before Claire kissed his neck and climbed off him. With nowhere else to put it, he fished around under the seat for an empty doughnut bag, dropped the condom in it and balled it up.

All he had to do was yank up his jeans, but he gave her an extra couple minutes in the foggy cocoon of the cab to get most of her clothes on before turning the defroster to high, just in case somebody *was* watching. She was laughing as she leaned down to find her boots, and he flipped on the dome light to help. Her left hand was braced against the dash and the unexpected glimpse of white skin where her wedding band had been killed any desire he'd had to laugh along with her.

He'd done it again, dammit. And he didn't feel any better about it this time than he had after the last time.

Claire finally got herself straightened out and flopped into her seat, buckling her seat belt. "I really needed that."

He turned off the dome light, thankful for the sudden blanket of darkness broken only by the dim dashboard lights. "Yeah, me too."

She was the one who took his hand this time and he started the drive back to her place with his head all screwed up. Part of him was happy and sated and wanted to curl up in Claire's bed and fall asleep. The other part was disgusted. He'd not only slept with his buddy's girl again, but he'd done it knowing it put his friendship with her back on shaky ground.

"So you'll call the dealership about Brendan's sled?" she asked after a few miles. "Soon? I really want to go riding with you."

A hard jab of grief hit him in the gut at the thought of trading in the sled, along with a fresh rush of guilt. Taking Brendan's girl. Getting rid of his sled. It was too much. "Yeah. I'll let you know what they say."

She didn't say anything else and, when she let go of his hand to hit the skip button on the CD player when a song came on she didn't like, he shifted his right hand to the steering wheel. She didn't seem to notice though. Just started singing along with the next song and pointing out her favorite Christmas lights as they passed the cheery houses.

Tightening his grip, he concentrated on the road and fought the urge to pull over so he could beat his head against the steering wheel. He'd managed to screw everything up this time, only this time it was worse. Not only was there no alcohol to blame, no matter how flimsy that excuse had been, but she didn't seem to have any regrets. He couldn't let her think they were starting anything.

When he finally pulled into her driveway, he put the truck in Park, wondering how the hell he was going to get himself out of this. He just wanted to go home, max out the iPod's volume and beat the crap out of the speed bag hanging in his basement for a while.

Claire was scowling up at her window, though, and not paying any attention to him. "I know I left the kitchen light on."

But the apartment was dark now, which meant he'd have to go upstairs with her. He shut off the truck and put his hand out. "Give me your keys."

She was on his heels as he went up the stairs and unlocked her door. The living room light went on when he flipped the switch and everything looked untouched. Moxie twisted around his ankles before moving on to Claire to be picked up and coddled. He peeked into her bathroom and bedroom and didn't find anything out of place, so he dragged the kitchen chair over to the sink and climbed up to remove the light bulb over it.

"Burned out. You got another one?"

"Over the microwave. Hold on."

He watched her as she set the cat down and stretched to reach the box of light bulbs. She looked…happy. Relaxed. And she smiled up at him as he took the bulb from her hand. "You're a pretty handy guy."

"Yeah." He took his time screwing in the new bulb and replacing the cover, but it was still only a few minutes before it was time to face the music.

She'd taken off her sweatshirt and was curled on the couch with her feet tucked under Moxie for warmth. Pausing in the act of reaching for the remote control, she gave him a funny look. "What's wrong?"

"I should get going. It's been a long night."

The happy glow faded a little, but she was still smiling. "Why don't you just stay here? There's no sense in making the drive home when you've got to go out early in the morning to finish up."

"I can't stay, Claire." And that pretty much killed the last of the happy on her face.

"Why?" He shrugged, not knowing what to say, but she shook her head. "Don't. Tell me why."

"I can't do this again. You and me, I mean. It's not right."

"You seemed to think it was pretty right a half hour ago."

"I want you. I still do, but…Brendan…" He didn't know how to explain it and all the words in the world wouldn't make it any easier. Probably just hurt more. "I have to go. I'll call you tomorrow maybe."

"Justin." He paused, his hand on the doorknob, but he didn't turn. "Don't come back."

CHAPTER SIX

Claire's body trembled with the effort it had taken to force the words out, but she wouldn't take them back.

Justin's hand slid off the doorknob as he slowly turned to face her. "Claire, don't do this."

Did he honestly think she *wanted* to kick him out of her life? He was her best friend. And, despite her best efforts to deny and deflect, he was the man she was falling in love with. Or maybe she'd always been in love with him but she'd blocked it out.

"I thought, after the Christmas party, we'd be okay," she said in a quiet voice. "I thought our friendship survived. And tonight, in your truck, I thought we'd had some time to come to grips with…whatever it is we're feeling and that we were taking a step forward together, but we're not. You're stuck riding some messed-up emotional rollercoaster and I want off."

"I'm not trying to hurt you."

"But you are. I've always loved you, Justin, but I think the *way* I love you is changing and it scares the hell out of me. Since you're not in the same place, you have to walk away now before it gets any worse. Please."

"You were a beautiful bride," he whispered.

The shift in the conversation put her off-balance and, almost involuntarily, she glanced at the formal wedding portrait of her and Brendan. After taking a second to calm herself, she looked back at Justin. "This isn't about the past. It's about right now."

"How can it not be about the past? I stood there, at my best friend's side, and watched you vow to love, honor and cherish him."

"'Til death we did part. I loved him, Justin. I still love him and if he'd lived I would have spent the rest of my life with him. But he died. That life is gone, but I'm still here and I have to make a new life. I want to make it with you."

"I can't. You're Brendan's wife, Claire. I can't get past that."

"No. I'm Brendan's widow. I'm not his wife anymore."

"But you were. I loved my best friend's wife. You know what kind of lowlife asshole that makes me? The worst kind, that's what."

I loved my best friend's wife. His words were slow to sink in and she was even slower to understand them. It would've made sense to her if he said *I made love to my best friend's widow.* She knew their relationships with Brendan messed with his head. He wasn't alone.

But he made it sound like he was in love with her. And had been since before Brendan died. That wasn't possible, though, because he was her best friend and she would have known if he had those kinds of feelings for her.

"You never betrayed him," she said, because she wasn't sure of much at the moment, but that was one thing she didn't doubt.

"I did. In my heart. And when I closed my eyes at night, I tried not to imagine making love to you, but I did it anyway. I tried *so* damn hard not to."

The emotional cost of that confession was written all over his face and she couldn't take it. She looked down at Moxie and stroked her fur, not sure if it was the cat she was trying to soothe or herself.

"You don't mean that, Justin." It couldn't be true because it changed everything she'd ever believed about their relationship.

"It's the truth."

"He's gone now."

"We both loved Brendan too much for him to ever be gone. I...I just can't do this."

"Then you have to go. I've had too much pain and unhappiness to hold on to something that hurts me, even if it's you."

"Don't. Please."

"I have to."

He looked like he had more to say—she could see it on his face—but then he opened the door and stepped out into the cold night. The first tear fell as he closed the door and, by the time the sound of his truck roaring up the street faded, she was bawling into the arm of the couch, Moxie trying to comfort her by batting at her hair.

Claire knew making Justin leave was the right thing to do, but she hadn't expected it to hurt quite so much. And she knew from experience it wasn't going to hurt just for a while. It was going to hurt every time she wanted to pick up the phone and call him, but couldn't. It was going to hurt every time she heard a joke she thought would make him laugh, but couldn't share it. It would hurt when there was a movie she knew they'd both love and she had to go to the theater without him.

Even if he came back, things would never be the same between them again. Now she knew he'd loved her—he'd used the past tense—and she loved him in the present tense, but he was right. They'd both loved Brendan too much for him to ever be gone. And, while she could accept she was lucky enough to love two great guys who happened to have been best friends, Justin couldn't.

When the tears had run their course, even temporarily, she spent a few minutes soothing Moxie and then washed her face. She turned on the radio to keep the silence at bay and then she grabbed a few of the empty shopping bags she always shoved under the kitchen sink and started gathering his belongings. There was no sense in having Justin's clothes and toiletries and miscellaneous belongings lying around when he was never going to crash on her couch again. Or sleep in her bed.

Unfortunately, the pain didn't ease over the next several days. With Christmas bearing down, it was an especially depressing time to be alone and nursing a tender heart. Concentrating on work helped and, with tax season right around the corner, there was plenty of that. Not having to leave her apartment much also helped, as did talking to her family on the phone. But she missed Justin too much to have more than a few minutes pass without thinking of him. Even Moxie seemed to miss him, judging by the way she'd pace in front of the door and then rub against the legs of the kitchen chair that had been "his."

Judy Rutledge called her bright and early Christmas Eve morning to invite her to meet for breakfast and Claire considered pleading a headache. But in the end she showered and got dressed, even putting on a little makeup, and headed down to the diner to meet her mother-in-law.

Judy had beat her there and Claire smiled as she slid into the booth. "I hope they've got a lot of coffee brewing."

She was rewarded with a look that could only be considered a maternal scan. "You look like you need it."

"You know how it is. Holiday exhaustion. And half my clients just realized it's the end of the year and they're panicking about taxes."

"You're not so busy you can't stop by the party tonight, I hope."

The party. Claire managed not to groan out loud, but she knew she'd be lucky to escape the diner without spilling her guts. Her mother-in-law had uncanny emotional radar and she didn't take "fine" for an answer.

"I'm not sure if I'll make it or not," she said honestly. She hadn't decided yet if she could face it. Either Justin would be there and she'd feel like crap seeing him again, or he wouldn't be there and she'd feel like crap knowing she'd come between him and the people he considered a second family. Neither really filled her with holiday spirit.

"I hope you'll try. It won't be the same without you."

Claire was saved having to respond to that by the waitress appearing to take their order, which required her to pretend she had an appetite. She figured an omelet and home fries would be easy to mangle on the plate, making it look as though she'd eaten more than she actually had.

Halfway through the meal and inane small talk, though, Judy set down her fork and gave her a hard look. "Tell me what's going on, Claire. Don't make keep trying to guess while imagining something horrible."

Looking her husband's mother in the eye made it seem a lot more horrible than it had seemed before, though. It was going to hurt, no matter how much she tried to hedge around the truth of the situation.

"Justin and I...we've had a falling-out of sorts."

"I thought it might have something to do with him. He hasn't quite been himself, either." Judy took a sip of her coffee, looking thoughtful. "It must be especially hard having a falling-out with a friend at Christmastime."

It was, though Claire only nodded, because it could always be worse. They'd both seen hard. Hard had been Judy's hand gripping hers at the funeral so tightly she thought their bones would crack.

"Claire." Judy said nothing else until she stopped fiddling with her home fries and looked up. "I hope you know Phil and I love you like a daughter, but that doesn't mean we expect you to spend the rest of your life mourning Brendan. You can talk to me, sweetie. I *want* you to talk to me."

"It's too messy." Claire shook her head, looking down into her nearly empty coffee cup. "It was just... I guess we were both lonely and we went to a Christmas party and had too much to drink and... It's just too messy."

She hated playing the alcohol card because it was a lie, but it was easier than trying to explain the tangle of emotions her relationship with Justin had become.

"You love Justin."

The statement, made so simply and without accusation, made Claire's throat close up and it was all she could do not to break down into tears. Her feelings for Justin were so complicated she hadn't thought it could be summed up so easily.

"But Brendan's coming between you," Judy continued.

"Brendan's not between us," Claire said, a little more sharply than she intended. She wouldn't share Justin's confession with Judy—that he'd loved his best friend's wife—because it might damage Justin's relationship with the Rutledges, but it was never far from her mind. "He's *with* us. In our hearts and our thoughts and he always will be because we loved him. I miss him every day, you know. So does Justin."

"I do know." Judy reached across the table and squeezed her hand. "I lost my son, but I don't know how it feels to lose my husband so I don't know the right words to say. But I hope you don't give up on Justin—or yourself—just because it's hard right now."

Sometimes it was *too* hard, but she didn't want to drag Judy any further into such a depressing topic. Especially the morning of her Christmas Eve party. "I'm not giving up on anything yet. But let's talk about something else. Since you always figure it out, what did Phil get you for Christmas this year?"

Justin stood with his hands shoved in his coat pockets, staring down at the block of polished granite. Brendan Rutledge. Beloved Son, Husband, Brother and Red Sox Fan.

He'd been sitting between Judy and Claire in the funeral director's office, holding their hands, while they went through the long, painful process of planning their goodbye. But it had been Phil, sitting with his arms wrapped around Brendan's sister and who'd been quiet up until the moment came to order the headstone, who had said his son would have wanted the world to know he was a Red Sox fan. The three women had laughed—weak, startled amusement that pierced through the suffocating blanket of unexpected, bone-deep grief.

Claire had wanted to add *friend,* for Justin's sake, but the funeral director was concerned about the amount of space on the small stone. Justin had squeezed her hand and told her *brother* said everything important about his relationship with Brendan.

He stared now at that word etched forever into granite. *Brother.* "I slept with your wife."

There was no clap of thunder. No lightning strike or howling winds or deluge of icy rain. Just silence and the beating of his heart.

"I tried not to. I tried so damn hard not to." He swallowed hard. "We tried to blame the booze at first. But we weren't drunk. It was just the excuse we used to make it okay. And… then we did it again."

He stopped. Blew out a breath. "I hurt her. You worshipped her and you made her laugh and smile and…I made her cry.

I think, more than anything, you'd kick my ass just for that. God, I wish you could kick my ass right now."

Justin heard a strangled sob behind him and turned to see Judy Rutledge standing a short distance behind him. Her face was pale and streaked with tears as her leather-gloved hands strangled the stems of a small Christmas bouquet. The guilt of hurting another woman Brendan had loved almost crippled him.

"He considered you his brother," she said in a small voice that hit him like a wrecking ball.

His shoulders hunched under his coat as he waited for the accusations and recriminations from the woman who'd been a second mother to him. He wouldn't try to defend what he'd done or hide from the pain. He deserved to hurt as much as she did. More. Because he'd betrayed her, too.

"I've loved you like a son, Justin. The boys. That's how Phil and I always referred to you. *The boys*. You were probably closer than any real brothers could have been. And he's gone now."

The agony in her voice and in her eyes made his heart clench and his throat close up until he could barely breathe. "I didn't want this to happen."

"But I still have you. I still have one of my boys and I have Claire, who will always be a second daughter to me. And seeing the two of you like this hurts me."

He shook his head, his hands curling into fists in his pockets. He didn't want her soft words and compassionate tears. She should be angry. She should pound her fists on his chest and yell at him for betraying her son's memory—for betraying Brendan's friendship.

Instead, she stepped forward and opened her arms, but he shook his head again. His vision blurred with unshed tears as she cradled his cheek with one of her hands.

"I get through each day by believing my son is in some wonderful better place," she said softly, but firmly. "I believe he can feel my love for him and, since I believe that, I also have to believe he can feel your pain. He loved you and Claire so much. Both of you hurting would make him unhappy."

"I slept with his wife," he whispered, and she dropped her hand.

She stepped around him and set the bouquet of cheery flowers at the base of her son's headstone. He watched her shoulders move under her coat as she took a deep breath and ran her fingers over Brendan's name.

Then she shoved her hands in her pockets and faced Justin again. "You have to stop telling yourself that. You have to stop *believing* it. You slept with Claire. You slept with the woman you love and who loves you and, as trite as it might sound, Brendan would want you both to move on. To be happy."

He might as well tell her the rest of it. Before she wished him any more happiness, she deserved to know it all. "I've always loved her, Mrs. R., even before he... Before the accident."

"If I believed for a second you had in any way betrayed my son, I wouldn't be able to look at your face, Justin McCormick. You know that, don't you?"

He nodded until she held his face between her hands again and made him look at her. "You can't choose who you love. And you can't will it away."

"I tried. I tried not to love her."

"And look where you've ended up. Both of you are miserable. Brendan might have been your best friend and Claire's husband, but he was *my* boy and I know—I believe in my heart—that he would consider the two of you being happy together a blessing."

He wanted to believe her. But he'd spent so many years telling himself his feelings for Claire were wrong, and the guilt wasn't a switch he could flip because Brendan's mom said it was okay. He wanted to, though, and for the first time he allowed himself to imagine telling Claire he loved her.

Mrs. Rutledge sniffed and then seemed to gather herself up emotionally. "Are you going to stop by the party tonight?"

"Probably not. I'm not very good company and I'm not really up to pretending I am."

"That's more or less what Claire said, too. You should go see her, Justin."

"I don't know." He wasn't sure he could give her what she needed.

The smile Judy gave him was warm, with only a hint of sadness. "You both lost Brendan. Do you really want to lose each other, too?"

As he drove home, that parting question wouldn't leave him alone. It echoed through his mind, over and over, until he wanted to beat his head against the steering wheel just to make it stop. He didn't know what he wanted to do, but there was one thing he knew for damn sure. He didn't want to lose Claire.

When the knock at the door came, Claire knew it was Justin. She recognized the sound of his truck pulling into the driveway. She knew the sound of his boots on the stairs. And she turned up the television, determined to continue crying her way through one of the greatest holiday comedies ever made, even though *National Lampoon's Christmas Vacation* wasn't the same without him.

Justin knocked again. She ignored it. Ignored the pounding on the door and the pounding in her heart and the godawful ache in the pit of her stomach.

She heard the scratching of metal against metal and the

ache intensified. His key wouldn't do him any good. She'd changed the locks.

He gave up after a few seconds and then resumed banging so hard she was surprised he didn't dent the metal. Or maybe he did. Right now, she didn't care. "Open the damn door, Claire, or I swear I'll kick it in."

Since he'd helped Brendan install the thing, she knew there wasn't much chance of that.

She heard him kick the bottom of the door—not in a real effort to kick it in, but in frustration. "Claire...please."

The change in his voice went straight to her heart. But if she let him in and he pulled her close only to shove her away again, she wasn't sure her heart could stand it. And he would because he couldn't separate his friendship with Brendan from his feelings for her.

"I'm not leaving, Claire. This time, I won't leave."

Considering how long he'd been standing outside her door in the frigid cold, she was starting to believe him. And her nerves weren't going to be able to stand much more, so she threw off the fleece blanket and walked to the door, flipped the deadbolt and opened it.

"I saw you first."

He looked like hell and her heart twisted for him. "What do you mean?"

"I saw you first." He reached for her face, but she took a step back. "You should have been mine, Claire, and I've lived with that for seven years."

"When did you see me first?"

"That night at the party, I'd been watching you and I was going to ask you to dance. But I made the mistake of going to take a leak first. When I came out, Brendan was talking to you. You were laughing and the chemistry was so obvious.

Later that night he told me he'd met the girl he was going to marry."

She tried to wrap her mind around what he was saying. "I never knew that. And Brendan didn't, either. Or he never said anything."

"I've spent the last two years telling myself I had to do right by my best friend's memory. But hurting you doesn't do right by him. Destroying myself doesn't do right by him."

"A few days ago you were calling yourself a lowlife asshole. Now, all of a sudden, it's okay?"

"I found out the hard way I can't live without you. And I realized Brendan would want us to be happy."

She shook her head, afraid he was simply at a high point on the emotional rollercoaster. "Until the next morning-after rolls around and you feel guilty and push me away again."

"I didn't realize it on my own. I had some help from Brendan's mom."

"You talked to Judy about…us?"

"Pretty sure I didn't tell her anything she didn't already know. Or suspect, anyway."

While Brendan's mother's blessing probably went a long way toward easing Justin's guilt, it was risky to hope it was some kind of magical wand that made everything better with a flick of the wrist and a bibbidi-bobbidi-boo. And it had hurt when he pulled away. A *lot*.

But her own conversation with Judy wouldn't stay buried in the back of her mind. *Don't give up on Justin—or yourself— just because it's hard right now.*

He took her hand and she watched as he ran his thumb over her knuckles because it was easier than looking him in the eye.

"I know I hurt you," he said quietly. "I'm sorry."

"The past few days of not having you at all hurt more than anything."

"I don't ever want to go through that again, Claire. It was pure hell." Every minute of that hell was as evident on his face as she was sure it was on hers. "I can't promise you there won't be times it's a little weird for me, but I *can* promise I won't walk away from you ever again."

Those were the words she thought she'd wanted to hear, but they weren't enough. "This isn't about Brendan and that's the problem. It has to be about us. You and me, Justin. Just us."

"I love you."

She froze, her heart pounding in her chest. "Justin, I—"

"I love you, Claire. If you take away everybody else and everything else and it's just you and me, that's all there is. All that's left is that I love you."

Looking into his eyes, that *was* all that was left. Maybe it wouldn't be magically easy, but he loved her and he could say it and that was enough. "I love you, too, but—"

"No but, Claire. I love you. You love me. And if we move just a little to the left, we'll be under the mistletoe."

"A little to the left, huh?"

"Yup. My left." He pulled her sideways so she had to shuffle her feet to stay upright. Looking up, he took her by the shoulders and lined her up beneath the sad-looking sprig. "Right there."

"I'm not letting you kiss me until we're finished talking about this. About the *but.*"

He slid his hands down her arms to her hands, where he threaded his fingers through hers. "Then let's talk about it."

"I want it all. Marriage and a house, whether it's yours or one we find together, and kids."

"Is that a proposal?"

"I guess it is. Will you marry me and have kids with me and kiss me under the mistletoe every Christmas?"

He closed his eyes for a second as the tension seemed to

drain out of his muscles, and then he was grinning and lifting her off her feet. "Yes, I want to marry you," he said just before he kissed her.

When he was finished taking her breath away, he set her back on her feet. "I'd like to stay tonight, if it's okay. Drive you down to your folks tomorrow and then stay tomorrow night. And the night after that."

"I'd like that."

He winced as Moxie started climbing his leg and, after disengaging her claws from his jeans, he cradled the cat and stroked her head.

"She missed you, you know. So did I."

"I won't walk away from you again, Claire. Ever." Then the television caught his attention and he smiled. "You're watching our movie."

They made it to the couch in time to watch the Griswold family's Christmas tree go up in flames and they were laughing as she curled up in his arms, nudging a reluctant Moxie out of her way. The cat sniffed and curled up in her lap.

"I love you," Justin said against her hair. "I've waited so long to say that you're probably going to get sick of hearing it."

"Never." She tilted her head back so he could kiss her. "Merry Christmas."

"Merry Christmas. And did I mention that I love you?"

★ ★ ★ ★ ★